the Sunshine Club

Center Point
Large Print

Also by Carolyn Brown and available from
Center Point Large Print:

The Lilac Bouquet
The Strawberry Hearts Diner
The Sometimes Sisters
Small Town Rumors
The Magnolia Inn
The Perfect Dress
The Empty Nesters
The Family Journal
Miss Janie's Girls
Hummingbird Lane
The Hope Chest

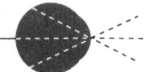

**This Large Print Book carries the
Seal of Approval of N.A.V.H.**

the Sunshine Club

CAROLYN BROWN

CENTER POINT LARGE PRINT
THORNDIKE, MAINE

This Center Point Large Print edition
is published in the year 2022 by arrangement with
Amazon Publishing, www.apub.com.

Originally published in the United States by
Amazon Publishing, 2021.

This is a work of fiction.
Names, characters, organizations, places,
events, and incidents are either products of the author's
imagination or are used fictitiously.

The text of this Large Print edition is unabridged.
In other aspects, this book may vary
from the original edition.
Printed in the United States of America
on permanent paper sourced using
environmentally responsible foresting methods.
Set in 16-point Times New Roman type.

ISBN: 978-1-63808-402-0

The Library of Congress has cataloged this record
under Library of Congress Control Number: 2022937406

To my daughter, Ginny Rucker,
for bringing me an old newspaper dated 1915,
which gave me the idea for *The Sunshine Club*

Chapter One

A lady sips good whiskey. She never throws it back like it is medicine. She loves Jesus, and she never gets a case of giggles at a funeral. Those were Aunt Bee's words, and Sissy had tried to abide by them, but sweet Jesus, this funeral was going to cause all kinds of talk in Newton, Texas. True enough, the town wasn't far from the Louisiana border, but Sissy would bet dollars to gator teeth that no one alive in the small town had ever marched from the funeral home to the cemetery behind a horse-drawn hearse. She wished that she had a flask of whiskey in her coat pocket that cold, miserable day. If she had a couple of shots, she would sip it like she should, and it might warm her insides when she and the rest of the procession left the funeral home and made their slow walk from the warm parlor to the graveyard in freezing rain and sleet.

If I giggle, you'll just have to forgive me, Sissy thought as she donned her long black coat and left to make the five-minute drive from Aunt Bee's house to the funeral home. She parked right beside her aunt's best friends, Ina Mae and Gussie, who had come together in Gussie's car.

"How are you holdin' up, *chère*?" Gussie gave her a quick hug.

"It's still kind of surreal," Sissy answered.

Ina Mae brushed a kiss across her cheek. "For us, too."

"I can't believe that she wanted a funeral like this," Sissy said as they made their way across the lawn. Frozen grass crinkled like wadded-up wrapping paper under her feet. "Or that she won't be here for Christmas. She loved the holiday season."

A tall man with a mop of gray hair opened the door that led into the funeral home parlor and stood to one side. "How you ladies holdin' up?" he asked.

"Not so well, Jimmy," Gussie answered. "We're all still in shock."

"It's tough when a loved one just drops like Blanche did, but at least she didn't suffer," Jimmy said in a soothing tone.

"Sissy, meet our former pastor, Jimmy Beauchamp. Jimmy, this is Blanche's niece, Sissy Ducaine," Ina Mae said.

Sissy shook hands with the guy. "Pleased to meet you."

"My pleasure," Jimmy said and dropped her hand. "I'm waiting on . . ."

The high-pitched sound of an ambulance filled the air, and Jimmy rolled his eyes. "Luke needs to be here, so I've been elected to go with her, and then take her home."

"Who?" Sissy asked.

8

"Elvira!" Ina Mae and Gussie said at the same time.

"We've got her in the office right now," Jimmy said. "It won't take long for us to clear out."

The ambulance came to a stop right outside the doors, and two guys wheeled in a gurney. One of them rolled his eyes at Jimmy.

"I hope she's okay," Sissy whispered.

"She's fine," Ina Mae said. "There's nothing wrong with her that a good swift kick in the butt wouldn't cure."

In minutes, the two fellows brought the gurney back out with a weeping woman lying on it. "Oh, my sweet Blanche. What will I ever do without you?" She reached out and grabbed Sissy's hand as they rolled her down the foyer. "You must be her niece. I'm so sorry to ruin the funeral, but she was such a dear friend. I was just overcome. Please call me if you need anything. She was kin to me at one time."

"We've got to go, Miz Jones," the EMT said.

"Maybe I'll meet Blanche in the by-and-by before the day is done." Elvira sighed.

Jimmy disappeared with them out into the freezing rain.

Gussie looped her arm into Sissy's. "Don't look so bewildered, chère. It's no surprise that Elvira had one of her spells this morning. She's the town hypochondriac and the biggest gossip in all of Newton."

9

"But she was Aunt Bee's friend, right? And how were they kin?" Sissy asked.

Ina Mae shook her head. "They were arch-enemies. We didn't invite her to join our Sunshine Club sixty years ago, and she's never forgiven us. And they are not kin. Blanche's ex-husband was like her third or fourth cousin. Let's go on into the chapel and pay our respects before they put Blanche into the hearse. You go in first, Sissy, and we'll come in right behind you. We will sit together on the front row of seats."

Sissy had never been to a jazz funeral, but that's what Aunt Bee had wanted, and her two best friends, the other two members of the Sunshine Club, had offered to arrange the whole thing. Every seat in the chapel was taken. The walls were lined with the overflow of folks, and the whole front of the room was filled with flowers and plants.

Both of Sissy's grandparents' funerals had been in a big church sanctuary when she was in her teens. When her parents passed a couple of years before, she'd had them cremated and scattered their ashes in the parking lot of the bar in Georgia where they'd met and fallen in love. Aunt Bee had flown in to be with her, and when it was done, they had gone into the bar and had a shot of whiskey to celebrate her folks' lives.

Every eye seemed to be on Sissy as she walked from the back of the chapel to the front and sat down in one of the three empty chairs. Gussie and Ina Mae took their places on either side of her, and the preacher stepped up to the lectern. Sissy stared up at him—black hair, clear blue eyes, a chiseled face that an artist would love—and waited for him to begin.

"We are gathered here today to pay our last respects to Blanche Ducaine, a pillar in our town and also in the Newton Community Church. Before we leave for the cemetery, I would like to read the obituary," the preacher said, and then cleared his throat. "Blanche Elizabeth Ducaine was born May 13, 1951, to the Reverend Delford Ducaine and his wife, Eva Ducaine, who both preceded her in death, as did her brother, Ford Ducaine, and his wife, Katy. She is survived by her niece, Martina Ducaine, also known as Sissy. Blanche grew up right here in Newton, Texas, and graduated from the Newton High School. She went on to college at the University of Louisiana at Lafayette, and then returned home to work her way up to hospital administrator at our hospital in town until she retired five years ago. She is also survived by two lifetime friends, Gussie Sadler and Ina Mae Garber. The family has asked for a few last minutes with Miz Ducaine. We'll give them their privacy, and then meet them outside." He nodded toward the congregation and then led the way outside.

Martina Ducaine—a therapist in Beau Bridge,

11

Louisiana, Sissy thought. *A professional woman who keeps her past tucked away from public view. Sissy Ducaine, the daughter of two rock musicians, who grew up in an RV traveling from gig to gig with her parents—a dysfunctional lifestyle that only a handful of people in Newton, Texas, knew about. Two people in one body.*

Sissy had loved her aunt Bee and had spent as much time as she could with her when she was a little girl. The fact that her aunt lived only two hours away was the reason she took the job in Beau Bridge, Louisiana, when she graduated from college—well, that, and the fact that Aunt Bee had paid for her to go to the University of Louisiana at Lafayette, the same university that she and her friends had attended. Aunt Bee had been the one who'd nicknamed her Sissy, and who loved her unconditionally.

Her aunt's sudden death had come as a shock, but it wasn't until that morning that it really sank in that she had no living relatives left. Knowing that and facing the massive job of getting her aunt's affairs in order, as well as the house cleaned out and ready to sell, was both overwhelming and bewildering. The only roots Sissy'd ever had were at Aunt Bee's place. She'd been homeschooled on the road and begged to go live with Aunt Bee when she reached high school age, but her parents wouldn't hear of it.

"All right, chère," Gussie said.

Sissy cocked her head to one side. "Are we ready to go to the cemetery?"

"No, darlin', we are going to tell Blanche goodbye now." Ina Mae stood and walked up to the open casket. "We decided to do things just a little different than a pure jazz funeral. We had some things to say, and we didn't want to talk to a closed casket at the cemetery."

Gussie stood up and patted Sissy on the shoulder. "You can go first, chère."

Sissy pushed up out of the chair but didn't go first as Gussie had suggested. She hung back for a few seconds before she went to stand between Ina Mae and Gussie. "Aunt Bee, I'm going to miss you so much. With your sass, I thought you'd still be kicking up your heels at your hundredth birthday party. I actually bought some paper plates a few weeks ago and stored them for your next birthday. I've always come to you for advice and to share good things with. Now where do I go? You've left me alone." Tears streamed down her cheeks, leaving black mascara tracks in their wake.

Gussie draped an arm around Sissy's shoulders and dabbed the tears away with a tissue. "Chère, you should have worn waterproof mascara today, but me and Ina Mae will take care of you, and don't you worry about being alone in this world. We are your family, and we'll always be here for you. Blanche was like a sister to me and Ina Mae, even if there wasn't a bit of DNA between us. We'll help you with anything you need."

Ina Mae took a step closer to Sissy and made it a three-way hug. "Darlin' girl, we'll all get through this together, and Gussie is wrong. We three were even closer than sisters. We were like triplets, and that makes you our niece, too."

Gussie focused on Blanche. "I'm too mad at you for dying to give you this last wish that you left in your letter, but I'm afraid if I don't do what you want, you'll haunt me the rest of my days." She pulled a small bottle of Jack Daniel's from her pocket and tucked it into the edge of the casket. "We made a pact when we were just teenagers that we would all go on the same day, and you've jumped the gun on me and Ina Mae. I may not forgive you, but we'll talk more about this when I make it up to the pearly gates."

Ina Mae pulled a .38-caliber bullet from her shoulder bag and slid it into Blanche's hand. "I don't like this one bit better than Gussie does. Who would have thought you'd go before us? You were the tall, skinny one that never had to take a pill for anything, and then you drop graveyard dead at the age of seventy with a heart attack. Well, here's the bullet I promised to put in your casket. I expect that you are planning to shoot Walter with it if he's in heaven, and then kick his sorry body out the pearly gates. I hope you do. This heart attack probably happened because you were married to that bastard for six weeks. It damaged your heart, didn't it?"

"You should've never married that sumbitch, Walter," Gussie whispered. "I'm not cussin,' Lord. I'm just callin' it like I see it. We should have kept to our promise to never let anyone but the three Js in our hearts." Gussie wiped her cheeks with the same tissue that she'd used on Sissy and then handed it to Ina Mae.

"Three Js?" Sissy asked.

"Jack Daniel's, Jim Beam, and Jesus," Gussie explained. "We decided that when we were sixteen and got our first taste of whiskey and sex. Blanche was the only one of us that ever gave marriage a try. Maybe Ina Mae is right—that six weeks of marriage caused her heart to be weak."

Ina Mae wiped away a tear with the tissue. "Or maybe Walter broke something inside her when he beat her so badly, and it didn't really shatter until she was seventy."

Sissy hadn't brought anything to put in the casket, or even thought about what she would say in the way of goodbye. She stared down at her aunt Bee again, lying there in her bright-red dress and with her dyed-red hair. "Nobody should leave their loved ones behind at the holiday season."

"Amen"—Ina Mae nodded and winked at Blanche—"and you're welcome. Me and Gussie had the hairdresser come in and cover up your roots. Maybe it was all that dye you've kept on

15

your hair since you found the first gray strand that gave you the heart attack."

The three of them stood there for several more minutes, arms laced together. And then Sissy took the tissue from Ina Mae. "I'm putting this in your casket so you can take all of our tears with you. I'd tell you to rest in peace, but I've got a feeling you're already causing some kind of mischief."

"That's perfect," Gussie said. "It's time to go now. The folks waiting outside are probably freezing their asses off." She reached down and touched Blanche's hand. "If you weren't already dead, I might shoot you myself, for making us walk all the way to the cemetery in this kind of weather."

Sissy had bought her long black coat for a winter conference she was supposed to attend in New York City, but then COVID-19 had put an end to that. She had never had occasion to wear it, either in south Texas or Louisiana, but when the weather turned so cold, she was more than glad to have it. Leave it to Aunt Bee to be buried on the day when the first freezing rain in fifty years hit Newton.

When they left the parlor and stepped out into the foyer, where the townspeople had lined up against the walls, the preacher nodded at the pallbearers. Several of the folks stepped up to shake Gussie's, Ina Mae's, and Sissy's hands, or to give them a hug and offer condolences. They introduced themselves to Sissy, but there was no way she would remember all those names. There were several couples who said they wouldn't be together if the ladies of the Sunshine Club hadn't played at a little matchmaking.

The pallbearers went inside and carried the casket out. Folks bowed their heads respectfully, but Sissy kept her eyes on the shiny red coffin—another of Aunt Bee's requests in the letter she'd left behind. Once they had slid the casket into the horse-drawn hearse, the preacher told everyone that it was now time for the first line.

Sissy had no idea where they got a shiny black hearse with glass sides so that the casket could be seen, or the two black horses with tall red plumes on their heads. But she knew in her heart that if Ina Mae and Gussie had needed to buy the whole getup for Blanche, they would have done it. The Newton High School band began to play a slow, mournful version of "Just a Closer Walk with Thee" and started the first line to the graveyard. The driver slapped the reins against the horses' flanks, and they plodded along behind the band. Hand in hand Sissy, Ina Mae, and Gussie all fell in behind the carriage, and the rest of the townsfolk followed them.

Bits of freezing rain pecked like cold BBs against Sissy's face. She hated to let go of the elderly ladies' hands, but she did so she could flip the hood on her coat up to cover her ears.

Her hands were getting numb, and her eyelashes felt like they were caked with ice, but there was nothing she could do about that.

With her free hand, Gussie brought a pair of black gloves from the pocket of her bright-red coat and handed them to Sissy. "Put these on. I always carry an extra pair. Blanche could have planned a better day than this. We haven't had snow or freezing rain in this part of the country since I was a little girl."

"Thank you," Sissy said. "Why did she want a jazz funeral anyway? Since Grandpa was a preacher, I figured she'd have a traditional service. I was pretty much blown away when y'all told me she wanted something like this."

"Lord, it's hard to breathe in this cold wind and rain. If you were here, Blanche, I would slap you silly," Ina Mae said.

Gussie drew the collar of her coat up around her neck. "I've got scarves in the hearse for when we do the second line. We kind of fixed things our way. Usually just the family goes in the first line, but Blanche wanted everyone to be there in both lines. I should've gotten them out before we left. You asked about why she wanted this kind of service, Sissy. Well, truth is, she loved anything Cajun or that had to do with Louisiana after we went to college over there, but the real story is that she wanted to go out with a splash."

"She was convinced that Ducaine was a Cajun

name. She probably told you that when she explained her love for anything with a Cajun flair when she decorated her house. We thought she'd change her mind after a few years about this kind of service, but she didn't." Ina Mae blinked back tears. "If I cry, I'll have ice on my cheeks."

"Strange thing is that we'd talked and laughed about it just a week before"—Gussie's voice cracked—"before she dropped right out there on the courthouse square. We were with her, sitting in the gazebo and talking about the cruise we planned to take in February."

"We might not even go now," Ina Mae said. "It just wouldn't be the same without Blanche."

"Of course you'll go," Sissy said. "Aunt Bee will come back and haunt the both of you if you don't go. I just wish Daddy could have been here. He idolized Aunt Bee for standing up to Grandpa. He would have probably wanted to play rock music on the way to the cemetery."

"We were sixteen when your daddy, Ford, was born. We always wondered if he'd follow in his father's footsteps and be a preacher. Blanche adored that child, and after her folks moved to Louisiana, she would bring him over here as often as she could to stay a few days with her. She also had a special place in her heart for your mother. She said that Katy was exactly what Ford needed to be happy, and that everyone's happy-ever-after didn't have to be conventional." Gussie sighed.

19

"When he got to be a teenager, he wanted to be a rock star. Blanche encouraged him to follow his dreams and her folks threw a fit. Then when she accepted Katy . . ." Ina Mae shook her head slowly. "Those were war years for sure. She hadn't ever gotten along with her parents—especially after she divorced Walter—but it was even worse after Ford and Katy got married. But that's a story for another day."

"I can believe that," Sissy said. "My mother told me a little bit about how Daddy's folks didn't accept her, and that made it easier for my parents to stay away from them. Of all the places my folks had gigs in during my childhood, the one I've loved the most was Aunt Bee's place right here in Newton."

Gussie almost smiled. "You're like your aunt Bee in that. And she also loved living in Louisiana."

"So did you," Ina Mae said and then turned around to face Sissy. "That's where she got in the habit of using the word *chère*."

"Well, it does sound better than *darlin'* or *sweetie pie*," Gussie protested. "It's got a soft, sweet sound to it."

Sissy glanced over her shoulder. "Those folks look a little embarrassed."

"They probably are, and I can imagine they're cussin' Blanche for making them walk in this cold rain." Gussie nodded.

"They might be fussin' right now, but they'll

be talking about it for years to come. That music is so sad . . ." Ina Mae wiped tears away with a white hankie she pulled from the pocket of her coat. "Got to dry them fast before they freeze. We are not supposed to shed a single tear at this funeral, and these hankies are for us to twirl at the second line, not wipe tears with. Don't you go tellin' on me, Sissy."

"I promise I won't say a word." Sissy had always wondered about their club, and this seemed like a good time to ask—maybe to take their minds away from the cold. "Aunt Bee told me that y'all formed the Sunshine Club when you were little girls and had kept it going for the rest of your lives. Why did you ever—"

Gussie butted in. "It was my idea. Some boys that had been our friends built a clubhouse and wrote on the outside, 'No Girls Allowed.' That made me so mad that I wanted to burn down their ratty old shack."

"No, you didn't," Ina Mae argued. "That was Blanche's idea. She thought because your daddy was the judge back then that he'd get us off if we got caught."

"Well," Gussie huffed, "she just said the words that were in my heart. Anyway, I asked Mama if we could use the old summer kitchen out back of our house to make a girls' clubhouse, and she said we could."

"Why did you name it the Sunshine Club?"

21

Sissy's toes were getting colder by the minute. She wished she had worn socks and boots, rather than high heels and no stockings.

"That was Gussie's mama's idea. She said us three girls were all rays of sunshine, so that would be a good idea for our club," Ina Mae answered. "And we've had a meeting in our club every Sunday for sixty years, and boys are still not allowed to step foot through the door. And now, just thinking about Blanche not being at our meeting this afternoon makes me all misty eyed."

"This isn't Sunday." Sissy could see the hearse headed for a green tent not far up ahead.

"No, but we have to meet today because that's in Blanche's letter," Ina Mae said. "Dammit! I'm crying again. Don't you dare tell Blanche, Gussie."

"I won't tattle on you, if you don't on me," Gussie said, and then turned to Sissy. "We have both cried until we had to put ice packs on our eyes this morning to make ourselves presentable at this service, but we vowed we'd do what Blanche wanted and not weep at the funeral."

The hearse stopped in front of a green tent set up with three chairs facing a platform wrapped in artificial turf. Ina Mae and Gussie sat down, leaving the middle chair for Sissy. She took her place and watched the pallbearers bring the casket out from the hearse and set it down. Fake green grass and an ice storm all at the same

22

time—that seemed like the story of Sissy's life. Two very different people—one professional, one as common as dirt. Hopefully, though, neither was fake or cold natured.

"Who are those pallbearers?" Sissy whispered to Gussie.

"The silver-haired one is the hospital administrator that took over when Blanche retired, and the others are either doctors or folks she worked with when she was working. She had a list of who we were supposed to ask to carry the casket," Gussie answered in a low voice.

"She didn't leave anything undone, did she?" Sissy's voice quivered.

"It'll be all right, chère." Gussie leaned over toward her and patted her on the arm as they waited for the rest of the people to gather round for the remainder of the service.

Sissy nodded and brought her head up at just the right angle to flip Gussie's big brimmed, black hat with its red rose on the side smack off her head, and sent it flying toward the preacher like a big-butted, black bird. Ina Mae reached up with a long arm and caught it in midair. She slapped it back down on Gussie's head and said in a low voice, "You are welcome."

Sissy heard muted giggles behind her, but she managed to get her serious face on when she remembered what Aunt Bee always said about being respectful at a funeral.

You would have thought it was a hoot if Gussie's big old hat had fallen right in the middle of your casket arrangement of white lilies. Lilies in the middle of winter. I wonder where on earth Gussie and Ina Mae found them, she thought as she stared at the casket.

The preacher cleared his throat and looked out over the crowd for a few seconds. "Miz Blanche Ducaine will be missed. She was a sweet lady who was an integral part of the church. She and her two friends cleaned it every Saturday morning . . ."

Daddy, you should be here, she thought. *You and Mama should be inheriting her house and setting down roots. You would both be over fifty, and this would be a good place for you to live.*

The preacher's voice faded into the background. Sissy remembered many times helping her aunt, Ina Mae, and Gussie tidy up the church on Saturday morning. She had picked gum and candy wrappers from the racks on the backs of the pews that held hymnbooks and even read a few notes from teenagers that weren't meant for her eyes. She hadn't minded helping out, especially since Aunt Bee always took her to the shooting range afterward and let her fire off a few rounds at the targets that were fastened on the ends of big round bales of hay.

She scolded herself for going down memory lane and not listening and tried to concentrate on the preacher. What had Gussie said his name was? Larry? No, that wasn't right. Liam? Sissy frowned, then caught herself just before she shouted out, "Luke." In her opinion, he was too tall, dark, and handsome to be a preacher. But then he did have piercing blue eyes that looked like they could see right into a person's soul. Her grandfather always said it was a preacher's job to help save souls, so maybe Luke's ability to see into a person's heart with those sexy blue eyes was a big help.

More than a hundred people stood behind her—at least that's how many she figured were back there. She could imagine their bones turning to pure ice and the lot of them freezing to death in an upright position. Folks in the southern part of Texas weren't used to this weather, and their thin coats probably did little to keep them warm. Sissy didn't have to imagine their sighs. Those were loud and clear.

"Why are so many people here? Were they all friends with Aunt Bee?" she whispered to Gussie.

"She always told everyone that, when she died, she was going to have a jazz funeral. No one believed her, and they've all come out today to see if me and Ina Mae would really do what she wanted," Gussie said out the side of her mouth. "There's no way they'd miss this, and besides, there's a potluck dinner after the burial."

That wasn't funny—but it was. Sissy buried her

face in the pretty white hankie that Gussie had tucked into her pocket on the way to the cemetery and hoped that all the folks behind her thought her shaking shoulders meant she was crying.

Oh, Aunt Bee, she thought. *Please, don't push the lid up on that casket and tell me I'm going to hell for laughing at your funeral. Like me, there were two sides to you. One was the religious side left over from your upbringing. You believed in Jesus and God, but not to the strict degree that your folks did. Then there was the fun-loving, ornery side. Neither of my sides are religious, but there's a touch of fun in the common one.*

Gussie bent forward and began to sob uncontrollably behind her big black hat. Ina Mae's hat almost lost the rose that was tacked to the side when she did the same. Sissy got control of herself and draped an arm around each of them. She sympathized with the loss of their best friend and sister, of the heart if not of the blood. As a therapist, she knew all about how hard losing a lifetime friend could be on seventy-year-old women and felt guilty about laughing.

Tears of humor turned into those of sadness and flowed down Sissy's cheeks. Then Ina Mae snorted, and Sissy realized they were giggling, and wondered if they had plumb lost their minds.

The preacher stopped, cleared his throat, and looked over at Ina Mae, Gussie, and Sissy. "I want to offer my services to all three of you if you need someone to talk to in your time of grief. Know that the entire church is here for you and will be praying earnestly that you will remember the good times you had with Blanche. Lunch will be served in the fellowship hall, and you are all invited to join us. Maybe each of you have a little memory you could share with Blanche's niece, Sissy, and her best friends, Ina Mae and Gussie, when you get a chance."

Sissy blinked several times as if trying to hold back the tears and nodded. "Thank you," she mouthed.

"Now for the march back to the church," Ina Mae said as she got to her feet. "I feel like one of them Popsicles Gussie's mama used to make for us. I'm too old to be dancin' in the freezin' rain, but if that's what Blanche wants, then that's what I'll do."

Sissy had lived in Beau Bridge, Louisiana, since she'd graduated from college, and folks often had this kind of service in that town. Still, she couldn't have imagined having a funeral like this for her parents when they were killed. Her grandfather had always seemed stiff and austere to Sissy. She could imagine him trying to dig his way up out of the grave to haunt her if she had done something like this for his son and daughter-in-law, even if he didn't like the woman who had caused their son not to go into the ministry like they'd wanted. Blaming his wife was a lot easier than putting the burden on their precious son's shoulders.

Maybe Aunt Bee had planned this just to make Sissy's grandfather mad. She could almost see her granddad standing just inside the pearly gates shaking his finger at Aunt Bee when she arrived. Sissy had been just a teenager when her grandparents both died within six months of each other, but before that happened she could remember the tension that filled the room when her dad and Aunt Bee came home for a few hours on Christmas—at least some of the years.

Gussie shook the preacher's hand and then went to the hearse. She opened the door and brought out three black lace umbrellas, each with a wide red ruffle around its outside edge, and handed one to Ina Mae and one to Sissy. "We got to do this part up in style. Get ready to do some fancy prancin' down the street for the second line. I'm going to change my end-of-life arrangements to have something like this, but I am not dyin' in the wintertime."

"Are you serious?" Sissy gasped.

"I'm as serious as my daddy was when he was sentencing a man to prison, and later in life when I did the same thing when I became a judge." Gussie popped the black lace umbrella open. "And, chère, you need a bit of color." She pulled three long red scarves from the hearse and passed them around. "After the lunch at the church, we'll go to my house and finish up the rest of Blanche's orders."

"There's more?" Sissy draped the scarf around her neck and then threw one end over her shoulder. That little bit of extra warmth was wonderful. "Thank you for this."

The band began to play a fast version of "When the Saints Go Marching In" and did some fancy stepping as they led the second line back to town.

Gussie twirled her umbrella and danced around in circles to the beat of the music. Ina Mae followed her lead. Sissy figured if two old ladies could move like that, then she might as well join them. Besides, a little movement might keep her from freezing plumb to death. She glanced behind her to see the preacher in the midst of the sober-acting folks. Maybe they were too cold and stiff for a proper second line, but Sissy Ducaine intended to send her aunt Bee off in style no matter what people thought of her. In Newton, she was Sissy, not the prim and proper Martina, anyway. She twirled the umbrella with one hand and her white hankie with the other as she dipped and swayed to the music's fast rhythm.

How Gussie and Ina Mae were still talking and laughing when they reached the church fellowship hall was a mystery to her. Her lungs were on fire from sucking in the cold air, and her hands were freezing even though she'd been wearing the gloves. Her feet felt like icicles on stilts. Never again would she wear four-inch heels during an ice storm.

"Well, butter my butt and call me a biscuit," Gussie said when they reached the church parking lot, where everyone was hurrying toward the fellowship hall.

"What?" Sissy smiled at the old adage she had heard Aunt Bee use before.

"I told you so." Ina Mae raised her chin a notch.

"Who told what?" Sissy asked.

"That right there"—Gussie pointed to a fairly new pickup truck—"is Jimmy's truck. That means the hospital has released Elvira and she's probably inside."

"I told you that she would be at the funeral home, but she'd pull something, so she didn't have to walk to the cemetery and back," Ina Mae said through clenched teeth. "What do you bet her appetite is really good for a woman who just had a heart attack."

"A *fake* heart attack," Gussie growled. "One of these days she's going to really have one and no one is going to believe her."

When they walked into the fellowship hall, sure enough there was Elvira standing behind the buffet table with a big smile on her face.

"See there, from a gurney to bossin' everyone who's brought food. Both sides of Elvira in one day," Ina Mae said.

Gussie took Sissy by the arm. "Come on over

here and see the memory table we set up. I need a minute to get my temper under control. This is Blanche's day, not Elvira's."

Sissy followed Gussie and Ina Mae's lead and hung her coat on a rack beside theirs, then followed them to a long table of pictures set against a far wall. There were photographs of all sizes taken of Aunt Bee, most of which she'd never even seen. Some with Ina Mae and Gussie, one or two with what she supposed would have been the doctors and nurses at the hospital where she had worked.

"You are the spittin' image of Blanche when she was your age," Gussie said.

Sissy had heard that comment often from her father and had always thought folks needed to have their eyes checked. Blanche had been a tall, lanky woman, and Sissy had to stretch or wear shoes with heels to be five-feet-three inches tall, and she was a little on the curvy side.

Ina Mae picked up a picture to study it closer. "This one was taken about the time that she was first promoted to hospital administrator. The youngest person ever to have that position and the first woman. She was about the age you are now when she got that promotion, and we were so proud of her."

Sissy could see the facial resemblance to herself in that particular picture. "That must have been before she started dyeing her hair red."

31

"She called it auburn." Gussie's chin quivered, but she soon got control. "You've got the same big green eyes and strawberry-blonde hair that she had before she found that first gray hair."

"She said she didn't intend to get old." Ina Mae ran a finger over Blanche's face. "And that hair dye was a cheap price to pay to stay young."

More people began pouring in from the cold, and several ladies went to the back of the room to join Elvira, who quickly told them what they were to do. In the south, everyone turned out for funerals, weddings, and church socials—and they all brought food. Aunt Bee would have been proud of the spread and all the folks who had braved the weather to see her off to eternity.

Gussie looped an arm in Sissy's and tugged. "Everyone is cold and hungry, chère, and they are all waiting for us to go first in the line because we are the family. We'll look at these pictures later."

"Let's get this over with," Ina Mae said out of the corner of her mouth, "so we can go get a shot of whiskey to warm my insides. I should've brought the flask that Blanche gave me for Christmas last year."

"Just lead the way and tell me what to do." Sissy sighed. "The only people I really know here are y'all, and I don't want to step on any toes."

"You've met a lot of them, but it will take time to put faces with names," Ina Mae said.

"No worries," Gussie said. "We'll take care of you like you was our own, which you are, since Blanche is . . . was . . . the only one of us privileged to have had a niece. We told her when you were born that she had to share, so we're collecting on that debt from now on."

Sissy wasn't sure if that was a good thing or something she should run from, but she trailed along to the buffet tables.

Chapter Two

Gussie argued with Ina Mae as she drove from the church to her house. "I think Blanche would be okay if we invited Sissy. After all, she's the only living relative any of us have. It won't seem right to just have two members in the Sunshine Club."

Ina Mae set her thin mouth in a firm line and shook her head. "She didn't leave it in her end-of-life letter." She grabbed the dashboard and squealed when Gussie slid around a stop sign. "Slow down, woman. The roads are slippery. We don't want to have another funeral in this kind of nasty weather."

"Or in any weather." Gussie got control of the vehicle. "The good Lord isn't finished with me yet, and my heart couldn't stand to lose you this soon after Blanche. And you'll be a hundred years old before God gets done with you." She gripped the steering wheel a little tighter.

"And what does that mean?" Ina Mae asked.

"That God don't want you, and the devil won't have you," Gussie told her as she tapped the brakes. The car slid right past the driveway, spun around in a complete circle, and was headed right back toward the house when it came to a stop.

"Holy hell!" Ina Mae panted as her hand went

to her chest. "I thought we was goners for sure. My heart hasn't beat this fast since we waited on the ambulance to come help Blanche, and Augusta Frances Sadler, I just saw my whole life flash before my eyes, and every bad thing I ever did, you and Blanche were right there with me. I guess you had better live to be a hundred, too."

Gussie's fingers were still glued to the steering wheel, but her heart was pounding like she'd just had hot sex, and that hadn't happened in years. "My head is still goin' around in circles, but at least we're headed in the right direction, and you're probably right about us being in on the bad stuff. We were there for the good stuff, too, I'll have you know."

Ina Mae started to open the car door, but Gussie managed to get a hand away from the steering wheel and grab her arm before she could get out. "What do you think you're doin'?"

"I'm walking from here to your house. We can't leave Sissy with no family at all, and you're about to kill both of us," Ina Mae answered.

"You're not leaving me in this car alone. The damned thing has a mind of its own, and I need some support if I'm to get it home. If I ever get it parked in the driveway, I'm not moving it until the roads are dry as a desert," Gussie declared.

"One more slip and slide, and I'm out of here." Ina Mae settled into the seat, but she put her hands over her eyes. "Next time I'm driving.

I don't know why you insist on these little lightweight cars. You need a big old truck like I drive. You can trust it to have a little traction."

"How many times do we need to fill up a gas hog like your truck when we take it on a trip?" Gussie eased down the road at less than five miles an hour.

"As many times as it takes if it saves our lives," Ina Mae argued, but she didn't take her hands from her eyes. "Are we there yet?"

"I'm turning into the driveway now," Gussie answered. "Keep your eyes covered until we get parked."

"I intend to," Ina Mae said. "You about scared the pee out of me. Next time my pucker power might give out, and I just got this suit out of the cleaner's. I don't want to have to take it back smelling like urine. If that news got out to Elvira, she would spread it all over town."

Gussie was almost afraid to tap the brakes again, but if she didn't, the car was going to slide right past the house and run smack into the clubhouse. Lord have mercy! If she destroyed the clubhouse, she would never hear the end of it from Ina Mae, and Blanche might rain fire and brimstone down from heaven upon her. She eased down on the brake and heaved a sigh of relief when the vehicle came to a stop.

"You can uncover your eyes now. We're safe," she said.

Ina Mae eased her hands away from her face and checked the rearview mirror on her side. "You didn't leave enough room for Sissy to park behind you."

"Hell's bells!" Gussie huffed.

Ina Mae got out of the car and held on to the door until she got her footing. "I see her. She's parking across the street in the courthouse spaces."

"Praise the Lord!" Gussie rolled her eyes upward. "We have to protect her, or Blanche will haunt us for sure."

Ina Mae slammed the door and waved at Sissy. "Stay on the grass," she yelled across the street. "It's not as slippery as the sidewalk. That thing looks like a death trap."

"Don't you talk about death right after a funeral," Gussie scolded her.

"You shush. Next time, I'm driving my truck," Ina Mae said.

"Your truck couldn't do a bit better than my car on these kinds of roads," Gussie said.

"I didn't hear you bitchin' about my truck when you wanted to go get that antique bed for your guest room that no one ever uses," Ina Mae smarted off.

"Whoa!" Gussie held up a palm. "We can only use bad words in the clubhouse, remember? And I think we should let Sissy be our new member."

"You're suggesting that we replace Blanche

before she's even cold in the ground?" Ina Mae narrowed her eyes and shook her head.

Gussie pursed her lips and slowly shook her head. "I'd say on a day like this she's plenty cold in the ground already. And for your information, Blanche is not replaceable. We'll never be able to put anyone in her place, but she wanted us to have the next part of her funeral day in the clubhouse. I don't know how to do that without inviting Sissy to join us."

"Nobody has ever been inside but us three," Ina Mae sighed.

"Well, we'd better make up our minds, because she's coming this way, and we're standing here freezing what's left of our asses off while we argue." Gussie shivered.

They'd made a pact when they were ten years old that no one, boys or other girls, or even parents, could ever come into the Sunshine Club. But down deep in her heart, Gussie knew that Blanche would approve of Sissy being allowed inside the old summer kitchen—at least this one time—for the remainder of her funeral service.

Ina Mae finally nodded. "If she didn't want us to do this, then she shouldn't have died and left us to make these hard decisions. I'm okay with inviting her inside just this one time."

Gussie held on to the side of the car with one hand and waved at Sissy with the other. "We're going to the clubhouse. Come join us."

Sissy nodded and followed them around the end of the house and back to the old summer kitchen. "Are you sure about this?" she asked. "Aunt Bee told me the rules of the clubhouse, and the first one is that no one other than you three can enter the place. I don't have to be here for the last part of Aunt Bee's wishes. I can wait in the house or go on home. I've got lots of stuff to go through, so . . ."

"You should be here." Gussie used a key to open the door and motioned Sissy inside. "We always said we were like a three-cord rope. One of our cords is gone"—her chin quivered again, but it had nothing to do with the cold weather—"and we're not ready to replace Blanche's third of that rope just yet, but since you're a part of Blanche, we think it's all right to let you in today."

"I'm honored and thank you." Sissy stepped inside the small building. "This heat feels so good."

"Take off your coat and warm your hands by the old heater over there in the corner." Ina Mae hung her coat on one of the three hooks beside the door.

Gussie wasn't sure whether Ina Mae would agree or not, but she took a deep breath and said, "You can hang yours on the end hook. That one belonged to your aunt Bee."

"Let's just leave that one empty," Sissy said.

39

"It's too sad to fill it right now. I'll just put my coat on the back of a kitchen chair."

"Maybe that's best." Gussie nodded as she put her heavy coat next to Ina Mae's. "Blanche left orders that we were not to grieve, but to get on with life, and that we were to do a few things after her funeral. To start with, we are to have a shot of whiskey in her honor."

Ina Mae pulled back a gingham checked curtain from a cabinet above an old wall-hung sink and took down a bottle of Jim Beam, one of Jack Daniel's, and three shot glasses. She set all of it in the middle of a wooden table that had lots of nicks and scratches. "I'm partial to Jim." She poured a shot and threw it back down her throat. "That's just to warm me up and get started. It's not part of the ritual for Blanche."

"Jack for me." Gussie crossed the room to where Ina Mae was pouring the liquor. "What are you drinking?"

"Jack, just like Aunt Bee liked," she answered. "Do we sit down or stand? Y'all have to tell me the rules. I don't want to do something that would upset Aunt Bee's plans."

"We'll stand for this first shot and then go sit on the sofa and the recliner," Gussie answered. "And, chère, I don't think you could upset your aunt Bee. She would be proud you are here with us."

Ina Mae poured three shot glasses full and held

hers up. "To Blanche, who was supposed to live another thirty years and then go to a nursing home with us so we could all raise hell together."

Sissy and Gussie picked up their glasses and they all three clinked them together and took a small sip.

"To Blanche"—Gussie held up her shot glass a second time—"a friend who took lots of our secrets to her grave and loved Jack as much as I do."

Ina Mae and Sissy touched their glasses to hers and they all took another sip.

Sissy raised her glass. "To Aunt Bee, who taught me to sip whiskey and enjoy every drop."

Another clink, and they all three drained the small shot glasses. Ina Mae set her empty glass on the table and said, "Now, we are supposed to leave these on the table and go sit on the sofa, where we are to share good memories we've had with Blanche."

"Get out our theme song and get it ready, Ina Mae, and reach me the tissues, because I'm going to cry. Blanche didn't say we couldn't bawl like babies when the jazz funeral was over," Gussie said.

Sissy wished that she could have another shot, but she determined that she would follow Ina Mae and Gussie's lead. Evidently, Aunt Bee's orders were to have one drink and then talk about the good times. "These glasses look old. Where did they come from?"

"We brought them back from our senior trip to Galveston. The class went down there for three days." Gussie picked up a box of tissues and carried them over to a well-worn old sofa. "That's a memory for sure, and, chère, we only use those little shot glasses for special times, like after an alumni reunion at the school when we always remember our senior trip, or on one of our birthdays, or to celebrate the day that Blanche got a divorce. One shot from them, and then we get out something bigger."

Sissy had thought she knew Aunt Bee, but evidently these three ladies had secrets no one else in the whole world was privy to.

"What's the story behind this bar?" She held up the little shot glass to get a better look at the logo on the side. "Did y'all barhop when you were younger? I bet Grandpa would turn over in his grave if he knew his daughter had ever been near a honky-tonk. My dad always said that his older sister had a wild side just like he did, but she was sly enough not to get caught."

Ina Mae laughed out loud as she brought out a CD and put it into a player on the top of the green refrigerator beside the stove. Then she took down three glasses that had once held jelly or preserves.

Sissy had a dozen or more just like them in her

own cabinet that she'd saved when she used all the grape jam out of them. "Garden Club crystal. That's what Aunt Bee called glasses like these."

"Yep, and they've held plenty of whiskey in their day. If we had a really bad week, we'd say we had to get out the Garden Club," Gussie said. "Don't get me wrong, chère, or think we're a bunch of alcoholics. We don't do this very often because we really don't like the aftereffects."

"But today we are honoring Aunt Bee, right?" Sissy asked.

"Absolutely and be damned to the consequences." Ina Mae poured four fingers of whiskey into two of the glasses. "Tonight we're going to talk about Blanche and tell stories and share happy times. And we're probably all going to get very drunk. I call shotgun on Gussie's sofa in her house. There is no way in hell I'm going to trust her to take me home, or myself to walk on slick roads, either. On Wednesday, the *Newton Weekly News* would have in big headlines across the top of the front page: Former Physician's Assistant Found Crawling Across Courthouse Lawn."

"And the subtitle would be Former county judge found passed out on her porch." Gussie giggled.

Sissy laughed with her. "If that happens, I'll frame a copy of it and hang it on the wall at Aunt Bee's house."

"Rest assured, there's no way any of us are

going farther than my house. There's four bedrooms upstairs. Y'all can choose a guest room. All we have to do is be able to climb the stairs, and I figure we can help each other. Besides, Blanche wants this Cajun wake, as she called it, to last until after church tomorrow."

Sissy jerked her head around and stammered, "I . . . can . . . drive . . ."

Gussie poured Jack Daniel's in the last empty glass and handed it off to her. "Rule number two was that we could cuss in the clubhouse, but we had to be dignified ladies anywhere else. Number three was that the person who tattled would join those boys." She pointed to the right of the fireplace, where an old door had been hung with "Boys Will Be Shot And Fed To The Coyotes" written below "The Sunshine Club." The letters had been purple at one time, but now they were faded.

Sissy read the sign and giggled. "Is that the original sign that y'all painted when you were little girls? Why did you replace it?"

"We lost the key, and we were older, so we decided to have a professional sign painter fix us up with a brand-new 'The Sunshine Club' on our door." Gussie sat down on the brown-and-gold plaid sofa and patted the spot beside her. "Blanche suggested we bring it in and use it like art. Other people might think it's trashy, but to us it's priceless."

Sissy sat down beside her and took the first sip of her whiskey from the jelly glass. "Tell me more about you three. I know you were good friends even back when you were little girls, but why did you all come back here after you graduated from college?"

"It was home," Gussie said. "I loved Louisiana, but I wanted to help the people in my own county, and Mama was still alive and needed me. I had a home right here, and I knew everyone."

"My grandmother was still living back then, and"—Ina Mae shrugged—"she wasn't in the best of health. Like Gussie, I had a home to go to, and Granny was glad to have me share it with her. After she was gone, I had the old place torn down and built myself a brand-new house in the same spot."

"And Aunt Bee?" Sissy asked.

"She had a job offer in Lafayette, but we couldn't bear to be split up. She moved back with us and stayed with me and Mama for a few months. Then she bought that house outside of town, and that's where she's lived since then," Gussie said.

"So basically you all wanted to help people?" Sissy asked.

"Yes, chère." Gussie raised her glass. "Just like you do. I was a lawyer for many years, and then Blanche talked me into putting my name in the election for county judge. I won by a landslide, probably because folks still remembered my daddy being a fair person when he was on the bench, and every election year after that . . ." Gussie stopped and took a sip of her whiskey. "Well, I just kept winning until I finally retired at sixty-five."

"And you, Ina Mae, what was your journey like from beginning to retirement?" Sissy asked.

"I started out as a registered nurse and kept taking courses until I got my physician's assistant license. Then I put in my own little clinic and sold it when I retired the same summer that Blanche and Gussie did," Ina Mae said. "We started school together, graduated together, went to college together, and retired at the same time. How are we going to go on without Blanche?"

"One day at a time," Sissy answered. "Tell me more about those shot glasses."

"Like I said, we were on our senior trip," Gussie said.

Sissy was glad she had changed the subject. If they started crying, she would, too, and according to Aunt Bee, they were supposed to be remembering good times.

"We were ready to set the world on fire," Gussie said. "If there'd been a bra burning on the courthouse lawn back then, all three of us would have been the first ones to toss ours into the blaze. We were liberated women, and we were going to prove it on our senior trip."

"We were in a hotel in Galveston right across the road from the beach. We had been to NASA that day. Bored. Me. To. Tears," Ina Mae said.

"It was called the Manned Spacecraft Center back then and everyone was all up in the air about a man walking on the moon. As Sophia on *The Golden Girls* used to say, 'Picture it,' " Gussie said. "Nineteen sixty-nine, two months before the moon walk. We got special permission to tour the Center. That was back before we ever heard of 'Houston, we have a problem.' "

Ina Mae hiccuped and then took another drink. "I didn't give a rat's tiny ass about all that stuff and neither did Blanche. I wasn't ever going up in space. Hell's bells, I couldn't get up to the second rung on a ladder without getting dizzy." She eased down in a wooden rocking chair that squeaked when she set it in motion.

"Curfew was ten o'clock." Gussie took up the story. "After the tour, we had supper at a seafood place with the whole group. Then we had a couple of hours to run around on the beach. At nine thirty, everyone was rounded up and we were all sent to our rooms. We had gotten to choose who we shared our rooms with, and normally it was two to the room, but we had an odd number of girls, so we three got to bunk up together."

When Gussie stopped talking to take a drink, Ina Mae went right on with the tale. "We passed bed check, and one of the parent sponsors turned out the lights. We waited until everyone was asleep, and then we snuck out of our room and went to a bar we had spotted just up the block. It was to be Blanche's last fling before she and Walter got married." Ina Mae giggled and pointed at Gussie. "This one sweet-talked the bartender into believing that we were twenty-one and this was a bachelorette party."

"It took a little more than words," Gussie admitted. "I had to undo enough buttons on my blouse to make that poor little guy drool. Not a one of us had ever drunk much before then, mainly because we couldn't buy it around here. To begin with, we were underage, and then everyone knows everything in this town. No one would think of selling us liquor back then. Everyone knew my daddy was the judge and Blanche's daddy was the preacher."

"And that my granny had a temper," Ina Mae added. "Gussie did manage to swipe a partial bottle of some kind of booze every time the judge had a party at his house."

"Hey, no one knew how much was drunk at those parties," Gussie said. "It was easy to wait until a bottle of whiskey was about half-full and then sneak it upstairs to my bedroom."

"Was that the first time you'd ever been to a bar?" Sissy asked.

"Yes, it was," Gussie answered. "We convinced ourselves that we could hold our liquor, but when we got back to the hotel, we couldn't remember where our room was. We thought it might be on the third floor, so we started there. We knew it had something to do with three, but we couldn't figure it out."

Sissy wished that she had a friend or two like these women. She had a few fairly close girlfriends—mostly women she worked with—and a couple she would even ask to be bridesmaids if and when she ever got married. But she hadn't shared secrets and sorrows so long with a single one that they could finish each other's sentences the way these two ladies did.

Ina Mae took a big swig of her whiskey. "We were afraid to try to open any other rooms with our key for fear we'd wake up one of the sponsors. If they caught us in that condition, we might lose our scholarships to college, and we'd all managed to get into the same school."

"What did you do?" Sissy asked.

"We crossed the road, shucked out of our clothes, and went skinny-dipping in the ocean." Gussie giggled, but soon she was crying again. "Dammit! Blanche! We had planned to go back to that beach and swim naked in the middle of the night again the summer when we'd been out of school sixty years. Now you're gone, and it won't be as much fun with just two of us."

"Sissy will go with us. She can be Blanche's proxy." Ina Mae held up her jelly glass in another toast. "Blanche would want us to follow through with all our plans."

"Oh, no!" Sissy shook her head. "If I got caught skinny-dippin', I could lose my license to practice family and marriage counseling."

"How do you do that anyway?" Gussie frowned. "You have never been married or had a family, so how can you know how to do therapy sessions for folks havin' domestic problems?"

"I studied all kinds of cases, so I understand their problems. I don't have to have the same issues." Sissy might not have had kids or a husband, but she'd come from a very different family, one that helped her understand the feelings of being alone and not living in a conventional home. She didn't want to talk about that this evening, however, so she deftly maneuvered the subject back to the senior class trip. "Please, tell me what happened next. Did you get caught?"

Gussie shook her head. "It's a wonder we didn't, but that chilly water sobered us right up. You wouldn't think that it would be that cold in May, but it was."

"Then"—Ina Mae took over the story again—"when we remembered that our room was number 333, we got tickled. Three floors up like we'd thought. Three threes all lined up to represent the three of us. How could we ever forget that number? But when we climbed the stairs up to the third floor, Blanche didn't have the key."

"Those were the days when most hotels had outside entrances, and most had real honest-to-God keys, not these newfangled plastic ones," Gussie explained. "So it wasn't like we had to pass through a lobby and chance meeting someone with our dripping-wet hair and damp clothing."

Sissy was so engrossed in the story that she didn't realize she had drunk all her whiskey until she looked down and the glass was empty. "Did you have to go wake up a sponsor after all?"

"Oh, no!" Ina Mae shook her head. "We went right back to the beach where we'd tossed our clothes. Thank God there was enough moonlight to help us find the key just layin' there like a piece of pure gold."

"I told both of them I could pick the lock with a bobby pin, but Blanche said we had to return the key to the sponsors at the end of the trip or they would ask questions," Gussie said. "There it was, shining in the moonlight like something out of a fairy tale. Blanche said it was an omen." Gussie finished off her whiskey and set the glass on the floor beside the sofa.

Sissy must have had a quizzical expression on her face because Ina Mae reached across the distance and patted her on the knee.

"The omen meant that our adventure was meant to be, or we wouldn't have found the key. We would have gotten caught, and our lives would have changed, because there would have been no way we could have all gone to college together," she said. "Gussie's daddy might have paid for her to go. Blanche's daddy would have sent her to a convent, and I'd have cleaned courthouse rooms like my granny did for the rest of my life."

"Baptists don't have convents." Sissy giggled. "And I didn't know that your grandmother worked at the courthouse."

"When we were little girls, we were convinced that they had a secret convent. When a girl got sent there, she never was allowed to leave and ended up dying in the place," Gussie told her.

"And my granny was strict, worked hard, and raised me right, but honey, I wanted more out of life than cleaning the courthouse," Ina Mae said.

"But evidently you didn't get caught. You all went on to be very productive women. Did you ever—"

"We were very careful," Gussie butted in before Sissy could finish. "And that wasn't the last time we got drunk. We paid the price for our choices a few times, as in a few hangovers, but finding that key was our lucky omen for the rest of our lives. That and having this clubhouse. We never got caught when we did something really . . ."

Ina Mae shot a look toward Gussie, and the two of them shared a moment that made Sissy wonder just how bad of a thing they had done. Did Aunt Bee know about it, or was she a part of it? One thing was for sure, Ina Mae didn't want Gussie to talk about it. That much Sissy could tell from that knowing look that passed between them.

"And we never got sent to the Baptist convent," Ina Mae giggled. "But getting back to the story, we had less than two hours' sleep when the sponsor gave us a wakeup call the next morning and said we had fifteen minutes to get loaded on the bus to go home," Ina Mae said. "That ringing phone sounded like it was inside my head and would never stop. God, I hate a hangover."

"Did anyone suspect that you'd gotten drunk?" Sissy asked.

"Nope," Gussie answered. "I imagine most of the kids had a slumber party in their rooms that last night, so we all tried to sleep on the way home, but I felt every single bump and rattle in that old yellow bus on that four-hour trip back home to Newton."

"How soon after that did Aunt Bee get married?" Sissy asked.

"Two weeks," Ina Mae answered. "What did she tell you about that time in her life?"

Sissy kicked off her shoes and drew her feet up on the sofa. Sleet still peppered against the windows, and when the north wind blew, the pecan tree limbs outside rattled together like the old skeleton in her high school science class. "She didn't tell me anything at all. I asked her about it, and she just said that I should be careful that I really know a guy before I get into bed with him, and to never live in the past but to move on from it."

Ina Mae locked eyes with Gussie, again, and they both nodded at the same time. Sissy figured they were deciding how much to tell her.

"Walter joined the army right out of high school and was sent to Vietnam," Ina Mae said. "He was injured after a year, and they gave him a discharge. He came home at Christmas and proposed to Blanche on Valentine's Day. He had gone to school with us, but he was a senior when we were freshmen. That made him about four years older, but he wasn't a stranger. At eighteen and twenty-two, that wasn't such a big age difference, and girls got married younger back then."

"He was very attentive to her, so neither me or Ina Mae thought he'd turn out to be an over-bearing bastard," Gussie said.

"Blanche thought she was in love," Ina Mae said. "And because she did, so did we. We came home and got all involved with the last-minute wedding preparations. Blanche's mama, Eva, was glad to see her getting married and settling down. Blanche wanted a small wedding, maybe just at the courthouse, but Eva would have no part of that—no, ma'am. She planned the biggest wedding Newton had seen in years. Blanche had the white dress and veil and a cake—the whole nine yards. Gussie and I were bridesmaids."

"She got married on June first. It's supposed to be good luck to get married in June, but after what happened in the next six weeks, we all decided that was a bunch of bullshit." Gussie shook her head at the memory. "I still get physically sick to my stomach thinking about it."

Sissy wanted to know more, but she didn't want to push. Both Gussie and Ina Mae had expressions on their faces that said the memory of those six weeks was painful.

Ina Mae nodded several times and said, "Blanche thought she would have the summer to settle into marriage. We'd all go to college in the fall, and Walter was going to use his GI Bill money to go with us. She'd live in a cute little apartment, and me and Ina Mae would go visit her and Walter every chance we got."

Gussie took another drink. "Those were the ugliest lilac-colored dresses in the whole world. We should've known right then that the marriage wouldn't last. Those things looked like they might have been popular in the forties."

"I thought Aunt Bee didn't like purple. Her favorite colors were baby blue and bright red," Sissy said.

"Eva . . . that would be Blanche's mother and your grandma . . . thought the lilac looked soft, like young ladies should wear to a wedding. Blanche didn't want anything like the wedding she actually had. Our dresses were hideous, but her wedding gown was so unlike her, it was downright pitiful," Ina Mae said. "Her dress had a Victorian collar and long sleeves, and a gazillion buttons up the back. It was fitting for a preacher's daughter, according to Eva, who thought we were all virgins. Walter was probably out of the mood for sex by the time he got all them buttons unfastened. Never thought of it, but that might be the reason he seemed to be angry about everything the whole time they were married."

Sissy could hold a couple of shots and maybe a beer in an evening, but she was beginning to get a little light-headed. "I thought you were teasing about having sex at sixteen."

"Oh, darlin', we never lie about liquor or sex. This was the age when we would've burned our bras and . . ." Ina Mae got up without weaving one little bit and headed over to the CD player, which looked to be at least thirty years old. "Time for our song, isn't it, Gussie?"

"Damn straight." Gussie grinned.

Sissy could have told them that there was a huge possibility that what Walter had seen in Vietnam had caused him to have PTSD, but that had all happened in the past. Hopefully, if he was still alive, he had gotten some help by now.

"This is '80's Ladies' by K. T. Oslin," Ina Mae explained as she started the music.

Sissy didn't remember ever hearing the song, but the first words sure did remind her of her aunt and her friends. The lyrics talked about being little girls during the fifties and getting stoned in the sixties.

"Is that the truth?" Sissy could feel her eyes popping out. "Did y'all get stoned in the sixties?"

"More like the early seventies, when we were in college," Ina Mae admitted. "And, darlin', we all inhaled."

Sissy's jaw dropped. "Are you serious?"

"Yep, we discovered weed in college, chère, and we wore miniskirts and went to activist demonstrations advocating equal rights for women students," Gussie answered. "In those days the dress code for the girls was a hell of a lot stricter than it was for the boys. We were banned from living off campus, but the guys could if they chose to do so, and drinking would get us kicked out of school, but the guys just got a slap on the wrist."

"If we'd gotten caught with weed in our room, we would have been sent home for sure," Ina Mae said. "The secret was not to get caught, so we hid our stash in Blanche's sanitary pad box." She added, "And the whiskey was put in my box."

Sissy glanced over at Gussie. She was too speechless to utter a single word.

"I kept the cigars in mine. I still enjoy a little Swisher Sweet on occasion."

"But we never 'inhaled' "—Ina Mae used air quotes on the last word—"or drank during the week when we needed to study. That was only on Friday night. Weekly tests were over, and that's when we let our hair down and got stoned and/or drunk."

"Why just on Friday?" Sissy had never touched weed or any type of drugs, but it wasn't really a shock to learn that her aunt Bee had done those things. So had Sissy's parents, but then, they were rock musicians. She knew what weed smelled like, and there was always liquor in the RV.

"Because on Saturday morning, we all had to come home to Newton for the weekend, and our folks would have disowned us for drinking or smoking weed," Ina Mae answered. "We only got to share a cigar—and we smoked them just to show all the men that we were as tough as they were—right here in the clubhouse."

"We didn't mix them. Weed on Friday. A cigar on Saturday evening. Alcohol on Sunday. We needed a little nip after spending the weekends with our folks," Gussie said.

"What about the smell of smoke on your clothes when you left the clubhouse?" Sissy asked.

"We blamed it on the guys we were talking to out on the courthouse lawn," Ina Mae answered.

"The song talks about getting through problems with men. Did you ever think about getting married?" Sissy asked.

"Not one time, but that didn't mean we didn't have issues with guys along the way," Ina Mae answered.

"The only thing I regret about not getting married is that, someday when I get old, I won't have a child to love like Blanche had with you." Gussie sighed.

Sissy said, "I'll always be here for you and Ina Mae. I need family, too."

"Thank you." Gussie moved over and gave her a sideways hug.

"I'm going to hold you to that," Ina Mae said.

"I promise," Sissy told them. "This song seems like it was written just for you."

"It came out in nineteen eighty-seven, when we were in our midthirties, and we've always believed that it *was* written just for us. It talks about one being pretty . . ." Gussie fluffed her gray hair and smiled. "That would be me. We were all smart, but the smartest one was Ina Mae. She got her master's degree and became a nurse and then a physician's assistant. She didn't stop studying and learning until we retired five years ago."

"That leaves Aunt Bee to be the borderline fool, then?" Sissy asked.

"That girl was smart and pretty, but good Lord, she knew how to have a good time," Ina Mae said, "and like the words say, she didn't mind crossing the border."

Gussie got up and began to weave to the music. "She was so much fun that we didn't care, and we were careful after our senior trip not to drink too much. Believe me, chère, your aunt Bee didn't need to visit with Jack Daniel's to have a good time."

"Thanks for sharing these memories with me. What else are we supposed to do tonight?" Sissy stood up but had to hold on to the back of the sofa for a few minutes before the room stopped spinning.

"Blanche said we're to listen to our theme song, which we did, drink a toast to her, and then remember the good times," Ina Mae answered. "Oh, and go to church tomorrow morning."

"I'm not so sure I'll be up to that," Sissy admitted. "I'm just a wee bit"—she held up her thumb and forefinger and left a half inch between them—"drunk off my ass. I should be getting back to Aunt Bee's place."

"That would be your place now," Gussie said, "and the instructions are that we're to stay at my house and all go to church together in the morning."

Sissy slumped back down on the sofa. "You didn't tell me why Aunt Bee got a divorce after just six weeks."

"Walter turned out to be a mean sumbitch," Ina Mae growled. "After they were married, he told Blanche she couldn't go to college, and that she was going to stay home right here in Newton and raise his babies. He got a disability check from the government, and he said that he could get a job doing yard work at the courthouse since she knew the judge and was friends with Gussie. Blanche told him they had agreed they would both go to college after they were married, and she wanted more out of life than just being a wife and mother."

"What happened?" Sissy asked.

"He jerked off his belt and commenced to whoopin' on her, sayin' that she would be a submissive wife like it says in the Bible, like her mama and like her daddy expected her to be," Ina Mae answered. "I still get mad at him every time I think about those days."

Sissy could feel her eyes popping out of her head. "That wasn't in the caveman days. Women went to school and worked outside the home. What did Aunt Bee do when he hit her?"

"She grabbed that belt from him and fought back, but he picked up a lamp, and after the first whack across her head that required thirteen stitches, she didn't have much fight left in her," Gussie said. "He ran out of the house, and she crawled to the phone and called me and Ina Mae. I called an ambulance and drove like a maniac getting to her house."

Sissy laid a hand on her shoulder. "You don't have to talk about it anymore."

61

"Yes, we do, and you deserve to know," Ina Mae said. "Gussie picked me up on the way, and when we got there Blanche was pale as a ghost and passed out on the floor. There was so much blood that we thought she was dead. We were afraid to touch her for fear we'd do more harm than good. Thank God the ambulance arrived just a few minutes later. I rode with her and held her hand the whole way and prayed that she wouldn't die."

"I followed them in my car, and we refused to leave her side in the emergency room and into a private room," Gussie said.

"What happened to Walter?" Sissy asked.

Gussie shrugged. "He was picked up later that night by the sheriff, spent a night in jail, and then skipped town. Blanche filed for an annulment, and my daddy signed the papers. That's when we made our rule that we'd never trust any men but Jim, Jack, and Jesus."

"We sat beside her bed for three days, but it took all summer for her to heal." Ina Mae doubled her right hand into a fist and slapped her left palm with it. "If hating Walter keeps me from going to heaven, then I'll just spend eternity in hell. I won't ever forgive him. I'm not sure Blanche ever got over it mentally. She never wanted to talk about it, so we didn't, but there were times when her eyes got that same haunted look in them she had when she woke up in the hospital. Her mama and daddy were mortified, and they moved over to Louisiana a couple of years later."

"We thought she would die," Gussie said, "and we tried to figure out a way to kill Walter without getting caught. Blanche said he wasn't worth a bullet or the time we'd have to spend in jail if we killed him, so we both promised that we wouldn't. But we all three decided that no man was ever going to treat any of us like that again. We started going to the shooting range when we got to college, and when we finished our education, we bought guns. We still make sure we can shoot the eyes out of a rattlesnake at twenty yards today, and we still practice every week after we clean the church."

"Those weren't happy memories, but you should know what happened," Ina Mae said. "We were only supposed to remember things that make us laugh tonight."

"Just one more thing . . ." Sissy could hear herself slurring her words. "Why didn't Aunt Bee go to jail if she fought back?"

"Because he damn near killed her, so there were no charges brought against her. She looked like she'd been the only chicken in a coyote fight, and . . . ," Gussie answered, "I declare this funeral is over. We need to find beds while we can still climb the stairs."

Sissy had counseled enough people to know

when there was more to the story. She also knew that they had to tell it in their own time and in their own way. Pushing just made them set their heels and refuse to say another word.

"That was a good theme song for y'all," Sissy said. "So this all went down in the summer of nineteen sixty-nine?"

"Yep, and when the church built the fellowship hall. I remember that because Blanche's daddy was so mad about her ruining the Ducaine name in Newton with the annulment that he said the church might not be able to afford to finish the fellowship hall. He said that he might lose members of his congregation over her being so bullheaded, and that Walter was right about her needing to be a submissive wife," Ina Mae said.

"Seemed like a lot of songs were good for us, even if they did come after the fact. Remember 'Goodbye Earl'?" Ina Mae rinsed out the glasses and put them in the dish drainer.

"I know that one." Sissy smiled. "I can just see y'all putting him in the trunk of a car and rolling him off into a river or a bayou for the gators to feast on."

Gussie gave Ina Mae another long, knowing look, and Sissy shivered. Had those two old gals really gotten rid of Walter back in the day?

"I'm even a little light-headed and I can hold my liquor better than either of these . . ." Ina Mae sighed. "Better than Blanche could or Gussie can."

"Hey, now!" Gussie scolded.

"I should really go home," Sissy said. "I didn't bring anything to spend the night."

"I've got everything you need, and you can wear that outfit you wore to the funeral to church in the morning. You didn't spill any whiskey on it, did you?" Gussie asked. "Bee would be disappointed if you wasted a drop of Jack Daniel's, and Luke might kick us all out of church if we came in smelling like booze."

"Not a bit." Sissy wasn't sure what Gussie meant when she said that she had everything that Sissy might need, but she knew she shouldn't drive all the way to Aunt Bee's house in the condition she was in—especially not on icy roads. And right then she didn't really care if Luke kicked them out of church. She would rather sleep in the next day than have to sit through a sermon anyway.

Later, when she crawled into a four-poster bed and closed her eyes, she dreamed of Gussie and Ina Mae stuffing a big guy in the trunk of a car and driving him out into the darkness.

Chapter Three

*E*very clack of Sissy's high heels on the hard wooden church floor that Sunday morning sounded like the beat of bass drums in her ears. The buzz of conversations all around her as folks poured into the church from Sunday school classes was as irritating as bees buzzing around her head. When she slid into the oak pew after Ina Mae and before Gussie, even her hip bones ached, and the sound her skirt made brushing across the varnish of the pew seemed to make her eyes vibrate.

I do not have a hangover. This was brought on from the cold I had to endure while walking to the cemetery on a sheet of ice and then back to the church, she thought.

I'd say that the visit you had with Jack Daniel's had a lot more to do with it than the cold. Aunt Bee was back in her head.

Then this is all your fault, Sissy argued.

A lady with gray hair all twisted up in a bun on top of her head turned around from the pew in front of them. Gussie flinched when the woman patted her on the knee. Sissy wasn't sure if it was because she didn't like the woman or if she was suffering from too much whiskey, too.

"That was quite a funeral yesterday," the woman whispered. "I was shocked"—she put a hand over her heart—"shocked to my roots that you and Ina Mae did such a thing. Poor Blanche was a preacher's daughter, for cryin' out loud."

"That wasn't their idea." Sissy's loud whisper rattled in her head like marbles in an empty soup can.

"Well, I'm doubly stunned that you would do such a thing," the woman hissed. "Your grandfather would be appalled."

"Wasn't her idea, either, Janelle." Ina Mae spoke up before Sissy could say a word. "Blanche left instructions about what she wanted, and we followed them to the letter."

And to the shots. Sissy sat on her hands to keep from pressing her fingertips against her temples.

"Had she lost her mind?" Janelle asked.

"Nope," Gussie said, "but I'm not sure we should be sittin' this close to you. Lightning is liable to shoot through the ceiling and strike you dead for the way you are passing down judgment on our dearly departed friend."

"Hmmph," Janelle snorted and whipped around to face the pulpit.

The woman wasted no time in whipping out her phone, and her chubby little thumbs flew as she sent a text to tattle on Blanche's niece. Small-town politics—that's why her parents never wanted to put down roots. Everyone knew everything about everyone and didn't mind telling everything they knew to anyone who would listen.

"Maybe we should have sat on the front row," Sissy whispered. "That way, no one could turn around and fuss at us, and we could slip out the side door when the service was over."

"No, ma'am!" Ina Mae shook her head. "This has been our pew since we were little girls, and no one in this building is making us leave, no matter how smart-ass they get with their remarks." She rolled her eyes toward the ceiling. "I'm not judging her, God. I'm just describing her ugly remarks."

"And we're going to hold our heads up no matter what," Gussie chuckled. "We did what Blanche wanted, and there's no shame in honoring our best friend the way she asked us to. After that hateful remark, I'm going to redo my end-of-life letter. I may have my funeral at the old bar and grill on the north side of town," she said loud enough that Janelle could hear it.

Janelle's back stiffened, and her thumbs worked even faster as she typed out a message to someone, who Sissy was sure would forward it to half the congregation.

"And," Gussie went on, "instead of flowers, I'll ask that everyone bring a roll of quarters for the jukebox."

Sissy giggled even though doing so made her

head hurt even worse. "If that's what you want, I'll be sure it gets done. What's the first song you want us to play?"

"That old one by Joe Diffie, God rest his soul," Gussie said. "The one called 'Prop Me Up Beside the Jukebox.' Like the lyrics say, put a shot of whiskey in my hand and have a big party."

Sissy was surprised that Janelle didn't fall out of the pew and have a seizure right there in the center aisle.

"You fix up your last-wish letter, and if I'm still on this earth, I'll make sure that's what we do," Ina Mae said.

"And I'll help her with it," Sissy declared.

"Good mornin', everyone!" Luke said in a chipper voice right into the microphone.

"Good morning," the congregation shouted back.

"Glad to see everyone here today. I, for one, am really grateful that the freezing rain has stopped, and that the sun is out bright and shiny today." Luke's deep voice seemed to bounce off the four walls—and maybe the ceiling as well— and reverberate in Sissy's ears. She was glad they weren't sitting on the front row. Her poor hungover head would have exploded before the end of the service.

"Our song director wasn't feeling well this morning," Luke said, "so I'll do my best to lead you in a congregational hymn to start our service off. Let's raise our voices all the way to heaven's doors as we sing number three hundred forty-two."

Gussie reached for a hymnbook and flinched as she flipped through the pages to find the right one. "Dammit, Blanche! You sure asked a lot of us friends."

"Amen." Ina Mae closed her eyes and shivered as the drummer of the church band did an intro to "There Is Power in the Blood."

Sissy had forgotten that this church had a full band and had to hold her hands in her lap to keep from covering her ears. *Good grief, Aunt Bee!* she thought. *If you were going to ask us to drink and remember stories, why did you also insist we go to church?*

You sow wild oats all week and go to church on Sunday to pray for a crop failure. Aunt Bee's voice was so clear in her head that she glanced around to see if the woman had been resurrected and was sitting behind them. If anyone could rise from the dead in today's world, it would be her aunt Bee for sure. *I had a wonderful funeral and an even better wake. Now it's time to repent and go forth cleansed. Two weeks' worth of wild oats would be tough for God to forgive.*

The bright sun shot through a side window, bouncing off a big silver urn filled with poinsettias on the altar and right into Sissy's bloodshot eyes. *I get the message. I won't get drunk on Saturday night again—at least, not for a long time.*

The song—and the torture—ended and Luke cleared his throat. Sissy checked her watch. Hopefully, Luke would keep his sermon to half an hour.

"Blanche Ducaine was a special friend of mine. She was an amazing person, and she loved a couple of hymns in particular. Those two songs have sparked my thoughts for my sermon. The first one is number seventy-three, 'It Is Well with My Soul.' This song talks about whether every-thing is peaceful, or when sorrows like billows roll, that God has taught us to say, 'It is well with my soul.' Blanche taught me that by her life, and I hope that I can show the same spirit to others. The last verse talks about the clouds rolling back, the trumpet sounding, and the Lord descending." He paused for a pregnant moment. "Even then it is well with my soul. Blanche was one of those people who lived her life the way she wanted and went out the way she wanted, and I truly believe that things were well with her soul."

Gussie leaned over and whispered, "I wonder if Janelle is feeling a little heat."

"I hope she's sittin' in boilin' water," Ina Mae said out the side of her mouth.

Sissy smiled even though just that much hurt her face. "Ouch!" she muttered.

"I know." Ina Mae patted her leg. "It really hurts to laugh, and I jump every time someone says 'Amen!' in a loud voice."

"Sneezing is a real bit—" Gussie paused. "A real stinker, too."

"The second song that Blanche loved is number one eighty-nine, 'From Every Stormy Wind.' If you will all turn to it, maybe we'll just sing it this morning, and think of Blanche while we do."

Knowing what she did now about her aunt Bee, Sissy could well understand why she liked it so much. Her aunt had faced stormy winds with that brief marriage and with her parents not supporting her. No wonder Aunt Bee had tried to be such a help to her own little brother, Ford, in spite of his choice of lifestyles. If it hadn't been for her friends, Gussie and Ina Mae, she would have been alone in a pretty horrible situation.

When the song ended, Sissy tried to listen to the rest of Luke's sermon about Jesus being there for us in the storms of life, but her mind kept wandering back to what she'd learned about Aunt Bee the day before. Jesus might have been there for her in a spiritual sense, but it was Gussie and Ina Mae who had taken care of her in a more pressing physical way.

Sissy liked to think that she would have the courage to have whatever kind of funeral she wanted, and to ask that her friends hold a wake in her honor like the three of them had done for Aunt Bee.

I hope wherever you are, you got to see that first line, the second line, and then everyone at the church, Aunt Bee, she thought. *I hope that Elvira's stunt even made you giggle, and that you enjoyed the wake we had at the Sunshine Club.*

There was something for everyone. Aunt Bee was back in her head. *Don't you worry, my child. I saw everything and loved it all, even Elvira's fake heart attack.*

"And now," Luke said, "I'm going to ask Brother Jimmy to give the benediction."

Ina Mae leaned just slightly and said, "You met him at the funeral home yesterday morning. He's Luke's uncle. Seemed fitting that we hire Luke when Jimmy left the pulpit. He is really quite handsome and charming, don't you think?"

"Which one?" Sissy asked.

"Luke!" Ina Mae said. "I hear he can cook, too."

"That's a good thing. He won't starve, then." Sissy might have a hangover, but she could smell a rat and its name was Ina Mae. Shame on her, trying to fix Sissy up with a preacher.

Brother Jimmy had a lot to be thankful for— the day, the message that morning, Blanche's friendship and contributions to the town, the fact that Jesus died for everyone's sins, just to name a few. When he finally said, "Amen," the congregation came alive, and everyone began to stir. The buzzing of conversations started again, and folks began to move out into the center aisle to file out of the church.

"I need a nap," Sissy whispered.

"Me too." Gussie yawned. "But before we get one, me and Ina Mae are going to the Hen's Nest for dinner today. They always serve turkey and dressing on Sunday. Want to join us?"

"Thanks, but no thanks," Sissy said. "I'm going home to sleep off this hangover."

Ina Mae stepped out into the aisle at the end of the string of people. "We'll be over first thing tomorrow morning to help you start going through things. How are you getting along with Danny Boy and Chester?"

"Don't know yet. I've just fed the birds and spent most of my time with y'all getting everything done like Aunt Bee wanted it," Sissy answered. "I'm still in shock. I was here for Thanksgiving with you three, and then in just a few days she's gone. It's all surreal even though we're past the funeral."

Elvira tapped Sissy on the arm, and said, "I'm so sorry about my dear friend Blanche. If you need anything, you just call me. I know all about cleaning out a house and getting it ready to sell."

"Thank you, but Gussie and Ina Mae have agreed to help me. I'm not so sure I'll sell the house. I may keep it for a vacation home," Sissy told her. "In that case, I wouldn't be getting rid of much of anything."

Elvira pursed her thin lips so tightly together that they almost disappeared. "Well, if you change

74

your mind, just call me. Gussie has my number." She sighed loudly and pushed her way forward through the people, who parted for her like she was Moses going through the Red Sea.

"Don't you let that soft little voice of hers fool you," Ina Mae whispered.

"Blanche would turn over in her grave if you let Elvira come into her house and go through her things," Gussie said out the side of her mouth. "And I might go back to the judge's bench and have you committed if you did something that crazy. Elvira would have something to say if Blanche's oven wasn't sparkling clean or there was a speck of dust on the bookshelf, and God help us all if she was allowed to get into the bedroom and found Blanche's red satin under britches. She'd have one of her fake heart attacks."

"Between spreading rumors and going to the emergency room, she's dug in deep in this church and is on the hiring committee. No one wants to cross her or get on her bad side. On second thought, maybe we should let her come to Blanche's. Maybe Danny Boy would bite her, and Chester would try to scratch her eyes out," Ina Mae said.

Aunt Bee had mentioned Elvira a few times in conversation, so Sissy knew that Gussie and Ina Mae weren't exaggerating. Still, it was tough to think of a little old gray-haired lady with such a soft voice being that mean.

"Do you really think Danny Boy would bite someone?" Sissy asked.

"Oh, yeah, he would," Ina Mae answered as they moved ahead a few feet. "What do you know about those two birds?"

"Aunt Bee told me that she almost killed Chester, so she had to adopt him, and that Danny Boy was a rescue bird from some guy here in town," Sissy answered. "She promised to tell me the stories, but it seemed like we always got sidetracked."

"She was driving home from the clubhouse meeting on July Fourth, and we had celebrated with too many shots of Jack." Ina Mae checked the ceiling before she went on. "Just making sure there's no lightning streaks coming down to strike me dead for talking about whiskey in church. The way Blanche told it is that a whole flock of chickens were in the middle of the road. She swerved to keep from hitting them, but the feathers flew when one big old red-and-yellow rooster flew up and hit her windshield. She felt so bad that she got out and took him home with her. The next day she took him to the vet, who said that his leg wasn't broken but his hip was hurt, and he'd never walk right again. Poor old thing limped so bad that she named him Chester, like the character on *Gunsmoke*."

"And the cockatiel?" Sissy asked as they neared the foyer, where Luke was shaking hands.

"He belonged to old Dusty Green, who owned a bar on the north side of town where we might have Gussie's funeral if she dies before I do. Dusty had a stroke last spring, and no one wanted the bird because he's got a nasty attitude, and he has to have his little shot of vodka at least once a day." Ina Mae laughed. "Blanche rationed him to one drink a day, but he'll beg for more. She felt sorry for Chester when she took him in and said that he looked lonely and refused to crow. That's why she decided to let Danny Boy come live with her. When the cockatiel arrived, Chester started crowing again. The two birds seem to get along fine. Danny Boy mimics Chester's crowing, but Chester hasn't learned to talk like Danny Boy does."

"It's strange that they like each other since Danny Boy is a house bird, and Chester is a yard bird," Sissy said. "I've heard Danny Boy mocking Chester's crowing and yet they are never really together, are they?"

"They visit through the living room window," Ina Mae answered. "Blanche said that Chester brags because he's got free rein of the yard and porch, and that Danny Boy tells him that he's the pretty boy."

They slowly made their way to where the preacher stood. It seemed like everyone wanted to chat that day, rather than just shake his hand and rush home to their pot roast dinners. Ina Mae finally got to the front of the line and stuck out her hand.

Luke shook with her and asked, "How are you holding up?"

"Sometimes good, most of the time not so good," Ina Mae admitted.

Gussie stepped around her and held her hand out. "But Blanche left explicit orders for us to get on with life."

"It's not easy," Luke said. "If there's anything at all that I can do, just call me."

"Thank you," Gussie said.

Then it was Sissy's turn to shake hands with him.

Luke's bright smile lit up his pale-blue eyes. "It's good to see you this morning."

He held Sissy's hand just a little longer than necessary and patted it with his other hand. Were those sparks she felt?

Impossible, she thought. She was just feeling the aftereffects of an unusual funeral and too much whiskey. No way would Sissy or Martina ever get vibes from a preacher. Not even a sexy one.

Chapter Four

*I*na Mae sank down on the sofa in the club-house. When they were little girls, she had felt more than a little out of place with Gussie and Blanche, what with Gussie's daddy being the judge and Blanche's the preacher where Ina Mae and her grandmother went to church. Ina Mae's grandmother was just one of the ladies on the cleaning crew at the courthouse. It wasn't until the incident with Walter that she began to really feel like she belonged with her two friends. "It just don't seem right without Blanche here. This is our very first ever meeting without her. She was alive and well last Sunday."

"We can't abandon our club." Gussie opened a package of chocolate cookies and set them on the coffee table. Then she poured two mugs full of coffee from a thermos. "That would make her sad. We vowed we'd meet every Sunday—rain, sleet, hail, or shine—and as long as we're alive, we're going to do just that. But I've got to admit, I keep looking for her to breeze in here with some excuse about Danny Boy, or Chester, or maybe even talking to Sissy on the phone to explain the reason why she's late to the meeting."

Ina Mae sighed as she dipped a cookie in her

coffee. Neither Blanche nor Gussie had ever made her feel inferior, but even something as simple as dipping a cookie in coffee reminded her of those days. "Blanche got me started doing this when we were just kids, and we weren't supposed to drink coffee. Granny said it would turn our toenails black. I used to check mine every night."

Gussie picked up the box of tissues from the table, set them beside the cookies, and took a seat on the other end of the sofa. "Good God, Ina Mae, you've made me go all weepy again"—she pulled out a couple of tissues and dabbed her eyes—"and it still hurts my head to cry or laugh or sneeze. Are you still as mad at her as I am, or have you moved on past this stage?"

"We've both been through the steps of grieving before when my granny and your mama passed away. We're in the anger stage. I'm thinking, maybe by Easter, we might get through all of the stages and accept that she's gone," Ina Mae answered. "But it will take years and years before I ever quit going to the phone to call her to come quick to the gazebo or to the clubhouse because we all need to talk." She took a deep breath and let it out slowly. "I've got a confession to make: when we were kids, I felt the difference between my world and yours and Blanche's."

"Well, I felt the difference, too. Blanche's daddy was our preacher, and my folks thought he hung the moon. And I loved your granny so much that I envied you sometimes. Ina Mae, I'm glad we don't have to get over being mad today." Gussie pushed her chin-length, gray hair back behind her ears. "Maybe we should both dye our hair red in honor of Blanche."

Ina Mae shook her head. "Not me. I'm convinced that in fifty years they're going to find that hair dye is the major cause of lots of diseases, like strokes and heart attacks. That might be the very thing that took Blanche from us. Just look at that bare spot on your bathroom vanity, and you can't argue with me. One glob the size of a dime got loose from her hair, and it ate through three coats of paint and one of varnish. You can't tell me that's good for your scalp. I'd rather adopt a crippled rooster than dye my hair red or any other color. I'm seventy years old, and I've earned every one of these gray hairs."

"Well, since you put it that way"—Gussie sighed—"this place seems like a tomb without Blanche. We should ask Sissy to join the Sunshine Club, so we'd have a third party. Don't seem right to have just two of us." Gussie looked over at the old door. "Remember the day we painted that? And I was jealous of you because you were so smart. I had to work for my grades. Everything came natural for you."

Ina Mae moved over to drape an arm around Gussie's shoulders. "Of course I remember. Like the song says, we were three little girls angry with a bunch of boys who wouldn't let us be in their club. But we need to remember something else, Gussie. We've still got each other and Sissy. Why would you say you were envious of me? We've got to move on whether we want to or not. Let's get the book out. We've done a lot of good in this town and looking at our victories will put us in a better mood."

When Gussie opened the old rolltop trunk sitting against the far wall, the smell of lilacs filled the room. "I'd forgotten that she kept a sachet in here along with our memories."

Ina Mae sucked in a lungful of air and tipped her sharp little chin up a notch. "She loved that scent, and we've got to stop weeping for Blanche. Granny always said that crying causes wrinkles, and God knows I've got enough of those already."

"Will this make you stop crying?" Gussie held up one of the dresses she and Ina Mae had worn when they were bridesmaids for Blanche. "They're even uglier than they were that day, more than fifty years after the fact. What on earth was her mama thinking when she made us wear these horrible things?"

Tears soon turned to giggles and then into guffaws.

"We should donate them to the high school drama club." Ina Mae wiped her wet cheeks with a tissue, only this time they weren't grieving tears. They were funny—ha ha—tears, as Blanche used to say. "All that netting and those big, droopy purple flowers at the neckline. Not even the school would want those hideous things hanging in their prop room."

Gussie put the dress back and brought out a thick book. "Let's start at the beginning."

"Yes"—Ina Mae patted the sofa beside her—"at the beginning and work our way through the book."

Gussie sat down and put the thick book in her lap. Ina Mae reached over and opened the first page, and they gazed down at the picture of the three of them at Blanche's wedding. The bride in her Victorian-style wedding dress made of satin that covered her skin from her neck to her toes, and her two friends in their ugly lilac outfits that looked like something that old women would have thrown in the trash can back in the forties.

"She wanted an eyelet lace dress with a blue satin ribbon around her waist." Ina Mae sighed again. "We designed it and our dresses right here in this clubhouse. We were going to wear blue eyelet lace minidresses with white sashes."

Gussie ran a finger across Blanche's face. "We were to go to the courthouse with her and Walter to be witnesses, and then we'd throw rice at them as they left on a little trip to Galveston."

"But Eva told her that people would say she

83

was pregnant if she had a hurry-up wedding like that, so we had to do the whole thing so her mama and daddy could save face. I wonder if they ever were sorry that they took up for Walter instead of Blanche when he beat her so bad."

"I don't think they were," Gussie sighed. "Once Blanche's daddy set his mind, you couldn't change it with a stick of dynamite."

Ina Mae turned the page, and there was a black-and-white photograph of Blanche standing in front of an arch decorated with purple flowers. "I'm glad the pictures aren't in color. All that purple would have made her look like she'd been propelled into a lilac bush."

Neither of them mentioned the place where a picture had gone missing, but Gussie remembered well the night they had removed the one of Walter and Blanche together. They had burned it with Blanche's dress, but she refused to let them put another photo in its place. She had said that it would remind her that she made a big mistake once in her lifetime, and to never make the same one again.

"We probably should have burned our dresses right along with hers," Gussie said and turned another page. Both of them reached out to gently touch Blanche's face in the photo.

"She had just come home from the hospital in this one," Ina Mae whispered. "I forget what a bad condition she was in until I see this."

Gussie had used her new Polaroid camera to produce a color picture of Blanche. After fifty years it had faded a lot. Gussie didn't need bright colors to remember Blanche's poor face, which had been covered with bruises. Or that she had walked slowly because her back still hurt so much. Even at that, Blanche had insisted that they take a picture of her and put it in the book. Then she had taken her wedding dress from the closet and told them to go out in her backyard and build a bonfire. While Ina Mae and Gussie got a blaze going, Blanche had cut her satin dress into shreds. She carried it out the back door and threw it into the fire, along with the only picture they had of her and Walter together.

"I'll never trust another man," she had declared as she watched the dress burn.

As they looked at the picture, the memory of the stench of burning satin came back to Gussie, making her cough.

"I can smell it, too." Ina Mae reached out and touched the picture of Blanche. She said, "That was not a good day, but it brought a measure of closure for Blanche. She looked so bad, but after we got done with the burning, she seemed better. I'm glad we stayed with her once she insisted on living in the house until we went to college."

"Of course we did—we were afraid that Walter would come back and finish the job he'd started," Gussie remembered. "But—"

Ina Mae cut her off. "We agreed to never talk about that again."

"We did, didn't we? Some things are better left unsaid. Her daddy should have hunted Walter down and made him pay, but he was too afraid of what people would say." Gussie turned another page. "Our first matchmaking wedding—Teresa and Billy are still married after forty years. Soon as that next great-grandbaby is born, we'll get to add a name to the list here at the bottom of their offspring. I'm glad this one lasted, since it was our first attempt at putting two people together. Do you realize that we are the prototype for those dating sites that are all the rage now? I liked our way of doing things better."

"Me too. It's a crazy world we're living in," Ina Mae agreed. "Do you think if we let Sissy into the club, she'll keep on going with our project when we're both gone?" She turned another page. "We didn't do so good with this couple, did we? Dorothy and Michael hit that crucial seven-year mark, and she got tired of his huntin' and fishin' and never being home with her. They didn't ever even have a child for us to list."

"Maybe if they had had children, they would have stuck together awhile longer, but we did our part," Gussie countered, wondering whether, if things had been different and she had married, it would have lasted. "They just didn't work at it. He didn't want to give up his ways, and she

86

couldn't live with them. Are you ready to invite Sissy into the club? After all, she is blood kin to Blanche."

"Let's make that decision when we're not still grieving." Ina Mae turned another page. "This couple might have made it if they had had a little therapy. Darlene and Oscar looked like they were in love that first year, but I think his mother got in the way. She never did think Darlene was good enough for her son."

Gussie snapped her fingers. "That's what we need! A good marriage to get our minds off Blanche leaving us. And we could use a family counselor in town. Our next project should be working toward getting Sissy to stay here. We'll play matchmaker, and the town will get a counselor at the same time. That would be a great way to get us through the grieving process, and"—she stopped to take a breath—"and we'd get to keep Sissy with us all the time."

Ina Mae closed the book long before they reached the end. "Matchmaking won't be the same without Blanche."

"We need something to take our minds off Blanche, don't we, and convincing Sissy to stay in Newton would be a good project for us, don't you think?" Gussie asked.

"A really good one," Ina Mae agreed, "but she's a part of a firm in Beau Bridge. She's using up every bit of her vacation time to take care of Blanche's affairs, and then she's planning on going back to her job."

"Then we've got six weeks, don't we? We've worked miracles in less time than that." Gussie's face lit up in a grin. "Now, what would make her stay on the Texas side of the border?"

Ina Mae shrugged. "Only thing I can think of is love, but this is the wrong time. She's grieving, and who on earth would we pair her up with?"

"That's right." Gussie nodded. "We need to get back into our job of matchmaking, and the rest will fall into place. We've always been good at this business."

"We should be," Ina Mae said. "We've been working at it for a long time. Who'd have thought that Blanche would ever want to see another woman get married? Crazy way to get closure, wasn't it?"

"Yes, it was," Gussie agreed, "but helping others get a happy-ever-after seemed to help her understand that all men weren't like Walter. Who's the lucky groom going to be for our Sissy? He has to be special because this is *our* girl we're talking about."

"We haven't devoted much time to the match-making since we all retired, so we might be a little rusty," Ina Mae reminded her. "With all this new technological stuff on the internet, our old-fashioned ways might be water under a bridge. But maybe it's like riding a bicycle. How many thirty- to thirty-five-year-old bachelors are left in Newton County?"

"Not many that we'd have in our family," Gussie answered, "but did you notice that Luke held Sissy's hand a little longer than necessary this morning? I think I saw a few sparks."

"No! No! No!" Ina Mae shook her head. "He's a preacher. You know how Blanche felt about being a preacher's daughter. If Sissy and Luke had kids—" She shuddered.

"What's wrong with that?" Gussie asked. "Things are different even for preachers' kids in today's world. Just think of it as our greatest challenge, and besides, times have changed. Preachers aren't as strict as they used to be when we were kids. I saw Luke playing basketball in the church fellowship hall last weekend when we were cleaning the church. He was in there with a bunch of teenagers, and he wasn't wearing a shirt." She fanned herself with her hand. "And, honey, he would make any woman swoon."

Ina Mae shook her head again. "I don't care if seeing him without a shirt would make Sissy's under britches crawl down around her ankles. Think of someone else."

The small summer kitchen had an old stove against the south wall. Beside it was a green Philco refrigerator that the girls had begged from Gussie's mama when she got a brand-new one back in 1960. It still kept beer, soft drinks, and

Kool-Aid cold just fine. Gussie stood up and crossed the room to get a pen and a sheet of paper from the top of the fridge.

"We'll make a list," she said. "We'll research every one of the guys before we start our project, and then we'll take a vote. I've got connections from my time on the bench, so I can find out anything on anyone."

Ina Mae's head started moving from side to side. "And I've got connections from the years I spent in the clinic. There's not much I don't know about anyone in this town. But voting won't work. Blanche was the deciding vote when we couldn't agree. If we disagree, we sure can't ask Sissy to make the decision for us when it involves the man we intend to wave our magic wand over."

"Then we'll have to agree." Gussie poised her pen over the paper. "Start talking. He has to be handsome and sweet, and we don't want someone who already has kids."

"Billy Bob Anderson?" Ina Mae suggested. "He's a lawyer . . ."

"No, ma'am!" Gussie said. "Billy Bob cheated on his last girlfriend. That's why they broke up. Once a cheater, always a cheater. How about Dr. Ford Lassiter?"

"Don't write his name. He takes too many trips to Vegas, and before I retired, I had to treat him for an STD. We can't take a chance on that." Ina

Mae flipped a couple of pages in the book and tapped the wedding picture in front of them. "Remember what happened to Callie and Freddy? He got to playin' around with hookers, and their marriage split because of it."

"Glad you've got the memory of an elephant," Gussie said. "If Luke wasn't a preacher, we would put him on the list, right?"

"Yes," Ina Mae said. "He's damn good-lookin', especially with those blue eyes, and I'm sure that he looked mighty fine without a shirt, so he'd appeal to a woman for sure, and I did see that bit of chemistry between them. But I'm still not sold on the idea."

Gussie started to write his name, but Ina Mae reached over and stopped her. "Let's think about it a little more. Right now, he's about the only one in town we'd even consider, but do we really want to do this? Sissy might never forgive us if she finds out, and Blanche left her in our care. And Luke might kick us out of church if he figures out what we're up to."

"Pssh!" Gussie wrote down his name. "We need this so we can get through this grief. Newton needs a therapist, Sissy needs a husband before she's too old to give us some grandkids, and Luke needs a decent wife. You know that Minnette Sullivan has been flirting with him. Blanche even mentioned that maybe we could come out of retirement just for Luke so Minnette wouldn't get her claws into him. Can you just see that woman as a preacher's wife? She's been wild as a March hare since she was thirteen."

"All right then," Ina Mae agreed with a long sigh. "You've made a good argument." She laid the book to the side. "I guess it's only right that we finish this book up with Sissy's wedding picture. Blanche's is on the first page and Sissy's would be on the last one, kind of like everything coming around in full circle."

Gussie wrote *Sissy/Martina Ducaine* under *Luke Beauchamp*, kissed the paper, and handed it to Ina Mae. She kissed it, folded the whole page neatly, and carried both it and the book back to the rolltop trunk. While she took care of that ritual, Gussie poured them each a shot of whiskey in their special glasses.

They stood in front of the trunk and touched their shot glasses over the top of it. "To happy-ever-after," they chanted together and threw back their shots in one big gulp.

"Where do we begin?" Ina Mae asked. "We've only got six weeks." They'd had the ritual, said the words, and had the shot of whiskey. It was done, and when Ina Mae committed to a matchmaking, she gave it her all.

"Might as well get started." Gussie took the two glasses to the old wall-hung sink beside the refrigerator and washed them. "Like John Wayne said, 'We're burnin' daylight.' "

• • •

Sissy kicked off her shoes at the door, went upstairs, and changed into a pair of buffalo-plaid flannel pajama pants and a long-sleeved thermal shirt. She made a trip through the bathroom and pushed bottles around in the medicine cabinet above the sink until she found the aspirin. She poured three into her hand, tossed them into her mouth, and chewed them up, then pulled one of Aunt Bee's tiny disposable cups from the dispenser on the wall and filled it with water three times before she got the taste out of her mouth.

"Vodka! It's vodka time." Danny Boy's voice rang out through the house, and then he crowed like Chester.

"I'm finding a home for you as soon as I can," Sissy muttered as she made her way down the stairs and into the kitchen.

That the nearest neighbors were a mile down the road was a good thing when Chester began to echo Danny Boy's crowing out on the front porch. Evidently, they had full-fledged contests, because Chester got louder with each crow.

"God, what have I gotten myself into?" Sissy groaned. "I've got two bad birds, a house full of stuff, and six weeks to get it cleaned out, unless I decide to keep this place. It would be nice to own my own house. Too bad it's not in Beau Bridge."

"Vodka! Time for a shot!" Danny Boy screeched even louder.

"What a way to spend the Christmas holidays, and use up all my vacation time. I'd be furious if this wasn't for you, Aunt Bee."

Don't rush into any decisions. Keep the place a year before you decide what to do with it, Aunt Bee's voice in her head reminded her.

She rustled around in the cabinet until she found a can of gumbo soup, which she heated up and carried to the living room. She'd have to make a trip to the grocery store tomorrow, but today, warm soup would do just fine, and then she was going to sleep off a hangover straight from hell.

"Out! Out! Get me out of here!" Danny Boy screeched, and ended with another crowing session. Not to be outdone, Chester came in right behind him.

"I may fry you both for supper if you don't stop," Sissy threatened as she set her soup on the coffee table and opened Danny Boy's cage.

The bird stepped out, flew down, and leaned over her soup as if he were going to taste it, then backed away. "Vodka! Spittin' dust! Need vodka!"

"Good grief! How did Aunt Bee live with you?" Sissy wondered how she could ever take the two birds back to Beau Bridge to live in her tiny one-bedroom apartment. The neighbors would complain about all the crowing, and the landlord would eventually toss her right out on the curb because of the complaints. She'd have to find good homes for them or else beg Ina Mae and Gussie to take care of them for her when she wasn't around.

"My apartment contract says no pets," she groaned. "I've got a two-story house, a crippled rooster, and an alcoholic bird. Aunt Bee, what have you done to me? If I follow your advice and keep this place a year, then I'll have to either get a sitter for the birds or else find homes for them."

Danny Boy flew over to sit on Sissy's shoulder and began whistling "Danny Boy." He kept that up for several minutes, stopped long enough to kiss her on the cheek, and then went back to his music. When he finished, he said, "Vodka!"

She finished off her soup and headed out of the living room. Danny Boy stayed on her shoulder as she walked down the hallway that went from one end of the house to the other, but when they reached the kitchen, he flew over to the counter below which Blanche kept the liquor. There he whistled a few more bars of "Danny Boy."

"Did the people who frequented the bar make you sing for your liquor?" Sissy asked.

She wasn't sure how much vodka to give the bird, or even if it would kill him, but right then, a funeral for the brightly colored cockatiel didn't seem like a bad idea at all. "All right, already!" she grumbled as she took a bottle of Smirnoff from behind the cabinet door and poured a little into a shallow bowl.

Danny Boy bobbed right over to it, drank it, and then said, "Nap time." He flew out of the kitchen, up the hallway toward his cage, and hopped inside.

Sissy hurried after him and closed the door and threw a towel over the birdcage. "That I can agree with," she said. "No crowing or whistling until I wake up." She stretched out on the blue velvet sofa and used the arm for a pillow.

More than an hour later, she awoke to both birds crowing and the doorbell ringing. She sat up straight and rubbed her eyes, then peeked out the big picture window to see Gussie and Ina Mae both peering back at her. The sight of their two noses pressed against the glass gave her a start, and she hopped to her feet. She jogged across the living room and the hallway that served as a foyer to unlock the front door. The sun was just a hint of an orange ball sinking fast out there on the western horizon.

"Come on in," she yawned.

"We wouldn't have stood out here in the cold and kept ringing the bell, but the screen was locked." Ina Mae came inside and removed her coat. "Blanche never locked her doors except at night. Brrr!" She shivered. "We aren't used to winters like this in southeast Texas. I don't know if it'll ever get warm again. Are you going to put up Blanche's Christmas tree? We usually go from house to house and help each other get our trees up, but we can't make up our minds if we should do that when we're grieving."

Gussie took off her coat and hung it on a hall tree hook beside Ina Mae's. "Be a shame to get rid of all of Blanche's antiques. I remember when we went all the way up to central Oklahoma to get this hall tree."

"We took my truck and made a four-day trip out of it." Ina Mae sighed. "Blanche loved her antiques."

"Can I get y'all something to drink—water, sweet tea?" Sissy asked as guilt settled over her worse than a cold, freezing rain. She wouldn't be able to get rid of a single thing if they got upset at just the thought of her selling or donating Aunt Bee's old furniture.

"Sweet tea would be nice," Gussie said.

"Out! Out! Get me out of here!" Danny Boy was definitely awake.

"I'll let him out." Ina Mae headed down the hall and made a left-hand turn into the living room with Gussie and Sissy right behind her. "He likes me. He tolerates Gussie, but he won't sit on her shoulder. We got this old library table from a place near Big Bend Park. That was another one of our short vacations. Who would have known that, years later, it would be a perfect place for Danny Boy's cage?"

More guilt jumped onto Sissy's shoulders, but she couldn't keep everything in the house—or could she? One year wouldn't hurt, now would it? She'd told patients not to make rash decisions during times of grief—to give things time to settle so there would be no regrets.

But were these old gals playing her? Something about their expressions, the way they kept exchanging long looks and sighing, said that they had something up their sleeves. She hadn't spent years getting her license in counseling for nothing.

If she didn't have to dive into all the nooks and crannies and try to decide what to get rid of and what to keep, it would simplify things. The place could be her vacation home or weekend place. It was less than a three-hour drive from Beau Bridge to Newton. She could easily come over on Fridays after work a couple of times a month and spend the whole weekend in the country. That way she could spend time with Gussie and Ina Mae and enjoy just being Sissy instead of Martina Ducaine, MFT (marriage and family therapist).

Another decision to be made, she thought as she put on a kettle of water to boil to make a pitcher of sweet tea. *But if I decided to do that, I would have to ask Ina Mae to come feed the birds every day, and that would take care of the animals while I was gone.*

"Something to think about." She got the box of tea bags from the cabinet and tossed four into a pitcher.

Gussie poked her head in the door. "Need any help?"

"Just waiting on the water to boil," Sissy answered. "There's chocolate chip cookies in the jar if y'all want a snack."

"Just tea for both of us. We ate our leftovers from lunch for our supper before we came over," Gussie said. "I'll finish making the tea. You should go upstairs and get dressed. Luke is coming over, too. He'll be here in about ten minutes."

"Why is he . . ." Sissy gasped. She looked like warmed-over hell on Sunday morning, and she was in no mood to have a guy in the house.

"We invited him. He's been begging for help with the Christmas program at church," Gussie answered. "He's bringing over a video of last year's program for us to watch. Ina Mae and I've gotten too old to be bending and stooping to help get things put together, so we volunteered you, chère. That way we can make suggestions about how to make it even better this year."

"But . . . why . . ." Sissy stammered, and then she remembered the vibes she'd just gotten from them, and Ina Mae *had* mentioned how good-looking Luke was. Did these two think they could fool her? She was a therapist, for goodness' sakes. She studied people, and if they wanted to play matchmaker to get over Blanche's death, then they should at least find someone other than a preacher for her. A preacher's wife had a lot of responsibility—more than she wanted to ever take on. Plus, if her grandfather had been right about the church's opinion, the wife should be submissive. There was entirely too much of Aunt Bee's blood in Sissy's veins for her to ever bow down to anyone.

"The best way to get to know folks in Newton is to work along beside them, and it's Christmastime, chère! Time to give back. Blanche would be so proud of you for donating your time to the Christmas program on her behalf," Gussie said. "Now, hurry on upstairs and put on some of them skinny jeans and a pretty sweater. You might want to brush out your hair. It looks a little like a mouse and Danny Boy had a fight in it. You got that beautiful thick hair from Blanche. I always wanted strawberry-blonde hair, but all I got was fine blonde hair that wouldn't hold a curl for anything. Run along. I've got this under control." Gussie picked up the teakettle and poured hot water over the tea bags and then threw a clean dish towel over the top so it could steep.

Sissy made her way out of the kitchen as if she had all the time in the world, but when she reached the stairs, she took them two at a time. She had peeled her shirt up over her head by the time she made it to her bedroom. She tossed it on the four-poster bed and slung her pajama pants in the same general area when she removed them.

What would it hurt to play along with them? Blanche had returned to her head. *They need something to dwell on right now. It would only be for a few weeks, and by then they'll be in better shape and you'll be back in Beau Bridge.*

"Oh, all right, I'll do it, but I don't have to like it." She could tell from Gussie's rapid-fire patter that the women were anxious. Sissy pulled a pair of skinny jeans and a green sweater from her suitcase and quickly put them on, then raced to the bathroom, where she touched up her makeup and brushed out her hair. "That will have to do," she muttered as she started down the stairs and realized that she was wearing one Betty Boop sock and one with Rudolph with his red nose on the toe. She turned around to go back up and find a matching pair, but before she'd taken a single step, the doorbell rang.

"Sissy, would you get that?" Ina Mae yelled.

"It's just socks, and it's not like this is a date," she said as she turned back around and headed for the door.

Chapter Five

*L*uke drew in a deep breath and let it out slowly as he waited for someone to answer the door. Blanche had been his favorite of the three ladies, and he'd visited the house often since he had taken the preaching job two years before. Yet going into the house without her being there reminded him of the first time he had gone into his grandmother's place after she had passed away. There was something about a silent house, the lack of something cooking or even the smell of that lemon cleaning stuff that Nana and Blanche used, that made walking into the house seem so final.

The floorboards of the old house gave testimony that someone was coming to the door. Luke pasted on a smile and got ready to greet whoever opened it, grateful that the house wouldn't be empty like his grandmother's had been right after she passed away and his mother sent him to get Nana's purse. He did not expect his chest to tighten or his pulse to race when that person turned out to be Sissy.

"Come on in out of the cold," she said. "Can I take your coat?"

"I'll just hang it on the hall tree, here, like

always." His deep voice sounded a few octaves too high in his own ears.

"Pretty boy!" Danny Boy was a blur of gray, white, and orange as he flew out of the living room and alighted on Luke's shoulder.

"Yes, you *are* a pretty boy." Luke ran a forefinger down the bird's back. "Are you missing Blanche as much as we are?"

"I don't know about him, but I sure do miss her," Sissy said. "I thought after the funeral that I'd have some measure of closure, but I still expect to hear her voice calling out to me from the kitchen, or see her rushing out of the living room to give me a hug. It seems like I had more peace in my heart when we buried my folks than I've got now. Is that crazy?"

Her big green eyes floated in tears, and she looked so vulnerable that Luke's first instinct was to take her in his arms for a comforting hug, but he couldn't very well do that with a bird on his shoulder. "You're a therapist, Sissy. You know these things take time, and each case is totally different. It might take weeks, or months, or even a year or two. Just hang on to the good memories that y'all shared. Those will help you get through the tough times."

"It's different when I'm helping folks than it is when it's me." She blinked several times. "Gussie is making sweet tea. Would you like some?"

"Love a glass." He removed a DVD from his

coat pocket and handed it to her. "And thank you for offering to help out with the Christmas program while you're here."

"You are welcome. We'll go into the living room and get this going. How long have you been here in Newton? I guess when I came over to see Aunt Bee, I never stayed over a Sunday, so I didn't hear you preach until today." She led the way from the foyer hallway and laid the DVD down next to the player beside the television. "Have a seat. I'll bring you a sweet tea."

He overheard her tell someone in the kitchen that he had arrived, and then the conversation became muffled. In a couple of minutes, she returned with two full glasses.

"Seems strange here without Blanche," he said.

Sissy handed him the glass in her left hand and sat down on the end of the sofa. "Do you think it will ever get any better? I feel like I should wait to make a decision about keeping or selling the place, but if it's always going to feel like this, I don't know that I can stand it."

"Maybe time will make it better," he said. "You asked how long I've been in town. It's two years." Luke sat down on the other end of the sofa. "This is my second Christmas here. I started my career in a small church in my hometown, Coushatta, Louisiana, down south of Shreveport. It was great to get to spend five years in a known church."

"Why did you come to Newton if you were at home in Coushatta?" Sissy asked.

"Brother Jimmy is my uncle. He was married to my aunt Ruthie. She died a couple of years ago, right about the time he decided to retire. He called me and said he felt like the church here needed some younger blood. I'd visited him often and always liked the people and the town, so I took the job when they offered it to me. Seemed like God was leading me here." Luke had never rambled on like that in his life. She had asked a simple question that required only a two-word answer, and he'd given her a short autobiography. What was it about this woman that turned a thirty-five-year-old man into a babbling idiot?

"And we're mighty glad that he did," Ina Mae said, coming in from the kitchen. "Our little church has grown a lot since you got here. Young folks that hadn't been attending regular services in years are coming to the Sunday morning services now."

"I'm working on getting someone to step in as youth minister," Luke said. "We can't pay them just yet, but as the church continues to grow, maybe later, we could give them a small stipend."

"Y'all get comfortable." Gussie brought in a tray with two more glasses of sweet tea and a plate of cookies on it. "I'll take the rocking chair since Ina Mae already has the recliner." She set the tray on the coffee table and picked up a glass for herself. "Let's get this show on the road."

Luke set his tea on the coffee table, stood up, and crossed the living room. He put the DVD into the machine and carried the remote back to the sofa. "We've got a lot of Christmas stuff in the storage room, but it's all pretty well worn out. There's not much money to put into this, so I hope you ladies can help me figure out a way to make our program nicer than last year on a nonexistent budget." There he went again, rattling on before they had even seen the video.

"Why don't you have what you need? Can't you take up a collection for it?" Sissy asked.

"Newton is a small town of just a little more than two thousand people. Granted, it's the county seat so that means something, but there's more than twenty churches in this town. That means even if we rake all the folks up from surrounding farm- and ranchland, none of us have big congregations, and our little community church is probably one of the smallest ones. I hate to burden the congregation with a collection for Christmas stuff," Luke answered.

"What's it like to be a minister in a small town like this?" Sissy asked.

"Fulfilling most of the time, but it does have its problems," Luke answered and then changed the subject, because he wasn't so sure he would be preaching until he retired. "But tonight, we're talking about how we can help our Christmas pageant without asking too much of our church family."

"We'll figure out something," Gussie said. "You're right about us needing a youth minister, and another thing we need is a good therapist in Newton. We've got entirely too many divorces going on for a town this small. If we had a marriage and family counselor in town, we might have more happy marriages. You know anyone over in Beau Bridge that might be interested in relocating, Sissy?"

Was that a blush turning Sissy's face red? What was going on that Luke didn't know about?

"You are so right," Luke agreed with a nod. "I worry about the couples that have gotten married in our own little church. I pray for them every night. It's tough making a go of it in today's world."

"Amen!" Ina Mae said. "Now, moving on to the problem at hand. We could have a Christmas drive that wouldn't involve money. I bet folks who have extra decorations would gladly donate them. Brother Jimmy and Paul have been doing some woodwork projects since they retired from the church. Maybe we could hit them up to make us a new manger scene or some cutouts of sheep and a new donkey for the program. Gussie and I could start making some calls around town. I bet, by the end of tomorrow, we've got more stuff than we need."

A grin lit up Luke's face. "I knew I'd get some ideas from y'all."

"We'll start right here with me," Gussie said. "A few years ago, I got a wild hair and decided to do my Christmas tree all up in red. All of those decorations and the tree that I used, because it came with all red lights on it, are stored in the attic. I'll drag them out and bring them to the church tomorrow."

Luke chuckled. "Do you ladies think we should put a tree up in the church that is totally red?"

"Jesus didn't condemn Mary Magdalene or the woman at the well," Ina Mae reminded him, "but if you think there could be talk, we can always decorate our tree with multicolored ornaments and gold tinsel to tone down the red."

"You are so right." Luke nodded.

"Blanche has got enough stuff to decorate the White House," Ina Mae said. "We're going to put up her tree tomorrow morning unless Sissy thinks it would be disrespectful so soon after the funeral, and what we don't use, maybe Sissy could donate to the cause."

"She didn't want us to mourn," Sissy said, "and one of the best memories I have with her is all of us getting together to decorate the trees. I'll be glad to donate what we don't use to the church, too. I think there's three trees in the attic. There's no way I'd need all of that stuff anyway."

Luke wasn't surprised at the sparks when they

shook hands. *I have to be careful,* he warned himself. *She's only here for a few weeks, and then I'll probably never see her again.*

Sissy caught a whiff of Luke's cologne when he held the remote out and pushed the button to start the show—something woodsy with a hint of vanilla. How in the world was she supposed to sit there only three feet from him and focus on an hour-long video?

And why am I feeling these things? she asked herself. *I should be mourning for Aunt Bee, not thinking of the preacher's pretty blue eyes.*

Luke hit the play button and a rather grainy video began to play. "I apologize for the quality of this. It was taken with a cell phone, but at least you can see what we've got to work with."

That everyone had tried to put on a nice pageant was evident. The little children had worn their Sunday best, and the adults in the manger scene did their part, but the props really were awful, and the timing getting from one scene to the next left a lot to be desired.

"That's pitiful," Gussie sighed. "I owe you an apology, Luke. You can drive around town and see all kinds of gorgeous decorations, and our church program looks like this? We'll rectify this, startin' tonight. You should start getting some decent stuff by morning, and promise me you'll throw away that pitiful tree in that video. It looks worse than the spindly little thing that Charlie Brown puts up."

"Didn't y'all go to the programs before now?" Sissy asked.

"Yes, but we spent the evening in the fellowship hall getting things ready for the potluck supper after the program," Ina Mae answered. "We haven't watched the show in years."

"Thank you. I knew y'all could come up with something to help out." Luke smiled.

"Nap time!" Danny Boy flew off Luke's shoulder and hopped back into his cage. Ina Mae jumped up from the recliner and closed the cage door, then covered him up.

I smell a fish for sure. From the way Gussie and Ina Mae keep looking at the two of us, there's no doubt that they're matchmaking. The corners of Sissy's mouth turned up in half a grin at the memory of what her mother used to say when something wasn't quite right.

Ina Mae knuckled her eyes. "You can turn that off now, Luke. The sound is horrible, and the picture is hurting my eyes. We know what we have to do, and I'm anxious to go home and get some calls made this evening."

"I should be going, then," Luke said.

"No need in you rushing off." Gussie got to her feet. "Blanche has lots of movies you kids can choose from this evening. We'll take care of the donation calls. Y'all two will have plenty

110

to do when the stuff starts coming in. Will you be in your office all day tomorrow, Luke? We'll need to tell the folks where to bring their things."

"I'll be there," Luke answered, "and I'll make sure all the doors are open. I'll ask Uncle Jimmy to help me clean out a Sunday school room to put everything in."

"I've got a better idea," Ina Mae said. "Sissy can help you with that job. I'm going to ask Brother Jimmy to build us a new stable and manger to lay baby Jesus in for the program, and you might do well to use the fellowship hall instead of a classroom. It's bigger and we can spread out more."

"Great idea," Luke agreed.

"And Paul can help Jimmy," Gussie said. "They are both at loose ends over holiday seasons without Nellie and Ruthie. Seems like Christmas always hits folks who've lost their spouses worse than any other time of the year." She shook her head. "I sure miss Ruthie. She was the best at organizing a funeral dinner, and Nellie was such a good receptionist at the health clinic."

The smell of fish gets stronger, Sissy thought.

"You kids enjoy the rest of the evening." Ina Mae headed out into the hallway. "We'll let ourselves out, and we'll plan on putting up your tree tomorrow evening, Sissy. I'll bring supper with me. You should join us, Luke. Y'all will be too tired to cook after a long day of sorting through things."

"I'd love to." Luke started to stand up.

"Six o'clock, then." Gussie followed Ina Mae. "This is a good evening to watch *Home Alone.* That always makes me laugh."

Sissy waited until she heard the car doors slam before she turned to face Luke. "If you need to go, I understand. They kind of railroaded you into staying for a movie."

"I can stay for a while," Luke said, "but do we have to watch that movie? Blanche and I watched *Die Hard* last year over the holiday season."

Sissy felt her eyes getting wider and wider. "Really? You're not trying to shock me?"

"Nope," Luke answered. "I'm a preacher, but I'm also a man, Sissy."

Sissy could almost hear the crackle of sparks in the room and could definitely feel a bit of a sizzle—no, that wasn't right. She could feel heat flooding her body just thinking about Luke and what being a man meant. A picture of him— tangled up in sheets, looking at her with desire in those sexy eyes—popped into her head. A blush crept up from her neck to her cheeks. She whipped around and went to put the movie in the DVD player.

"*Die Hard* it is." If he was testing her to see if she would say she didn't want to watch that movie, then she was about to fail the test in more ways than one. She loved the film, and she was adult enough that she could watch it with a preacher. "Looks like she's got all five."

"We don't have time for a marathon, but the first one should be fun, unless you *want* to watch Hallmark Christmas movies, or . . ."

Sissy shook her head. "I like action movies just fine. *Shooter* is one of my favorites, too. I've got good memories of coming to see Aunt Bee and watching shoot-'em-ups, car chases, and bad guys getting theirs."

She still couldn't believe that a preacher would watch R-rated movies with the kind of language the character John McClane used in them.

"But before we watch the movie," Luke said, "tell me what you were like in high school. Were you a Hallmark movie girl then, or did you like action films?"

"You first." She brought the remote control back to the sofa and sat down on the other end from him. "Were you an athlete? Maybe the quarterback of the football team? Or the star of the basketball team?"

"I was a little bit of a dork. I liked music more than sports, played in the band and the piano in church, and was on the academic team," he answered. "Your turn."

"I didn't get to go to high school," she said. "I was homeschooled my whole life. I took a few concurrent online courses, though, so when

I started college, I already had a full semester finished."

"Sounds like you were pretty smart. Where did you live?" Luke asked.

"In an RV, so everywhere, I guess," she answered. "Surely Aunt Bee talked about her brother, Ford."

"Just that you were his daughter, and someday when you came to visit, I would have to meet you," Luke said.

"My folks were rock musicians. I was raised in the storeroom of bars for the most part. When I was about twelve, they let me stay in the RV and study at night, but Mama came to check on me between sets," she said.

"Sounds like an exciting life," Luke said.

Sissy sure hadn't expected him to say that, and for a few seconds she was stunned. "And after high school? Did you go straight to seminary school?" she asked.

"No, I went into the army, got sent to Afghanistan, and we watched a lot of movies in the evenings. *Die Hard* was one of our favorites," he answered.

"How long were you in the service?" Sissy asked. At one time she'd thought about enlisting since her folks didn't have the money for her to go to college. Then Aunt Bee had offered to pay her tuition.

"Six years," Luke answered. "I served as chaplain the last three, came home, and used my GI Bill to go to seminary, and I already told you the rest."

"I'll get us a refill on our tea," she said as she picked up the tray, "and get out some more cookies. Once the movie starts, neither of us will want to pause it."

Should she offer him a drink or maybe a beer? No, definitely not. That would be taking things way too far, but she did eye the few drops of vodka left in Danny Boy's bowl as she passed by.

She was refilling their tea glasses when she remembered that Ina Mae and Gussie were playing matchmaker. Evidently, they had picked up on the subtle vibes, or maybe since she was the only family they had left, they wanted her to stay in Newton, and to them love was the answer.

I thought I was doing a fine job of hiding the sparks, she thought.

Not so! the aggravating voice in her head argued. *You were as jittery as a schoolgirl, and you kept sneaking looks at him. He is one sexy guy, isn't he?*

"He's a preacher," she muttered.

He's a man first—remember?

She couldn't argue with that, so she picked up the tray, carried it back to the living room, and set it on the table. "I'm ready when you are."

"Sissy, if you are uncomfortable with me being here or if—"

She held up a palm. "There's a long evening ahead of us. We might as well enjoy a movie together. Besides, we both miss Aunt Bee. I could sure use the company."

"I was hoping you'd say that." He smiled again. "Being the pastor of a small church in a little town is a tough job sometimes. Folks want to put me up on a pedestal. I even got a gentle reprimand from the deacons a couple of weeks ago for playing basketball shirtless with a bunch of the young guys."

"How are you going to reach them if you set yourself apart from them?" she asked.

"Exactly, and besides"—there was that smile again—"I like playing basketball, and someone has to be skins. We were inside the fellowship hall, and we'd pushed the tables all back to one side. It's not like we were outside in the cold. Maybe pretty soon, someone will step up and offer to be the youth director."

"Are you still going to play ball with the kids, even then?" she asked.

"Yes"—he nodded—"but I'll probably be on the shirts side instead of the skins. That should make the deacons a little bit happier. Here we go." He hit the play button. "I don't suppose they'd be happy about me watching an R-rated movie with a beautiful woman and no chaperones, either."

"God knows and sees what we're doing," Sissy

told him. "It's not anyone else's business." He'd called her beautiful, so maybe he felt the same vibes that she had. If so, that called for even more introspection on her part. She didn't want to hurt him, and yet she knew from her sessions with folks who had tried to make long-distance relationships work that it was one tough job.

"I like the way you think." Luke kicked off his shoes and propped his feet on the end of the coffee table and then pulled them back with a jump. "I'm sorry. I should've asked if this was all right. Blanche and I used the table for a hassock all the time."

Sissy stretched her legs out and so he followed her lead. "So did we." She didn't tell him that she and Aunt Bee usually had a glass of wine in their hands, instead of sweet tea.

She stole quick glances at Luke all through the movie. He reminded her of someone with his chiseled features and dark hair, but she couldn't put a finger on who. Not until she caught the right angle when he laughed at something on the screen. He looked a lot like Matt Bomer, who played Neal on *White Collar*. She owned every season of that series on DVD and binge-watched them at least once a year.

In her opinion, they should make that show a must-watch for graduate therapy classes. The dynamics of the whole cast, such polarized personalities, purely good or evil, were fascinating.

What made them tick? What was in their backgrounds to define them?

The movie was coming to an end, so she shook the thoughts of her favorite series from her head and focused on the last few scenes, where Bruce Willis's character, John, single-handedly showed the villains that good would prevail.

"And the good guys win again." Luke pumped his fist in the air. "On that note, I should be going, but I do have one favor to ask of you since you're going to be at the church tomorrow."

Sissy turned to look at him. "Someone getting married and you need a witness?"

"No, but there's this young married couple. They were pregnant when they got married, and they're having a really tough time of it. They're still trying to get used to each other while both working long hours and not spending much time together. I can't pay you, but would you . . ." He paused. "They want to talk to me in the morning, and I think a therapist could help so much more than I can."

"I'd be glad to counsel them pro bono." She wondered if she should bring her work life into her Sissy life, but if someone needed her help, she couldn't say no. "Don't know if I can be much help. That first year is tough enough without dealing with a baby on the way and the hormones, the adjustments, and all that entails, but I'll do my best."

"Thank you so much." Luke put his shoes on and stood up. "I always felt like I could be myself here at Blanche's house. She reminded me of my grandmother, and she was my sounding board for any problems I had. I'm going to really miss her, but getting to sit here tonight with you and just watch an old movie was great. Thank you for that as well as in advance for the therapy session for Annabelle and Wesley."

Sissy walked him out to the hallway and stood to the side while he put on his coat. "I've always felt the same way about coming to visit Aunt Bee. The house seemed so empty when I walked into it after"—she paused—"well, you know. It's like a ghost of a place, with all the life gone from it. I always had a FaceTime with her on Saturday mornings while we had our coffee. It's still surreal. One Saturday she's telling me jokes, and the next, I'm walking behind a horse-drawn carriage."

"Just teaches us that time isn't guaranteed, and we should make the most of every hour of every day." Luke opened the door, and a gust of cold wind swept through the long hallway. "I'll open the church at eight in the morning. Wesley works the night shift at the hospital as an orderly. You think you could visit with them when he gets off work at nine?"

"I'll be there," Sissy assured him.

"See you then. Have a good night, and thanks

119

again," he said and waved as he disappeared into the darkness.

"Thank you for keeping me company." Sissy raised her voice, but the noise of a truck engine probably covered up the sound. She stood on the other side of the screen door for a few minutes, then closed and locked the heavy wooden door and headed up the stairs. Aunt Bee loved all things antique, so the walls were covered in paper with a twining rose pattern that looked like it had come out of the *Great Gatsby* era. She sat down on the bed and replayed the feelings she had had all evening, from that little sizzle when Luke said he was a man as well as a preacher, to the moment he left—when his eyes looked less like a preacher's than a man's.

How do you know what a preacher's eyes look like? Aunt Bee was so clear in her head that she glanced out the open door, thinking that she might see her coming across the hall.

"I don't know much about preachers, but I have dated a few guys, and I know what hungry eyes look like," Sissy answered. *I'm not talking about wanting to eat food.*

She was still thinking about Luke's eyes when her cell phone rang and startled her. For just a split second, she thought it might be Luke, and hoped that God didn't give preachers the ability to read minds. She grabbed it from the nightstand without even looking at the caller ID. "Hello," she said.

"Was the movie good?" Ina Mae asked.

"Yes, it was great," Sissy said.

"I've got you on speaker so Gussie can hear," Ina Mae said. "We just wanted you to know that we've got twenty people willing to help with the new church decorations, and if you need anything beyond what is donated, Gussie and I will provide the funds to cover that. The stuff will be starting to come in tomorrow morning, so you and Luke will be busy all week."

"I'm also doing some pro bono counseling for a couple named Annabelle and Wesley. Know anything about them?" Sissy pulled the chain to turn on the antique lamp beside her bed.

"Oh, chère." Gussie sighed. "That little couple so needs some help. Annabelle just got out of high school in May, and his folks didn't think she was good enough for Wesley, so they cut him off financially. It's a shame, because he had high hopes of being a doctor. He's working at the hospital as an orderly, and she works at the doughnut shop on the north side of the square. Bless their hearts. I'm glad you're going to help them."

"Thanks for telling me that," Sissy said. "I hope they can keep their eyes open long enough to talk to me."

"I hope they listen to you and appreciate that

121

you're not going to charge them," Ina Mae told her. "They're such good kids, but they have a lot of hurdles to overcome. Will you tell us how it all goes?"

"Can't," Sissy answered. "What they tell me has to stay between us. I could lose my license if I said a word."

"Understandable," Gussie said. "Then we'll just hope for the best. Get some sleep, chère. We'll see you tomorrow evening. I'm glad Luke is joining us. We need a tall man to help decorate Blanche's tree. I swear to God, she only bought that big house with its twelve-foot ceilings so she could have a ten-foot Christmas tree. I'm glad that Luke will be there to crawl up on the ladder to work on the top of it. Good night."

"Good night to both of you," Sissy said and ended the call.

Poor darlings were lost without Blanche, so she didn't mind so much if they wanted to play matchmaker. They wouldn't succeed for many reasons, but mostly because she loved her job in Beau Bridge and she had no intention of leaving the area. When Luke talked about Newton, there was something in his tone that said he really liked the town, and he'd shown that he cared about his little church family when he asked for their help with the pageant. No doubt about it, Luke had put down roots in Newton, and she wouldn't be a bit surprised if he was there until he retired—

that was, if the deacons didn't catch him playing basketball without a shirt again.

She smiled at that visual, and then wondered exactly what he would look like with his bare chest showing. Would it be covered in soft, dark hair? Did he have a six-pack? He'd worn a button-up shirt and jeans that evening, so she couldn't tell much about what was under all the clothing.

Maybe she *should* keep the house pretty much intact for the next year. That way she wouldn't have to move furniture and clean out drawers and closets—and the attic. She shivered at the thought of going up there, where there might be spiders or mice, or both.

If she listened to her own advice and waited a year before she made any rash decisions, she would have several weeks to try to find closure for the loss of Aunt Bee.

Chapter Six

Sissy awoke the next morning to Chester crowing out on the porch and Danny Boy echoing every single one of those sounds from inside the house. She looked at the clock, groaned, and crammed a pillow over her head. Her alarm was set for seven and even that was early when she was using up her vacation days. Getting up while it was still dark should be a sin, and the price of repentance should be the sacrifice of two awful birds. Their incessant noise didn't let up, so she sat up in bed, threw off the covers, and yawned.

"All right, I'm up," she moaned. "Remind me to find good homes for you two before I go back to Louisiana—or maybe just homes. Right now, I don't care if your new place is so whoopee-good or not."

She put on a pot of coffee and then took a cup full of chicken feed to the front porch to fill Chester's feeding dish. Danny Boy stopped crowing when Chester did, and was now alternating between telling everyone where to go and screaming to be let out. Sissy jerked the towel off his cage and laid it to the side, then opened his cage door. The bird looked downright cocky as he pranced outside, said, "Pretty boy," and flew over to the window ledge.

Sissy poured herself a cup of coffee and carried it to the kitchen table. The empty tea glasses and plate of leftover cookies were still there, so she picked up a chocolate chip cookie and dipped it in her coffee. Her phone pinged about the time she was about to take a bite, and the noise startled her so badly that she dropped the soggy cookie back into the mug.

"Three messages before six o'clock," she muttered as she tapped the screen. "I just talked to Ina Mae and Gussie last night, so it shouldn't be either of them." But she was wrong. The first two were from Ina Mae, sent at five thirty that morning, asking if she would give her a call when she was awake.

The next one was from Luke. Number one was just short of an apology: I hope it's all right that I got your number from Gussie. Can you be at the church at 8:30 instead of nine?

"Sure, why not?" She sent back a yes and dipped another cookie into the hot coffee.

Danny Boy flew into the room and circled around the ceiling twice before he landed on the table, dragged a cookie over to the end, and held it down with his claw. "Pretty boy," he said.

"Just how many words do you know?" Sissy asked.

He ignored her and hopped over to dip his beak

into her mug and eat the floating bits of cookie. "Good stuff, Blanche!"

"Well, there's some I haven't heard," she said.

"Dammit! That's hot!" His voice wasn't the same, but the inflection was just like Aunt Bee was sitting across the table from her. Evidently, she hadn't saved all her cuss words for the clubhouse.

"Maybe I won't give you away after all." Sissy chuckled. "As long as you're alive, I don't have to say goodbye to Aunt Bee."

She pushed back her chair and put the dirty glasses in the dishwasher and the remainder of the cookies in a baggie that went into the pantry. While she was there, she made a list of what she needed to buy at the store on her way home that evening. Mainly just staples like flour, sugar, and cornmeal, but she had opened the last package of cookies, so she put them on the list along with chocolate ice cream.

That done, and the dirty plate put into the dishwasher, she headed back upstairs. She had always loved the old claw-foot tub in the bathroom at the end of the upstairs hallway. She was still grumbling about being awakened so early, but it was nice to get a long bath that morning without having to rush. From the window at the end of the tub, she watched the sun come up—starting as nothing more than a bit of orange on the eastern horizon that painted the sky in an array of colors.

"I don't get a view like this anywhere in my apartment in Beau Bridge," she muttered. "My tub is so shallow that I can't sink down to my neck in warm water and bubbles. I could keep this place just for this tub."

By the time she finished her bath and got dressed, she decided that getting up early wasn't such a bad idea. She hadn't had to rush at all that morning. She grabbed one of Aunt Bee's cardigans from the hall tree, put it on, and rolled up the sleeves. She slung her purse over her shoulder and opened the door to find Chester roosting on the porch rail. He turned his head to glare at her.

"Don't look at me that way," she said. "You're still alive and living in the lap of luxury one more day, but there's still no guarantees for tomorrow, so be nice to me, or I won't feed you in the morning."

"Are you Miz Ducaine?" A young man opened the church door for Sissy.

"Yes, I am." She flashed a smile, hoping to calm his nerves.

He wore dark-green scrubs the color of his eyes, and just looking at him told Sissy that he was nervous about this visit. "I'm Wesley McKay and this is my wife, Annabelle."

"I'm pleased to meet you both," Sissy said.

"Luke said to tell you that we can have our

visit in the nursery." Annabelle's eyes darted around instead of looking right at Sissy. "He said he'll be back in a few minutes." A T-shirt with a bakery logo stretched tightly over her very pregnant stomach. A few strands of red hair had escaped her ponytail, and her blue eyes looked both worried and tired.

"That's great. If y'all will lead the way, I'll follow. I have no idea where the nursery is," Sissy said, hoping her smile and voice put them somewhat at ease.

They had started down the aisle in the sanctuary with Sissy behind them when she got an idea. "Hey, wait just a minute, please. Before we have a visit, I want Wesley to go stand in the place where he stood on your wedding day, and Annabelle, I want you to go back to the door and come down the aisle very slowly."

"Why?" Wesley asked.

"Before we even talk, I want you to remember that day. While she's walking toward you, think about all the love you had for each other, the funny things that happened, the plans you made," Sissy told them both. "I'm going to sit right here on this pew and wait."

"This sounds a little crazy," Wesley said.

Annabelle laid a hand on her bulging belly. "I sure don't feel like a pretty bride."

"For the next five minutes, Wesley is a nervous but handsome groom, and you are the beautiful

128

woman he's in love with." Sissy reached over to the back pew and handed Annabelle a Bible. "Pretend this is your bouquet."

"I've got doughnut stains on my shirt, and my hair is a mess," Annabelle whispered, but she took the Bible from Sissy's hands.

Sissy had barely gotten seated when Luke slid in beside her. "What's going on?"

"A little role-playing," she whispered. "Remembering how much they were in love on their wedding day will make things easier when they talk to me."

"That is a great idea," Luke said. "They said they could only spare thirty minutes. Wesley's just off work and needs to get some rest."

"That's long enough for this first time," Sissy said.

"Oh!" Luke raised an eyebrow. "Is there going to be a second time?"

Sparks flitted around them like butterflies around a flower bed in the spring. Sissy grabbed on to the feeling and held it close to her heart. Preacher, man, or both, she was attracted to Luke like she'd never been to a guy before.

"I'll be here six weeks. As long as you let me use the nursery for sessions, I'd be glad to see them a few more times," she whispered and deliberately gave the couple a little time alone before she went forward. "Time to go. Where do you want me after I finish talking to them?"

"I'll be somewhere in the church," Luke answered. "You've got my number. Just give me a call."

"Will do." She stood up and made her way to the front of the church, where the young couple were hugging each other. "Did you recapture that love?"

"I think we did," Wesley said.

"I know I did." Annabelle grinned and appeared a lot more at ease. "Can we go to the nursery now?"

"Lead the way, and I will follow," Sissy said. When they reached the right place, Wesley opened the door and stood to one side to let the ladies enter first. Sissy noticed that he draped an arm around Annabelle's shoulders as they entered the room filled with two baby beds, a couple of rocking chairs, and a basket of toys in the corner.

Any of this set your biological clock to ticking? Aunt Bee was back for a visit.

An instant picture of a baby with dark hair and blue eyes popped into Sissy's head. She quickly hit a mental "Delete" button and concentrated on Wesley and Annabelle.

"Why don't y'all sit in the two rocking chairs, and I'll just pop open a folding chair?" Sissy suggested.

They were six feet apart when they sat down. Sissy picked up a stuffed bunny from one of the cribs and set it in the middle of the open distance.

130

"Now I want you to stand up and move your chairs closer so that the arms are touching. I figure that bunny is about halfway."

Wesley hopped up and said, "I'll move both of them. They're kind of heavy."

"No, I want Annabelle to move hers," Sissy said. "She can scoot it, or if it is really too heavy, she'll ask for your help."

Annabelle bent over her big belly and had no trouble moving the chair over. "What do we do with the bunny now? We might rock on it if we aren't careful, and now it's been on the floor, so it should be washed before a baby plays with it."

Sissy picked the toy up and tossed it into a laundry basket over in the corner of the room. With that attitude, Annabelle would be a good little mother who thought of keeping things clean for her baby.

Sissy sat back down in her chair and said, "Annabelle, I want you to look at Wesley and tell him what your top problem is."

"Can I just look at you?" Annabelle asked. "We fight about these same things every day, and I can see by his expression that it upsets him when I fuss about this thing."

That statement told Sissy a little more about Annabelle. She loved Wesley enough that it actually hurt her when they argued, and yet at the same time the problem was something that was causing friction between them.

"No, I want you to look at him, and, Wesley, I want you to really listen," Sissy said.

Annabelle sucked in a lungful of air, let it out slowly, and then grimaced. "Okay, you already know this, but just so Miz Ducaine can understand the issue, I hate going to your folks' every Sunday for dinner. They made it clear that they didn't like me when they refused to continue paying for your college. You were going to be a doctor, and now, you're working as an orderly in a hospital because we got pregnant and you insisted on marrying me. I told you that we could just live together, or that we could even wait until you got through school to get married."

"I want to be a part of my baby's life," Wes said, "and yours. I want us to be a couple."

"But," Annabelle went on, "Sunday is our only day off from our jobs together, and I'd like to spend it doing something other than being miserable and then coming home to cry until bedtime." Tears hung on her eyelashes.

Sissy pushed up out of her chair and handed Annabelle a whole box of tissues. "Now, Wesley, you respond to her problem."

"I want to keep the lines of communication open between us and my parents. I want them to see that Annabelle is a good person and that she will be a good mother. They have to spend time around her to know that, and they *are* our baby's grandparents . . ."

"Your mother told me that she was too young to be a grandmother and not to ever ask her to babysit for us." Annabelle dabbed at her eyes.

Wesley closed his eyes for a moment, as if choosing his words wisely. "Annabelle's mother told us that she'd keep the baby so we wouldn't have to pay a sitter, but my mom works every day at the law firm. She wouldn't have time to keep a baby. She always throws her mother up to me when we argue. It's like comparing apples to watermelons."

"That's something to talk about another day," Sissy said. "Working through problems takes time and patience. Let's try to solve one issue each week. This time let's take care of Annabelle's feeling that she's not wanted at your folks' house. She wants to spend more time with you, and less with your parents on your day off. You want to keep the lines of communication open between you and your folks. How about a compromise? First, I want you to remember the feeling you had when you were in the sanctuary a little while ago. Annabelle wants that once a week."

"What are we supposed to do?" Wesley sighed.

"When you pushed your chairs together, you were willing to take care of Annabelle's for her," Sissy answered.

"What's that got to do with all this?" Wesley asked.

"That tells me that you are willing to go the

extra mile, and that Annabelle is willing to do her fifty percent," Sissy said. "Why don't you visit your folks one Sunday a month? Annabelle is right in wanting time with you. You need that to build a solid foundation for a marriage. You are right in wanting to not cut your parents out of your life. On the Sundays that you don't go to your parents', you should vow to each other that that is your day, and you are going to spend it together without outside influences—not Annabelle's mother or either of your friends. It doesn't matter if you take a walk around the courthouse square or watch movies on television all day. What you do isn't important. What is important is that you spend the day with each other and reignite the fire of your love. That's the big thing for that day. Wesley, you aren't to feel guilty or to throw it up to Annabelle that you would rather be having a fine meal at your folks' house instead of eating bologna sandwiches. Annabelle, on the one Sunday a month that you go to his folks', you shouldn't come home griping about the way they've acted. Think y'all can do that?"

Wesley nodded. "We were there yesterday. I'll tell Mother we won't be back until the first Sunday in the New Year."

"Thank you." Annabelle smiled. "What about Christmas?"

Sissy held up a palm. "That will be next week's problem. One step at a time. You will have spent a whole day together before I see you again. We'll talk about the holidays that day. The first year of marriage is an adjustment in the best of circumstances. You have come from very different backgrounds, but you love each other. I could see it when you were in the sanctuary. Each day make sure you tell each other— and mean it—those three magic words: 'I love you.' "

"Thank you." Annabelle tried to get up from the chair.

Wesley hopped up and extended both hands. "How about I start right now. I love you, darlin'."

"I love you, too, but marriage is tough," she said.

"It really is," Sissy said, "and it requires a lot of hard work, but the benefits are worth it."

Worth it for a preacher and the daughter of a couple of hippie rock band people? the pesky voice in her head asked.

The question made Sissy uncomfortable. She was willing to admit there was an attraction there, but marriage? That would demand more than just hard work. Their backgrounds were even more different than Annabelle's and Wesley's, so Sissy could only imagine the problems.

"Thank you, Miz Ducaine," they said at the same time and then smiled at each other.

They left—still holding hands. They had barely cleared the room when Jimmy Beauchamp, the former preacher, came into the room and settled into a rocking chair. The worried look in his green eyes left no doubt in Sissy's mind that something was bothering him.

"Paul and I just brought a pickup-load of stuff to donate to the Christmas cause, and we're going to build a new manger scene this week," he said. "Paul had to get on back home. Lucas asked me to tell you that he had to make a run to the hospital. Elvira thinks she's having a heart attack again, and she wants him beside her if she dies."

"Again?" Sissy asked. "Didn't she just have one the day of the funeral? How often do these things happen?"

"She's got an acute case of hypochondria. I can't count how many times I had to go to the hospital and sit with her until the doctor released her to go home. When the phone would ring late at night, Ruthie would always ask if it was Elvira," Jimmy answered.

"She needs help," Sissy said.

"Amen to that," Jimmy agreed, "but while there's just me and you in the church, I wanted to talk to you. I should've gotten some therapy when Ruthie died, but I just couldn't admit that I needed to talk to anyone. Paul had been through the same thing a few years before, so I did visit with him, but this is something that . . ." He grimaced. "Well, I still love my wife, but . . ." He

136

paused and closed his eyes as if he couldn't face saying the words.

"But you'd like to move on, right?" Sissy asked.

Jimmy crossed one long leg over the other and sighed. "Ruthie has been gone for two years. Paul's wife passed away five years ago. We're both seventy-five years old, and we enjoy working in the woodshop together and going fishing, but . . ."

"You're lonely for female companionship, and you feel guilty, right?" Sissy finished the sentence for him.

Jimmy nodded. "I'm not sure I'd ever remarry, but it would be nice just to go to dinner with a lady, or maybe even . . ." He paused.

"Watch a movie together?" Sissy thought of how much she'd enjoyed watching *Die Hard* with Luke the night before. Hearing his laughter at some of the parts and seeing him sit on the edge of the sofa during the dramatic parts was so much fun.

"Yes, that's it, but even sitting here today, even just talking about that, makes me feel guilty," Jimmy said. "Like I'm cheating on Ruthie."

"Did she love you?" Sissy asked.

"Of course she did. We were married almost fifty years." Jimmy sounded a little offended.

"Would she want you to be happy?" Sissy asked.

"I see where you are going with this," Jimmy said. "You just conned an old preacher into seeing things in the right light. What do I owe you?" He started to pull his wallet from his hip pocket.

Sissy shook her head and held up a palm. "You don't owe me anything. We were just having a visit. And even a man of God needs fresh eyes on a problem every now and then," she told him, "and seventy-five is the new late fifties and early sixties. You are only as old as you feel."

Turnabout is fair play. What are you going to do with his information? Blanche's giggle was so plain that Sissy glanced over her shoulder.

She almost snapped her fingers when she realized what her aunt Bee was talking about. Ina Mae and Gussie were playing matchmaker, and Blanche had just given Sissy license to do the same. If they could try to put Sissy and Luke together, then she could throw Jimmy and Paul into the mix and see what shook out. Plus, that would give them something and someone to help them get over Blanche's shocking death, and also help Jimmy and Paul take a step toward moving on. It was a win-win-win situation all the way around.

Jimmy started to stand up, but then settled back into the chair. "I haven't even put up a tree since Ruthie passed away. I miss those times when we decorated the house together, but it's no fun to do all those things all alone."

"Ina Mae is making supper for us, and we're decorating Aunt Bee's tree tonight. You and Paul should come over and help us. Putting a few ornaments on the tree and stringing some lights might help you find closure. Goodness knows, we can use some tall guys to help us. Aunt Bee has a ten-foot tree; there's no way any of us can reach the top of it without a ladder, and I'm not about to let Ina Mae and Gussie go climbing up on one," Sissy said. "Luke is coming to help, but we could never have too many tall guys."

This time Jimmy did get to his feet. "Thank you for the invitation. If you think it will help, we'll be there."

"Of course it will. Remember, I'm the therapist." Sissy stood up and walked to the door with him. "What did y'all bring to the church today?"

"Two trees, and a bunch of decorations, plus some old red drapes that Ruthie liked to use at Christmas. I thought you might find a use for them," he answered.

"I think I already know exactly what to do with them." Sissy remembered the video of last year's pageant and how they'd had to keep moving some of the props out and more in to take their place before the next group could do their parts. "Thank you so much for everything, including coming to our aid this evening. Be there about six?"

"Yes, ma'am. Can we bring anything?" Jimmy asked.

Sissy followed him out into the hallway and then into the sanctuary. "Just a healthy appetite and some long arms, and we'll appreciate the help so much. Oh, one more thing." She frowned. "You do know that Danny Boy has a colorful vocabulary, right?"

"We all do at times." Jimmy waved over his shoulder.

Oh, yes, Aunt Bee, turnabout is definitely fair play, she thought.

"I'm really dyin' this time, Brother Luke," Elvira groaned. "I feel the life ebbin' out of me. Pray over me and ask God to receive my soul into the gates of heaven."

Luke bowed his head, but before he could say a word, a nurse came into the emergency room cubicle with a set of papers in her hands. "Miz Elvira, you've got an abundance of gas, most likely coming from what you ate yesterday. You're not having a heart attack. Your blood tests came back, and everything is normal, so we're releasing you to go home. Do you have a driver?" she asked and then realized that Luke was in the cubicle. "Oh, didn't see you there. Hello, Luke."

"Hi, Martha." He smiled at one of the members of his congregation.

"Luke will drive me," Elvira sighed. "Maybe

I got food poisoning from the Hen's Nest. I had Sunday dinner there."

"You have no signs of food poisoning." The nurse winked at Luke. "The doctor has ordered this to help with your problem." She handed her a glass with green liquid in it. "We call it a green lizard, and it will make you feel better by the time you get home."

Elvira turned up the glass, drank the medicine, and shivered. "That tastes awful."

"Most medicine does," Martha said. "Now, Luke will step out and let you get dressed in private. I'll stay right here in case you need help."

"I can dress myself," Elvira snapped at her.

"I'm so glad. It's good to see folks your age doing for themselves and not in nursing homes. With no family in town, if you had a stroke or heart attack, you might not be able to live alone anymore," Martha suggested.

Luke hoped that Elvira got that message, but he figured it flew over her head like a hard winter wind.

Another long sigh from Elvira filled the tiny cubicle as Luke pulled back the curtains and stepped out. "Are you sure that the EKG didn't show something horrible wrong with me?"

"Positive, ma'am," Martha said.

Luke waited outside the curtains, and in a few minutes Martha came out, shaking her head.

"One of these days she's going to cry wolf one too many times."

"Maybe she needs some therapy sessions," Luke suggested.

"At her age, I doubt they'd do much good. She's been like this for as long as I've known her, and I'm lookin' forty right in the eye. What she needs is something to keep her so busy that it wears her out and she doesn't have time to even think about her imagined ailments," Martha said. "See you in church on Sunday. Until then, we'll hope that Elvira doesn't have another episode."

"From your lips to God's ears," Luke said with a chuckle.

Elvira marched out of the cubicle with her shoulders squared back. Not one hair was out of place, and her makeup didn't have a smear. Evidently, she had wanted to approach heaven's doors looking her best. Didn't folks understand that their physical bodies ended with their last breath, and all that went to meet the Master was their spirits?

"I think from now on, I'm calling an ambulance from Jasper to come get me and take me to one of their hospitals. These people wouldn't know a heart attack if it jumped up and bit them on the hind end. They wanted me to ride in a wheelchair out to your car. If I'm not having a heart attack, then I can walk myself out. They even made me sign a release form before they'd let me go on my own," she grumbled as she stomped across the floor and outside.

Luke ran ahead and opened his car door for her, made sure she was settled in, and then closed it. He had learned that being a minister involved more than getting sermons ready for Sunday morning and Wednesday night. The scripture said that we shouldn't be hateful or mean to those who had a weak spot. Elvira most likely just wanted attention. Too bad she and her husband had divorced ten years ago, and yet in some measure, Luke could understand the stress of living with someone like her on a daily basis.

"Do you need to make any stops along the way?" Luke asked as he slid in behind the steering wheel.

"No." Elvira laid the back of her hand on her forehead. "Just take me home so I can lay down and rest until this colon problem solves itself. It's so painful that I'll probably just spend the day in bed. That medicine Martha gave me was awful. I'm not sure it's going to help at all."

"Yes, ma'am." Luke had never truly appreciated his grandmother enough. She had been eighty years old when she passed away, and she'd still been mowing her own lawn, making a garden, and quilting. She never complained and always had cake or pie or cookies ready—just in case someone stopped by.

He parked in the driveway beside Elvira's

house and hurried around the car to help her out, gently slipping his hand under her elbow and escorting her up the steps to the porch.

"Thank you, Luke." Elvira's sigh could have been heard halfway down the block. "Most people don't understand how hard it is to be sickly. I'm glad you do."

"I'll send up extra prayers for you." Luke waited until she was inside the house before he turned around and headed back to his car.

I'm going to ask God to make you understand that you need friends. You are pushing those you have away with your hypochondria and bossiness, he thought as he got into his car.

An idea popped into his head as if God had answered his prayer right then and there. He got out of his vehicle, jogged back to the house, rang the doorbell, and shivered as he waited.

Elvira opened the door with a quizzical expression on her face. "Did you forget something?"

"No, but could I come in for just a minute?" he asked.

She swung the door open wide and smiled. "Of course. Can I make you a cup of tea or get you a bottle of water or sweet tea? Let me take your coat."

"I can't stay that long." He stepped inside out of the bitter cold wind. "We're trying to get a better Christmas pageant together at the church. I'm sure you've been called about donations."

"Oh, yes, and I've got them gathered up. Paul is going to pick them up this afternoon," Elvira answered.

"My uncle Jimmy just this morning donated a bunch of red drapes, and I'm sure we're going to need them fashioned into curtains for the stage. I heard that you used to be a pretty fine seamstress. Would you feel up to doing some sewing for the church?" Luke asked.

"Oh, my! Yes!" Elvira said. "Maybe I'll just bring my donations myself this afternoon, and we can talk about what needs to be done. My sewing machine is portable, so I can put it in the car, too."

"That would be great," Luke said, "and while you're there, how are you at decorating a Christmas tree for the foyer?"

Elvira's eyes lit up like she'd just won a million-dollar check from a magazine company. "I would just love to do that." She pointed across the room at her own tree. "I'm good at sewing *and* at decorating. I'm willing to help any way I can. Of course, if you need someone to supervise the whole pageant, I could probably do that, too."

"I'll be taking care of the supervision, but your tree is beautiful. I figured you'd be just the one to ask to help out with the curtains and the foyer tree," Luke said. "I've got to get back now, but we'll see you in a little while."

Elvira opened the door for him. "I'll be there soon as I get done with my lunch."

"Don't let this wind blow you away," he teased.

"I'm stronger than I look." She smiled again and then closed the door behind him.

He got into his car and drove four blocks to the church and rushed in the back door to find Sissy coming out of the nursery. "I'm so sorry that I couldn't be here for the therapy session. I had to leave in a hurry. Elvira had another episode."

"Is she all right?" Sissy asked.

"She's got acute hypochondria." Luke removed his coat and hung it on a hook beside the door. "She just sits around and worries about having a heart attack or cancer or something. I'm not a therapist, but I think it's for attention."

"Yep." Sissy nodded. "That's usually the case. It's a vicious cycle. A person doesn't have any hobbies or anything to keep them busy, so they create health issues so maybe someone, anyone at all, will pay attention to them. Then because of the way they're always so tied up in their health, what friends they have tend to slip away and not want to have anything to do with them."

"That's exactly right," Luke said. "She's coming to the church this afternoon to bring her donations for the Christmas program. Would you help me figure out what we're going to do with the curtains Uncle Jimmy donated, so we can tell her how to stitch them up? We could discuss

146

it over lunch if you can stick around that long?"

"Over lunch?" Sissy asked.

"I ordered a couple of pizzas to be delivered at noon for whoever was here helping," he said.

Her eyes met his. "Right now, it's just me and you. Everyone else has gone home."

For a split second he had a rare breathless moment when he felt as if he were drowning in her mossy green eyes, but he blinked and looked away before he lost the ability to think straight. "Then we should have plenty. There's soft drinks, water, and sweet tea in the kitchen." His voice sounded strange in his own ears.

"Sounds great to me," she said. "Do you think Elvira would go for a couple of therapy sessions?"

"Not if she knew about it," Luke answered.

"Then we'll make sure it's a secret." Sissy grinned.

Chapter Seven

The warmth of that moment when she and Luke locked gazes stayed with Sissy all the way to the fellowship hall. He made a phone call as soon as they got into the kitchen area and asked that the pizza delivery person bring the order to the back door.

"Have a seat anywhere." With a wave of his hand, he motioned toward the tables in the dimly lit fellowship hall and the brighter kitchen area. "What can I get you to drink?"

"Diet anything?" she asked. "If not, sweet tea will do fine."

"One diet anything coming right up and one sweet tea." He opened the refrigerator and brought out two bottles.

Sissy sat down at a table with four chairs around it and tried to collect her thoughts. He was going to ask her about the curtains, and she'd had an idea when Jimmy mentioned them, but now her mind was blank. Why did just stealing glances at Luke turn her brain to jelly?

He set the two drinks on the table and took his phone from his hip pocket. "Great timing. Just got a text that the delivery guy is in the driveway. I got a pepperoni and a meat lover's. I should have asked if you were a vegetarian."

"Not me," Sissy said. "I like meat too well to go down that path."

"I have no beef—pun unintended—with folks who eat different than I do"—he chuckled—"but I like pizza and burgers too well to try that." He headed to the door, paid the kid, and brought two big boxes of pizza to the table.

"Smells delicious," Sissy said.

"Mind if I say grace before we eat?" he asked.

"Not one bit," she answered.

Luke sat down, bowed his head, and said a short prayer. Then he flipped the boxes open and motioned for her to help herself first.

"Shall we talk about those curtains while we eat?" Sissy asked.

Luke hopped up. "I forgot the plates and napkins. Do you need a fork? We've got leftovers from a birthday party and from the big Easter egg hunt we had at the church last spring. It's not like a five-star restaurant, but it is colorful."

Sissy shook her head. "Pizza is finger food."

"Woman after my heart." He brought two red plastic disposable plates and a fistful of napkins with Easter eggs printed on them to the table.

He had said it in jest, but it flushed her with warmth anyway. She hadn't dated in more than a year, not because of any traumatic event like a horrible breakup or a cheating boyfriend. She blamed it on her job. She found herself analyzing any man she went out with, or even had a fairly long-term relationship with, which in her world meant three to five dates. She always tried to fix the guys she dated, and that led to arguments and eventually breakups. Most usually, she was glad to see things come to an end, so she had never experienced the weeping, lying around in pajamas, and eating ice cream to ease her emotional pain that seemed to come from that kind of thing.

"Ladies first," Luke said.

Sissy took a slice of each pizza and laid them on her plate, then opened her diet root beer. "Thank you for dinner."

"Hey, you're supplying supper. Dinner is the least I can do." He took two pieces of meat lover's out of the box and put them on his plate. "I get lots of invitations for Sunday dinners but not so many for supper. I guess folks think that preachers are only hungry after a sermon. Two nights in a row at Blanche's place—no, that would be your home now—is quite a treat."

"It might be Aunt Bee's house for a long time. I don't know what I'm going to do with the place, but I have decided not to do anything until after the holidays." Sissy bit into a slice.

"Sounds good. Now, Elvira and the curtains," he said. "I'm also hoping that if we can keep her busy at something other than worrying about her health, she won't be calling the ambulance two or three times a week."

Sissy would rather have heard more about Luke than about Elvira's imagined illnesses, but then, maybe she should just enjoy his company and leave analyzing him up to God. "Well, I was thinking that maybe we could string a cord or a rod or whatever Jimmy and Paul can come up with and separate the stage into thirds. The front portion would have a decorated tree on about a third of the space. The youngest kids could do their little part there. Then we would close those curtains and open the second ones to reveal the older kids doing their songs and readings."

"Then we would close them and the last third would be the nativity scene, where I read the story of Jesus's birth," Luke said. "That's genius, but I see a problem there. The stage isn't big enough to do all that, and we'd still have to move the props from the older kids' part of the pageant. Santa Claus and reindeer don't have much to do with the manger scene."

Sissy took a sip of her root beer, and her eyes lit up. "What if we use the choir loft for the nativity scene? We could string a set of curtains up in front of it, and the floor is slightly raised, so it would make that part extra special. That would leave the lectern open for readings and the deacon's bench for the two Sunday school teachers to sit on after their classes do their parts."

"That's a great idea." Luke locked eyes with

her over the top of the pizza boxes and even more electricity flickered between them than before.

"So we probably don't need the curtains cut off, but if Elvira would remove the pleats at the top and put loops or wooden hooks on them, it would make them easy to slide," Sissy suggested.

"You are amazing, Sissy Ducaine." Luke raised a brow and smiled at her.

There was that warm flush again. Sissy took a sip of her cold soda, hoping that the red of the blush didn't reach her cheeks and cause her faint freckles to pop out even worse.

She'd finished off her second piece of pizza when the door from the sanctuary into the fellowship hall opened, and Elvira peeked around the edge.

"Luke, are you in here?" she called out.

"Yes, Sissy and I just finished having pizza. You want a slice?" Luke answered.

"I'd love one." Elvira removed her coat as she crossed the room. "I can't eat a whole pizza by myself, so I seldom get it."

"Tea, water, or soda?" Luke asked.

"Coke would be great." She hung her coat on the back of a chair and sat down.

Luke opened a bottle for her and set it on the table. "I hate to leave good company, but I really should go to my office. I've got several more folks bringing in decorations this afternoon.

Sissy, can you tell Elvira what we want done with all those curtains?"

"Sure." She nodded.

"See y'all later." Luke started out of the room, then turned around. "Elvira, if you'll give me your car keys, I'll unload what you brought."

Elvira fetched them out of her coat pocket and tossed them toward him. "It's in the trunk. Mostly, they are lights and ornaments, so you could just put them in the foyer where you want me to work on a tree."

"Will do," Luke said.

Elvira picked up a piece of meat-lover's pizza and took a bite. "Mmmm." She made appreciative noises. "While I eat, Sissy, you could draw out what you're going to do with the curtains, so I'll have an idea."

Sissy unfolded a napkin and then pushed back her chair. She stood up and went to the kitchen, where she rustled around in a drawer until she found a sharpened pencil and went back to the table. "This is kind of what we've got in mind . . ." She described the scenes as she drew out a rough idea of the stage and the curtains.

"We'll need ropes here and here," Elvira said, "that can be taken down afterwards. They would be an eyesore if we left them up all year. The ceiling up at the stage area is ten feet tall, and I remember the curtains that Ruthie put up for the holidays. Doing all that work at home for just a month seemed pretentious for a preacher's wife, but then she did teach the senior citizens' Sunday school class and had the Christmas dinner for us out there." Elvira sighed. "She had twelve-foot ceilings in her old farmhouse, so we'll have plenty to cut off at the top to make loops for sliding . . ." She went on to talk about the logistics of the dimensions.

Listening to Elvira rattle on as she made drawings for the project made it hard for Sissy to even believe that, just hours ago, the woman had been in the emergency room with chest pain, but the little dig about Ruthie proved Ina Mae and Gussie's story about gossip. Sissy had worked with hypochondriacs before, and getting them to realize they had a problem was tricky at best. Her therapist brain went into overdrive. Elvira's posture and the way she kept eyeing Sissy to see what her reactions were said that the woman had control issues and was probably manipulative. That wasn't unusual with hypochondriacs, but it sure made helping the patient a tougher job.

Be careful. Blanche's voice was loud and clear in Sissy's head.

Elvira wolfed down another piece of pizza, talking between bites about her plans, and then she pushed back her chair and said in a bossy tone, "Let's get busy on that tree."

Sissy hadn't thought that she'd be helping the woman decorate a tree, but then maybe if they worked together, she could get a more accurate read on her. "I'm ready when you are." She closed the lids on the pizza boxes and carried the dirty plates and empty bottles to the trash can.

"I just love Christmas. I'm hoping that Luke asks me to take over Blanche's Sunday school class. She taught the kindergarteners, and I just love little kids. Never got to have any of my own. Granted, Blanche was a preacher's daughter, but"—she lowered her voice and looked around the room—"she didn't act like one all the time. I never understood why she was asked to teach them."

"Oh, really?" Sissy raised an eyebrow and took a deep breath before she spoke, but her tone was still icy cold. "You do know that she was my aunt and that I loved her dearly, don't you?"

"Of course you did, and I'm sure she loved you." Elvira smiled ever so sweetly. "But Blanche had two sides, especially when she was young. She was married to my cousin, Walter. He was a wonderful man, just so sweet and kind, and he loved Blanche so much. He came home from that awful war with anger in his heart. If it hadn't been for the war, he would have never hit Blanche."

Blaming someone else and never being accountable for mistakes was another problem some hypochondriacs had. The best Sissy might be able to do was simply to help keep Elvira so busy that she didn't have so many fake episodes.

"God says I have to forgive her, so I have," Elvira sighed and laid a hand over her heart.

Sissy was afraid that the woman would have a heart attack—fake or otherwise—right there in the center aisle of the church. She made sure her phone was in her pocket so she could call 911 if Elvira fell down on the floor and started moaning. Talk about causing trouble—*well, Luke, I reminded her that Blanche was my aunt, and she grabbed her chest and had a heart attack.*

Sissy breathed a little easier when Elvira removed her hand, smiled, and changed the subject.

"We'll put the tree together first, and then we'll start decorating it. I imagine that either Gussie or Ina Mae will want to teach that class, since that will help them keep Blanche alive in their minds. I'm a little older than they are, and of course I'm sure I read my Bible more than either of them, so I'm more qualified. And I love children. None of those three who had their Sunshine Club"—she said the words like they were dirty—"ever had kids."

"I can't believe you are older than they are." Sissy tried to steer the conversation in a different direction. "Have you lived here in Newton your whole life?"

Elvira fluffed up her gray hair. "All of us—Blanche, Gussie, and Ina Mae—were born in this town and most likely will finish our days right here. It's still hard for me to think about poor Blanche dropping with a heart attack at seventy."

Sissy could hear the envy in Elvira's tone. Didn't she realize just how serious a real heart attack was, and how it would disrupt her lifestyle *if* she even survived?

"Those three were still in junior high when I graduated from high school. I've always looked younger than I am." She smiled so big that the wrinkles around her eyes deepened. "I'd been married five years when they went off to college. It was too bad that Walter and Blanche didn't make a go of it, but"—she lowered her voice—"I knew from the beginning that he wasn't going to put up with Blanche's bluntness. A man likes to think he's the boss, even if he's not. I'm not speaking ill of the dead, and to tell the truth, I always envied Blanche. She had a backbone of steel. But she shouldn't have pushed Walter into a corner. Even a rat will fight if it's cornered."

Sissy tried diverting her away from Blanche. There was no way Sissy was going to agree with anything against her aunt Bee, but she didn't want to make Elvira stroke out, either.

"So all of you were little girls together until you became a teenager?" Sissy opened the box and removed the older-model tree that required limbs to be put on individually.

"Oh, no! There was no room in the Sunshine Club for anyone but the three of them. Besides, *they* were just little girls. I'm older than they are, remember. Not that I wanted to be in their silly old club anyway." The wistfulness in her tone did not match her words. "I hear that they did all kinds of wicked things, like listen to loud music and drink and even use swear words, in their clubhouse."

Sissy wouldn't affirm and couldn't deny the accusation, so she simply asked, "Are you sure you're up to all this hard work? Luke told me you were in the hospital this morning."

"I'm fine," Elvira said. "They gave me a clean bill of health. People just don't know how hard it is to be afraid of dying all alone. My husband of forty years got middle-age-crazy ten years ago and left me. I have no living relatives. Even my sweet cousin Walter has gone on to heaven, so I'm by myself. I have my church family, and God bless Luke for always being there to sit with me when I have one of my sinking spells."

If thunder and lightning begins to rain down from the sky, we'll know that Aunt Bee found Walter in heaven. It might be best for him if he didn't get past the pearly gates. Hell would be better than dealing with Aunt Bee when she's angry.

"I've got to make a run to the ladies' room," Sissy said. "Will you be all right for a few minutes?"

"You go right on." Elvira patted her on the shoulder. "I'll just get the ornament boxes opened up and the lights out while you're gone. Although you are kin to Blanche, I think we might be friends."

What an honor, Sissy thought, then felt guilty. The woman needed friends. The trouble was that she wanted to use them, boss them, and manipulate them into doing for her.

Sissy stopped in her tracks when she opened the door into the bathroom and found she was in a lovely sitting room complete with a rose-colored velvet sofa flanked by two matching wingback chairs. A lovely silk flower arrangement graced the middle of an oval glass-topped coffee table that sat in the center of the seating area. Another door led into the actual bathroom, where four stalls were lined up on one side and a vanity with as many sinks took up the other side of the long, narrow room. Sissy chose the first stall, and when she was done, she washed her hands, stuck them under a turbo air dryer, and then went back out to the sitting room.

The sofa was every bit as comfortable as it looked when she eased down in the corner of it. She pulled out her phone and called Ina Mae.

"Hey, how's it going at the church? I'm putting you on speaker. Gussie is here with me. We got her tree done this morning, and now, we're working on mine," Ina Mae said.

"Going fine. I'm glad that you're both there. Do either of you want to take over Blanche's

Sunday school class?" Sissy asked. "And who did the ladies' room in this bathroom? It's the prettiest place in the whole church."

"Gussie had it done. The previous bathroom was downright ugly," Ina Mae answered. "We thought it would be nice for ladies who were nursing babies to have a place to go, and we even had a speaker put in there so they can listen to the sermon."

"That's so sweet," Sissy said and then gasped. "It's not a two-way thing, is it? Someone in the foyer can't hear me talking, can they?"

"Oh, hell no!" Gussie laughed out loud. "A bawling baby would be distracting during church services. Some women just leave their kids in the nursery, but others bring them into the sanctuary. The pretty bathroom serves two purposes. It's a place to take a baby to nurse, and it can be used to take a child for a little discipline."

Sissy almost wiped her brow in relief. "Now, about the Sunday school class?"

"Not me!" Gussie said from the background. "Blanche was the one of us who loved little kids. She would have taken you and raised you if your dad and mama would have allowed it. I'm not like her. I never know how to talk to kids, and since we've got you, I don't even regret not having any of my own."

"Me either," Ina Mae chimed in. "Is Luke about to ask one of us to do that? I'd hate to tell him no, but I sure don't want the responsibility of having to teach snotty-nosed kids every single Sunday morning."

"Ina Mae!" Sissy scolded.

"Darlin', it's wintertime, and that means colds and runny noses," Ina Mae defended her statement. "Why are you askin'?"

"Well, Elvira . . ." She went on to tell them what was happening. "She wants to teach that class, but I didn't want to say anything to Luke if one of y'all wanted it because Blanche had taught it."

"Elvira is welcome to it," Gussie said. "Maybe if she finds enough to keep her busy, she won't have a heart attack or a stroke every week, but if she tries to get me to talk trash about Blanche, she might wish she had a heart attack when I get done with her."

"I just keep steering the conversation away from Aunt Bee," Sissy said.

"You are a good woman, Sissy," Ina Mae said. "But be careful. She's known for sucking up to a person and clinging to them until she smothers them nearly to death."

"I suppose that means you aren't going to take her into the clubhouse, then," Sissy teased.

"That wouldn't be no, but hell no!" Gussie shouted. "And don't you go inviting her to come help decorate the Christmas tree with us tonigh either."

Sissy chuckled and then said, "Which would you rather have—Elvira to come and help us, or Jimmy and Paul?"

"Jimmy and Paul any day of the week," Gussie answered.

"We can use some tall guys to help us, and I've got plenty of food," Ina Mae said.

"I was going to bring the leftover pizza home," Sissy said.

"You send that pizza home with Elvira, and we'll all pray she don't get a gas bubble from it and think she's dyin' again," Ina Mae said.

"All right then, I'll see y'all about six," Sissy said.

"Be careful what you say to Elvira. She loves to spread rumors, and she usually puts a spin on them to make herself look like a martyr," Ina Mae warned and then ended the call.

Sissy enjoyed the peace and quiet for another minute and then she stood up and left the pretty bathroom. She was halfway across the sanctuary when she heard footsteps behind her and got that fluttery feeling that told her Luke was in the area. She glanced over her shoulder and wasn't a bit surprised to see him coming out of his office.

"How's it going?" he called out.

Sissy sat down on the end of one of the old oak pews and slid down a little way to leave room for im. In a few long strides he was there and had t down beside her.

"Did Elvira go home?" he asked.

"No, she's busy in the foyer. I've invited Jimmy and Paul to help us out tonight, and Elvira wants to teach Blanche's Sunday school class. That's up to you, but she needs friends, and maybe little kids would be a good place to start. It would give her something to do and look forward to."

"Sounds like a great idea to me. I didn't really know who to ask to step into Blanche's shoes and take over that class. Should I go ask her now so that she can be getting them ready for the Christmas program?" Luke asked.

"That's your bailiwick," Sissy said. "I'm just passing on information for you to do with as you choose."

"Can you pass on anything about the therapy session for Wes and Annabelle?" he asked.

"I can tell you that they seem to be eager to try to get along better," Sissy said. "Statistics are stacked against them, so it's going to take a lot of work on both their parts. I should probably get on back to Elvira."

"I'll come with you to ask her right now," Luke said with a bright smile on his face. "Thank you for getting that question answered, and for doing all this on your vacation time. If you were to decide to get rid of all Blanche's stuff and sell the house, I'll be glad to help you."

Sissy turned sideways so that their faces were just inches apart. "Would you take Danny Boy?

He thinks you're a pretty boy. You might teach him to pray."

"Nope," Luke said. "He's talking about himself when he says 'pretty boy.' And that bird spent too much time in a bar to learn to pray. Besides, what would happen if one of my congregation saw me buying gallons of cheap vodka at the liquor store? Think they'd ever believe that I was purchasing it for a cockatiel?"

Luke got to his feet and Sissy walked along beside him down the center aisle to the foyer. Elvira looked up from unwrapping ornaments and smiled. "I got the tree put together, and we're ready to put the lights on it."

"I'm finished with my work in the office," Luke said. "I'll help do this and then maybe we'll have time to put up one on the stage before we stop for the day." He glanced over at Sissy. "Shall I wrap the lights around my arms, and you follow along behind me to situate them on the branches?"

"Sure thing." Sissy nodded. "Elvira, would you please stand back a little way and supervise so we get them just right? This is the first tree that folks will see when they come into the church."

Elvira cut her eyes around at Sissy. "I've got a wonderful eye for getting things just right. That's why Luke can depend on me . . ."

Every time Sissy reached out to get a bulb to fasten to a branch as Luke went around the tree, her hand brushed against his, and another little burst of sparks danced around the foyer. Was it a sin to feel like that in a church house?

"Oh, and before we get going on this and forget," Luke said as he came around from the back side of the tree. "There's something I need to ask you, Elvira. Would you consider taking over the kindergarten Sunday school class? I understand if it's too much for you with your health problems, but I think you'd make an amazing teacher."

Her hand went to her chest and her eyes widened. "Oh! My! Goodness! I would just love to teach the little darlings. I was just telling Sissy a little while ago that I would love to have that job. Can I go get the class materials from the office today so I can be ready on Sunday? And do I get to take care of their little part in the Christmas program, too?"

"Of course," Luke said as he started back around the tree, giving Sissy time to position each and every light. "I thought they could sing two songs. The choice is yours, and you can work with them here at the church. I believe there's about a dozen kids that age."

"Would it be all right if I ask their parents to bring them to my house? We could have a little party with cookies and treats, and I can give them all a little gift right after the program." Elvira's expression was rather childish.

Sissy wondered if she'd done the right thing by

talking to Luke about Elvira teaching the class. If she tried to dig her way into the parents' lives, that could cause trouble in the church.

"It's your class," Luke said. "You can practice wherever you want. As far as gifts, just don't go overboard."

Sissy's fingertips brushed against Luke's firm arm when she hung the next light. How could there be so many vibes when she had known Luke only a short while? Evidently, he didn't have a girlfriend in the wings, or else Ina Mae and Gussie wouldn't be trying to play matchmaker for them. Still, he might not feel the same things she did, so she warned herself to be careful.

Gussie used her key to let herself and Ina Mae into Blanche's house, took one look at the rubber boots sitting beside the hall tree, and burst into tears. "I bought those boots for her last Christmas. She wore them outside to feed Chester. God, it's tough being an old woman in a small town like this. When I was the judge, I had a purpose. Now, it just seems like . . ." She pulled a tissue from her oversize black purse and blew her nose. "I'm rambling like a fool. Blanche would throw a hissy fit over a damn pair of boots making me cry."

Ina Mae slipped an arm around Gussie's shoulders. "Do you think we retired too early? Seems like we're just waiting to join Blanche in the hereafter."

"Yes." Gussie nodded. "I wish none of us had ever retired. You and I are left with a big hole in our lives. No job to give us purpose. Club falling apart. But"—she shrugged off Ina Mae's arm and removed her coat—"I refuse to get old, and we're going to enjoy our retirement."

"That's the spirit." Ina Mae hung her coat on the hall tree and led the way into the living room. "Think of it like this—we had those years with Blanche when we could go when we wanted and stay up as late as we wanted because none of us had to work the next day."

Gussie flopped down on the sofa. "I want Blanche back. It's always been the three of us, and I love you, Ina Mae, but I feel lost."

"Me too," Ina Mae said. "I broke down this morning when I poured my coffee. She got me the mug when we all three went over to Beau Bridge the last time. Remember that shopping trip we had? You tried on a purple suit, and Blanche said you looked like a giant grape."

"I remember, and you can't make me feel better," Gussie said. "I've half a mind to hang out my shingle and go back to work."

"You will not!" Ina Mae said. "We are going to get past this, and we're going to get Luke and Sissy together. They're going to have half a dozen babies, because Sissy will want more than one since she was raised as an only child and didn't like it. Then our lives will be busy again."

Gussie appreciated Ina Mae trying to make her feel better, and she really did want to find closure, but her heart wasn't cooperating one little bit. "Thanks for trying to cheer me up. All I can see is that a third of us is gone. No one can ever fill Blanche's place. Remember when we started the club? We were only ten years old. We've been together through wars, rumors of wars, bad presidents, good presidents, and even a divorce and a near murder of one man who badly deserved it."

Ina Mae led her to the kitchen and made her sit down at the table. "Sixty years of livin', but she wouldn't want us to die with her. We've got to be sure that Sissy and Luke get together so we can enjoy the grandbabies for Blanche."

Gussie threw her head back on the sofa and closed her eyes. "We were supposed to all die on the same day."

Ina Mae air slapped Gussie on the arm. "And just where would that leave our sweet Sissy? She wouldn't have anyone to help her find a happy-ever-after."

"We volunteered her at the church so she would be near Luke all the time, and now Elvira is there." Gussie pulled a tissue from a box on the end table and blew her nose. "What if she gets involved with trying to cure Elvira and doesn't have time for us? You know how clingy that woman has always been, and she'll stick to

Sissy like glue, telling her all her ailments and problems. She didn't want us to hire Luke to begin with, but now she's adopted him as her personal savior when it comes to getting attention for her heart attacks. She's not going to like it if our matchmaking starts to work and she loses him."

"Sissy is a therapist," Ina Mae reminded Gussie, "and she will see right through any bullcrap that Elvira puts out. Sissy belongs to us. She's our child as much as if we'd birthed her ourselves. There's no way Elvira can take that from us . . ." Ina Mae stopped and grabbed her head.

"Sweet Jesus!" Gussie squealed. "Are you having a stroke and leaving me on this earth all alone?"

"No, I just had a bad thought," Ina Mae answered. "What if that hussy undoes what we're trying to do because she wants Luke to still be at her beck and call?"

"She better not. I'm not a bit afraid to punch her lights out," Gussie declared. "Let's figure out ways to keep her from being around them so much. How about we ask her to help us clean the church on Saturday? You know how she loves to gossip. She'll tell us all about what's going on between Luke and Sissy, and having something to do that day might keep her out of the emergency room."

Ina Mae took her hand away from her head and

nodded. "That sounds like a good idea. I'm going out to bring in the food. You think about what else we can do to put Luke and Sissy together while I'm gone, and we'll compare notes while the casserole heats up in the oven."

Gussie wasn't a daily prayer–type woman, not even when she had had a hard case back in her working days. She always figured God had enough on his plate taking care of her and Blanche and Ina Mae. But that evening, she sent up a prayer asking that the good Lord wouldn't forsake her and would help give her ideas to help Luke and Sissy see that they should be together.

"I've got an idea!" Ina Mae said when she came in with a box of food in her arms. "Come on in the kitchen. We can insist that they go to the shooting range with us, and then we'll make dinner right here at Blanche's place and play board games until midnight."

Gussie followed Ina Mae into the kitchen, opened the cabinet doors, and took down six plates.

"We could invite both of them to go to the Hen's Nest with us on Sunday," Gussie said.

"Great idea." Ina Mae nodded. "If they're seen together at the Hen's Nest, rumors will spread that they're dating. And when we're cleaning the church with Elvira on Saturday morning, we can let it slip that they have a date to do some target practice that afternoon out back of Blanche's place. She'll help spread that tidbit, and then they'll be at the café on Sunday—two times in one weekend. That way we can see if we're right about her wanting to keep them apart."

"And tonight! That makes at least three times in one week." Gussie set the plates on the end of the bar. "The other four days they'll be at the church working on Christmas stuff."

Ina Mae finished unloading the box she'd carried in. "We should volunteer a couple of those days so we can keep steering them in the right direction, and we could keep an eye on Elvira, and squash any malicious rumors she starts."

Gussie nodded in agreement. "I just realized I'm past denial and being angry, and I've gone over to the other stage of grief. I can't remember what it is, but it's worse than PMS and hot flashes. Instead of weeping, I feel kind of numb."

"I'm in the same boat you are, but we've got a matchmaking job to do. Blanche would be disappointed if we didn't see to it that Sissy comes home for good. She wouldn't have left her the house and all her possessions if she didn't intend for her to at least think about putting down permanent roots." Ina Mae opened the refrigerator door and brought out two kinds of pickles. "Get down the divided dish so we don't mix dill and bread-and-butter pickles together."

"We used that pickle dish at Thanksgiving." Gussie sighed. "I remember Blanche telling me to get it down because Sissy likes it."

"Out, out, out!" Danny Boy began to scream.

"I really don't like that bird, especially when he gets in the way of one of my memories," Gussie growled. "Will I go to jail if I shoot him?"

"He's not worth wastin' a bullet on," Ina Mae told her. "Probably be too tough to fry and eat if we killed him. If our best-laid plans with Sissy don't pan out, let's give him to Elvira."

Gussie's giggle turned into a guffaw, and soon she was wiping tears again. "I swear to God, you'd think I was going through menopause again the way I go from laughing to crying in an instant."

"Shut your mouth!" Ina Mae scolded. "I don't even want to think about hot flashes and those emotional roller coasters we were on about twenty years ago. Those were miserable days."

"That's the gospel truth." Gussie remembered all three of them going through those emotional days. If she had had to endure that alone, she would have gone crazy for sure. "Just thinking about it is scary. I'm supposed to be the strong one of the three of us, and here I am, blubbering like a baby that can't have a lollipop."

"Gussie, I love you like a sister, but you never were the strong one." Ina Mae gave her a sideways hug. "Blanche was our strength. I was the organizer, and you were the glue that held us all together."

"Well, I sure don't feel like I'm holding much

together today." Gussie tossed her tissue in the trash, and heaved a heavy sigh. "Today is tougher than when the doctor came down that hallway and told us that he couldn't save her."

"It's the second day after the funeral." Ina Mae took her by the hand and led her over to the table. "Granny always said that the second day after a surgery or a sickness was the worst one. I guess it could stand true for grieving as well as ailments."

"Your Granny Jewel was so smart. I loved her sayings." Gussie visualized the tall, thin gray-haired lady with a stern look and kind eyes. "She bossed all three of us like we belonged to her."

"I still miss her." Ina Mae waved her hand around as if she were warding off memories. "We can't think about her, or your folks, either, right now, or we'll both be crying when the kids get here. Sissy needs our support, not for us to be a couple of blubbering old women."

Gussie straightened her back and gave a quick nod. Like their song said, one was smart, and Ina Mae had always been the smartest one of the three of them. "You are right. If she sees us weepin', she'll feel like she has to comfort us, and we should be helping her get through this grieving process." She shook her finger at Ina Mae. "And don't you be calling us old. You're only as old as you feel, and I'm just twenty-five."

"You are full of bullshit!" Ina Mae said. "We're both seventy and this next summer we'll be livin' on borrowed time. We only get three score and ten, so every day from now on is a blessing. We'll just have to be as strong as Blanche. Shhh . . ." She put her finger to her lips. "I hear a car door slamming. Sissy is home."

The front door opened and closed. Danny Boy must have heard it because he began alternately crowing and saying, "Out. Let me out."

"Just a minute," Sissy yelled. "Where is everyone?"

"In the kitchen and in the cage," Ina Mae answered.

There was no sound of footsteps going toward either room on the hardwood floors or the noise of someone climbing the stairs. Gussie cocked her head to one side and strained her ears even more. "Something's wrong." She headed out of the kitchen with Ina Mae right behind her.

They found Sissy crumpled up on the floor, her knees drawn up to her chin and tears dripping off her jaw. "I saw her coat hanging there, and for a minute, I thought . . . ," she stammered. "I thought . . ." She sobbed so hard that her shoulders shook. "I thought she was still with us."

Gussie dropped down on one side of her, and Ina Mae went straight to the kitchen and brought back a whole roll of paper towels. Then she sat down on the other side of Sissy.

Gussie rolled off a couple of towels and dried Sissy's cheeks. "Ina Mae says it's the second-day syndrome."

"What's that?" Sissy asked.

Ina Mae explained what her grandmother had told her. "We've all been weepy today. Blanche was our strong person, both in the Sunshine Club and in life. She would have taken the bull by the horns and spit in his eye, and here we are sobbing."

"It's part of the process, and they went over that in several of my courses," Sissy said, "but it seems to be the little things that set me off. Like today, there was a Christmas ornament that reminded me of one that she used to always let me hang on the tree. It's . . ." She teared up again.

Ina Mae patted her on the shoulder. "It's the one that's shaped like Tinker Bell, right? She bought it the year she took you to Disney World."

"That's the one," Sissy said with a nod. "Christmas was Aunt Bee's favorite holiday. We can't be acting like this."

"That's easier said than done," Gussie said as she wiped at her cheeks with an already wet paper towel. "You go on upstairs and wash your face, chère." Just knowing that she had helped Sissy gave her a new lease on the evening. She could make it through the rest of the day because she was the glue that held everyone together—Ina Mae said so, and she was never wrong.

"What about you two?" Sissy asked.

"We'll use the little half bath off the utility room," Ina Mae answered. "Now, go. We've got them wimpy men arriving in fifteen minutes. They'll all three run away if they see a single tear."

"Yes, ma'am." Sissy smiled.

"That's my girl," Gussie said. "We are strong. We are smart."

"Isn't that a line from *The Help*?" Sissy asked as she stood and started up the stairs.

"Pretty close and very true," Gussie answered. "We'll have to watch that movie together sometime before you go back to Beau Bridge."

"It's a date." Sissy took the stairs two at a time.

Ina Mae's knees popped when she got to her feet. "Bones are getting old," she said as she picked up the paper towels with one hand and extended the other one to Gussie.

Gussie put her hand in Ina Mae's and let her pull her up. "Isn't that the truth? But I intend to let them get a lot older before I retire my bones for good. Do you realize that we just proved that we are strong enough to help each other, just like always? I think Blanche has left us some of her strength because she knows we'll need it to help Sissy."

"And to make one more match before we officially retire a second time," Ina Mae whispered.

"Amen!" Gussie hoped she was right, because right then she felt more like a limp dishrag than a strong and smart woman. But even a limp dishrag is good for something, she told herself.

Chapter Eight

Sissy figured she had a few minutes, so she threw the lid of her suitcase back, then opened the closet door and started hanging up her clothing. Hopefully, a mundane job like that would take her mind off Aunt Bee. She had gotten most of her things put away when she noticed a plastic bag on the shelf. She pulled it down and found a pair of pajamas with Rudolph on them, a bottle of her favorite perfume, and a gift card to a restaurant over in Beau Bridge.

Sissy's parents never made a big deal out of holidays, but then, how could they? The RV barely had room for three people. There was simply no place to put a tree, but when they got to come to Aunt Bee's—well, that was a different story. Aunt Bee always read the story of Christmas to her, both the imaginary one with Santa Claus and the religious one about Jesus. There was a huge tree that reached all the way to heaven in the living room and presents underneath it, and Christmas dinner was something out of a fairy tale book.

"I can't sell this place," she muttered. "How could I ever have even thought that I could? This is where so many of my memories are."

More tears welled up in her eyes and spilled down over her cheeks. She wiped them away and fussed at herself, "No more crying, not even when we put the tree up."

The idea of a tree brought back a memory that put a smile on her face. She had been about five years old, and it was one of those years when they couldn't come see Aunt Bee. They were somewhere in California doing a weeklong gig, and from there they were going to Las Vegas. She had whined about not getting to go see Aunt Bee, and her father had drawn a tree on a green box that whiskey came in and cut it out. He taped it to the RV door and told her to decorate it any way she wanted. She spent hours coloring ornaments and pasting them to her tree, and then her mother topped it with a star covered in gold glitter. Every year from then on, she had a paper tree in the RV, and a present to open on Christmas morning whether they were able to go to Newton, Texas, or not.

"You tried"—Sissy's heart clenched—"to make my life a little more normal, and I love both of you for that."

She slid the bags with her presents back up onto the shelf and noticed some things on the other end. She pulled them down to find one bag with a sticky note on it saying "Gussie." The other bag said "Ina Mae."

She peeked inside each one to find matching

T-shirts, which read "I Love Jesus, but I Drink a Little."

She held the shirts to her chest and giggled, breaking the ache in her heart for her parents and her aunt Bee. "Oh, Aunt Bee, what do I do with all this? I knew that y'all exchanged presents, but I had no idea they were gag gifts."

You wrap them up and put them under the tree. What good is Christmas without presents? And you are not alone. I've left Gussie and Ina Mae just for you! Aunt Bee's voice was clear in her head. Sissy nodded in agreement. "And since I haven't bought anything for you, I'm going to pour out a bottle of Jack Daniel's on your grave, and I'll have a drink while I'm doing it for us to celebrate Christmas together. And I'll take Gussie and Ina Mae with me."

She put all the presents back into the closet and unloaded the rest of the items in her suitcase into a dresser drawer. She really should make a trip back to her apartment sometime that week for a few more clothes, she thought. When she had packed, she had been so rattled that the only nice outfit she'd brought was the one for the funeral. If she was going to be in church every Sunday, she needed more than what she had brought with her.

Or you could just go down to the boutique on the square and purchase a couple of outfits. Aunt Bee was right back in her head.

"That would save wasting a whole day of traveling." She hadn't thought about her job or her clients since she had arrived in Newton, but now both came rushing back to her mind. Was sixteen-year-old Katrina doing better accepting her parents' divorce? Was Raymond moving on from finding out that his son wasn't his blood kin, but the result of one of his ex-wife's affairs? Had Betty, her assistant, remembered to send out the midmonth bills?

She picked up the phone and called Betty's cell phone.

"Hello," Betty answered.

"Betty, I hope it's all right that I called your personal phone. This is Martina"—saying her professional name sounded strange in Sissy's ears—"checking in to see how things are going. I can update files and send our bills from here if—"

"I told you when you left to call me anytime," Betty said, "and I meant it. The boss lady figured you would be calling before long. She said to tell you that you are on vacation and that we've got everything under control. Your clients are seeing other therapists while you are gone, and everything is going well. We'll be closing for the two weeks of Christmas and New Year's just like always, so you don't worry about things here," Betty said. "But from me to you, I miss you."

"I miss y'all, too," Sissy said. "Thanks for

taking care of everything, and tell our boss lady, Miz Lacy, hello and thank you."

"You are welcome," Betty said. "How are you holding up?"

"Some days not so good. Others are pretty decent," Sissy admitted.

"Well, if you need to talk, I'm here," Betty said.

"Thank you for that," Sissy said. "I appreciate it. Have a great Christmas."

"You too. See you in a few weeks," Betty said.

She ended the call and went to the bathroom to freshen up. She grimaced when she saw her reflection in the mirror. Her eyes were swollen and red, her hair a mess from getting tangled in the two Christmas trees she and Elvira had decorated that day, and she had a pizza stain on her shirt from that last piece that she ate in the middle of the afternoon.

She jerked off her shirt, wet a washcloth with cold water and held it on her eyes with one hand, and brushed out her hair with her other one. She applied a little makeup and then rushed back to her bedroom to find a clean T-shirt. When she checked her reflection in the vanity mirror again, she frowned.

"Not much better, but at least my shirt is clean," she said.

The doorbell rang at the same time she reached the bottom stair. She slung the door open to find all three men standing on the porch.

"Come in." She smiled when she thought of those two shirts in the closet.

Jimmy came in first, took his coat off, and hung it on the hall tree; then Paul did the same thing. Luke followed their lead, but when they headed for the living room, he hung back for a moment.

"I just wanted to thank you for what you did for Elvira today. She can be a real pain in the neck, but I appreciate your efforts," Luke said. "She tends to want to get too involved too fast with folks."

"She needs to be needed, and she is a pain, but in a place a lot lower than the neck," Sissy teased and then grew serious. "We all want someone to give us a purpose in life. What did you tell her?"

Luke's clear blue eyes were mesmerizing, and Sissy had to fight the urge to reach up and touch the five-o'clock shadow on his chiseled face.

"I reminded her about the seminar we put everyone through about our responsibilities as Sunday school teachers. She assured me that she didn't need a refresher course, since she'd taken it a few years ago, and that she would remember the rules. Back then we had an opening for the junior high kids' class, and she wanted that one, but I thought they could relate better to someone a little younger," Luke said. "It's sure nicer to hear her happy than to listen to her whine in the emergency room."

Sissy gave him a brief nod. "Everyone needs

friends to share their joys and half their sorrows. Maybe these small children will help her even more than adult friends. We'd better get on into the kitchen, or there won't be any of that Mexican chicken casserole left."

"Oh, they won't eat without grace." Luke grinned. "Not when there are two preachers in the house."

"I forgot about that." Sissy took a step toward the kitchen, tripped over Aunt Bee's rubber boots, and was on her way for a nasty fall when Luke reached out and grabbed her.

Her heart pounded so hard inside her chest that she couldn't breathe. She wasn't sure if it was the adrenaline rush from a near fall into the hall tree, or if it was the fact that she was pressed up against Luke with her arms tight around his neck. She should let go, she knew, but her knees were still shaking.

"Thank you," she gasped and eased her hold on his neck.

"I don't get to save a damsel in distress very often," he teased as he removed his hands from around her waist and took a couple of steps back. "Consider it payback for making Elvira happy and for counseling with Wes and Annabelle."

"Out! Vodka, please," Danny Boy screeched.

"It *is* after five." Luke chuckled.

"According to Jimmy Buffett, it's always after five somewhere, but don't tell Danny Boy that."

Sissy led the way to the living room, where she let Danny Boy out of his cage.

"Supper is on the bar!" Gussie called out.

Danny Boy stepped out of his cage like a prince and then flew straight to the kitchen.

"Dang bird!" Gussie fumed.

"He just wants his before-dinner cock-tail." Jimmy chuckled. "After all, he is a cock-a-tiel."

Gussie air slapped at his arm. "You haven't lost your sense of humor one bit."

Flirting was the same at most every age, and Sissy recognized it as one little step forward in her own matchmaking business.

"I'll get down the vodka," Ina Mae offered. "At least if he's drinking, he won't be crowing like Chester while you're saying grace, Jimmy."

"I thought that honor went to the preacher in charge," Paul said.

"Maybe since there's two preachers in the house, the senior one should do the honors," Ina Mae said as she poured a little vodka into Danny Boy's bowl. "Think you might need a little shot of this before you talk to God?"

Paul laughed out loud and then said, "Old age hasn't changed you a bit, Ina Mae. You've always been outspoken, but that means folks know where they stand with you."

"Don't call me old." Ina Mae's eyes glittered. "You're older than I am, and always will be."

"Darlin', we're both as old as dirt. Why, I

remember back before eight-track tapes were invented, and when television channels went off the air at ten o'clock at night," Paul said.

"And when phones had cords, and hamburgers cost a quarter," Jimmy chimed in.

"And when both of you walked a mile in the snow to school," Gussie added.

"Uphill both ways." Ina Mae giggled.

Sissy wanted to hug herself for asking Jimmy and Paul to join them that evening. Ina Mae's eyes were lively as she flirted—whether she would ever admit that or not—with Paul. And Gussie's tone had gone from melancholy to spirited. This matchmaking among senior citizens was downright fun.

"I bet you all four rode dinosaurs to the football games on Friday nights," Luke said.

"Mine was named Flame," Jimmy answered.

"Mine was Spike." Paul cracked a smile.

"We better forget about the good old days and someone better say grace before Danny Boy finishes his drink and starts crowing," Gussie said.

"And before the food gets cold," Ina Mae added.

Heads bowed and Jimmy said a short prayer that ended with an amen and Danny Boy crowing at the same time.

"Barely made it." Jimmy stepped up to be first in line.

Paul fell in behind him. "Maybe his crowing is his way of praying."

"If that's the case, then maybe I should start crowing when Luke asks me to deliver the benediction after Sunday morning services," Jimmy joked.

"I dare you," Gussie said with a grin. "I'll even put an extra ten dollars in the collection plate to hear you do that."

"You heard the lady." Jimmy loaded up his plate. "I can make money for the church if I crow out a prayer."

Paul nudged him on the shoulder. "You reckon these folks will come see you in rehab if you take that dare?"

"I will, and I'll drag all the rest with me," Ina Mae said. "Elvira will have a real heart attack and learn what it feels like, so it will be worth it."

"Silverware and napkins are already on the table"—Gussie pointed to the dining room— "and I double dare you now that Elvira is in the picture."

Luke leaned over and whispered in Sissy's ear, "Remind me to never ask one of those two to give the benediction again."

His warm breath on her neck sent shivers down her spine, but she shook her head slowly. "Not me. I want to hear Jimmy crow."

"That sounds like Blanche," Luke said.

"Thank you," Sissy told him with a broad

smile. "Best compliment I've had in days."

"Maybe we should have done the decorating first," Jimmy said. "After a big supper like this, I may need a nap."

"Me too," Paul agreed. "I've got a nerve on the bottom of my stomach. When too much food lands on the nerve, it pulls my eyelids shut."

"And then you snore, right?" Ina Mae asked.

"A gentleman never snores and tells," Paul said with a chuckle.

Sissy was almost jealous that the seniors were getting in more flirting than she and Luke.

"Never fear the big bad snore," Gussie said. "We will save dessert and coffee until the tree is finished."

"I made blackberry cobbler, and we can have it with or without ice cream," Ina Mae said. "That will give y'all something to look forward to while you're putting ornaments on top of the tree, and maybe keep you from falling asleep on the ladder and falling off."

"Elvira would be so upset if one of you got to go to the emergency room instead of her," Gussie teased.

Luke lowered his voice and asked Sissy, "If I ask Uncle Jimmy to deliver the benediction so you can hear him crow, do I get a shot of vodka?"

"That's only for birds that sleep in a cage," Sissy said.

"Guess that leaves me out, then. I never could even yodel." Luke filled his plate and carried it to the table.

Sissy filled six glasses with ice and took them to the dining room, then went back for a pitcher of sweet tea and one of lemonade. Luke set his plate down and turned around just in time to take them from her.

"Let me help with that," he said. "I'll pour so you can get your plate ready."

"Thank you," Sissy said with another smile.

With all the banter and the smell of good food, the whole feeling in the house had changed. It was almost as if Aunt Bee were still there with them. Sissy knew she wasn't there in body, but a little of the sadness left her heart.

"This is delicious," Jimmy said.

"Ina Mae and Gussie put it all together," Sissy called out from the kitchen.

"Good home-cooked food can't be beat," Paul said.

"Amen to that," Sissy said.

Gussie nudged her with a hip bump. "You look happier."

"So do both of you," Sissy said. "We needed company to bring us out of the doldrums."

Gussie flashed a bright smile her way. "What do you think of us asking Elvira to help us clean the church on Saturday mornings? As a therapist, do you think it would help her? Or is she too old

189

for us to be putting that kind of responsibility on her?"

Ina Mae dipped up casserole on her plate. "Give it some thought while we eat supper."

"Don't have to," Sissy said. "That's a wonderful idea. But don't go thinking that you'll ever get her into the Sunshine Club. She told me today that y'all cuss and"—Sissy lowered her voice—"and even drink sometimes, and she could never be a part of something like that."

Ina Mae sucked in air and let it out in a whoosh. "She doesn't have a thing to worry about. I'd ask Paul or Jimmy or both to join the club before I would her, and we made a pact that no boys—or men, at this stage of our lives—would ever set foot in our clubhouse."

Sissy dropped her tone to a whisper. "I believe she might have been flirting a little with Jimmy and Paul." She figured all was fair in love, war, and matchmaking.

"Those poor men," Gussie groaned. "We'll be at the church every day this week to protect them."

A sin of omission wasn't as much of a sin as an outright lie, Ina Mae thought.

"Why don't you two sit at the ends of the table?" Sissy suggested. "Jimmy and Paul have claimed the far side. That way you can talk old dinosaur stuff with them, and Luke and I sit beside each other."

Ina Mae sneaked a sly wink at Gussie and then said, "Whatever you think is best, Sissy. This is your house now. I was thinking that the two preachers might take the ends, but since they want to sit together, Gussie and I will be glad to be the important ones tonight."

"You always will be in my eyes," Sissy said.

"Aww, that's so sweet." Ina Mae gave her a quick hug.

"Truth is truth, no matter if you serve it up plain or cover it in chocolate," Sissy quoted something from her aunt Bee.

"Or bullcrap." Gussie nodded. "Thank you for loving us."

"Right back at you," Sissy said as she headed back to the dining room.

Ina Mae took her plate to the table and looked around at all the friends, old and new, gathered. For the first time since Blanche died, Ina Mae was truly happy, and she knew that Blanche wouldn't want her to feel guilty about it, either.

"Is it rude to take second helpings?" Jimmy asked. "I love Mexican food any way you cook it."

"Ina Mae brings this to church socials," Gussie said. "We'll have one after the Christmas program."

"I remember," Paul said. "I always looked forward to it. It's probably wrong to admit it, but sometimes I even wished for a funeral dinner so I could have a few spoonsful of it."

191

"Paul Landry!" Ina Mae scolded. "If you liked it that much, all you had to do was ask, and I would have made one just for you."

"For real?" Paul asked.

"Yes, for real." Ina Mae wondered if Paul had been living on takeout and microwavable dinners since Nellie passed away.

"Then I want one for New Year's Day," Paul said.

"Nope, that's the day we all gather for black-eyed peas, turnip greens, and sauerkraut cooked with a pork roast," Gussie told them.

And a casserole, Ina Mae thought, *if Paul wants one.*

"I understand the peas and greens, and I love sauerkraut, but why serve it on New Year's?" Jimmy asked.

"My granny's daddy came from Pennsylvania, up there in Yankee country, and they had sauerkraut and pork for New Year's dinner. Every strand of kraut stood for a dollar bill that you would earn in the next year. Her mama was a Texan. That meant peas and turnip greens or spinach, so we had both," Ina Mae said.

"Sounds like a fine dinner to me." Paul picked up his empty plate and headed to the kitchen with Jimmy. "Does that *all gather* mean all of us?"

"Of course it does," Sissy said. "Mark it on your calendar."

"We'll be here." Jimmy brought his second

plate of food to the table. "But speaking of calendars, we've also got it marked that we'll be in and out of the church until the pageant is over. Will y'all be helping?"

"Yep, we will," Gussie answered. "Starting tomorrow morning, we plan to be there."

"We're hoping to put the new shed for the manger scene together and bring it to the church tomorrow." Paul sat down beside Jimmy. "It's no big deal. Just a back and two sides. We'll cover the top with hay and strew some on the floor around the actual manger. I'm glad to have something to do during this season. It was Nellie's favorite time of the year, and . . ."

Ina Mae reached over and laid a hand on his shoulder. "We understand. This was Blanche's favorite, too, and there's an emptiness about it."

"Amen!" Jimmy said. "But it is looking brighter now that we've got some plans to keep us busy and the promise of good food in the future."

"Hear, hear!" Luke raised his glass in a toast. "To old friends, new friends, those who have left us, and to wonderful days ahead."

They all held up their glasses, and those who were close enough clinked them with each other.

"Talking about those who have passed on, I understand that Elvira had another visit to the ER today," Jimmy said.

"Yes, but . . ." Luke went on to tell how Sissy

had helped by suggesting that Elvira take over Blanche's Sunday school class.

"While we're on that subject," Ina Mae said, "Gussie and I were thinking we would ask her to help clean the church on Saturdays, Luke. Think she's up to it?"

"She graduated the same year Jimmy and I did," Paul said. "I don't think of myself as old at all at seventy-five. And if I can help build a shed for the manger scene, I reckon Elvira can dust a few pews and sweep up the floor of the sanctuary."

"Elvira has always been . . ." Ina Mae paused and pursed her lips together. "She's always been just like she is right now. You can't change a leopard's spots."

"Amen to that," Jimmy said. "Ruthie tried to help her by befriending her, but Elvira got too clingy. When she backed away, Elvira spread rumors about her."

"Bless her heart," Ina Mae said with a chuckle. "She's been a gossip hound since she was a kid."

"Are y'all looking for someone to step into Blanche's shoes?" Luke asked.

"Heaven forbid!" Gussie shivered.

"Well, you said 'bless her heart,' " Luke said.

"Didn't your mama teach you what that saying means?" Gussie asked.

"I don't think she did," Luke answered.

"One use means that you truly want her to be

blessed," Paul explained. "The other way, which is said in a different tone, means something like flipping someone off."

"I'll have to be careful with my tone," Luke chuckled.

"That's right, and you should have your mouth washed out with soap for making a suggestion that we bring Elvira into the Sunshine Club." Ina Mae shot a dirty look down the table toward Luke.

Luke laughed and soon the whole table was in an uproar. When it settled down, Ina Mae wiped tears from her face. "I needed that so badly today, but, Luke, you can rest assured that Blanche's boots are too big for Elvira or anyone else to fill."

"Amen!" Luke said in agreement.

Chapter Nine

Aunt Bee had always kept a spotless house. Her method was to clean one room a day except for the dining room and kitchen. Those she tidied up on the same day, and then she started all over again. The attic was a different matter. The attic resembled what Sissy imagined a metropolitan dump ground might look like if it were elevated to a third story and covered with a roof. Even as a child, when she got to spend a couple of days with Aunt Bee, she had imagined that spiders lived in every corner of the spooky attic—they skittered about on the narrow stairs and even on the creaking floor. In her mind, they hung upside down from the bare rafters like bats and waited to jump into her hair.

Since it was now her house, she felt as if she should go up there with Gussie to find the Christmas tree and the rest of the decorations, but she kept a constant watch, shifting her eyes from one side of the jumbled mess to the other while she and Gussie searched for all the stuff they needed.

"I'm telling you one thing," Sissy said. "If scanning this place for spiders is exercise, then I'm earning a double portion of blackberry cobbler when we finish putting up the tree."

"I swear to God on the Bible," Gussie huffed after she'd moved a stack of ratty old quilts off to one side, "that I put that box right here in the middle of the room last year when we put everything away."

"What is all this stuff and where did it come from?" Sissy asked. "It's been years and years since I've been up here. I never did like this place, but I don't remember this much junk."

"Blanche was a hoarder of sorts." Gussie held up a half-gallon jar full of empty thread spools. "According to her, these are going to be worth a fortune someday."

"I'm not ever selling this place, because if I did, then I'd have to clear out all this stuff," Sissy declared, "and after Christmas, the decorations and tree are going into one of the spare bedroom closets."

"Good luck with that," Gussie almost snorted. "The closets look just about like this. Her house has always been spotless, but her closets and this attic? They are the stuff that nightmares are made of." She shuddered. "Except for the one in your bedroom. She always wanted you to have plenty of room to hang up your things and store your suitcase when you came to visit."

Do we all have two sides? Sissy wondered. *I'm Martina at my job, and I'd never tell any of my colleagues that my nickname is Sissy. When*

I come here, I'm Sissy. Aunt Bee was a strong, independent woman on the outside just like I am as Martina. But the inside of her most likely looked like her attic—an unorganized mess that came from never really dealing with what happened when Walter abused her.

Sissy gave that some thought as she moved a box marked "Coloring Books" over to one side and then opened it to see if that was something she should donate to the church. "Oh, my!" she gasped.

"Did you find the tree?" Gussie stopped and turned around to face Sissy.

"No, I found a box of old coloring books that Aunt Bee and I did together from the time I was old enough to hold a crayon," Sissy answered.

"I remember when she put those up here," Gussie said. "She told me that living in an RV didn't allow you to hang on to keepsakes. That someday you would want to have some stuff from the past to show your children."

"She thought of everything, didn't she?" Sissy carefully put the lid back on the box and set it aside. Someday, she would come back to the attic and see what other keepsakes Aunt Bee had left for her.

"Roots," Gussie said. "Everyone needs roots and keepsakes to ground them. I found it!" She pumped her fist in the air.

Her squeal startled Sissy so badly that she

straightened up and bumped her head on one of the rafters. Stunned, she sat down in an old rocking chair and the whole thing gave way and dropped her right onto the rough floor.

Gussie hurried over to her side. "Are you okay? Was it a spider?"

"No, just lost my footing and then broke this rocking chair," Sissy answered. "Why did you ask about spiders?"

"Instinct, I guess," Gussie answered. "Blanche was terrified of them. That's probably why she kept such a spotless house, and never wanted to come clean this messy attic up. I'm glad that after my mama passed, I cleaned out the attic once and for all. I never, ever go up there for anything. I'm not afraid of spiders, but mice are a different matter. Look here." She pointed toward a corner. "I found the tree and all the decorations right where Ina Mae and I put them last year. Guess my memory isn't what it used to be."

Sissy stood up. "A lot has happened since then, and we're all still in shock. We can't expect everything to be normal. Not even when we're doing what she wants us to do. Now, how do we get all this down the narrow stairs?"

"Fire brigade!" Gussie yelled down the narrow steps to the open door. "We're ready. Come on up here. The door is open. Put Luke at the end. He's young, so he can run up and down the stairs better than the rest of us."

"Where do you want me?" Sissy asked.

"About halfway down the attic stairs," Gussie answered. "I'll hand the boxes to you. You'll pass them to Ina Mae, and . . ."

"I see. It really *is* just like a fire brigade." Sissy was more than glad to get even that far down from the attic.

When everybody was in place, the process of getting things from the attic to the living room started. After fifteen minutes, Gussie called out, "Last box!"

"I've got the music ready for the player," Ina Mae said. "We always have Christmas music while we are decorating."

Sissy wondered if she could sneak a shot of rum into her cup of eggnog. Preachers in the house or not, she felt like she deserved it after being in the attic.

Not even a few drops of Bacardi will erase that mess you've seen up there from your mind, the niggling voice in her head said.

Yes, but I did find the coloring books, and that means I've got keepsakes, she argued.

Sissy started the rest of the way down the stairs with Gussie right behind her. By the time they reached the living room, the guys had opened the long, narrow box and were already assembling the tree.

"We'll unpack the decorations while you guys get the tree up," Ina Mae said. "Gussie, you start on that box marked 'Lights.' Sissy, you can undo the one with the garland in it, and I'll start unpacking the ornaments. I was the one who put them away, so I'll remember how to take them out."

"Ma'am! Yes, ma'am." Gussie saluted smartly.

"Don't be a smart-ass," Ina Mae fussed at Gussie. "You know I'm right. You never have liked to take orders. Just because you were the one who thought about forming the Sunshine Club, you thought you should be able to boss everyone around."

"Did not!" A wide grin broke out over Gussie's face.

"Did too!" Ina Mae giggled. "Put on the music and do your job, or I'll tattle on you to Blanche and she'll come haunt you tonight."

"Is this part of the ritual?" Luke whispered to Sissy.

"I've only been here a few times when we put up the tree, but they always argued back then," Sissy answered.

For the first time, she realized that each of the friends had a definite place within the confines of the Sunshine Club. Ina Mae was the organizer. Gussie was the bossy glue. Aunt Bee had to have been the strong one who wasn't afraid to have a good time or lead the other two right into temptation like the song implied. No wonder they had managed to remain such good friends all their lives. Each of them depended on the other two for what was lacking in their own personalities. Together, they quite literally made up one whole being. Sissy had seen that kind of dynamic only in twins and triplets, and most of the time they were identical.

Gussie crossed the room to the CD player and pushed a button. Sissy was surprised when the first song that played was Brenda Lee's "Rockin' Around the Christmas Tree."

The guys had the tree all put together by the time "Grandma Got Run Over by a Reindeer" started. Jimmy and Paul did a little jig to the music, to celebrate having part of the job done.

"I haven't had this much fun in years." Jimmy grabbed Gussie's hand and spun her around a few times.

Not to be outdone, Paul did the same with Ina Mae, and all four of them were panting when the song ended.

Sissy glanced over at Luke, who just shook his head. "We've got our work cut out for us raising these senior citizens."

"Who are you calling old?" Ina Mae asked. "I didn't see either of you dancing."

George Strait's voice filled the room with "Christmas Cookies." Luke held out his hand to Sissy, and not to be outdone by the older couples, she didn't hesitate for a minute. Luke two-stepped her around the room to the whole song.

The lyrics talked about how every time a batch went into the oven, that meant fifteen minutes for kissing and hugging. Luke bent her backward and said, "And that's the truth."

Sissy hadn't danced in years, but she managed to keep up until the end of the song, when Luke spun her out and brought her back to his chest. "Thank you for the dance, Miz Ducaine," he said.

Her heart beat so fast that she was afraid everyone in the room could see it thumping under her T-shirt, and she could barely breathe out, "You are very welcome. I didn't know that preachers could dance like that."

"I'm full of surprises," he said with a big smile.

The very next song was "Santa Claus Is Comin' (In a Boogie Woogie Choo Choo Train)."

"Are y'all going to try to show us up with this one?" Sissy asked.

"Nope, I'm too old to dance anymore, and too young to jitterbug," Jimmy answered. "Let's get back to the tree. I hear some blackberry cobbler calling my name."

"The two young'uns here"—Ina Mae gestured toward Sissy and Luke—"can put the lights on now. I bought a pre-lit tree years ago, but Blanche and Gussie refused to have anything but the old-fashioned kind. These are probably the very strings that were on her tree when she was a little girl."

"Yep, and so are mine," Gussie agreed. "It's

getting tougher and tougher to find replacement bulbs, though."

"Ruthie was the same way." Jimmy smiled. "I even bought her a new pre-lit tree just before she took sick. She made me return the thing—said it was too modern. She wouldn't give up her memories, no matter what everyone else had."

"Nellie liked the holidays, but she was more like Ina Mae," Paul said. "She liked things easy-peasy."

Ina Mae eased the lights out of a box. "Nellie and I had a lot in common. Now get over here, Luke. You're going to hold these and Sissy is going to put them on the tree."

Luke stretched out his arms and Ina Mae looped the lights around them. "Uncle Jimmy, you probably should get the ladder ready for when we reach the top. I've got a good reach, but it don't go that far."

"Oh, I thought you were ten feet tall and bulletproof," Sissy teased as she bent over and clipped the first light to one of the bottom limbs.

"Try six feet, two inches, but don't test out that bulletproof theory. God is still working on me." He took another step and waited for her to put more lights on the tree.

She felt more than a little guilty for flirting, but then she caught a look that passed between Ina Mae and Gussie and decided that if a little flirtation made them get past the grief, even for a little while, it was worth it. And if Jimmy and Paul threw in a measure of help, too—well, that just made it doubly worth it.

With Ina Mae's bossing, they had the tree done by nine o'clock, except for the star at the top.

"You should put it on this year," Gussie said as she handed the antique gold star to Sissy.

Luke held the ladder steady, and Sissy affixed the star to the very top of the tree. When she started back down the ladder, Luke let go and put his hands on her waist to steady her.

Her pulse did double time, and her breath caught in her chest at his touch—even through her T-shirt. "Thank you. My middle name is not Grace."

"Doesn't need to be," he said just for her ears. "As beautiful as you are, you don't have to be graceful."

"Who's going to plug in the lights for the first time?" Paul glanced over at Ina Mae.

"That would be Sissy," she answered. "Her house, her tree, her privilege."

"I want you to do it. I want to stand back here like when I was a little girl and get the full effect of the magic," Sissy said.

"All right then." Ina Mae nodded. "We'll do a countdown like Blanche did. Ten, nine, eight . . ."

Sissy held her breath, just like she had as a child. When Ina Mae got to one and flipped the switch, Sissy let it all out in a whoosh. For a moment everyone was quiet, lost in the beauty of the moment, and then Danny Boy said, "Dammit, Ina Mae and Gussie!"

"Blanche likes it." Gussie giggled.

"Sorry about that." Sissy blushed.

"We've heard far worse." Jimmy chuckled.

"Out. Vodka!" Danny Boy crowed a couple of times, and then said, "Turn out the lights. The party's over."

"Not until I get my part of that cobbler," Paul said.

"You'll have to learn patience if you're going to run with this group," Luke told Danny Boy.

"And you've had your vodka for today," Sissy added.

The four older folks headed for the kitchen, but Sissy stood in the middle of the floor, still mesmerized by the tree, and the whole evening for that matter. She belonged right here, but how in the world could she leave her clients and her colleagues back in Beau Bridge?

"It's pretty, but not as beautiful as you are." Luke slipped his arm around her waist.

"Thank you, but—"

"There are no *buts* tonight, just *ands,*" he said.

"What does that mean?" Sissy liked sharing the moment with him, the feeling down deep of just simply enjoying a Christmas tree.

"*But* means adverse. *And* means addition,"

Luke said. "I don't want anything negative between us, just positive."

"That's pretty sweet," she said.

Paul poked his head around the door. "You kids going to have cobbler and ice cream with us?"

"See there," Luke said, "*and* ice cream. Addition, not subtraction."

"Yes, we are," Sissy said, "and maybe a cup of coffee, too."

Luke ushered her out of the living room with his hand on her lower back. "Now you are getting the idea."

"Thank you, ladies, for supper and such a fun night," Jimmy was saying when Luke and Sissy reached the kitchen. "I'm of a mind to put up a tree at my house now. I think Ruthie might like that."

"I know Nellie would," Paul agreed.

"We'll repay the favor," Ina Mae said, "by helping y'all since you helped us."

"That would be great," Jimmy said. "We'll decide what evening would be best and make it a date for all six of us."

Danny Boy started whistling "The Party's Over" again.

"Give us time to finish our cobbler," Gussie fussed at the bird. "It's not even ten o'clock, and I know Blanche didn't go to bed this early. The rooster might, but you're a honky-tonk bird."

"Dammit, Ina Mae and Gussie!" Danny Boy said.

"I should get one of those birds." Jimmy chuckled.

"I'll give you that one if you want him," Sissy offered.

"No, you wouldn't," Luke said. "He sounds too much like Blanche when he says certain things. You'd never give him away."

Sissy gave him a shoulder bump. "You are so right, but I can threaten him with it when he wakes me up before daylight."

As soon as they had finished their cobbler and coffee, Jimmy covered a yawn with his hand. "One more time, thank you all for this wonderful evening. We'll be looking forward to more of the same in the future, but bedtime is sneaking up on me. I'm going to call it a night."

"I'll add my thanks to Uncle Jimmy's for an amazing evening." Luke carried his dirty bowl to the sink and then followed Jimmy out of the kitchen. "I'll see y'all sometime tomorrow at the church to help with decorations, right?"

Gussie, Paul, and Ina Mae were right behind him. "I'll be at the church, but not very early, and, Ina Mae, don't you dare wake me at the crack of dawn."

Ina Mae tossed Gussie's coat toward her and then removed hers from the hall tree. "Wouldn't dream of it, Miss Grouchy Butt."

Sissy walked them all to the door and watched until the car and truck lights were out of sight, then went back to stare at the tree some more. "Oh, Aunt Bee, you would have loved this day. I hate that I have to say that in past tense."

"Vodka!" Danny Boy yelled.

"You were quiet for the most part, but you did cuss. It's a toss-up whether you deserve another drink," she told him.

"Love Jesus. Cuss a little," he said as he flew to the kitchen.

"Did Aunt Bee teach you that?" Sissy asked Danny Boy. "I bet that's why she had those T-shirts made for Ina Mae and Gussie."

The bird landed beside his small bowl on the cabinet. Sissy poured a few drops of vodka into the bowl and then poured herself a glass of white wine.

"Everything is moving at warp speed," she said. "I can't think straight, and I'm trained to compartmentalize things. What's the matter with me? I'm talking to a bird and falling for a preacher."

Danny Boy finished his vodka, flew over to alight on her shoulder, and then began whistling "Danny Boy." Sissy began to think of the lyrics as she listened to him. The part that said something about one of them going and the other staying stuck in her mind.

"Why start something that can't be finished,

especially when I'm in this vulnerable state of mind?" she whispered. "I've just lost my last living relative, and it's probably that I'm just looking for something or someone to fill this big hole in my heart at Aunt Bee's passing."

Danny Boy's head bobbed up and down as if he agreed with her. "Dammit, Ina Mae and Gussie!" he screeched and kissed Sissy on the cheek.

"All right, Aunt Bee," Sissy said. "I get the message. I'm supposed to depend on your two friends to fill the empty space in my heart, and in turn, that will help them reach some measure of closure, right?"

The bird gave her another kiss and flew back to the living room. Sissy picked up her glass of wine and followed him. Danny Boy flew to the tree and landed on a limb.

"So, this is where you intend to sleep tonight, is it?" Sissy asked.

She got no response, so she switched off the lights on the tree and then both lamps that were on the end tables and climbed the stairs to the second floor. When she passed by Aunt Bee's bedroom, she cracked the door for the first time and peeked inside. Nothing had changed since she had been in town the last time. The queen-size, four-poster bed took up a large chunk of the room. Yellow floral paper covered the walls. A bottle of Aunt Bee's favorite perfume still sat on the dresser, along with a tarnished silver hairbrush and its matching mirror.

"I shouldn't leave this room as a shrine to you, Aunt Bee, but I'm not ready to go through your things." She took a sip of her wine and let the memories wash over her like baptism waters. She had always felt like a princess when Aunt Bee brushed the tangles from her hair with that brush.

"And when you let me crawl into the bed with you on stormy nights," Sissy said out loud. "What do I do now when it thunders? Not real thunder, but the emotional kind. I've always talked to you about everything. Who am I going to vent to now?"

Chapter Ten

Gussie awoke on Tuesday morning and switched off the alarm. She had dreamed about her father that night. He had been standing in the room smiling at her and Jimmy dancing around the living room, and she had the feeling like that had pleased him.

Other than the four years she spent in Lafayette in college, she had always lived in this same house since her mama brought her home from the hospital. When she decided to pursue her law degree, she chose a school close enough to home that she could commute, just so she wouldn't be away from Blanche and Ina Mae. She wished that her father had been there the day she hung out her shingle in a little storefront on the town square, but at least she had the memory of her mother's happy face from that day.

"Was I being silly carrying on like that with Jimmy?" she asked as she slung her legs over the side of the bed.

Who gives a damn? If you were having fun, that's what matters, Blanche's voice chided. *Life is short. Enjoy every moment.*

She reached for her phone and hit speed dial for Ina Mae.

"Good mornin', sleepyhead," Ina Mae said. "I've been up for an hour and got a load of laundry done. Plus, I fixed us a sack lunch to have at the church around noon. I should get extra stars in my crown because I made enough to feed Elvira, too."

Gussie yawned. "You should have to take Chester to your house if Sissy doesn't stay in town. You're always up before dawn anyway, so his crowing wouldn't bother you. And, chère, if that woman even sneezes this afternoon, she'll blame your sandwiches for poisoning her."

"I'll take Chester if you agree to take that pesky house bird," Ina Mae shot back. "And don't give me any ideas about my sandwiches!"

"Oh, we could never split the birds up. They'd grieve themselves to death, and Blanche would come back to haunt us both. I'll take the high road and let you have both of them," Gussie teased.

"That's so kind of you!" Ina Mae's tone dripped sarcasm. "We'd better both work real hard at keeping Sissy in town, or else those birds are going to accidentally get turned loose, maybe in Elvira's house."

Gussie put the phone on speaker mode and straightened her bed as she talked. "That's funny, but I don't want to talk about the birds. Did you notice the way Sissy and Luke were flirting last night?"

"No," Ina Mae answered, "I was too busy watching Jimmy make goo-goo eyes at you."

"And what about you and Paul?" Gussie asked. "I haven't heard that man string together more than a dozen words in years, and yet he talked to you all evening." She headed for the kitchen. "But forget about us and think about Sissy and Luke. Our matchmaking is looking like a big success. Did you see the way he was looking at her all evening?"

"Nothing escapes these old eyes," Ina Mae declared. "We just got to keep getting them in the same place and love will do the rest."

"From your lips to God's ears," Gussie said.

"Or maybe to Blanche's ears if she's got any pull with those folks in heaven," Ina Mae told her. "See you at the church. Bet I beat you there."

"I bet Elvira beats us both." Gussie got down the oatmeal from the cabinet.

"Probably so," Ina Mae said. "Bye now!"

Gussie told her goodbye and ended the call. "I hate goodbyes," she said as she poured the instant oatmeal in a bowl and added water.

After breakfast, Gussie climbed the stairs back to her bedroom and opened her closet doors. She took out a pair of plain jeans, but she chose a cute little Christmas sweater, and took a little more care with her makeup.

"It's not for Jimmy," she declared as she applied bright-red lipstick. "This color matches

214

my sweater and keeps me from looking so pale."

Yeah, right! Ina Mae's voice was so clear that she whipped around to see if her friend had sneaked into the house.

Gussie drove from her house to the church that morning even though it was only a couple of blocks away. She told herself it was because a cold wind had picked up from the north, but the real reason was that she didn't want her hair to look like it had suffered through a tornado—just in case Jimmy was there. She might be seventy, but it felt good to think a man might be interested. She parked the car close to the back door into the fellowship hall and dashed inside.

"Well, well, well!" Ina Mae raised an eyebrow. "You got all dressed up just to work on curtains."

Gussie removed her coat and then eyed Ina Mae from toe to top. "Looks like I'm not the only one."

"I thought it would make me less depressed if I put on a little makeup and a bright-colored sweater. After all, I only get to wear my Christmas sweaters for one month out of the year," Ina Mae said.

"I'll go with that same excuse, too, then," Gussie said with a big grin. "Where's Elvira? I expected her to be here bossing everyone around before the crack of dawn."

"Well"—Ina Mae did a head wiggle—"if that woman thinks for a single second that she can boss me, she can spin around and call the ambulance to take her right back to the hospital. I'm not following her damn orders."

"No cussin' in the church—only in the clubhouse," Gussie reminded her.

"Oh, hush!" Ina Mae said.

As if on cue, the woman burst through the side door that led into the church and set a box on one of the tables. "I made banana bread, pumpkin bread, and cranberry orange this morning. I brought cream cheese spread and whipped butter to go on it."

"She's trying to steal your boyfriend," Ina Mae whispered out the side of her mouth.

Gussie nudged her with a shoulder. "Or maybe she's got her eye on yours."

"That's so sweet of you, Elvira." Ina Mae's tone was saccharine sweet. "I brought sandwiches for our lunch, and some bought cookies, but your homemade quick breads sound so much better."

Elvira sighed. "I was hoping that you would agree to spring for pizza since I brought snacks and dessert."

Gussie shot half a grin over at Ina Mae. Who was going to win this battle? Who would get to wear the bossy crown for the day?

"If you really want pizza, then you can order yourself one of those little personal pan pies." The saccharine was still in her voice. "Gussie and I love chicken salad sandwiches with bread-and-butter pickles on the side."

Another long sigh. "Well, since you went to all the trouble to make them, I suppose it would be rude of me not to eat with you. Maybe we can have pizza tomorrow?"

"That sounds great." Ina Mae nodded. "I'll bring the snacks and dessert and you can order the pizza."

And the crown goes to Ina Mae! Gussie thought.

Elvira set her thin mouth in a firm line and changed the subject. "Did y'all hear about Anna-belle and Wesley? They aren't going to his folks' house for dinner on Sundays anymore. I bet he leaves her and moves back home. I heard that Sissy told them to try that. What was she thinking?"

Anger rose up from Gussie's toes to her face, heating it bright red. "She was thinking that she might save their marriage, I'm sure. If folks compromised more, relationships might be saved."

"Oh, dear!" Elvira laid a hand on her forehead. "I didn't mean to step on your toes."

"The hell you didn't," Ina Mae said under her breath.

"Let's get busy on our curtains and forget about what I said." Elvira turned toward the table where her sewing machine had been set up.

"Good morning!" Jimmy's voice filled the

room when he and Paul came through the back door.

That jerked Gussie right out of the thought of snatching Elvira bald-headed, and she whipped around to see Jimmy and Paul each bringing a wooden cutout of a life-size lamb into the fellowship hall.

"We got these done this morning, but we're lousy at painting, so we're hoping you ladies can take care of making them look like lambs when you finish up with the curtains." Paul laid his lamb down on the table. "When you get done, we'll put the props on the back so they will stand up."

Jimmy put the one he was carrying down on one of the other long tables and sniffed the air. "Is that something pumpkin I smell?"

"No, it's bananas," Paul told him.

"It's both," Elvira said in a sweet little innocent voice. "Help yourselves. I already sliced it up and wrapped each piece individually so they wouldn't dry out through the day. Cream cheese and butter are in the plastic containers."

Gussie had a flash of pure jealousy, which was something she hadn't felt for at least twenty years. She might be willing to be nice to Elvira for Sissy's sake, and not even send her out of the church bald-headed, but the woman wasn't going to step in and flirt with Jimmy and Paul. Folks say that the way to a man's heart is through his stomach. With Elvira, the way to get rid of Luke, should he pay more attention to Sissy than to Elvira, would be to shake a piece of pumpkin bread in front of Jimmy and Paul. They were both on the hiring committee, and if she could sway their votes, she would have a majority of three out of the five.

"I guess we've got double duty," Ina Mae whispered. "We got to get Luke and Sissy together and keep Elvira from snagging one of these good men."

"We just need to keep Elvira so busy she doesn't set her sights on them for their votes on the hiring committee if she decides to get rid of Luke and find a new preacher to sit with her in the ER," Gussie said out the side of her mouth. And then she said in a louder voice, "Of course we'll paint the little lambs, but I'm thinking maybe we should buy one of those fleecy throws and use the backsides to make them look more real. Then all we'd have to do would be paint the noses and eyes, and maybe the inside of their ears."

"Wonderful idea." Elvira nodded. "I've even got two or three of those at home that aren't as soft as they were when they were new. I'll drive back to the house and get them right now. Anyone need anything else while I'm gone?"

"Not a thing," Gussie said. *But if you could get lost and never find your way back, that would be nice. I know enough about sewing to redo those curtains, and I can make banana bread, too.*

Jimmy spread cream cheese over several slices of pumpkin bread and put them on a paper plate. "Here you go, ladies," he said, "and might I add that you both look lovely today?"

"Thank you," Gussie said.

"And might I add"—Paul picked up a piece of bread—"needs more pecans and it's just a little dry."

"I was thinking the same thing. One should never be stingy with pecans when we have so many growing in our part of the world," Gussie agreed.

"Amen to that," Paul said. "I picked up a hundred pounds off my trees alone. Back to what I was saying. We noticed y'all are trying to get Luke and Sissy together. We think it's a great idea and want to offer to help any way we can."

"I've been praying that God would send someone to Luke," Jimmy said. "I feel like he's answered my prayers, but God never refuses a little help from us. If we all four pool our ideas, maybe we can move things along without them knowing that we're meddling."

Ina Mae headed for the kitchen. "Was it that obvious that we're trying to get them together?"

"Only to us two old widowers who don't have much of a life of our own." Jimmy picked up a slice of banana bread from the plate and handed it to Gussie. "Sissy would make a great preacher's wife, and Luke needs someone in his life. He's too young to be as lonely as me and Paul get at times."

"We agree with y'all," Paul said.

"We thought maybe we'd do some skeet shooting on Saturday and invite the kids and you ladies," Jimmy said. "We know that you do some target-practice weekends, so would it be possible to combine the two things into one?"

"Sounds great to me." Ina Mae carried a tray with four cups of coffee on it from the kitchen. "The kids won't figure out that we're trying to play matchmaker if we switch off on ideas and events."

"Where are you planning to do this skeet shooting?" Gussie was all for anything that would help keep Sissy in Newton, even sharing the job with the two guys.

Paul reached for a piece of the cranberry orange bread. "This one is still a little dry, too. Ina Mae, tell me what it needs."

"I make mine with cream cheese to make it moist," Ina Mae answered. "We usually target practice out behind Blanche's house. I bet Sissy won't mind if we set things up for skeet at her place. Still seems funny to call it her place."

"I'll ask Sissy just to be polite, but I'm sure she'll say yes." Gussie tasted the cranberry orange bread. "I like this one better than the other two, but I use a rum glaze on mine. I should make some for our skeet shooting on Saturday."

"I'll be looking forward to it. Ruthie used to make rum cakes at Christmas, and they were amazing," Jimmy said.

"I remember her bringing her cake to our ladies' auxiliary party every year, but we were careful who we told that it had rum in it," Gussie told him. "Elvira, for one, would have had one of her spells if she'd known she was eating something with alcohol in it."

"Yep, she would have for sure," Ina Mae added. "We're going to tell the kids that the skeet shooting was y'all's idea."

"Which it is, so you won't be sinning." Paul nodded in agreement. "Can we have a cup of coffee to go? We've got more work to do this afternoon."

"Sure thing," Ina Mae answered.

"And we kind of thought after we shot some skeet on Saturday that we would bring over some T-bones and grill them, if that's all right." Paul raked his fingers through his thin hair. "You treated us when we put up the Christmas tree, so we'd like to repay the favor."

"That would be great. We'll throw some potatoes in the oven to bake, make a salad and a dessert, and the kids will never know what we're up to." Gussie could visualize the fellowship hall all decorated for a wedding. White tablecloths would cover round tables for eight with center-pieces of lilies.

"We have to be sneaky, or they might set their heels." Jimmy went to the kitchen, where he poured coffee in a couple of to-go cups and carried them back to the work area. "We should get back to work. Tell Elvira thanks for the snack and thank you two for letting us meddle in your matchmaking. This is putting some life back in our old hearts."

"See y'all in a little while," Paul said.

"We'll be right here, making curtains and woolly lambs," Gussie told him.

As soon as the two men were out of the room, Ina Mae poked Gussie on the arm. "You were flirting! I haven't seen you all spicy like that in at least twenty years."

"I was not flirting. I was planning our match-making business," Gussie protested.

"Hello!" Elvira came through the back door with an armload of furry throws. "Did I miss anything?"

"Nothing at all," Ina Mae and Gussie said at the same time.

Sissy left the lawyer's office in a daze. She'd never dreamed that Aunt Bee was wealthy, or that she would be leaving so much to Sissy when she passed away. The lawyer, Mr. Lawrence, had explained it all to her, then turned over four bank accounts—one checking that had a modest amount in it compared to the savings accounts, which boggled her mind. And there were interest payments on investments that came in every month that exceeded what Sissy made in six months' time.

She needed to think, and yet her mind was spinning out of control. Her parents should be inheriting all this. They could live so well in Aunt Bee's house, and would be able to have all those things they'd sacrificed for their careers through the years.

We sacrificed nothing, her mother whispered in her head. *We are happy with our lives.*

Sissy remembered trying to talk them into renting an apartment in Beau Bridge and maybe teaching voice and guitar lessons instead of gigging. She'd used the phrase *sacrificed a home and roots,* and her mother had said those exact words.

And we even got to leave this world together, so don't feel guilty, her mother said and then she was gone.

"I wanted more time with you and Daddy," Sissy said as she crossed the courthouse lawn and sat down in the gazebo. At night, the place was all lit up in twinkling lights, but even in the day, the magnolia trees were wrapped in sparkly red and green tinsel. The cedar trees at the four corners of the Veterans' Memorial monument were all aglitter with multicolored ornaments and silver tinsel.

"I think you would have been happy here," she said, but then shook her head. Who was she kidding? She was happy in Newton because it was where Aunt Bee lived, and that meant a real house, with real furniture, and a room of her own instead of lowering the kitchen table every night and arranging the pillows around the booth to make a bed for herself.

She wrapped her coat around her and pulled her stocking hat down over her ears. Aunt Bee and her friends had played on this courthouse lawn when they were little girls, while Sissy had always loved the gazebo and found it to be a peaceful place to catch her breath after jogging a few laps around the courthouse square.

The north wind whipped a few dead magnolia leaves around in a circle about her feet, and the lights wrapped around the gazebo swayed back and forth. She lost track of time as she sat there trying to make sense of everything the lawyer told her. Sissy didn't have to work another day in her life, but she loved helping people. All the decisions she would have to make bewildered her; she wished that she could pick up her cell phone and call her parents for advice.

"Hey, there's a warm church about two blocks from here." Luke startled her when he sat down beside her.

"Where did you come from?" she asked.

"I had to go to the courthouse to file some

papers," he answered. "My truck is parked right there." He pointed. "Didn't mean to scare you. Why are you sitting out here in the cold wind?"

"I just needed a place to think," Sissy said. "I saw the lawyer about Aunt Bee's estate this morning."

"Do you need time alone, or want some company?" Luke asked.

"I could use some company," she said, relieved to have someone to talk to.

"Then how about we drive to the Dairy Queen and get some hot chocolate. Your lips are turning blue." Luke stood up and extended a hand.

"That sounds wonderful," she said as she put her hand in his and let him pull her to a standing position. "Your hands are so warm. I should have worn gloves."

"We hardly ever need gloves this far south." He kept her hand in his all the way to his truck.

"This has been quite a week," she said.

He opened the truck door for her. "Seems like it. A lot of sadness with losing Blanche, but a lot of good things have happened, too. You've been here to help all of us through the tough times. You're helping Wes and Annabelle. I could go on and on."

"Thank you for that, but you've all helped me, and Wes and Annabelle just need a few little pushes. They'll be fine. My mind was blown away at the lawyer's office today, Luke." Sissy was glad to be able to share the news she'd just gotten. "Aunt Bee had more than a house and two ornery birds."

Luke started the engine and turned the heat up to the max. "I'm not surprised. She was the administrator of the hospital for years, and she told me that she had invested well."

"That she did . . ." Sissy sighed. "I had no idea that she had so much saved or so much still coming in."

"And you wouldn't ever have to work again, if you didn't want to, right?" Luke started the engine and pulled away from the curb.

"I guess so, but I love helping people," she answered.

"Me too, and I understand," Luke told her, "because Uncle Jimmy and Aunt Ruthie didn't have kids, either, and when Aunt Ruthie died, Uncle Jimmy turned all of her oil royalties over to me. He said he had plenty to live on for the next hundred years and didn't need the money, and that it would all be mine when he was gone anyway. I don't have to preach, Sissy. I do it because I want to help people," he said. "I put all my salary back into the collection plate, but no one knows that."

"But all this stuff for the Christmas program . . . ," she started.

"Folks feel good when they help, and besides, Ina Mae and Gussie needed something to take their minds off Blanche's sudden death," he said.

"Then we got Elvira, Uncle Jimmy, and Paul involved, and it just got better and better."

"You are pretty spectacular," she said.

"Thank you, but I'm not fishing for compliments. I'm just sharing it with you so that you can see common people like me and you don't have to act like we're all that and—"

"A bag of potato chips," she finished the sentence for him.

"You got it!" He held up his palm to high-five with her.

She slapped his hand with hers. "Thanks for telling me that. It helps."

"Just live your life in whatever way that brings you peace. That's what Blanche did." He made a couple of turns and headed toward the Dairy Queen.

"You sure you aren't a therapist?" she asked.

"Nope, just a country preacher, but I do try to counsel anyone in my congregation when they need it," he answered as he pulled into the parking lot. "Drive through or go in and sit down?"

"Drive through," she answered.

He drove around the store to the window and ordered two large cups of hot chocolate. He handed the first cup of hot chocolate that came through the window over to her, took the second one for himself, and pulled back out onto the road. "Want to talk some more or go to the church and help get things done?"

"Talk some more," she answered. "Let's drive to the park and watch the ducks while we drink this chocolate. One of the things Aunt Bee and I always did when I came for a visit was a trip to the park to feed the ducks."

"That's a good thing to remember." Luke took a sip of his hot chocolate. "This hits the spot on a cold day. Aunt Ruthie and I used to do the same thing, even after I was grown. The last time was the Christmas before she died. The temperature was seventy degrees, and we didn't even need a jacket."

He drove a couple of blocks from the Dairy Queen and parked his truck beside a pavilion with three picnic tables under it. A small creek ran through that area, and ducks of every color and size either floated in the water or waddled around the park pecking at the ground.

"Do you feel . . . ," she stammered and blushed.

"This attraction between us?" he finished for her. "Yes, I do. What do you think we should do about it?"

"When did you first notice it? Do you think it's because we're both vulnerable? Aunt Bee was my last living relative, and she was your good friend, so are we feeling something real, or just reaching out for life?" she asked.

"I got a little tongue-tied when I saw you at the funeral," he admitted. "In my opinion, the fact that we are so vulnerable has nothing to do with what we are feeling. What we do with it is up to us. What do you want to do?" He unfastened his seat belt and turned to face her.

Sissy wanted to kiss him—that's what she wanted—just to see if it would be as hot as she thought it would, but there were at least three other cars parked not far from them. If playing basketball with no shirt on could cause a problem for him with the deacons, making out in broad daylight would stir up a huge hornet's nest.

"I would like . . ." She paused, searching for the right words. "I would like to . . ."

Luke set his hot chocolate in the drink holder in the door, leaned across the console, and cupped her cheeks in his hands. He brought her lips to his in a fiery kiss. Every hormone in Sissy's body begged for more, but the kiss ended, leaving her limp and more than a little weak in the knees.

"That's what I've wanted to do since I first laid eyes on you," he whispered.

"And?" she gasped.

"And it was as awesome as I thought it would be." He grinned. "I may never want to taste hot chocolate except on your lips again."

"So there's going to be another kiss?" she teased.

"I sure hope so," he answered.

Chapter Eleven

Sissy could tell the moment Ina Mae walked into the house on Saturday afternoon that something wasn't right. Her face was drawn, and her eyes had a blank look to them that Sissy had seen too many times in folks who were in deep depression. Her first thought was that something had happened to Gussie.

"Are you all right?" Sissy asked, pushing back her thoughts. "Can I get you something to drink?"

Ina Mae hung her coat on the hall tree and went straight to the living room, where she plopped down on the end of the sofa. "Not long ago we had Blanche's funeral, and here we are carrying on like she didn't mean a thing to us. We put up our Christmas trees and we have even let men into our lives. All three of us swore off men more than a decade ago."

"I thought you did that when Walter abused Aunt Bee." Sissy sat down beside Ina Mae.

"We swore off husbands then. We had men in our lives, discreetly, and none as far as the world knew, but we told each other nearly everything," Ina Mae said. "I had a special friend that I met in college. We got together every few months for a long weekend. Is what I'm about to tell you privileged, and you can't repeat it?"

"If you are my client, it is," Sissy said.

Ina Mae pulled a handful of change from the pocket of her jeans. "If I give you this, does that make me your client?"

"There's paperwork to fill out, but for today, this will do." Sissy bit back a smile.

Ina Mae laid four quarters, a dime, and a penny on the coffee table. "Only Gussie and Blanche knew about Edward."

"I'm sure Aunt Bee wouldn't have minded if you decided to get married." Sissy looked at the coins. Was there an omen hiding in a dollar and eleven cents? Didn't 111 have to mean something?

"I couldn't marry Edward," Ina Mae said. "He was already married. His wife had a stroke when she was in her early thirties and was in a nursing home. He had to stay married to her for insurance reasons. That was fine with me because I didn't ever want a husband, not after the misery Walter caused Blanche."

"Do you still see Edward?" Sissy asked.

"He was twenty years older than me, and he died ten years ago—just dropped dead one day with a heart attack, and his wife died the very next day." Ina Mae sighed. "I mourned that man for a solid year, and here I am . . ." She took a deep breath and let it out slowly. "Here I am, acting like Blanche wasn't even as important as Edward, and she was so much more."

"Aunt Bee would want you to move on and live out the rest of your life in happiness instead of sinking into this depression," Sissy told her. "I'm going to bring you a glass of—"

"Vodka! Out! Out! Dammit, Ina Mae," Danny Boy screeched from his cage.

"Tea!" Sissy finished her sentence.

"You better let Danny Boy out first or he won't ever shut up. He sounds just like Blanche when he fusses about me or Gussie." Ina Mae's smile still had sadness in it. "How do I get rid of this guilt, Sissy?"

"That's a good question." Sissy got up and opened Danny Boy's cage. "I've been feeling the same way. Why should I be anything but sad? My mind keeps telling me that I should be mourning for Aunt Bee, and I do miss her so much. My heart says that she wouldn't want any of us to grieve at all. She was like that—full of life and love—and she wouldn't want us to stop living. If anything, she would tell us that life is uncertain and we should enjoy every single second to the fullest."

"Easy to say, hard to do." Ina Mae got to her feet and followed Sissy into the kitchen.

"Yes, ma'am, it is." Sissy nodded as she poured a little vodka into Danny Boy's bowl and then brought out a pitcher of freshly made sweet tea from the refrigerator. "Now what's this about allowing guys into your life?"

"Jimmy and Paul." Ina Mae filled two glasses with ice. "I don't know how to . . . well, it's like this . . . ," she stammered. "It's nice to have them to talk to, but . . ."

Sissy filled two glasses with sweet tea. "But you feel like being around them means you're replacing Aunt Bee?"

Ina Mae snapped her fingers. "That's it. I've been trying to figure out why it don't feel right, and that's it."

"I've had the same feeling about Luke," Sissy admitted. "Am I really attracted to him, or am I using him to fill the hole that losing Aunt Bee left in my heart?"

"Blanche liked Luke." Ina Mae patted Sissy on the shoulder. "She said if she'd ever had a son, she would have liked him to be just like Luke— that he wasn't a hard-shelled preacher like her daddy had been."

Sissy carried the glasses to the table and motioned for Ina Mae to sit down. "I can understand that."

Ina Mae took a long drink of her tea. "You are really attracted to him?"

"What woman wouldn't be?" Sissy asked. "He's good-looking, kind, and sweet, and he has an awesome sense of humor."

"Yep," Ina Mae agreed. "And there's several women around town who have been wanting a chance to be a preacher's wife. Minnette Sullivan is out in the lead. She would be at the church every day working on the Christmas stuff if she wasn't already wrangling two jobs. She works in admissions at the hospital from Monday through Friday, and then she's a bartender at the Magnolia Bar and Grill down south of town on Friday and Saturday night."

"Who are we talking about?" Gussie breezed into the kitchen.

"I didn't hear you coming in," Sissy said. "Want a glass of tea?"

"Yes, I do, but I'll get it myself," Gussie answered. "Y'all just stay seated. Did I hear Minnette's name? And what's this I'm hearing about you and Luke at the park earlier this week? Did he really kiss you?"

A scalding-hot blush rushed from Sissy's neck to her cheeks. "The gossip vine is getting slow. That happened in the middle of the week, and it's just now getting out?"

Gussie brought her tea to the table. "Details. We want to hear the whole story."

Just remembering the way Luke's kiss had made her feel jacked Sissy's pulse up a few notches. "That might betray confidentiality . . . ," she joked.

"Bullcrap!" Ina Mae butted in. "Don't you try to get out of this by teasing us about confidentiality laws. He's not your client, and besides all that, even if he was, you've been in the clubhouse. That means you are obligated to tell us everything, and besides, I paid you money, so what's said in this kitchen stays in this kitchen."

"Okay!" Sissy had been itching to tell someone about kissing Luke ever since it happened. She had even talked to Aunt Bee about it, but her aunt must have been off in a distant corner of heaven talking to her brother, because she didn't have a single thing to say about it.

"We're waiting," Gussie said. "The guys will all be here pretty soon, so start talking."

"We admitted that there was chemistry between us. He kissed me, and then we went to the church and worked all afternoon. I had a lot of business to take care of the rest of the week. We've texted, and he's called me to talk an hour or so every evening, and that's all there is to it." Sissy stopped for a drink of tea.

"Did you have phone sex?" Ina Mae asked.

"No, we did not! Luke is a preacher." Sissy gasped.

"Yep, and preachers have desires just like any other man. At least that's an assumption. How else would they ever have kids if they never had sex?" Gussie asked.

"I bet Minnette would have phone sex with him any old time, and she would tell everyone in town about it the second she hung up. How did it feel when he kissed you? Did your knees go weak? Do you like talking to him at night? Are you looking forward to seeing him again?" Ina Mae spit out questions so fast that it sent Sissy's head into a spin.

"Okay," Sissy said, "my knees did go weak, and the kiss was . . . well, let's just say it affected me like no other kiss has ever done. I love talking to him at night. We have so much in common, and he's easy to talk to. And yes, I'm looking forward to seeing him today. That old saying about being out of sight, out of mind isn't working for me."

"Now, that's what we wanted to hear," Gussie said.

A hard knock took all three women's attention to the front door. "We'll save any more talk of this until later," Gussie said. "It looks like our skeet-shooting buddies are here."

"Y'all come on in," Ina Mae yelled down the hallway. "We're in the kitchen."

"Jimmy's out back getting the machinery set up. You ladies have shotguns?" Paul asked as he entered the kitchen and handed Ina Mae a large plastic container. "You can use ours if you don't."

"We have our own guns," Gussie answered, "and we'll be out soon as we get our coats on."

"What is this?" Ina Mae set the container on the counter.

"Steaks, marinating in Jimmy's special sauce," Paul answered. "They don't need to be refrigerated. See y'all outside in a few minutes."

"Nap time!" Danny Boy said and flew out into the hallway from the kitchen. "Pretty boy!" he crooned the minute he saw Luke and landed on his shoulder. He picked at the hair above Luke's ear, gave him kisses on the cheek, and repeated the phrase over and over.

"I'll get him back in his cage and then come outside with the ladies," Luke said. "Afternoon, ladies."

"Pretty boy," Danny Boy said again.

"Good to see you, Luke," Ina Mae said.

"Glad you could join us." Gussie beamed.

Sissy could see from the looks they gave each other that Gussie and Ina Mae were downright proud of themselves for their matchmaking.

Luke stopped beside Sissy's chair and laid a hand on her shoulder. "Are you ready to show off your shooting skills? I've got to admit that mine are rusty."

"I am if you are." Sissy would far rather test his kissing skills a little more than his ability to shoot a clay pigeon.

"Pretty boy! Pretty boy!" Danny Boy crooned and then began whistling his song.

"Of course you are a pretty boy," Luke chuckled as he carried him on his shoulder back to the living room.

"I don't think he's talking about himself," Sissy said from the doorway. "He never says that unless he's sitting on your shoulder. If he was a girl, I'd think he had a crush on you."

"Maybe he's just feeling the need to change his lifestyle and start praying instead of swearing." Luke opened the door to the antique cage and the bird flew right inside.

"Dammit, Ina Mae and Gussie!" Danny Boy said as he tucked his head under a wing.

"Guess he's not quite ready to repent of his sins just yet," Sissy said.

She wore a faded red sweatshirt and jeans that hugged every curve. Her strawberry-blonde hair had been pulled up into a knot on top of her head, and her makeup had worn off, showing a faint sprinkling of freckles across her nose. Luke thought she was even more gorgeous than she had been in the dress she'd worn to church the previous Sunday.

"Looks like you might be right." He covered up the birdcage with a towel. "But I'll keep hoping that I can turn him to Jesus."

"Sweet Jesus!" Danny Boy said and started whistling "One Day at a Time."

"That's a new one. I've never heard him whistle that one before," Sissy said. Even Danny Boy had two sides, just like she did—one for the bird who was raised in a bar, the other for the bird who came to live with Aunt Bee. How many times had she played that religious song to him before he started to whistle the tune?

"Blanche was working on helping him turn his life around," Luke told her. "She used to play that song at least once a day. She was trying to change him from being a bar bird into a respectable old boy. Shall we go join the others?"

"We might ought to." Sissy thought again of how much she would rather stay inside and make out with him. "It's already all over town that we shared a kiss. We wouldn't want to ruin your reputation by spending too much time alone."

"If that happens, I trust that you will make an honest man out of me," Luke teased.

"We won't even know if you're pregnant for a few weeks, so we don't have to worry about shopping for your wedding dress for a while," she teased back.

In a few long strides, he crossed the room and took her hand in his. "I'll remember to take my birth control pill every morning so that doesn't happen."

Her laughter filled the house and his heart.

Now that's what I want to hear, Blanche's voice whispered in his ear.

Me too, and for longer than just today, he thought, *but I'm a patient man, and she needs to get over your passing before we get serious about this chemistry between us.*

Don't wait too long, Blanche cautioned.

Sissy stopped giggling and stared right into his

eyes. "What's wrong? You were laughing with me, and then . . ."

"I was arguing with Blanche," he admitted.

"I understand." She nodded. "I've been doing a lot of that lately, too. She's never had a lot of patience, but since she passed, it feels like she's got even less."

Gussie stuck her head in the back door and yelled, "You kids going to come out here and shoot with us or stay in the house all day? We're ready to start, but Jimmy says he's going first and that he will outdo us all."

"On our way." Luke raised his voice. "Want to make a wager on who hits the most clay pigeons?"

Both of Sissy's eyebrows shot up. "Preachers don't gamble. Is this just between us or does it include the whole bunch?"

"Just us, and no money is involved so it's not technically gambling. If I win, I get to take you out for Sunday dinner. If you win, you owe me two kisses," he answered.

"You're on." She stuck out her right hand. "And you'd better be sure your credit card isn't maxed out, because I love food."

"I like a woman who isn't shy about eating." He shook with her and then raised her hand to his lips for a kiss. "I'll look forward to those kisses."

"Not as much as I look forward to dinner." She led the way outside.

"Pull!" Jimmy yelled, and a few seconds later the sound of a shotgun blast filled the air. The clay pigeon fell from the sky in too many pieces to count. "Gussie, write down one for me. I'm on my way to outshooting all of you today."

Gussie wrote Jimmy's name down in her notebook, and then put a mark after it before she handed it off to Sissy. "My turn," she said as she picked up her shotgun from a long table. "Pull!"

The clay pigeon went flying into the sky. She fired when it reached its highest point and it disappeared in a cloud of dust. "And that's one for me."

"Nice gun you got there," Jimmy said.

"Thanks. Santa Claus brought one to each of us—Blanche, Ina Mae, and me—last Christmas. We haven't had much time to practice with them," Gussie told him and then turned to focus on Sissy. "Why didn't you bring Blanche's out with you?"

"Her guns are all in the safe, but I don't know the combination," Sissy answered.

"I'll go get it for you while the rest of them have a turn," Gussie offered.

"No," Sissy told her. "I'll get it. Just tell me how to open the safe. I'll need that info if I ever need to get into the safe again anyway."

"You can use my shotgun, if you aren't used to the new one," Luke said.

"I reckon there's not much difference in any

of them," Sissy said, "but thanks anyway. I'll be right back."

Sissy punched in 51351—Blanche's birthday—and turned the handle. The safe opened right up, and there, among an arsenal of other guns, was Aunt Bee's fancy Beretta with the engraved silver on the stock. She picked up the gun, tucked it under her arm, and then noticed Aunt Bee's jewelry case on the top shelf. She took a moment to peek inside the familiar little wooden chest, where Aunt Bee kept what she called her good jewelry. There weren't many pieces, but the ruby pendant had always been a favorite of Sissy's. She closed the box and returned it to its right place.

She had shot skeet with the ladies only one time before, and that was back when she was eighteen. She wasn't too bad with a pistol or a rifle when she was shooting at a still target, but hitting that clay pigeon on her first shot had been pure luck. There was no way she was going to win the bet with Luke, but it didn't matter if she won or lost; she would kiss him anyway—just thinking about that made her feel all tingly inside.

"Wish me luck, because I'm going to need it, Aunt Bee," she said as she picked up a box of shells sitting beside the jewelry box. She carried the gun outside and got in line behind Luke. He shot his clay pigeon out of the sky, but when she threw up the shotgun, aimed, and fired, the red clay disc soared out of sight and fell without a scratch to the ground.

"I'm winning." Luke winked at Sissy.

"Maybe in some bet you two have going, but in the big picture, I'm going to win this contest," Jimmy said.

"In your dreams," Gussie told him. "I can shoot the eyeballs out of a rattlesnake at a hundred yards with a pistol. I've never met a clay pigeon I couldn't send to the earth in dozens of pieces."

"We'll see about that." Jimmy raised his thick gray eyebrows at her.

Sissy's own matchmaking was working, by golly! Her first attempt at doing what her aunt Bee, Gussie, and Ina Mae did was going to be a success. It might not result in weddings, but at their age, new strong friendships would be enough for Sissy.

Aunt Bee popped into her head. *And their plan to put you and Luke together is working, too.*

"For a little while," she whispered.

"That's right," Gussie said right beside Sissy. "We'll see who's ahead when we've killed all those clay pigeons."

You belong here in Newton, Texas. Luke needs you. Ina Mae and Gussie need you. It's no small thing to be needed, Aunt Bee continued. *Put that under your cap and think about it.*

Yes, ma'am, I will. Sissy glanced over at Luke

244

to find him staring right at her. Did he really need her, or did she need him, and would the attraction between them disappear once they got over losing Aunt Bee?

All five of the others hit their targets when it was their turn, but Sissy missed hers by a couple of country miles for the second time.

"I think I'm ahead in this battle." Luke raised up two fingers on one hand and made a fist with the other. "It's two and zero."

"Hey, the purpose is to kill the chunk of clay, isn't it?" Sissy declared. "I scared it so bad that it fell to the ground and broke into as many pieces as y'all's did when you shot them, so I should get half a point for that."

"Sorry, baby girl." Ina Mae reloaded her gun. "That's not the way it works."

"Aunt Bee would have given me a little credit," Sissy insisted.

"Blanche wouldn't have given you squat, and you know it," Gussie informed her. "She hated to lose and didn't give a single inch when it came to any competition."

"Pull!" Jimmy yelled and missed his target that time.

"Looks like you're down one," Gussie said.

"Arthritis is getting my shoulder." He laid his shotgun down and rubbed the shoulder. "My gun has more kick than those things you women are shooting."

"Pull!" Gussie yelled, and Paul sent one flying. She missed hers that time, too, and stomped her foot. "Dammit to hell! That rotten wind blew something in my eye just when I zeroed in on the target."

Sissy jerked her head around to see how Jimmy and Luke would respond to Gussie cussing like that, but neither of them blinked an eye.

"Excuses, excuses," Sissy said with a giggle.

Gussie and Jimmy both gave her the old stink eye. In her books that was a good thing. They were standing together against her, which meant her plan really was still working.

"Wait until you're old," Jimmy started.

"And your body tells you that you can't hit every target," Gussie finished.

"To begin with"—Sissy shook her finger at them—"neither of you are old, and to end with, I'll have to practice a lot to ever be as good as any of y'all. And one more thing. There's just one clay pigeon left in the box. I think that I should get one last chance since I haven't hit one all evening."

"Fair enough," Luke agreed.

"It's getting dark anyway, so we should be thinking about getting some steaks on the grill," Paul said.

"Dammit!" Ina Mae swore and then clamped a hand over her mouth. "I forgot to put potatoes in the oven to bake."

Sissy didn't even bother to look at the two preachers this time when Ina Mae swore. Evidently, they weren't as stiff necked as her grandfather had been.

Thinking of that made her remember Aunt Bee's comment about sowing wild oats on Saturday and then going to church to pray for a crop failure on Sunday morning.

I do not intend to repent for the kisses I will give Luke, or to think about the rumors that going to dinner with him will cause, she thought. *I'm going to enjoy every minute that I spend with him.*

"No worries," Jimmy said. "You get them washed, and I'll cut them up, put some green beans and onions on top of them, and cook them on the grill."

"I thought cussin' was reserved for the clubhouse," Sissy whispered to Ina Mae and Gussie.

"It is except when my pseudo dementia kicks in." Ina Mae picked up her gun and took a step toward the house.

"And when I miss a target. Blanche wasn't the only one who hated to lose," Gussie added.

Sissy got her gun in the right position and then yelled for Jimmy to pull. She aimed, squeezed the trigger, and hit the pigeon dead on. The thing disappeared like it had never been there.

"You did it! You hit one!" Luke took the gun from her, laid it on the table, and then picked her up and swung her around until they were both dizzy.

"You still owe me kisses," he whispered for her ears only.

"Not to worry, I pay my debts." She held on to him so that she wouldn't fall flat on her butt.

"What did he say to you?" Gussie asked when they all headed toward the house.

"That was classified," Sissy answered with a grin.

Dark had settled on Newton, Texas, that evening when everyone started home. Chester had found a place in the corner of the porch and had his head tucked under a wing. Danny Boy had evidently gone to roost, too, because he wasn't cussing, whistling a hymn, or screaming for vodka.

Luke lingered behind on the porch until the taillights of the older folks' vehicles were completely out of sight; then he caged Sissy against the wall with a hand on either side of her shoulders. "I believe you owe me something, ma'am."

"Oh, yeah?" she asked. "And what would that be?"

"Dinner." He kissed the tender spot on the side of her neck. "And two kisses if you lost, which you did."

She stiffened her knees to keep from sinking. "Does that count as one?" she asked breathlessly.

"No, ma'am." His lips moved up to her cheek. "The deal is that you kiss me."

"Well, I wouldn't want it said that I reneged on a bet, especially to a preacher," she said.

He kissed both her eyelids. "Even a preacher needs to be loved, darlin'."

Luke needs you. Aunt Bee's words flashed through her mind as she wrapped her arms around his neck and went up on tiptoe. She moistened her mouth with the tip of her tongue and tangled her fingertips in his thick, dark hair. Their lips met in a steaming-hot kiss that left her leaning against him for support.

"That was one. Now, where's the second one?" Luke's drawl was deeper, almost hungry sounding.

"Coming right up. Would you like fries with that?" Sissy teased.

"No, ma'am. Just another of those fiery kisses will do fine," he answered.

The second one was even hotter than the first, and she was on the verge of dragging him back into the house to see where a third one might lead when he took a step back. "You lost. I won. I will take you to dinner after church tomorrow."

"As in a date?" she asked.

"Yes." He was breathing just as hard as she was.

"I'd love to go," she said.

"Great!" he said. "Good night, Sissy. This has

been an amazing day. No, I take that back. It's been awesome ever since I met you. God is helping both of us get through this tough time."

"You are so right," she whispered.

"See you tomorrow in church?" he asked as he started down the porch steps.

"Oh, yeah!" She watched him walk out to his truck, get inside it, and drive away, and then she went inside, closed the door, and slid down the back side of it. "Good God, Aunt Bee, what am I going to do? Do I really belong here? Is it time for me to put down permanent roots right here in Newton, Texas, and if so, what do I do about my job in Beau Bridge?"

Her phone rang, and for a minute, she wondered if her aunt had a hotline from heaven back to earth. She fished it out of her hip pocket and said, "Hello," without even checking to see who was calling.

"Gussie and I are at her place. I've got you on speaker," Ina Mae said. "We forgot to ask you to go to dinner at the Hen's Nest with us tomorrow after church."

"Can't," Sissy said.

"You can take a nap after we eat," Gussie argued.

"I can't go with you because Luke asked me to dinner, and it's a date, and yes, he kissed me good night. I know you're dying to ask, and I might as well tell you or else you'll pull out that Sunshine

Club card and make me 'fess up anyway"—she ran out of breath and stopped to suck in another lungful—"and Aunt Bee keeps popping into my head with advice. I don't know if it's really her, or if it's just my subconscious telling me what I really want to hear."

"Whew!" Gussie said. "Slow down, girl, and catch a breath. You're still reeling from kissing on Luke. Want us to come back over there? Blanche has been pestering both of us, too."

"It's late, and we've got church tomorrow," Sissy answered. "Maybe we can have a visit tomorrow afternoon and compare notes?"

"Not on your life," Ina Mae said. "We're not butting in on yours and Luke's time. We can talk Monday. Good night and sweet dreams."

"Same to you," Sissy said.

She'd no sooner ended the call than the phone rang again. When she saw Luke's name pop up, she took a deep breath and answered. "Did you forget something?"

"No, I just wanted to hear your voice one more time before I go to bed," he said.

"That's pretty romantic." She could have sat right there and listened to him talk in that slow southern drawl for hours.

"Hey, even a preacher can have a romantic bone," he chuckled. "I can't wait to see you in church tomorrow morning."

"I'll be the one in the blue sweater sitting

251

beside Ina Mae and Gussie." She didn't want to end the call.

"I'll be the one behind the lectern, trying to keep my mind on my sermon," he said. "It's getting late. This really should be good night."

"Night." She ended the call and started up to her bedroom. "Aunt Bee, where are you? I could use some advice right now."

Evidently, Aunt Bee had gone to bed, if there was such a thing as sleeping in heaven, or maybe she felt like she'd given all the advice that Sissy needed, because she didn't have anything else to say.

Chapter Twelve

*E*very head in the restaurant turned when the waitress showed Luke and Sissy to a table in the back corner. Cell phones came out of pockets and purses, and Sissy could practically hear the buzz in the air as the towers outside town heated up to the frying point with so much use.

"If the cell towers blow up, are they going to blame us for it?" Sissy asked.

Luke seated her and then took his chair. "Looks like my sermon on minding your own business went right over the tops of some folks' heads this morning. But if they put us in handcuffs for having dinner together, I'm not saying a word until they put it in writing that we can share a prison cell."

"That would really cause the phone towers to fry." Sissy didn't confess that she hadn't listened so well, either. Her mind kept wandering back to the kisses she and Luke had shared and to the friendship she had built with Ina Mae and Gussie in the past couple of weeks. The two ladies had always been like aunts to her, but these past days they had formed a bond that was unlike anything she had with any of her other friends or acquaintances.

She wondered if they might eventually ask her to agree to join their club and wasn't sure how she would answer them if they did. She thought she might say yes, so that Aunt Bee's legacy could live on, but then she was afraid they would never get over losing their best friend if she did.

Luke reached across the table and laid a hand on hers. "Earth to Sissy."

She blinked a couple of times and suddenly there was no one else in the restaurant. Gossip didn't matter. All worry and thoughts disappeared. There was just the two of them in a cute little restaurant with fake sunflowers in quart jars sitting on red-and-white checkered tablecloths.

"Sorry, I was thinking about Ina Mae and Gussie." She wondered if they had a magic wand in the antique chest with that book. If they waved it over a couple, they lost all ability to think about anything but each other.

"Dammit, Ina Mae and Gussie!" Luke mimicked Danny Boy. "I was hoping that you were having a mental replay of our kisses like I was."

"You make a great Danny Boy." Sissy smiled. "And yes, I was also thinking of the effect those kisses had on me."

"Want to elaborate on that?" Luke seemed to be ignoring everyone in the restaurant and focusing solely on her.

"Do you know that Ina Mae and Gussie are trying to play matchmaker for the two of us?"

she asked. "They used to do a lot of that kind of thing when Aunt Bee was alive."

A middle-aged lady with "Delores" written on her name tag came over to their table and laid a menu in front of each of them. "What can I get you to drink?"

"Sweet tea," Sissy said, "and I don't need the menu. If the special today is turkey and dressing, that's what I want."

"Same here." Luke handed the menus back to her.

"That's easy enough," she said, "and by the way, I sure enjoyed your sermon this morning. It's tough for me to get to services since I'm open seven days a week, but I appreciate having that call-in number so I can listen while I work."

"Thank you," Luke said. "I set that up for the folks who have trouble getting out. I'm glad that it's a help to you, too."

"It really is," Delores said and turned to go wait on another bunch of folks coming into the restaurant. "I'll have your dinner out in a few minutes."

Luke gave Sissy's hand a gentle squeeze. "Yes, I realized early on that they were trying to get us together, but so are Uncle Jimmy and Paul. They try to be subtle, but I can see right through them."

"Well, for your information, I've turned the tables on them," Sissy confessed.

"Now, that got past me," Luke chuckled. "But it's a good thing. Those old guys have been lonely, and it's good to see them both smiling again. Now, let's talk about you for a while. What made you go into your field of work?"

"Do you know anything about my family?" Sissy asked.

"I know that Blanche worked her way up at the hospital until she was the head administrator over the whole thing," Luke answered, "and that her father was our church's minister until after she graduated from high school. There were a couple of preachers between him and Uncle Jimmy, and then I was offered the job. Did I tell you that committee I interviewed with had a problem with hiring a single man?" He shrugged. "But that's about me, and right now we're talking about you."

"My dad was one of those *oops* babies, born when Aunt Bee was sixteen years old, and he kind of followed in his sister's rebellious footsteps. I guess you could say he was a true preacher's kid," Sissy said. "He met my mother in a bar. She was the singer in a rock band, and he was the lead guitar player in the one about to go on stage after her group finished their set."

Sissy could understand why the hiring committee might have a problem with asking Luke to take over the church, but in her eyes, it would have had more to do with the fact that he was so sexy rather than him being single.

"How long was it before they got married?" Luke asked.

Sissy's shoulders raised in a half shrug. "Two weeks later they went to the courthouse somewhere in Florida. The story sounded like a fairy tale when I was a little girl—love at first sight. A quick trip to stand before the judge and vow to love each other forever."

Luke's eyes met hers across the table. "And now? Do you still believe it was a happy-ever-after fairy tale?"

"Maybe." She could hardly string two thoughts together when she felt as if she were drowning in his blue eyes. "I don't know." She blinked and looked over his shoulder at the folks at the next table, who were whispering behind their menus. "Mama said it was, right up until the last time I saw her."

"I believe that happy-ever-after exists, but only if two people work at it," Luke said.

Sissy nodded in agreement. "My folks really did love each other. There was no doubt about that. Mama walked away from her band to marry him and then go on the road with *his band* that whittled down to just the two of them within a couple of months. I'm not totally sure that I wasn't one of those *oops* babies, too. Yet they didn't give up their lifestyle just because they had me. I was raised and schooled in an RV that they drove from one gig to the next. The only time I slept in a house that didn't have wheels was when I got to visit Aunt Bee. I've asked myself why I went into this field, and I guess it was because I wanted to help other people who had an unusual start, maybe even those who came out of unconventional families like mine."

Luke reached around the sunflowers and took her hand in his again. "You do a fine job. I wish we had someone like you in this little town. We might save a lot of marriages and stave off a few divorces. I try to counsel with each couple before they get married, but most of the time I don't feel like I'm doing much good."

"It usually takes more than one or two sessions to get through to folks." She pulled her hand free when Delores brought their food so the woman could set the hot plates on the table.

"Enjoy!" Delores said and then hurried back to the cash register so a family could pay their bill.

Luke picked up the saltshaker and shook it over his food. "Need some?"

She nodded and took it from him. "Aunt Bee was an amazing cook. She taught me everything I know. My mama was good at opening cans and making sandwiches. Daddy could make good hot dogs and burgers if the place where we parked the RV had a grill."

"Blanche made lots of meals for me," Luke said, "and if you can cook like she did, I might drop down on my knees and propose to you right here and now."

Not even a big gulp of her iced tea quenched

the heat Sissy experienced at that thought, even though she knew he was teasing. "If you're planning to do that, maybe you'd better call for all the ambulances in Newton County to head this way, because all these nosy folks around us will begin to drop like flies from pure shock. The hospital will be so full that Elvira will have to put off having her spell."

"Guess you've got a point there." Luke chuckled and forked some turkey into his mouth.

Sissy slathered butter on her hot roll and wondered what she would have done if Luke really had proposed. Of course, here in the restaurant it would have been a big joke, but when and if it should become real, how would she answer?

Ina Mae slumped down on the sofa in the clubhouse and sighed. "It's not the same anymore. Instead of looking forward to coming here today, I dreaded it."

Gussie tossed her coat on the rocking chair and eased down on the other end of the sofa. "Take off your coat, or you'll get too hot and get pneumonia. I don't want to be holding down this club by myself, and you're too skinny to survive being sick."

"What's that supposed to mean?" Ina Mae slipped her coat off, threw it toward the rocking chair, and missed. "See there. We aren't even hanging them on the hooks anymore because it reminds us that Blanche's would be empty. Should we ask Sissy for one of Blanche's coats to hang up there?"

Gussie shook her head. "That's morbid, and what I meant was that a person needs a little extra meat on their bones so that if they get sick and lose a bunch of weight, it don't kill them."

"Then I'd better not get sick. I've been tall and skinny my whole life." Ina Mae sighed again.

"We'll get through this tough time," Gussie said.

"No, we won't," Ina Mae argued. "Not until we admit that Blanche is gone, and we quit trying to keep her alive through the club."

"You want to dissolve our club?" Gussie's expression registered pure anger. "We've had this club for sixty years. What would we do without it? It's been the very core of our friendship."

"But what do we do *with* it? Maybe we should just end it," Ina Mae huffed.

"I'm not ready to do that." Gussie crossed her arms over her chest. "I still think we should invite Sissy."

"And I still vote that we don't make any rash decisions right now."

"I do agree with you about dreading to come out here today," Gussie said. "Let's go in the house and not have our meetings here until after the new year. We can decide what to do after we think about it awhile."

Ina Mae got to her feet and picked up her coat from the floor. "I can live with that. We can catch up on gossip in the house as well as we can out here."

"Yes, we can." Gussie turned off the heat, put on her coat, and led the way out of the old building. "Kind of seems like the end of an era, doesn't it?"

"Yep, but maybe if we can convince Sissy to stick around, it will be the beginning of a new one," Ina Mae said.

Gussie opened the door into the kitchen at the same time the house phone rang. She hurried over to the cabinet, picked up the cordless phone, and threw her coat over the back of a chair.

"Hello," she answered.

"This is Elvira. Did you know that . . ."

Gussie put the phone on speaker and motioned for Ina Mae to sit down at the table with her.

". . . that Luke and Sissy had dinner together at the Hen's Nest? He was holding her hand on the table, and people are saying that they've been seen kissing. He's a preacher, for God's sake. I knew when we hired him two years ago it was a mistake. I was on the committee, and I voted against it. A preacher should be settled and married, maybe even have kids. If his uncle hadn't been on the committee, he would have never gotten voted in."

Ina Mae leaned past the lazy Susan and spoke

into the phone. "Yes, we knew that they were having dinner together, and we knew that he'd kissed her. And, Elvira, just how does a preacher get married and have kids if he doesn't date? Sissy is a good woman, and she's helping in the church. What more could we ask for?"

"They are both adults. Just exactly what have you got against Sissy? You've been singing her praises for days, and now you're going to turn your back on her?" Gussie asked.

"Well, we all know that Blanche had a wild streak, and that her little brother was even wilder. He even had a rock band and raised Sissy on the road," Elvira said, "and as much as I like Sissy, the apple doesn't fall far from the tree. She's just not a suitable wife for our pastor—and Luke isn't acting respectable enough for our flock."

Ina Mae saw red—literally, little red spots appeared in front of her eyes. "Well, then how about we all three meet up at her place in an hour and have us an intervention? *You* can tell Sissy that we don't want her in our church or dating our preacher, and maybe it would be best if she went on back to Beau Bridge before dark. Then you can take Blanche's rooster and cockatiel home with you, since this is all your idea, and they'll need a home when Sissy leaves Newton."

"Oh, no! I couldn't do that." Elvira began to backpedal. "I've got two cats. I can't have birds of any kind in this house, especially one that cusses and drinks. Oh, dear, I think I'm having chest pains."

Gussie raised both eyebrows and threw up her palms in a dramatic gesture. "If you get sick, then you won't be able to work at the church tomorrow, and we don't know how to sew those curtains like you do. And if you've got something to say to our Sissy, then at least have the damn guts to say it to her face and not gossip behind her back."

"I agree with everything Gussie just said." Ina Mae glared at the phone.

"Well, I never," Elvira gasped. "You both have your heads stuck in the sand. And don't you dare touch my curtains. I'll be there tomorrow, but don't plan on me eating lunch with you or cleaning the church with you again, either."

"That's fine by me." Gussie's tone shot up a few octaves.

"And I want it on record that I really don't like Luke and Sissy dating. They can be friends, but not a couple," Elvira said.

"I'll tell her myself, and we'll fix him up with Minnette Sullivan for next Sunday. Would you like that better?" Ina Mae's voice was as cold as ice.

"No! That girl works in a bar two nights a week. We can't have that. I'll make a list of women that would be suitable and bring it tomorrow. We can look over it together then. Bye now." Elvira ended the call.

"We knew it was coming," Gussie said, "but we didn't think it would be quite this soon."

"We saved Luke a trip to the hospital, so we'll count today as a good one." Ina Mae slapped the table with both hands.

"I could strangle that bitch and enjoy watching her turn blue," Gussie declared. "I need a shot of whiskey to get the taste of that conversation out of my mouth."

"Pour me one, too," Ina Mae said. "I'll go find us something on the television."

"Put on a football game. If the Cowboys are playing, I'll put five dollars on them to win." Gussie headed to the antique pie safe where she kept the liquor.

"They're not worth crap this year, so I'll take your bet. Whatever made us think we could even be semi-friends with that woman?" Ina Mae picked up the remote and found the channel where the Cowboys were playing.

"We were trying to help Sissy and Luke, but they don't need our help anymore. They've got this on their own." Gussie brought two triple shots of whiskey to the living room and handed one to Ina Mae.

Ina Mae took a sip and then took her cell phone from the pocket of her cardigan. "I'm going to call Sissy and see if she wants to come over."

"But we won't say a word about Elvira's phone call, will we?" Gussie asked.

"Mum's the word." Ina Mae pretended to zip her mouth.

Sissy answered on the second ring, which meant that she wasn't in bed with Luke—yet.

"Hello, Ina Mae," Sissy said.

"Do you like football?" Ina Mae asked.

"Love it," Sissy said. "Are the Cowboys playing? What channel?"

"Is Luke with you?" Ina Mae cocked an eyebrow.

"Nope," Sissy answered. "He had an emergency call to the hospital."

"Was it for Delman Throckmorton? Did he die? Or did Elvira succumb to another fake spell?" Ina Mae asked.

"Delman's wife said he'd taken a turn for the worse and was asking for Luke to come pray for him. Do you know him? And what made you think that Elvira might have another episode?" Sissy asked.

"Known the Throckmorton family all my life," Ina Mae answered. "We'll probably have to clean all our stuff out of the fellowship hall tomorrow if he doesn't make it through the night. There'll be a funeral about Wednesday, and we'll need to have a family dinner afterwards. And it's been quite a while since Elvira had her last spell. If she thinks Delman's family is getting attention, that might bring one on. Did Luke kiss you goodbye at the door?"

"Is that why you really called?" Sissy laughed.

"That sound tells me that he did. Come on over and have a drink with us and root for the Cowboys," Ina Mae said. "We're at Gussie's house. Throw on some sweatpants so you'll be comfortable and bring the rest of that rocky road ice cream that's in the freezer."

"I'll be there in ten minutes." Sissy ended the call.

"Hey, Gussie," Ina Mae yelled. "Pour another drink. Sissy is coming over."

"Luke with her?"

"No, he's at the hospital with Delman," Ina Mae answered.

"His poor wife." Gussie shook her head seriously. "I've got a lasagna in the freezer. I can take it to her tomorrow if Delman doesn't make it through the night."

"I'll make a cobbler," Ina Mae said. "Folks our age seem to be dropping like flies all around us."

Gussie lifted her drink and held it up for a toast. "That's why we need to make the most of every day."

"Amen!" Ina Mae touched her glass to Gussie's and then took a sip. "We should've waited on Sissy to do that."

"Who says we'll only have one?" Gussie asked.

Chapter Thirteen

Warm sunshine pouring through the bedroom window woke Sissy on Monday morning. For a moment she thought it was spring or summer. Then she sat up in bed and remembered that it was really the middle of December. She glanced at the clock and groaned. She had a counseling session with Wesley and Annabelle in thirty minutes. No time to lollygag—one of Aunt Bee's favorite words—around that morning. She had to hustle and forget all about morning coffee or even a quick breakfast bar. Hopefully, there would be some snacks in the fellowship hall and coffee brewing. If not, as soon as the session was over, she'd make a run to the Dairy Queen and get a breakfast meal deal.

She jerked on a pair of jeans and a sweatshirt, pulled her hair up into a ponytail, and brushed her teeth. Then she drove ten miles over the speed limit getting to the church and arrived at the same time Wesley and Annabelle pulled into the parking lot.

"Good morning," she called out and waved.

They both waved as Wesley opened the truck door for his wife, helped her out, and then held her hand all the way into the church.

Sissy let them go on inside ahead of her and she trailed along behind them, watching their body language. They both looked tired, and Annabelle was doing the eight-months-pregnant waddle. When Sissy reached the nursery, they had moved the two rocking chairs close together and were still holding hands. Sissy pulled a folding chair over from between the two baby beds and sat down.

"What kind of week have y'all had?" she asked.

Annabelle's eyes misted over but she didn't cry. "The doctor said that I can't work anymore until after the baby comes. I'm not on bed rest, but I have to keep my feet up as much as possible."

"I've taken on a few extra shifts to make up for the money that she would have brought in," Wesley said.

"How do you feel about all this, Annabelle?" Sissy asked.

"I feel guilty and lonely and scared," Annabelle answered, "but we can live on soup and crackers if we have to."

"I could ask my folks for a loan but . . ." Wesley shrugged.

"They wouldn't give it to us, and you know it," Annabelle told him, "and my folks just don't have any extra to help us with, but we'll make it."

"Do y'all live in an apartment or a house?" Sissy asked.

"A little house back behind where Miss Gussie

lives," Wesley answered. "There's not many apartments in Newton, other than a few that's up over garages. The only one that we looked at had roaches, and the rent was even higher than the place we have."

"All right, let's talk about yesterday," Sissy said. "Y'all had a day to yourselves, right?"

Annabelle shook her head slowly from side to side. "My doctor told me on Friday that I couldn't work anymore, so Wes did a double shift on Sunday. He gets time and a half for weekends. I feel so guilty. I was supposed to work right up until the baby came, and now, Wes is having to carry the whole load."

"Don't worry, darlin'." Wes patted her hand. "We'll manage."

"So, what do y'all want to talk about today?" Sissy asked.

"We were supposed to discuss the holidays," Wes said, "but that's not a problem anymore. I can get double time if I work on a holiday, so I signed up for Christmas Eve, Christmas, and New Year's, all three."

"I'll spend the day at my mother's or else in our house waiting for Wes to come home. If we can afford it, I'll make a special little dinner for us," Annabelle said.

Sissy's mind spun around in circles, trying to figure out a way to help these two kids without anyone ever knowing that she had done so.

"I imagine that Gussie, Ina Mae, and I will have more food than we could possibly eat, so why don't we bring over some leftovers for y'all to heat up on those holidays?" Sissy asked. "And I bet the church has a food chain where folks sign up to bring in supper for you each day. Want me to ask Luke about it? Better yet, I imagine Gussie would know."

Annabelle glanced over at Wes. "We wouldn't want to be a bother to anyone."

"From what I've seen, you've got a good church family here," Sissy said.

"Then thank you," Annabelle said. "We appreciate that and look forward to it. We don't have much more to talk about, and Wes has to grab a little sleep before he goes back at three today to work the night shift."

"Can we talk again next Monday?" Sissy asked. "If you don't feel like coming to the church, I'll be glad to come to your house for a visit and bring anything you need. Just call me"—she pulled a card from her purse and wrote her cell number on the back—"anytime, night or day."

"That's so sweet." Annabelle teared up. "Don't mind me. I cry about everything these days."

"Which is completely normal," Sissy assured her.

"Thank you"—Wesley stood up—"for the offer, and for checking about food. That will help us a lot."

"You are so welcome. See you next week, unless you need me sooner. If you get lonely and just want to talk, please call me."

As soon as they left, Sissy took her phone out and scrolled down to find Luke's number.

"Hey, Sissy! I thought you were in a therapy session with Wes and Annabelle this morning," he answered.

"It got cut short. I need to talk to you. I'm in the nursery," she said.

"Be there in a minute, but are you trying to tell me something? Are we having a baby?" he teased.

"Only if kisses produce them," she said. "Then we might be having quadruplets."

"I always wanted a big family." He sounded like he was already jogging.

Before she could say another word, the door swung open, and he rushed inside, picked her up out of the chair, and swung her around like he'd done when she finally shot a clay pigeon from the sky. "You've made me the happiest man in the world."

"You are crazy," she laughed. "We both know it takes more than kisses to make babies."

He set her down in one of the rocking chairs and fell into the other one, panting like he'd run a mile instead of just from his office.

"Good thing no one is here but us," she said. "The way you're breathing, they'd swear we'd been doing evil stuff right here in the church."

"Is what they might suspect really evil?" he asked.

"Of course not," she answered.

"It's a beautiful thing that God created for a man and woman in love."

"Yes, it is," Sissy agreed, "but let's not talk sex right now. I want to help Annabelle and Wesley. To begin with, they need immediate help, as in food brought in, and I'll ask Gussie to put together a group willing to take casseroles or supper to their house each evening since Annabelle has been home with her feet up. But for long-term aid, I want to do something much bigger, and I need some help figuring out how to do it anonymously."

"What have you got in mind?" Luke asked.

"I'd like to pay their rent up for a few months and give them a gift certificate to the grocery store, and maybe one to the Hen's Nest for an evening out," she said. "I know it's temporary help for now, but maybe we could figure out a way to help them so they wouldn't need financial help anymore later on. I'm hoping that you have ways to do things like that. Am I right?"

"I do." He nodded.

"If they had those two things taken care of, maybe Wesley wouldn't have to work so hard and could enjoy the baby a little more," Sissy said.

"That's a pretty nice thing you're offering,"

Luke said. "I'd like to help with it, too. How about we share the expense?"

"That is so sweet, Luke," she said. "If you can take care of it anonymously, I'll write you a check for whatever my half is. I didn't want to pry, but I don't know what they've got for the new baby. The ladies' auxiliary might be able to put together a little baby shower to surprise Annabelle with at her house."

"I've said it before, and I'll say it again: you are amazing, Sissy." Luke's grin couldn't have been broader. "Blanche would be proud of you, and, honey, she would have been offering the same things if she were still here with us."

"How will you do this?" she asked.

"I have my ways, and this is the season of miracles and magic," Luke answered.

"How soon can you make it all happen?" she asked.

"Is tonight soon enough?" He leaned over and kissed her on the cheek.

Sissy nodded. "You're an awesome man, Luke Beauchamp."

"That's good to know." He tucked a piece of hair behind her ear and stood up. "I've got a meeting with the deacons in ten minutes. As soon as that's over, I will make this happen, and they will never know where it came from, so they won't be able to refuse it. You, Sissy Ducaine, are an angel this day."

"Don't get the halo and wings out just yet," she told him. "Tomorrow you might change your mind and need horns and a pitchfork."

"We've all got two sides. If we were angels all the time, God would take us on to heaven, and personally, I want to stick around a little longer and get to know you a lot better," he said on his way out of the room.

"Same here," she murmured.

She set the rocker in motion with her foot. "Aunt Bee, I hope you're good with the way I just spent some of your money."

Proud of you, darlin' girl. Her aunt popped into her head for just a moment.

The door swung open again, and she looked up, half expecting to see Luke returning, but it was Gussie, and she turned around and yelled, "I found her. She's in the nursery."

Ina Mae hollered back, "I'm on the way."

"What's going on?" Sissy asked.

Gussie sat down in the rocking chair next to her. "Delman passed away about thirty minutes ago."

Ina Mae rushed inside and slumped down in a folding chair.

"Do I need to come help clean up the fellowship hall?" Sissy asked.

"We can still work in there today and tomorrow, and we should have the curtains done by then," Gussie said. "It's a good thing we haven't got all the pageant stuff set up. That wouldn't be right for a funeral, and to tell the truth, I'm not sure I'm up for another one this quick after Blanche's. Me and Ina Mae will probably man the kitchen for the family dinner rather than attending the service."

"I'm sure folks will understand," Sissy said. "I'll help in the kitchen, too."

"Thank you," Ina Mae said, "but that's not why we're here. The big Newton Christmas Parade and Festival is this Saturday. Parade is in the afternoon and then the festival runs all evening, until midnight sometimes."

"Delman and Lizzy, his wife, always ran the crawdad boil booth. That's one of the fundraisers for the missionaries from our church," Gussie said. "We've always helped with it, but we had thought we'd bow out this year and let some of the younger crowd take over."

"I'll help with it. If y'all can cook 'em, I can sell 'em and take the money," Sissy offered.

"It takes at least four people, five is better," Ina Mae told her.

"Then we'll ask Luke and Jimmy and Paul to help us," Sissy said. "That will give us six, and some strong guys to do the heavy lifting."

"I don't know why we didn't think of asking them," Gussie said. "They're supposed to bring us a donkey to paint this afternoon. I'll talk to them about it. We were so rattled this morning that we couldn't think straight, what with the upcoming funeral and now this thing with the festival."

"Speak for yourself," Ina Mae scolded. "I had enough sense about me to tell you there was no way we were asking Elvira to help."

They were still bantering when they left, and Sissy got comfortable in the rocking chair again. With counseling Annabelle and Wes, and now needing to help with the festival and funeral, she was entangling herself in the town of Newton—and it felt pretty good.

She stood up and headed back to the fellowship hall to help with a couple of little cutouts of sheep, but her mind was on the festival. The only regret she had was that she wouldn't be attending it with her aunt.

But you'll have my best friends and Luke, Aunt Bee reminded her.

"And I'll tell you all about it when it's over," Sissy promised, and hoped that she wasn't going crazy, hearing voices and talking back to them.

Chapter Fourteen

Sissy missed Luke.

This was the second day that she hadn't seen him in person, except that time across the sanctuary when he was leaving to go to Delman and Lizzy's house to talk about funeral arrangements. Supporting the family of the deceased was his job, and Sissy admired him for taking care of his responsibilities with so much love and patience.

Now the funeral was over, and the last of the folks were leaving the fellowship hall. She had joined Ina Mae and Gussie in the kitchen and was helping wash empty casserole pans and set them to the side for the owners to pick up. They had reached a lull in their chore when Sissy let out a long sigh.

"Thinking about Blanche?" Gussie asked.

"Now I feel really guilty because I wasn't thinking about her." Sissy sighed again. "Actually, I was thinking about how much I missed being around Luke this week. We've barely seen each other in passing these past few days. He's been so busy with the funeral stuff that he's only texted me a couple of times, and we've only talked on the phone once. I'm a damned therapist, and here I am mooning around like a high school sophomore. Maybe it's a lesson in what it means to be a minister's wife and figuring out if that's what I want in the long run. If it's not, then why even consider a second date?"

"Surely you've missed a boyfriend in past relationships." Ina Mae sat down in one of the folding chairs that were lined up against the wall. "Y'all might as well take advantage of this breather and have a seat."

Gussie sat down and smoothed the front of her bibbed apron. "Do you always go into a relationship with marriage in mind?"

Sissy took the chair between Ina Mae and Gussie and thought about the symbolism even in that simple act. They were both more than forty years older than she was, but somehow, she'd never been as comfortable with anyone as she was with them and her aunt Bee. She had no doubt that they would have her back if anyone said a harsh word about her, and heaven forbid if anyone hurt her.

"Well?" Gussie's tone said she was impatient.

"Sorry, I was thinking about what good friends y'all are to me," Sissy admitted.

Ina Mae laid a hand on her shoulder. "Honey, we're not just friends. We are family whether we share DNA or not."

Gussie patted her on the knee. "You are an old soul, like Blanche was. Lord, I hate putting her in the past tense."

"I always thought of Aunt Bee as a rebel child, not an old soul," Sissy said.

"She was that, too, but she was one of those people who analyzed everything, especially after Walter. That experience changed all of us and yet drew us closer together than we'd ever been," Gussie told her. "Why don't you just enjoy dating Luke and let this play out a little at a time, rather than worrying about where it's going?"

"I'm just not wired like that," Sissy answered. "I don't waste my time and energy on something that has no future. I made that mistake with a guy my freshman year in college and threw away two years of my life. When I go into something, I look ahead five years, ten years, and even twenty and ask myself where this is going to be at that time."

"Did you enjoy the relationship? Did he make you laugh? Do you have good memories from it?" Ina Mae shot questions at her so fast that Sissy's head was spinning.

"Yes, yes, and yes," Sissy finally answered. "But—"

Gussie butted in before she could say another word. "That's where you went wrong. Love and real friendship have no *buts*."

"I can agree with that"—Sissy nodded—"and I was going to say, *but* I never missed that guy. He would go home to Clinton, Oklahoma, for the holidays, and I'd come to Aunt Bee's or else go spend some time on the road with my folks. We talked on the phone and sent texts, but I didn't ache for him or miss him so much."

"Do you think you're missing Luke because he came along and filled the hole that Blanche's passing left in your heart? Maybe when you go back to Beau Bridge in a few weeks, this thing you have with him will fade," Ina Mae suggested.

What was going on here? Sissy wondered. They were supposed to be matchmaking, weren't they, or had she read that wrong? Her training didn't often fail her, but maybe her instincts were off, what with the shock of Aunt Bee's passing so suddenly.

"I was dating a guy when Mama and Daddy were killed. We were apart for more than a week, and I didn't miss him, either, so I don't think that's the problem." Sissy frowned. "But why Luke?"

"The heart wants what the heart wants," Ina Mae told her.

"The heart has no eyes or ears. It only has feeling," Gussie said. "If you listen to it, you'll never get off on the wrong path. Listen to us, chère. We know what we're talking about. We're not just pretty faces."

"Did either of you ever consider being therapists or counselors?" Sissy managed a weak smile.

Gussie shook her head and stood up to go back

to the sink when Elvira brought in two more casserole dishes. "I knew I was going to be a lawyer from the day that we went to the hospital to see Blanche after Walter beat her. I was going to help other women get justice when that happened to them."

"And I knew I was going into the medical field for the same reason," Ina Mae answered as she got to her feet. "Blanche had always said that she wanted to go into hospital administration with a minor in medical business, and she did just that. She wanted to help people, but in a different way than her father did with his ministry. If she had listened to Walter, she would have never fulfilled her dream."

"My husband didn't want me to work outside the home, but I did do some babysitting in my house for many years. And of course, I had my work on the committee to hire or fire preachers." Elvira gave Gussie a long look. "I see another dish has been cleaned out. Delman and Lizzy had a big family. That means a lot of work at the dinner, but I'm not one to complain about helping others." She left the kitchen and returned to the fellowship hall.

"Bless her heart," Ina Mae said. "If there's a crown in heaven for the person on earth who was . . ."

"Was so determined to be a martyr, she'll get it for sure," Gussie finished the sentence for her.

"Hey." Luke poked his head in the door. "I just got a call from Annabelle. She's at the hospital. She and Wes would like for us to be there. It might be hours, but . . ."

"We're about done here," Gussie said. "Go on, and call us when the baby is born. Ina Mae and I have got a surprise baby shower in the works. Guess we'll have it now when she takes the baby home."

Sissy removed her apron. "Thank you. Thank you, for everything."

She dashed across the room to where Luke waited. He took her hand in his and led her to his truck, then opened the door for her.

"Today has been better than the day of Aunt Bee's funeral," she said as she settled into the already warm passenger seat. Luke seemed to think of everything. No wonder everyone loved him.

"I missed you these past days." Luke leaned in and kissed her on the cheek, then closed the door and jogged around the back side of the truck. When he slid in behind the wheel, he reached across the console and ran his hand down her cheek. "I mean it, Sissy. I really missed you, but I had so much to do."

She laid her hand on his. "I've kept busy, but I missed you, too."

"I miss my folks, but this is something deeper, something I've never experienced before," Luke said.

"I know exactly what you mean," she agreed. "It's a whole new experience for me, too."

"Speaking of parents, mine are coming to visit over the Christmas holiday. They'll be here for the Christmas pageant, and then they'll spend a day or two with me," he said. "I can't wait for you to meet them, or better yet, for them to meet you. I would have told you sooner, but they only called me just before the funeral. Dad didn't know if he could get off from his job right here at the holidays, but everything worked out for him."

Sissy expected her stomach to knot up in a pretzel like it had in the past when one of her boyfriends wanted her to meet the parents. She'd always counseled clients that it was a big step, but this was different. Meeting his folks in a church full of people wasn't the same as sitting down to dinner with just the four of them. They would be introduced to so many folks that evening at the potluck that they wouldn't even remember all the names or faces.

"I miss Blanche," Luke went on, "because she was like a grandmother to me. As a therapist, what do you think this dull ache I have when you aren't around means?"

"I can help other folks with their problems, but when it comes to me and you, I'm kind of flying blind. I missed you, too, and it's a whole different feeling than when my folks, my grandparents, or even Aunt Bee was taken from me," she admitted.

Luke removed his hand and backed out of the parking lot. "I'm glad that we can be honest with each other. I hate playing mind games."

"Me too," she said. "If everyone could be honest about their feelings, and then try to work on the problem areas, I would be out of a job. It might be worth it, though. Speaking of therapy, was Annabelle worried or upset? The baby is coming early, isn't it? Bless her heart, she needs someone to support her. I don't understand Wes's folks. He's their child, for God's sake."

"She sounded fine," Luke answered. "She apologized for even calling, but she wanted to see you, and said that you told her after their Monday session that she could call on you anytime."

"Oh, no!" Sissy threw her hand over her mouth. "I left my phone in my purse and it was all the way across the room. If she tried to call, I didn't hear."

"It's all right. She got a hold of me, and we're on the way," Luke said. "Wes is working, and his shift doesn't end until three. Her mother had to leave yesterday because Annabelle's grandmother had a mild heart attack and is in the hospital in Jasper, so she can't be here. And Wes's parents— well, you know the story there. I'm in total agreement with you in not understanding how they can treat him like they have."

"Did you take care of those other things we talked about for them?" she asked.

"I got that finished up, and we'll talk about your half after the baby gets here. I've been too busy to tally up what all we spent. I roughly figured a year's worth of groceries and put that much into an account at the local market for them. We paid a year's rent and gave them two certificates for dinners at the Hen's Nest. I went ahead and prepaid their electric and water bills for six months, too. If you don't want . . ." He drove from the church to the hospital in less than five minutes and snagged a parking spot not far from the front doors.

"No!" She held up both palms. "I'd do it all without splitting the cost with you. I thought of something else. What do you think of sending Wes a scholarship for online classes to continue his education toward being a doctor?"

Luke turned off the engine and unfastened his seat belt. "I like the way you think. For now, let's go have a baby."

Sissy undid her seat belt. "Good thing the gossip vine didn't hear you say that."

Luke chuckled as he got out of the truck and raced around it to help her out. "That rumor mill is going to be the death of me," he said when he opened the door. "The deacons met with me about the way the gossip is spreading through town about us. They're commiserating with me, but then they said that the taint of a bad reputation is as bad as having one, so that I should be very careful."

"Should we stop seeing each other?" she asked.

"No, ma'am." He slipped her hand into his. "I pick my battles, but this one I don't intend to back down from." He led her to the front door and discovered that one of the volunteers at the front desk was a member of his congregation. "Hello, Betty Jane. We're here to see Annabelle McKay. I just need her room number in the maternity ward."

"That would be 214." Betty Jane's lipstick had run into the wrinkles around her mouth, and gray was showing at the roots of her jet-black hair. She gave Sissy a sideways glance that didn't take a rocket scientist to figure out and pointed to her left. "Elevator and stairs are both that way."

"Thank you." Luke smiled. "And thanks for the nice donation you made to the church for the decorations. They're coming along very well with all the help we've had."

Betty Jane smiled, deepening the wrinkles around her mouth. "I heard that Elvira hasn't been back to the ER in a few days. You're doing a good thing, Luke." She gave Sissy another long look. "Just be careful that you don't ruin it. We'd hate to lose you, and even though Elvira has stayed well"—she air quoted the last word—"for a while, we all know that she loves rumors as much as heart attacks."

"I'll be there as long as God needs me. When He doesn't, I expect I'll follow His will for me." Luke grinned. "See you in church tonight?"

"I'll be there." She nodded and then focused on the lady who had stepped up behind Luke and Sissy.

Luke led Sissy toward the elevator and pushed the button to the second floor. Sissy waited until they were inside to say anything, but she couldn't hold it in any longer. "I will not be the cause of you getting fired, and I'm not a bad person. So, what's these people's problem with us seeing each other? We are two grown, responsible adults."

"The sins of the fathers," Luke said. "Everyone in town knows about your parents' choice of lifestyle. That doesn't make it right, but it is what it is. I do *not* intend to let any of them bully me. I like you, Sissy. I missed you a lot these past couple of days, and that tells me there is something important and special between us. I've trusted in God to steer me in the right direction for most of my adult life. If He doesn't want me to preach at this church, or anymore for that matter, then I'll do something else. I've thought about putting in a soup kitchen for the local people, but I just didn't have the time to do that and preach, too."

The elevator stopped, and he stood to the side to let her exit first. They found Annabelle's room and Sissy knocked gently on the door.

"Come on in," Annabelle called out.

Sissy peeked into the room before she threw the door open. "I've got Luke with me."

"I'm decent. Come on in." Annabelle motioned to them with a hand. "They gave me the drugs. I don't feel anything now. Listen to the baby's heartbeat." She pointed to the machine beside her bed. "She's going to be a strong girl, and the doctor says she's measuring about seven pounds. Her lungs are good, and I should be able to take her home, even though she's a little early. I'm so glad you came. Wes has popped in and out when he has break time, and he'll be back soon as he gets off work. Listen to me rattling on and on. Y'all have a seat. I've got so much to tell you, Miz Ducaine. You said I could call . . ."

"Sissy. Just call me Sissy like all my friends do." She slipped her hand out of Luke's and sat down in a rocking chair beside Annabelle's bed.

"I was going to wait and tell you at our session next Monday, but I'm kind of lonely here all by myself. I'm sorry if I interrupted something important," Annabelle said.

"Not one thing. I'm glad to get to sit with you until Wes gets off, or even until the baby girl arrives," Sissy assured her.

"We got a Christmas miracle this week," Annabelle blurted out. "Wes didn't want to accept it at first, but there was no way to give any of it back."

"What kind of miracle?" Sissy hoped that she looked genuinely surprised.

"Our rent has been paid for a year, and we've got a credit at the grocery store that will last for months. After Wes works the shifts for the holidays, he gets to go to day shifts, and guess what, they gave him a week off with pay for paternity leave. We also got a notice from the utility companies that our bills have been paid up for six months there. Do you know what that means?"

"That you and Wes get to spend more time together and enjoy this baby?" Sissy asked.

"Yes!" Annabelle's eyes got all misty. "I can't imagine who did this, but I'm glad I don't know, because Wes is a real stickler about charity cases."

"I would imagine that whoever did it would have told you if they wanted you to know, and they would probably want you to pay it forward someday when you are able to do so," Luke said.

"That's what I'd say, too, as your therapist and as your friend," Sissy told her.

"I like that we're friends," Annabelle said. "Now that Wes has figured out that we have to take the help, it's like a weight is lifted off his shoulders. He's even talking about taking some online courses to finish his first degree. And all this help means I can stay home with the baby for a little while instead of going back to work in a few weeks."

Luke pulled a chair over closer to Sissy and

sat down beside her. "Did you ever think about college or more education?"

Annabelle sighed and nodded at the same time. "I had a scholarship for two full years to study nursing. Wes was going to be a doctor and open up a practice for families, and I was going to be his nurse, but then we got pregnant and everything changed. I needed to work to help support us, and his folks refused to pay for his education."

"There's lots of scholarships out there for folks like you and Wes," Luke said. "I could look into them for you if you'd like."

"For real!" Her big brown eyes widened. "You mean like we could both . . . ?" She stammered, "Yes, please. That's not charity. It's scholarships, right? Wes's folks look down on folks who take charity, and they would . . ." She frowned. "You understand, right?"

"Absolutely," Sissy answered.

Wes popped his head into the door and then came on in. "Hello. Thank y'all for coming to sit with her. She was getting lonely, and we sure appreciate the support. Just another hour until my shift changes, darlin'. Are you okay? Are you hurting?"

"I'm fine," Annabelle said.

Wes crossed the room and kissed her on the forehead. "The nurse just told me you're dilated to four and progressing just fine. There's a pool going among the nurses and orderlies. We're all putting in a dollar and whoever gets closest to the delivery time wins it all. I said five thirty, and if we win, we get ten dollars, so keep that in mind, sweetheart." He brushed her hair back with his hand.

"I told them about our Christmas miracle, and Luke has an idea, Wes." Annabelle wrapped her arms around his neck and kissed him on the mouth. "He knows how to get scholarships for both of us to take online courses."

Wes jerked his head around so fast that a strand of his dark hair fell over his eyes. "Are you serious? When my folks stopped paying for my tuition and books, I was told that even though I had high grades, they made way too much money for me to have financial help."

"You are a married man now, and not a dependent of theirs. There are scholarships out there that are given on grades, not income. Would you mind if I looked into them for you?" Luke asked.

"No, sir!" Wes said. "If I'm only working one day shift five days a week, I could do online classes at night with no problem. I have two years already done, so I just need two more to finish my first degree, and then . . ." He paused. "I'm getting ahead of myself. Just let me know if you need anything from me. My break time is over. I'll be back soon, darlin'." He gave his wife another kiss and hurried out of the room.

Luke pushed up out of his chair and asked, "Can I get either of you something from the vending machine? I need a root beer."

"I would love one," Sissy said, "but whoa! Will it bother you if we have something in front of you, Annabelle?"

"Not one bit," she said. "I've got my ice chips right here."

"Be back soon, then." Luke disappeared out into the hallway.

"What are you going to name the baby?" Sissy asked.

"Since she's coming right here at the holiday season, we thought maybe Holly Belle would be sweet," Annabelle said. "Holly for Christmas and Belle for me, but I do like Atticus. That's what we picked out when we first found out we were pregnant. Of course, we'd call a girl Atty."

"Just so long as the two of you agree on the name and it doesn't become a matter of contention or a regret later on, then you do whatever you want. You are the ones who'll be getting up with her at night, changing a multitude of diapers, and living with her through the terrible twos and then even the more terrible teenage years," Sissy said.

"Thank you for that," Annabelle said. "What's your name? Is it really Sissy?"

"Sissy is just a nickname," she answered. "I'm not even sure where I got it, since I don't have siblings. My real name is Martina Blanche Ducaine. My grandmother on my mother's side was Martina. Blanche was for my aunt Bee, of course, since my daddy loved his big sister."

"Do you like your name?" Annabelle asked.

Sissy raised a shoulder in a semi-shrug when she thought about how different she felt when she was Sissy and when she was Martina. "I didn't ever attend public school or have playdates, so I never really thought about my name. I'm not sure I even noticed it until I went to college and the professors called me by my first name. I was just Sissy. The people I work with and my friends in Beau Bridge call me Martina. I've gotten used to it, but when I come to Newton, I'm Sissy. I like it better. Seems more personal," she answered.

"My granny calls me Annie." Annabelle smiled. "I kind of like it, but Wes says Annabelle sounds like a queen's name, so he tells me that I'm his queen."

"That's really sweet." If anyone could beat the statistics of a teenage marriage lasting, these two might wind up at the top of the list.

Annabelle winced and said, "I'm feeling some pressure."

Sissy got up to go get a nurse, but met Wes and Luke coming back in before she reached the door.

"They said I could take off half an hour early, since I didn't take a lunch break today," Wes said.

"We've been monitoring your contractions

from the desk," the nurse told her. "It looks like it's time to push."

"Already?" Annabelle laid a hand on her belly. "All I feel is a little pressure."

"The drugs are wonderful." The nurse smiled.

"We'll be in the waiting room," Luke said.

Annabelle's expression changed from happy to fearful. "Please stay until she's here, Sissy," she begged. "I want you to see her."

"I'll be right down the hall," Sissy told her. "I want to see her before I go home, but, Wes, if it's time to push, I think you might have lost that ten-dollar pot."

"Gladly, if this can just be over for Annabelle," he said.

Luke escorted Sissy to the empty waiting room and over to two chairs by the window.

"Is this where y'all waited when Aunt Bee had the heart attack?" she asked.

He shook his head. "No, this is the maternity ward waiting room. We were in a different one. This is actually the first time I've been asked to wait for a baby since I've been in Newton. Most of the time, I'm sitting in a place with a family who is waiting for a loved one to take that step from earth into eternity. Usually, they only let one or two at a time into the room to tell the person goodbye."

"Were you here when Aunt Bee died?" Sissy asked.

Luke took her hand in his and rested it on his knee. "She was gone when I got here. The doctors said that the heart attack killed her instantly, and that she felt no pain, but they tried to revive her for several minutes before they sent her on to the funeral home."

"I'm glad she didn't suffer," Sissy said.

"Where were you when you got the news?" Luke asked.

"Alone in my apartment. I threw stuff into my suitcase. The rain and sleet had already started, but that seemed like nothing compared to the black hole in my chest," she answered.

"I'm sorry you had to go through all that all by yourself." He made gentle circles on the back of her hand with his thumb. "You've got friends and family here in Newton, Sissy. You don't have to ever be alone again."

"I've got friends in Beau Bridge," she said, "just a different kind than what I've got here. But thank you," she whispered. "There's something about death, and yet so . . . I can't think of the right word . . . about birth."

"One life ends, and another begins?" Luke asked.

"Yes, that's it in a nutshell," she answered.

"Sometimes God gives us an end so we can have a better beginning," Luke said.

"Are we talking about a new baby being born, or a soup kitchen?" Sissy asked.

"Maybe both," he said. "Would it be rude of me to lean back and catch forty winks while we wait on this baby? I've been up late for the past three nights trying to comfort Lizzy and the family, and I'm so sleepy."

"Not one bit. I'm too excited to sleep, but you can even lean on my shoulder."

"Wake me in half an hour." He leaned over and rested his head on her shoulder.

Perfect fit! Aunt Bee popped into her head for just those two words.

Sissy caught a whiff of the shaving lotion remnants he had slapped on his face that morning. It was different from the kind that her father had worn, but it reminded her of the early mornings when her father would pick her up from the pallet in the storage room of a bar and carry her out to the RV. He smelled like cigarette smoke and whiskey for the most part, but there would still be a little bit of the Stetson he had applied when he and her mother got dressed for the gig.

Sure, she had lived a very different life from most kids, but never once did she doubt that her parents loved her. She shifted her eyes over to a table in the far corner that had children's books scattered over the top. How many big brothers and sisters had read those books, or had them read to them as they waited with aunts, uncles, or grandparents for a new sibling to be born? Sissy had been born in a clinic in Memphis, Tennessee, at eight o'clock in the morning. Her mother and father had played a gig and left the bar six hours before. The next day, her father had taken her mother to the RV, and they had traveled to Hurricane Mills, where they had another gig two days later. Having a baby didn't slow her mama down one bit. Sissy couldn't help but wonder if she would be that strong when she'd had a child.

When, not if, I have a child, and I want more than one. I want my baby to have a sibling. Someone to argue with and stand up for him or her if need be. Life was lonely for me. I want a big family. Besides—she smiled to herself—*if there's only one child, Ina Mae and Gussie will fight over it.*

Wes threw the door open at exactly four o'clock and yelled, "I'm a father. My baby girl is here. You can come to the room and see her in about fifteen minutes."

"What?" Luke's head shot up. "Who? When?"

"The baby is here," Sissy told him. "Evidently, just before four o'clock."

"Is she all right?" He combed his hair with his fingertips.

"Wes looked pretty happy, so I'd say that she's fine," Sissy answered.

Luke covered a yawn with his hand. "When will they have her in the nursery so we can see her?"

"In just a few minutes, only we'll be seeing

her in the room. Nowadays, they put a baby on a mother's chest as soon as they get it cleaned up. They call it skin-on-skin bonding time," she explained.

"How do you know all this?" Luke asked.

"I'm a therapist," she said with a smile. "Did you have a good nap?"

"The best. Your shoulder is the best pillow I've ever slept on. Do you think I could borrow it more often?" he asked.

"Are you flirting with me, Luke Beauchamp?" Sissy raised an eyebrow.

"Yep, I am," Luke said. "Now about borrowing your shoulder?"

"Sorry, if you take the shoulder, you have to take all of me," she answered.

Before he could say anything else, Wes came back to the door and motioned for them to follow him. Still wearing the scrubs he'd worn to work that morning, he led them back to the room and passed out yellow masks.

"For the baby's safety," he said.

Sissy went straight to the bed, where the new baby was lying against Annabelle's bare chest. The two of them were covered with a sheet, but the new baby's sweet little head was visible. She had dark hair and big round eyes, and Sissy hoped that she grew up to be as strong as her mother.

Be strong and do things your way. Don't give a

flip about what other people do or don't do. Your life is yours. You make your own path. Sissy's mother's advice from when she was going off to college came back to her mind.

"Be strong, beautiful baby girl," Sissy said. "Your life is yours. Make your own path," she whispered.

"That's so sweet," Annabelle said.

"That's what my mama told me when I left for college," Sissy said.

"Have you decided on a name?" Luke asked.

"Holly Martina," Annabelle answered.

Luke reached out and touched the baby's hand and she wrapped her tiny fingers around his.

"We decided it sounded like a good strong name that she could grow into." Annabelle beamed.

"Oh. My. Goodness," Sissy said. "That's quite an honor."

"It's for you and for both our mothers. My mama is Tina and Wes's mother is Marsha," Annabelle told her.

"I want a dozen of those," Luke whispered as he looked down on the little dark-haired baby.

"Not me." Annabelle kissed her new baby daughter on the top of the head. "One's enough for a long time."

I'll take that dozen, Sissy thought as she slipped her hand into Luke's.

Chapter Fifteen

Unlike the day of Blanche's funeral, the weather cooperated on the day of the Newton Christmas Festival. Even though a gentle breeze made the lights around the gazebo and the war memorial dance, the temperature was a lovely seventy degrees, and there wasn't a cloud in the sky.

Luke and Sissy watched the parade from their booth set up at the southwest corner of the courthouse square. Starting at a side street, the high school band, dressed in their purple uniforms and playing the high school fight song for the Newton Eagles, led the procession.

"I missed this," Sissy said.

"Parades?" Gussie and Ina Mae left their posts in the crawdad boil booth and went to stand beside Luke and Sissy.

"No, the whole high school thing. Being in the band, or on the debate team, or even having friends that came over in the evenings to experiment with makeup and talk about clothes," Sissy answered.

"It's overrated," Jimmy said from the other side of the booth. "What you just said is a fairy tale. Most kids are insecure whether they're popular or not."

"Oh, I don't know." Paul left his station and stood beside Ina Mae. "I have some good memories of when you and I were in high school."

"So you weren't the popular kids?" Sissy asked.

"Oh, no!" Jimmy chuckled. "We were the nerds who went to church on Sunday and didn't drink on Saturday nights."

Luke draped an arm around Sissy's shoulders. "I kind of envy you getting to travel all over the nation, and not have to clean your room or worry about deadlines on essays."

"For real?" Sissy couldn't believe anyone would want that kind of life.

"Sounds like a simple life," Luke said.

"It was that for sure. When I went to college and had a room all to myself, it was almost scary," Sissy admitted.

"Did you make friends there?" Gussie asked.

"More like acquaintances," Sissy answered. "But like you said, I've got friends and family right here in Newton. Hey, look at that float with Santa Claus on it. Mama used to take me to whatever mall was in the area when Santa was going to be there. I'd sit on his knee and tell him what I wanted."

"And what was that?" Gussie asked.

"The last year before I had to admit there was no real Santa, I asked for a bicycle," Sissy answered just as the bicycle brigade headed down the street. Kids of all ages rode every kind of decorated bike imaginable. There were even a few tricycles with little kids on them and fathers running along beside.

"Did you get one?" Luke asked.

"Yes, and Daddy even bought a rack for the back of the RV so we could take it with us everywhere. Just riding it around in the parks where we stopped was sheer freedom," Sissy answered.

"Hey . . ." She nudged Luke with her shoulder. "Why aren't you on one of the church floats?"

"Because I'm helping with this crawdad boil," he said. "And before you ask about the horses"— he pointed to about twenty horses, all decked out with ribbons braided into their manes and tails—"I don't ride. Do you?"

She shook her head. "Nope, not me. I'm not afraid of them, but if I'm going to ride something, I'd rather have my bike or maybe"—she paused—"a motorcycle."

"You really are kin to Blanche. She told me that if she was younger, or if she could talk Gussie and Ina Mae into getting one, she would buy a Harley," Luke said.

"She tried, but we vetoed that," Gussie said.

"Ah, come on," Jimmy teased, "if I got one with a little sidecar, would you go for a ride with me?"

"Nope." Gussie eyed him. "At best it would mess up my hair, and at the worst, a bug would fly up my nose, and I'd cough myself to death. I

302

don't want my obituary to say that a gnat or a fly killed me, and that I died with windblown hair."

Jimmy chuckled. "Prominent former county judge met her match, not in a hardened criminal, but in a common housefly. How about the Sky Ride over there, will you go on that with me when we get done here? It's enclosed, and I promise to protect you from evil bugs of any kind."

"I might think about that," Gussie agreed, "but first we've got lots of crawdads to boil, so we'd better get back to work. Those police cars coming around the corner signal the end of the parade, and the people will hit this booth fast and furious really soon."

Eight-foot tables had been set up to form a square. Jimmy and Paul manned the back table, where four big pots of hot water and crab boil seasoning were already boiling and ready to drop the crawdads into. Gussie took care of the table where small whole potatoes boiled in seasoned water and corn on the cob cooked in a second pot. Every so often she threw in a handful of crawdads just for flavor. The table facing the street had big flat pans waiting to be filled with cooked crawdads, corn, and potatoes.

"This reminds me of Times Square in New York City," Sissy said as she slipped a bibbed apron over her head and wrapped the strings around her waist, tying them in the front.

"How's that?" Gussie asked.

"Mama and Daddy took me to Times Square when one gig was over. Nobody sleeps in New York City—at least that's what it seemed like to me. So many people milling around in the middle of the night. Our RV was in a parking garage—top level—and I didn't like sleeping there. There was so much noise, sirens going off all night long, and cars coming and going. I was glad we didn't have to go back for another gig right there in the city. I liked the towns where we had an RV park to go to after the bars closed down."

Luke slipped an apron over his head. "Did you see Elmo begging for money on Times Square, trying to make folks pay to take their picture with him?"

"Oh, yeah." Sissy nodded. "He tried to get Mama to take a picture of me with him, but I didn't want to. I'd much rather be right here at this festival than back there."

"Of course you would. Newton is the best-kept secret in the whole world." Jimmy dipped up crawdads, corn, and potatoes into one of the large stainless steel serving pans. "We'll cook 'em. You kids get over there and serve 'em."

"I'll take the money." Ina Mae opened a small cash box and got ready for the rush.

"Jingle bells, jingle bells," Luke sang along with the Christmas music blasting from the courthouse steps as he dipped up crawdads into a paper container and handed it off to Sissy.

She hummed along with him as she added a small ear of corn and a potato and gave it to a teenage customer. "Sauces are right down there by Ina Mae. She'll take your money."

"After this we're going to get tacos," the teenager told his friend.

"Not me," the other kid said. "I'm going to use every dime I've got on crawdads. My mama makes mean tacos, but she hates the smell of fish in the house." They were still arguing about how to spend their money when they moved away.

The line behind them reached all the way to the end of the block, and kept Paul, Jimmy, and Gussie hustling to keep the three large serving pans filled. Sissy had wondered while the parade was going on if they'd have to hawk their wares, maybe yelling that they had crawdads for sale, but not so. The line to get a basket of them seemed to stretch all the way out to the western horizon, where the sun set in a bright-orange ball that put even more sparkles on the ornaments and lights decorating the booths, the Ferris wheel, and all the kiddie rides.

"Our missionaries are going to be very happy," Gussie said.

"I'm happy," Luke said. "This is so much fun. I want to do this every year with all y'all."

"Me too," Sissy said. "And before the night ends, I want to ride on the Ferris wheel."

"It's a date, but they don't call it a Ferris wheel.

It's called a Sky Ride because all the seats are enclosed." Luke nodded toward her as he dipped up another order. "When we run out of crawdads, we'll take in the carnival. I'll even treat you to cotton candy."

"Now that's my idea of a knight in shining armor." She bumped him with her hip. Sissy liked being Sissy for more than a day or two at a time, and more than she ever had liked being Martina.

"Never been called that before, but I'll be glad to own the title. Since I don't have a white horse to sweep you away on, how about we go on the Sky Ride?" Luke asked.

"I haven't been on a Ferris wheel since I was about twelve years old." Sissy noticed the looks passing between all four of the older folks. "I think we should all have a ride on the wheel before we leave tonight. How about it?"

"I'm game," Jimmy said with a wide grin. "How about you, Gussie? Want to take a ride with me? I might even buy you some cotton candy."

She nodded toward the fancy Sky Ride. "We can't let these young'uns get ahead of us. I'd love to take a ride on that thing."

"Ina Mae?" Paul raised an eyebrow. "Are we going to be the only ones on the ground?"

"I'm in," Ina Mae said, "but let's go Dutch. You pay for the ride. I'll buy the cotton candy."

"That could cause Elvira and Janelle both to

306

have real heart attacks," Luke whispered to Sissy.

"Aren't they cute together?" Sissy whispered back.

"Thank you again." He kissed her on the cheek. "I haven't seen those two old guys so full of life in years, and this is just what Gussie and Ina Mae needed."

"Yep, it is." Sissy scooped up the last of the crawdads in her pan and caught a look from the elderly lady who was next in line and giving her the old stink eye. Sissy gave the lady a few extra crawdads from Luke's pan and then whispered for Luke's ears only, "Who was that lady, and why is she giving me a go-to-hell look?"

"That's Nadine," he answered. "She's one of the members of the hiring committee. She and Elvira were against hiring me because I'm single. But like my mama says, what will be will be, and what won't be—well, I'll accept it and move on. But tonight, I'm going to kiss you when we reach the top of the wheel, and we're going to share cotton candy. Nothing is going to spoil that."

At just after nine o'clock, the music from the courthouse steps stopped, and the mayor of Newton stood next to the band with a microphone in his hands. "Good evening, everyone. Has this been a good festival?" he asked.

A few folks yelled. A few more whistled.

"If you're having a good time, remember me on Election Day," he teased, "but for tonight, let's give everyone who made this festival possible a big hand." He started the applause and kept it going for a full minute before he raised his hands to quiet the crowd.

"As you all know, the Christmas Festival Committee gives a cash prize of one hundred dollars to the best decorated house and lawn each year. The second prize is fifty dollars and the third is a dinner for two at the Hen's Nest," he said. "I'm proud of our town for keeping the tradition of the Christmas Festival going. The only years since we began the festival in 1940 that we couldn't have one were during World War II and the Korean War. I know some folks refer to the latter as a conflict, but if our boys fought and died over there, then I'm going to call it a war, just like I refer to what happened in Vietnam as a war."

The noise of another round of applause filled the air. When it died down, the mayor said, "The third prize this year goes to Amos and Lydia Gunter. Y'all come on up here and get this certificate and enjoy your free meal. The second one, for a fifty-dollar bill"—he waved the envelope in the air—"goes to Elvira Jones. She always has a lovely yard whether it's holiday time or not. And the big prize goes to Delores Adams for the Hen's Nest. We know it's not a yard, but it's a highlight of the whole town. Guy Williams has asked all y'all to go to the gazebo so he can take your picture for this week's newspaper. We'll be closing down the carnival and the festival at midnight just in case there's a risk any of our cars might turn into pumpkins. Y'all enjoy the rest of the evening, and thanks again to all of you for supporting Newton, Texas."

"Lord, we'll never hear the end of Elvira's bragging now," Ina Mae groaned.

"Speak of the devil." Gussie nodded toward the folks who were headed toward the gazebo.

"Look at that strut," Ina Mae said. "I swear, she looks like a little banty rooster."

"Or maybe Danny Boy after he's had a shot of vodka," Gussie said.

"That's it, folks." Jimmy dipped up the last of the crawdads into a pan. "When those are sold, we are done."

"Came out about even," Gussie said. "We're out of corn and potatoes, too."

"We've had an amazing night," Ina Mae said. "I'm pretty sure we've broken last year's record."

"Our missionaries will appreciate every bit of it." Luke served a couple more customers. "This should be about enough for half a dozen more and then we will have sold out."

"And it's been so much fun," Sissy declared. "This kind of thing is what you miss if you don't have a home with a foundation."

"Then stick around," Luke said. "Newton could use a therapist, and—"

Before he could finish, Elvira rushed up to the stand and waved her envelope around. "I can't believe I won this. I'm going to spend every bit of it on a new flannel board for my Sunday school classroom."

"That's really sweet of you," Luke said.

Elvira raised her chin a notch. "Gussie, you really should decorate your place a little better. It's right across the street from the square, and it's been declared a historical home."

"There's a tree in the window and a wreath on my door," Gussie said. "That's more than enough to have to take down and store when the holiday is over. You deserve the second-place honor. Maybe next year you'll even get first place if you aren't too sick to decorate."

Sissy bit the inside of her lip to keep from giggling, but the humble insult seemed to blow over the woman's head like a tornado over a chicken coop.

Elvira looked over her shoulder and set her mouth in a firm line. She was about to say something when Myrtle, one of Elvira's cousins who looked enough like her to be a sister, laid a hand on her shoulder. "You deserved first place. It's not right to call the contest Newton's Best-Decorated Homes and give the big prize to a business."

"Maybe they should make two contests next year. One for businesses and one for homes," Jimmy suggested.

"That's right!" Elvira jacked up her chin another half an inch and all the wrinkles in her neck disappeared. "I would have gotten first prize if there had been a division like that."

"At least Delores and her restaurant realize that when you have a business or live on the square"—Myrtle gave Gussie a lengthy, cold glare—"you should make an effort to help make the town pretty."

"Thank you!" Elvira's head bobbed. "I appreciate that so much, Myrtle. Would you like to share a basket of crawdads with me to celebrate my win?"

"I'd love to, and I'll even treat as a congratulations," Myrtle said. "I've been needing to talk to you anyway. Give us two baskets and add an extra corn to both. I do love the flavor when it's cooked in crab boil."

"Yes, ma'am." Sissy dipped up extra in each basket and handed them to the ladies. "Y'all enjoy. Are you going to ride that fancy Ferris wheel before you go home?"

"Oh, Lord, no!" Elvira grabbed her chest with her free hand. "That thing isn't for old folks. It would give me a heart attack for sure."

"Guess we're young folks, then," Jimmy chuckled as he emptied the big pots of water and set the empties in the bed of his truck.

"Lots of crazy things going on tonight." Myrtle paid for the food.

"I agree." Elvira nodded. "Let's take this over to the gazebo. We can watch all the people from there and talk in private."

Gussie wiped down her table and helped Jimmy fold it while Paul took care of three of the others. "There go two peas in a pod," she whispered.

"Not to worry," Jimmy said. "In a week's time they'll be at each other's throats. I've seen it happen more than once."

"Small-town politics." Gussie sighed. "But even with them, I'd take Newton over any other place in Texas."

"She's got a burr in her granny panties, but we don't need to talk about that tonight," Ina Mae added. "Let's finish getting this booth broken down and into Jimmy's truck, so we can catch a ride on the Ferris wheel or Sky Rocket or whatever you kids call it. If it goes around and lets us see the stars, I call it a Ferris wheel."

"Fair enough," Luke said and then leaned over to whisper in Sissy's ear. "What's on your mind?"

She brought his ear down to her mouth and cupped her hand over it. "Whether Jimmy is going to kiss Gussie when they reach the top of the ride."

Luke burst out laughing so hard that not only did the four elderly folks turn around to stare at him, but the people in the booths on either side of theirs looked that way, too.

Evidently, Sissy thought, *preachers are supposed*

312

to be dull as ditchwater all the time as well as celibate.

Luke stepped up to the young man who was taking the money for the Ferris wheel and handed him enough money to cover all six of them. "Y'all can divide up however you want, but I'm sitting with Sissy."

"Welcome to the Sky Ride," the teenage boy said as he opened the door to the bucket and let them get seated and seat belts fastened.

"Could you stop it at the top for a few minutes so we can be up among the stars?" Luke asked before the guy closed the door.

"Be glad to." He nodded.

"That's every bit as romantic as riding up on a white horse and saving the damsel in distress," Sissy said.

Luke pulled her a little closer to his side. "If you're afraid of heights, I'll hold you tight and let you hide your face in my shoulder if you need to. That's what knights do when their ladies are afraid."

"And I thought chivalry was dead," she teased.

The bucket moved up a notch and Luke slipped his arm around Sissy. "Oh, no." He brushed a soft kiss across her cheek. "It will always be alive and kicking in our world."

"I hope so." Sissy snuggled in closer to him. "But those old women over there in the gazebo sure look like they'd like to take your sword and chop your head off with it."

"They're not looking at us, darlin'. The new gossip of the week is about Uncle Jimmy and Paul getting involved with Gussie and Ina Mae."

"Hey! Your uncle could do a lot worse than Gussie. Want me to fix him up with Elvira?" Sissy teased. "He could sit with her at the hospital, or maybe help take down all nine thousand cutout things in her yard."

"He's already had his fill of that job." Luke gave her shoulders a gentle squeeze. "And you've got a bit of a fireball hiding under your angel wings, don't you? I love Gussie and Ina Mae both. And they're all four good for each other, but I don't mind sharing some of this heat from rumors with them." The bucket swayed a little as it moved up another notch so Jimmy and Gussie could get into their places. "Here we go, and I want to talk about the stars and us, not worry about gossip."

"They are beautiful," Sissy said. "Mama and I used to lay outside on a pallet after she and Daddy had finished a gig and tell stories about the stars."

"Like looking at clouds and telling stories about what they're shaped like? When Daddy took me and Mama camping, we would do that," Luke said. "I bet there were nights that we were looking at the same sky and didn't even know it.

Did you ever get lonely being an only child?"

"Yes, definitely," Sissy answered. "I begged for a baby brother or sister but Daddy always said there wasn't room for another body in the RV."

"My folks just said that God evidently only wanted them to have one child, or He would have blessed them with another one," Luke told her. "I used to shake my fist at the sky and tell God that I didn't like Him because He wouldn't let my mama have a dozen kids."

"God wasn't a part of my life when I was a kid," Sissy told him. "I blamed the RV and rock music for the fact that I didn't have siblings until Mama told me that I was a miracle baby. She had been told that she could never have children at all."

"Did you listen to rock music?"

"No," she answered. "To my folks' dismay, I only listened to country music. How about you? Did you only listen to gospel?"

Luke chuckled. "I listened to soft rock and alternative country. I can't imagine growing up without church and gospel music, though," he said.

"I can't imagine growing up in a house without wheels. When I started college and had a room that was as big as the whole RV all to myself, I felt guilty." Sissy lifted her face to the stars. "Just look at all of them, Luke. This is . . ." She stopped and looked right up into his eyes. "There are no words."

"I see beauty beyond the stars right here beside me," he said as he leaned over and kissed her. She smelled like a mixture of crab boil and perfume, and her lips were slightly cold. Luke's senses were reeling when the kiss ended.

"I thought we were waiting until we got to the top," she said.

He nuzzled the inside of her neck. "One for this little stop, one for the next, and when we get to the top, we'll just make out all the way to the bottom."

"You really think that will get you brownie points with the deacons?" she asked.

"I'm." He tipped up her chin again. "Not." He kissed her on the tip of the nose. "One bit." His lips moved to her eyelids, where he brushed soft kisses on both of them. "Worried about." He felt her shiver when he made it to her forehead. "Deacons." His lips barely touched hers, and then he moved back. "God knows what I'm doing, and He hasn't told me to quit." His mouth covered hers in a long, passionate kiss that went on until they reached the top of the Sky Ride.

"Sweet Jesus," she panted.

"I can agree wholeheartedly." Luke winked at her. "Jesus is sweet, and I appreciate him for bringing you into my life, but right now, look at those stars."

Chapter Sixteen

Sissy plopped down in a velvet wingback chair at Gussie's house on Sunday afternoon and sighed so loudly that both the older women stopped what they were doing and rushed over to sit down on the matching sofa in front of her. Everything had moved so fast these past days that she felt discombobulated, as Aunt Bee used to say. Sissy had always loved that word, but seldom got to use it.

"Did you and Luke have a fight?" Ina Mae asked. "Please tell me it isn't so."

Gussie looked like she might cry. "Did you break up? Did he hurt your feelings? Did he say something about all these rumors?"

"Whoa!" Sissy held up a palm. "We didn't fight or even argue, and I know there's rumors, but we thought y'all might take some of the heat off us since you were seen with Jimmy and Paul all evening."

"We would if we could," Ina Mae said. "But it seems like Elvira isn't going to let this alone."

"What's all this gossip going to mean for Luke's job?" Sissy asked.

Gussie got up and started for the kitchen.

"Where is she going?" Sissy asked.

"This requires a shot of whiskey," Ina Mae answered. "It's not pretty, and we're scared that you'll take it the wrong way and run back to Beau Bridge."

"That bad, huh?" After the way cell phones had appeared out of thin air that day when she and Luke had gone to the Hen's Nest for Sunday dinner, Sissy couldn't say that she was a bit surprised.

Gussie returned with three shot glasses and two bottles of whiskey—one of Jim Beam and one of Jack Daniel's. She poured each one and passed them around. "Take a sip so what we have to say won't be so bitter in your mouth."

Sissy took a sip and felt the warmth of Jack Daniel's slide all the way to her stomach. "I can't drink a lot because I'm supposed to sit with Luke in the middle of the church tonight when the kids have their dress rehearsal for the program on Wednesday. Can't you just see the deacons and Elvira if I arrived with whiskey on my breath? They might just shoot me on the spot."

"No one"—Ina Mae's expression went dead serious—"is ever going to hurt you, neither physically nor your feelings. Gussie and I will take care of them if they do."

Sissy took another sip. "Are you stalling?"

"I promised Gussie that I would keep my mouth shut about the gossip and about other things. This is, after all, the holiday season, and we should be happy, not dwell on rumors and the past," Ina Mae said.

"Does it have to do with Luke's parents? They're coming tomorrow and will be here a few days. I got to admit that I'm scared to meet them."

"Becky and Tom are good people," Ina Mae said. "You don't have anything to worry about from them, and this is just rumors so . . ."

"So, where there's smoke, there's often fire," Sissy said. "My mind will probably worry a mole hill into a real mountain if you don't tell me what you know."

"Okay, but, Gussie, you can't be mad at me," Ina Mae said. "You might not know it, Sissy, but she and Blanche were both a handful when they were angry."

"Is, not were, where I'm concerned," Gussie said, "but the cat is out of the bag, so we might as well tell her what's being said."

"Elvira is stirring up trouble, and now she has Nadine and Myrtle both on her side. In her way of thinking, a preacher should be married, settled, and a couple of kids wouldn't hurt before he's given a church. How he's supposed to do that without dating is a mystery."

"They all think that you and Luke shouldn't be showing affection in public." Gussie sighed. "They're all in a tizz because he kissed you on the Sky Ride last night."

319

"Maybe she'd be happier if you just took things to the bedroom and tangled up the sheets," Ina Mae grumbled.

"Pull down the blinds if you do," Gussie teased.

Sissy giggled at the visual that brought about and blushed at the same time. "Luke and I've talked about this. He says that we don't hide things from God, so why hide them from people?"

"Amen!" Gussie said. "But there's more. The deacons seem to think that kisses and hand holding before marriage is just as bad as having wild, passionate sex. I could tell them a thing or two."

Ina Mae pursed her lips tightly together. "Sex is way better, and yes, I'm speaking from experience."

Sissy's smile faded. "I will not be the reason that Luke has to quit the ministry or move to another town. He loves what he's doing. As much as I like him, I don't want him to resent me for being the one to destroy his life."

"What are you going to do?" Gussie asked.

"I want to spend Christmas with y'all, and all these petty people aren't going to run me off. But after the holidays, I'm going home to Beau Bridge for a few days. I need to make a decision about where I'm going to live and what I'm going to do if I decide to move here permanently." Sissy had made up her mind, and as much as she loved Ina Mae and Gussie, they weren't going to change it.

"Luke is a grown man. I don't think he would ever resent you," Ina Mae said.

"Don't let a bunch of small-town rumors run you off," Gussie said.

"I won't." Sissy downed the rest of her whiskey. "I promise I'll make my decision based on what my own heart wants, not the spitefulness of a bunch of gossips."

Gussie poured herself another drink and threw it back. "Are you leaning one way or the other right now? We don't want to influence you, but we can't imagine not having you close to us all the time, not just on weekends."

"You know that in Beau Bridge, I'm Martina or Ms. Ducaine. Here I'm Sissy," she answered.

"What's that got to do with anything?" Gussie asked.

"Since spending time here . . ." She paused. "Everyone has two sides or maybe even more. One side they show to the public. One they keep inside for the closest of friends, and sometimes a third side that is only for themselves. Martina Ducaine is an independent, well-respected, and well-educated woman, and I worked hard for that. But I keep asking myself if that's all I want to be, or do I want to be Sissy, who's a bit of a free bird like her parents?"

"Can't you be both?" Ina Mae asked.

"Maybe . . . ," she sighed. "But I'm not sure I know how to be both in one place. If I come back here, do I want to put in a therapy clinic, or just do pro bono work for people who need help? There's a lot of decisions to make, and I really need a little alone time. That's why I'm going back to Beau Bridge for a few days."

"I understand," Ina Mae said. "And there's one more thing we need to talk about. Gussie and I have decided that you should know about Walter."

Sissy wondered what he had to do with making up her mind to either stay in Newton or just use Aunt Bee's place. Was he buried under her future weekend getaway? "What"—she frowned—"has Walter got to do with me and Luke's job?"

"Not one thing, but me and Gussie don't want to think about you being gone, and we want to tell you that story, so you'll understand how much you mean to us," Ina Mae said. "We've never shared it with another human being, not even Blanche, and we want you to understand just how much we mean it when we say that no one better ever hurt you."

Sissy's therapist mind went into overdrive. They shared every little detail of everything with each other, so why would they leave Blanche out of the story about Walter? Were they going to need legal help dealing with something that had happened more than fifty years ago? So many questions and not a single answer that made sense other than the fact these two old women had taken care of the person who had hurt her aunt Bee.

"We shared everything with each other," Ina Mae said, "but she wasn't strong enough to know about Walter, not when it happened. And then when she was, too much time had passed to bring up his name." Ina Mae turned toward Gussie. "Get out your purse and give Sissy some money so that she's your therapist and what we're going to tell her is confidential. I gave her a dollar and eleven cents because that's what I had in my pocket."

Gussie whipped a five-dollar bill from her pocket and laid it on the coffee table. "I was going to put this in the offering plate this morning, but I was mad at Elvira and just passed it on without giving anything to the church."

"Why? God didn't cause Elvira to be the way she is, and He probably wouldn't even condone her attitude," Sissy said.

"It's not hers I was worried about," Gussie said. "It was mine. Why give anything to the church when I was so angry? God loves a cheerful giver, not a hateful one. Is what we say now confidential?"

"Yes, it is." Sissy bit back a smile. "But you don't have to give me money. In order for what we talk about to be classified by law, there would have to be papers signed, and we'd have to discuss each part of our relationship."

"Sounds like a marriage to me." Gussie picked up the money and put it back in her purse. "For it to be recognized as a relationship, there's paperwork and a courthouse involved."

"I'm not taking back my money," Ina Mae said. "I'm going to pretend it buys me immunity."

"We kind of got to talking about Walter when Elvira put you and Luke down," Ina Mae explained. "Walter is, or rather was, her cousin. His mama and Elvira's were second or third cousins. We never can figure out all the connections, but they were kinfolks."

"She told me that he was her relative when we were working on the Christmas decorations." Sissy wondered if they had really killed Walter. Ina Mae had said Walter *was her cousin,* and maybe she hadn't been teasing about immunity but meant it. Sissy began to try to figure out just how much trouble she would be in if she didn't report a murder.

"After he abused Blanche," Gussie started and then poured herself a third shot, "me and Ina Mae expected her daddy to, at least, have a face-off with Walter and threaten him or tell him what he thought of him. But your grandfather asked Blanche what she'd done wrong to upset her husband, and when she told him, he gave her a lecture about being a submissive wife and letting

324

Walter be the boss of the family. In his opinion, married women had a duty to their husband and home and shouldn't think about going to college."

When Gussie picked up her drink, Ina Mae said, "The sheriff had put him in jail, and your grandfather paid his bail and told everyone that Walter had become his son when he married Blanche. He even said that he would counsel with them to keep them together."

"Holy crap! Did Aunt Bee know about that?" Sissy asked.

"She did." Ina Mae nodded. "That's why she refused to go live with her folks anymore. She stayed in her own house, and either me or Gussie or both of us stayed with her. Then we all three went to college together, and she stored what we didn't need in the Sunshine Clubhouse."

"Did Walter go to prison after he faced the judge? Wasn't that your father, Gussie?" Sissy understood a little more of why there was so much tension in her grandparents' house when her folks took her to visit them. That poor family—every one of them, including her father—had needed counseling.

"My daddy never heard the case or passed judgment," Gussie answered.

"Walter went to the hospital down in Jasper," Ina Mae said through clenched teeth. No doubt about it—she still carried a big grudge toward the man.

"Remember us telling you about the boys who were our childhood friends building a clubhouse and not letting us be a part of it?" Ina Mae asked.

Sissy's brows knit into a single line. "They put 'No Girls Allowed' on the door, right? That's why y'all started the Sunshine Club."

"That's right," Gussie said, "but they bragged that they had a pair of brass knuckles in the clubhouse that they stole from one of their fathers, and that they kept a bat in there, just in case a girl thought she was brave enough to come through the door."

Sissy's mouth went dry. "You killed Walter?"

"Not quite," Gussie answered. "But we borrowed those knuckles and that bat to even out the fact that he was bigger than us. I put them back when we were done with them. The boys had forsaken that old shack when they found out how much fun chasing girls and drinking booze was, so nobody ever missed them, and as luck would have it, their clubhouse burned down the next week."

"Did y'all do that?" Sissy asked.

"Yep." Ina Mae nodded.

"We figured that would get rid of any evidence, and we were right," Gussie went on. "Soon as Blanche's daddy bailed him out of jail, he went to Dusty Green's bar. We waited for him to come out and told him that Blanche wanted to see him."

"He was drunk and cussing her for putting him in jail," Ina Mae said.

"We put him in my car and took him to the woods. When we got done making him look as bad as Blanche did, we drove him to the hospital in Jasper and we tossed him out at the emergency room doors," Gussie said. "I still don't feel guilty about any of it other than not telling Blanche, but it does feel good to tell you."

"He never brought charges against either or both of you?" Sissy breathed a sigh of relief that she didn't have to cover up a murder, but how in the hell had someone like Walter let them get away with that?

"Think about it, chère," Gussie said. "He was the hero of Newton, gone off to war and came home wounded. Was he going to tell anyone that *two girls* beat the crap out of him?"

"Where did he go when he left the hospital? Elvira mentioned that he had died." *Thank God they didn't kill him,* Sissy thought.

"He moved to California and married a woman out there," Gussie said. "He died about five years ago from liver problems. Guess he drank too much."

"Thank you for taking me into your confidence," Sissy said, "and for being a family."

"Hmmph," Ina Mae snorted. "I don't believe that DNA stuff makes families. The heart is what makes folks kin to each other."

"Amen!" Sissy raised her empty glass in a toast. "What did Aunt Bee say when she found out he was dead?"

"Blanche said that she had buried that part of her life years ago, and that whether he lived or died made no difference to her," Gussie answered.

Ina Mae picked up the remote and turned on the television. "Enough about all that. Let's watch something funny and get that taste out of our mouths."

Get the memory out of your heads is more like it. Too many times to count, Sissy had seen and helped people through abuse in her counseling. She'd seen victims who never got over it, and others who had come out stronger on the other side. Evidently, Aunt Bee had been one of the latter group, and her therapy had been in Sunday meetings at the Sunshine Club.

A rerun of *The Golden Girls* was on television, and Sissy realized that the dynamics between those women were exactly what she had seen in the members of the Sunshine Club. Ina Mae was tall and gray haired like Dorothy. Her aunt Bee had worn her hair short and had a somewhat perfectionistic attitude like the character Blanche. That left Rose and Sophia. Gussie was neither, but more a mixture of a smart-mouthed woman like Dorothy and a southern belle like Blanche.

"I love this show. I want to grow up and be just

328

like Sophia." Gussie poured herself one more drink.

"I always thought you were more like Blanche, the character in the show, not our best friend," Ina Mae said. "All southern sass, and when we were younger . . ."

Gussie leaned forward and shot a dirty look past Sissy. "That'll be enough of that. Who says I'm too old to do what I did when I was younger?"

"Jimmy and Gussie sittin' in a tree," Ina Mae started.

Gussie shook a finger at Ina Mae. "Enough of that, too, or I'll start telling your secrets. Blanche took a lot to the grave with her, but there's enough left in my head to scorch the paper off these walls if I start talking."

"Did the writers for *The Golden Girls* interview y'all?" Sissy joked. "If this show had been rebooted, they could have used you three women, and called it *The Sunshine Club*."

"No, but if they had, the show would have been even better," Gussie replied.

"I have no doubt about that," Sissy agreed.

Chapter Seventeen

Sissy popped her hands on her hips after throwing another sweater on the bed. She had tried on everything in her closet and was digging through Aunt Bee's things on Wednesday evening when her phone pinged. A pile of red and green Christmas sweaters had reached an unstable height on Aunt Bee's four-poster bed. Her phone pinged again, and she searched the dresser, the nightstand, and even the floor but couldn't find it; then she remembered tossing it on the bed when she started trying on sweaters. She moved the pile to the other end of the bed, and sure enough there was her cell phone with a message from Luke: **My folks have arrived. Program starts in 30 minutes.**

Her thumbs were a blur as she typed: **Be there in twenty.**

"No pressure at all," she muttered as she tossed the phone to the side and stared at her reflection in the round mirror above an antique vanity. Trying on so many sweaters had caused her hair to fly out like she'd stuck her finger in a hot light socket. She had decided on a pair of black slacks, but suddenly they didn't look dressy enough, and none of the sweaters appealed to her.

With a long sigh, she went back to her bedroom,

dragged out the black dress she had worn to Aunt Bee's funeral, and slipped it over her head.

"This is what I get for not going home to Beau Bridge for more clothes or not shopping right here in Newton," she said as she picked up the hair spray and tamed her hair. Since she was short on time, she pulled it all back into a bun at the nape of her neck. "I look like I'm on the way to your funeral again, Aunt Bee, not a Christmas pageant."

Wear my emeralds or the rubies, Aunt Bee whispered.

Sissy had forgotten about Aunt Bee's jewelry, but she did remember that the jewelry box with her better things was kept in the gun safe downstairs. She picked up her high-heeled shoes and took the steps two at a time.

"Vodka!" Danny Boy screeched and then began to whistle "One Day at a Time."

"That's an oxymoron if I've ever heard one. Whistling a hymn and begging for vodka. You could have been kept in a politician's house instead of a bar with that attitude. You'll have to wait until I get home this evening for your drink." Sissy poked the buttons to open the safe, turned the handle, and nothing happened. "Dammit!" she fussed.

"Dammit, Ina Mae and Gussie!" Danny Boy said in Aunt Bee's voice, and began to whistle "Turn Out the Lights."

"That won't work, either, but it could be lights out for good if Luke's parents hate me." Sissy tried again and this time the safe opened. She took out the jewelry box and pulled out a strand of emeralds set in gold.

She held it up to her neck and checked her reflection in the tiny mirror on the hall tree. "This is a bit too much for a church pageant."

The next thing she picked up was a ruby teardrop hanging from a white gold chain.

"I like this one better." She quickly fastened it around her neck and then saw the matching earrings. "Thank you, Aunt Bee."

Now, go get my red-and-green plaid shawl. It's in the closet under the stairwell. You loved it when you were a little girl.

"I'd forgotten all about it." Sissy put the earrings on and returned the box to the safe. Then she found the shawl, slipped it around her shoulders, and put on her high-heeled shoes.

Finding a parking spot when she reached the church took longer than the short drive from Aunt Bee's house, but when she was circling the lot for the third time, she noticed someone waving at her in the rearview mirror. She braked, came to a stop, and realized that Luke was motioning for her to go around to the back of the church.

She followed his instructions, and he guided her into a space right beside his truck, then ran over and opened the door for her. The moment she stepped out, he wrapped her up in his arms and hugged her tightly. "I can't wait until this holiday is over so we can spend more time together without so many people around us."

"Me too," she said.

He tucked a fist under her chin and kissed her. "That will hold me until later."

"I need one more since I'm going to meet your folks." She brought his lips to hers for a second kiss.

Her heart thumped and her pulse raced as she took a step back, and he looped her arm into his. "We've got about five minutes to get you seated. Gussie and Ina Mae have saved you a place. My folks are sitting with them, and by the way, you look stunning tonight."

"Thank you. You clean up pretty good yourself." She was almost thirty years old and had met guys' parents before, so why was she suddenly so nervous?

"Awww, shucks!" Luke drawled. "I'm just a country preacher. It's the suit that makes me look a little better."

"I've seen lots of men in suits, so I disagree." Sissy blinked when he opened the side door into the church. Bright lights seemed to be everywhere— on the Christmas tree in the far corner, wrapped around the flowerpots of the three poinsettias decorating the altar, and even hanging from the red curtain backdrop. This pageant was certainly going to outshine the one on the video that Luke had brought to the house.

The low buzz of conversation had filled the sanctuary when Sissy and Luke first walked in, but now even the little kids seemed to be frozen in a soundless time warp that reminded Sissy of a still from a movie. Luke walked with her down the center aisle and seated her at the end of a pew beside Gussie, then went to stand behind the lectern.

"Welcome to our Christmas program this evening." He leaned into the microphone, but he kept his eyes on Sissy. "I'd especially like to thank my folks for driving down from Coushatta, Louisiana, this evening. Those of you who haven't met them, please take time to say hello at the reception in the fellowship hall when our program is finished. We've had a lot of help with this program, and I want to thank each person who donated materials, time, and effort for our pageant this year. I believe it just may be the best one ever. Now, I'll turn this over to Elvira Jones, who is in charge of the first part of the program, and I'm going to sit with all y'all in the audience and enjoy the evening."

"Make room," Gussie whispered as she scooted down closer to Ina Mae.

Sissy slid down as far as she could so that Luke could squeeze into the corner of the pew beside her. He draped an arm across the back of the pew, rested his hand on her shoulder, and whispered in her ear, "I think this year's video is going to outdo last year's by a country mile."

"Let's hope so." Sissy tried to concentrate on Elvira's little Sunday school class singing about Rudolph, but it wasn't easy with her entire side pressed up against Luke's. The children kept messing with the red noses that Elvira had put on them. One little boy stopped and scratched his butt, and the little girl beside him slapped his hand and shook her head without missing a single word of the song.

Sissy had to give credit where it was due. The children—boys and girls alike—were dressed in jeans and white shirts. Elvira had either made or bought red velvet vests for each of them, and they were all wearing cute little Santa hats with jingle bells sewn around the edges for the second song. There was no class distinction that way. Rich, poor, or somewhere in between, the kids all looked alike. The old girl might be a gossip and a busybody, among other things, but she had done a good thing.

"I'm glad Elvira's back is turned to face the kids in her Sunday school class," Gussie whispered. "She'd have a fake heart attack for sure if she could see you practically sitting in Luke's lap."

"Probably so, but if she's talking about me and Luke, she's leaving you and Jimmy alone," Sissy teased.

"Amen to that." Gussie giggled under her breath and led the applause when the second song had finished.

When her part of the program was over, Elvira introduced the next group, gave Luke a lengthy glare, and then sat down like a queen bee on the deacon's bench facing the congregation. In Sissy's opinion, everyone wore many hats. Gussie had been a lawyer and judge. She was a member of the Sunshine Club, a fantastic friend, one of the pillars of Newton, and among all that she was a surrogate aunt to Sissy. Ina Mae had been a nurse and a physician's assistant, and wrangled as many hats as Gussie did.

Now, Elvira? she thought.

Some folks can't be fixed. You know that from your job, Aunt Bee reminded her.

Luke leaned over and said in a low voice, "That little girl on the end of the row was my favorite. She reminded me of you with those big eyes and that light-red hair."

Sissy's therapist hat was gone in a split second, and she forgot all about Elvira and everyone else in the church when she watched the little girl skip down the center aisle to sit with her parents. Sissy wondered what it would have been like to have had parents like that. Her mother and father had loved her. She had no doubts about that, but instead of participating in a church Christmas program when she was kindergarten age, she had been curled up on a pallet with a stack of books in the storage room of whatever bar her folks were playing a gig in that night.

A teenage boy pulled back the curtain to reveal an older group of kids, maybe up to age eleven. The church pianist played the prelude to "Silent Night."

Sissy had watched all this in the dress rehearsal, but tonight it seemed as if the whole program had been sprinkled with magic dust. The kids were on their best behavior, and it was coming together like clockwork.

"Elvira is not happy," Sissy whispered to Gussie.

Luke must have heard her, because he leaned over and said, "Don't let her or anyone else destroy the pure joy of this program."

"What Luke said," Gussie said out the side of her mouth.

If they can do that, then I can, too, Sissy thought and leaned over closer to him and brushed a soft kiss across his cheek. "Thank you," she said.

Of the group of them, Luke was really good at wearing whatever hat he needed for the time at hand. Sissy had never known or counseled with anyone who had such a positive outlook on life as Luke did. That came from growing up in a functional family that sure didn't need counseling. Sissy had rarely seen those kinds of folks in today's crazy world.

Luke gave her shoulder a gentle squeeze, and

Sissy closed everyone and everything out of her mind as she watched the rest of the program. Seeing the magic of Christmas with Luke and through his eyes made every song and every reading even more special.

When the last carol had been sung, the last reading was finished, and everyone had been invited to go see Santa Claus in the fellowship hall, Gussie nudged Sissy. "We done good. This program outshines that poor pitiful one that we saw in the video."

"I agree," Sissy said.

"I'm so glad you're here with us, and, chère, don't let anything Elvira says or does ruin your evening with Luke."

"Meeting Luke's folks is scarier than Elvira," Sissy said out the side of her mouth.

"Don't worry about that. Just be yourself. You do look gorgeous tonight." Gussie stood up with a slight groan. "Knees aren't what they used to be, but I refuse to get old. Blanche would be glad that you're wearing her rubies. She always said that jewelry was made to show off, not lay in a box collecting dust."

Sissy felt a slight touch on her arm and looked up to see Luke with a hand extended to help her up. She put her hand in his and had just made it to a standing position when a tall woman and even taller man stopped right in front of them. The man stuck out his hand and said, "I'm Tom,

Luke's father, and this is his mother, Becky. Luke has told us all about you, and we're glad to meet you."

As Sissy shook hands with him, she felt like she had known the man for a long time. *Transference of a kind,* she told herself. *I know his son, and he looks like Luke will thirty years down the road.* "It's my pleasure. I can sure tell that you're Luke's father."

"Except for the eyes. He got my blue eyes." Becky stepped up to embrace Sissy in a tight hug. "I like hugs, not handshakes."

"Yes, ma'am. Me too." Sissy hugged her back and then stepped away.

"See, I told you so," Gussie said in a low voice right behind Sissy.

Becky looped her arm in Sissy's and started down the aisle. Sissy could hear Gussie and Ina Mae rustle as they followed behind. "You and I don't have a lot of time to get to know each other while we're here, but we're having our traditional Christmas dinner tomorrow at the parsonage, and we'd love for you to join us. Ham and all the trimmings."

"But tomorrow is just the twenty-third," Sissy said.

"Yes, it is," Becky answered, "but we've always volunteered at the soup kitchen in Shreveport on Christmas Eve and Christmas Day. We started doing that when Luke was just a baby. It was our way of giving back since God had given us a child. We had tried for seven years before Luke came along."

That explains a lot, Sissy thought.

"We also have a tradition," Gussie said. "We always have our big meal on Christmas Eve at Blanche's place, but we wouldn't mind pushing it ahead a day. Ham and all the trimmings for us, too. Why don't we all meet up there in the morning and fix the meal together? We can plan the menu while Santa Claus is giving out treats and gifts to the kids."

"I would love that," Becky said. "Luke has so little in the way of pots and pans and decent dishes to work with. He's never been materialistic, but he could invest in a decent pan to cook a ham in. I hate using all disposable stuff, but . . ." She shrugged.

When they were in the fellowship hall, Becky gave Sissy another hug and said, "It looks like we will have most of tomorrow to visit as we cook dinner. That will be so much fun, but right now, there are some folks I need to say hello to, so excuse me, please."

"How about we all gather at nine in the morning for coffee and doughnuts?" Gussie chimed in from a few feet away.

"That sounds wonderful," Becky said. "Is it all right if I invite Jimmy?"

"Yes, of course, and we'll tell Paul Landry to

join us, too. That'll make eight around the table," Ina Mae answered.

"Paul is a good friend of ours, too, so thanks for thinking of him," Becky said and crossed the room to where Tom and Luke were deep in conversation.

Sissy looked around the room. "Where is Jimmy?"

"Getting his Santa Claus suit on," Gussie said. "He'll arrive with a big 'Ho-ho-ho' in a few minutes and give out sacks of candy and presents to all the children."

Ina Mae pointed over to a corner, where a wingback chair waited. Presents wrapped up in red and green paper were stacked under the tree, and paper sacks with candy canes attached to the outside waited on a nearby table.

"What is all that?" Sissy asked.

"Each year, the Sunshine Club donates a stuffed animal to each of the kids. The gift shop wraps them for us. Red for boys. Green for girls. But no one else knows where they come from, so shhhh . . ." Ina Mae put a finger over her lips. "Blanche came up with the idea years and years ago, and I know she'd be proud that we're carrying it on."

"That's pretty awesome," Sissy said, but her eyes were on Luke, who was crossing the floor toward them.

"I hear we're having dinner at your house."

When he reached her side, he slipped an arm around her waist. "Thank you so much. Mama gripes because I don't have decent things to cook with, and besides, it'll be fun with all of us around the table. Oh, and my folks think you're beautiful, and Mama says she can tell that you are an old soul just from talking to you those few minutes."

Sissy felt the blush creeping into her cheeks and tried to curtail it, but she couldn't.

"Of course they do," Ina Mae chuckled. "They're not blind. Let's have some cookies and hot chocolate while we wait on Santa Claus to get here." She took Gussie by the arm and pulled her over toward the refreshment table, leaving Luke and Sissy alone in the kitchen.

"Why don't we step outside for a breath of fresh air." Luke removed his hand from Sissy's waist and led her out the kitchen door. "I wanted to ask if it would be all right with you if I ask Uncle Jimmy to bring his skeet-shooting equipment tomorrow. That would give us guys something to do while you ladies cook dinner."

"Of course," Sissy said, "but you didn't have to ask."

"Yes, I did. I would never want you to think I take you, your house, or even your cussin' bird for granted, Sissy. You mean too much to me for that to ever happen." He took her in his arms and held her close. "Just hugging you and feeling your heart beating in unison with mine feels so right."

Are you for real or is this a line? Sissy thought for a split second, and then his lips were on hers and she forgot about everything else.

Chapter Eighteen

Sissy had just put on a pot of coffee and fed the birds when she heard the noise of a car out on the gravel driveway. She hurriedly checked the time on her phone—seven a.m.—and ran to the living room window to see who was arriving two full hours early.

"Thank God!" She didn't even know she was holding her breath until she let out a loud whoosh of air. She rushed to the door and threw it open for Ina Mae, who was carrying two large brown bags of groceries into the house.

"You look like crap, girl." Ina Mae went straight to the kitchen. "Gussie will be here with the doughnuts in a few minutes. We wanted time to get a little brunch set up before the rest get here."

"Bless your hearts." Sissy ignored the comment about her looks because it was the gospel truth. She'd seen her reflection in the mirror that morning as she brushed her teeth. "I thought maybe Luke's folks were arriving early, and I'm not nearly ready for them. What's the news today about me and Luke, or better yet about Jimmy and Gussie?"

Gussie came in the front door with a sack of groceries in one arm and a box of doughnuts in the other.

"Sorry to tell you, but you and Luke take top billing these days. You left the reception and went outside, and your lips were bee stung when you came back in, and Luke had lipstick on his face. I'm just glad you both were dressed, or Elvira would have had you going to the drugstore for a pregnancy test." Ina Mae began to unload the food from the bag. "No matter the outcome, if Luke's zipper had been down, or his shirttail untucked, they would have tarred you with hot chocolate and feathered you with cookie crumbs and rode the both of you out of town in Santa's sleigh."

Sissy poured two cups of coffee and handed one to Ina Mae. "You are so funny, Ina Mae. You should have been a comedian instead of a physician's assistant. But in all seriousness, the deacons are going to fire him, aren't they?" Her hands trembled, and she spilled coffee on the cabinet. Her chest tightened at the thought.

Gussie grabbed a paper towel and wiped it up. "Stop worrying, chère. Everything always works out for the best."

Sissy thought of a dozen or more instances in her profession when things had not worked out for the best—times when she couldn't help her client work through their issues and how she had felt like a failure. She had to remember to take a breath.

"If Elvira has her way, they will fire Luke,

or rather, since his contract is up at the end of this year, they will simply not rehire him." Ina Mae removed cheese, eggs, and bacon from a bag and set it all on the cabinet. "But while she's spreading love with the little children and breathing fire about you and Luke at the same time, she's not in the emergency room begging for a stroke or a heart attack, so all is well."

"What's all that for?" Sissy took a sip of her coffee.

Ina Mae reached into the cabinet and took down a big bowl and a casserole dish. "I make a mean breakfast omelet. We thought we'd serve that and hot biscuits along with the doughnuts for brunch."

"Good coffee," Gussie said as she brought out a skillet and began chopping the bacon into small pieces. "Blanche must've taught you how to make it. She always said anything that didn't melt the silver off a spoon was just murdered water."

"Yes, she did, but I think you're trying to avoid telling me more about the deacons," Sissy said.

"I heard that Elvira is spreading rumors that the committee will probably be looking for a new preacher by the first of the year," Ina Mae said. "I thought maybe Jimmy could step up until they found a new one, if worse comes to worst, but she doesn't like the fact that he and Paul have been hanging around with us. I guess the three of us are just a bunch of horrible women. But hey, it's kind of nice to know that I'm not over the hill, and God only knows that I'm in excellent company."

That settled it for sure. Sissy was definitely going home to Beau Bridge come Christmas evening. She needed time away from all the gossip, and Luke needed time away from her.

"Thanks for being honest with me," Sissy said.

"Friends are always honest, even if it hurts for a little while, but, honey, you just remember that me and Gussie have three sharpened shovels in the pantry at the Sunshine Clubhouse. We might be honest, but we'll help you bury a body if we need to," Ina Mae assured her. "Now, you best get on upstairs and make yourself presentable. I'm going to get my casserole ready for the oven and open up a couple of cans of biscuits."

"Yes, ma'am." Sissy managed a grin, but she already missed Luke as she climbed the stairs. She didn't want to leave this wonderful house and go back to her small apartment. Not even the thought of saying goodbye to the pesky birds seemed like a good thing, and she needed to ask Ina Mae and Gussie if they would mind the birds for a few days. Once in her room, she dragged out her suitcase and set it by the bed. She'd start packing that evening when everyone went home. No use in putting it off, and if she had things ready to go after she had spent Christmas with

Gussie and Ina Mae, it would make things easier.

She pulled on a pair of skinny jeans and topped them with a red shirt—after all, this was Christmas. One look in the mirror told her that she'd have to tuck all her hair up into a messy bun because she sure didn't have time to do anything else with it.

"Holy crap on a cracker!" she muttered as she realized that she would be having dinner, and a holiday meal at that, with Luke's parents. She should be dressed for that in something fancier than jeans and a shirt. Maybe she should plan an outfit change before they sat down to dinner.

"Too late to worry about all that now," Sissy said as she whipped her hair up, sprayed a touch of perfume onto her wrists and rubbed them together like Aunt Bee had taught her to do, and raced downstairs in her bare feet.

The aroma of bacon and coffee mixed together floated across the hallway as she made her way to the kitchen. Through the window in the back door, she could see Jimmy and Paul setting up the skeet equipment in the backyard.

This was the life Sissy wanted. Friends, family, and possibly even future family if things kept going so well, all around her. She wrapped her arms around herself in a tight hug. If only Aunt Bee were here, things would be absolutely perfect.

I am with you always, no matter what. Just look around you and feel my love and spirit. Aunt Bee had told her that when she cried so many times at having to leave after a visit.

"What can I do to help?" Sissy asked around the lump in her throat.

Gussie handed her a cute little bright-red apron decorated with Mrs. Santa Claus on the front. "You can put this on and set the table. I called Amelia, who owns the Newton Boutique, and asked if she had four left, and if she did, would she open up early and sell them to me. Saw them in the window during the festival parade and thought they'd be cute for us three. Then we added Becky to the mix, so I bought Amelia's last four."

"Remember, the Christmas dishes are in the buffet, and the red chargers are in the middle drawer with the tablecloth and napkins," Ina Mae said.

"Yes, ma'am." Sissy put the apron over her head, and suddenly the fact that she wasn't dressed up really didn't matter. They were going to use the fancy dishes and napkins and sit at a table that didn't have to be broken down later to make a bed for her. Those had always been her favorite things about Christmas—that and the feeling she had anytime she got to come see Aunt Bee. Maybe her aunt had been right—no matter where or what, she was really with Sissy. And she had a pretty new apron to dress up the day, so everything was fine!

"Thank you for the apron. I feel all special and pretty now."

"You didn't before?" Ina Mae asked.

"Honestly, I did not! What if Becky gets all dressed up for this dinner?" Sissy asked. "What if she believes the rumors and thinks I'm about to ruin her son's life?"

Gussie shot Ina Mae a nasty look. "We weren't going to say anything about that today."

"She asked, and one of the club rules is that we don't lie." Ina Mae added the crispy bacon to the eggs and then covered it all with a bag of grated cheese. "Besides, she's a big girl and a smart one. She'll take care of this like Blanche would."

Sissy couldn't help but wonder exactly how Aunt Bee would approach something like a town that was most likely split down the middle on the issue of whether or not to fire a preacher. Elvira was leading the pack of those who wanted Luke gone, and Jimmy would be pulling for him on the other side. To Sissy, it looked like the child's game of tug-of-war, and the frail Elvira was showing everyone just how much power she really had.

She got out the pretty red Christmas cloth and made sure each side was draped evenly all around the dining room table. The last time she had done this, there had been only four to pull up chairs around the table. Today, all eight chairs would be filled, but there would still be an empty spot in her heart, because Aunt Bee wasn't physically there to eat with them—even if she had said she would be with Sissy no matter what. Maybe that's why Ina Mae and Gussie were busying themselves with making a nice brunch. They didn't want to think about the fact that Blanche wouldn't be with them this year, either.

Next, she took eight red enameled chargers from the drawer and placed three on one side, three on the other and one at each end of the table. She remembered asking Aunt Bee why she always made such a fancy table for Christmas.

"Because you are special to me," Aunt Bee had answered, "and I want to do something just for you to show you how much I love you. I know your mama uses a lot of paper plates, and that's perfectly okay. Living in an RV and traveling from place to place can't be easy for her, but once in a while, it's nice to sit down to a table that's as pretty as you are."

That memory caused still another lump in Sissy's throat, so she forced herself to think about the song about the eighties ladies and began to hum it.

Gussie whipped around and smiled. "What brought that song to your mind?"

"Just thinking about the story y'all shared with me about your senior trip, and the line from the song that talks about burning bras and bridges. Aunt Bee told me that . . ." She went on to tell

351

them how she had cried as a child when it was time to leave.

"I like that," Ina Mae said. "Does she talk to you?"

"Oh, yeah," Sissy answered, "and I hope she always does."

"Me too." Gussie nodded. "Here lately she's been telling me that she doesn't care if we dissolve our clubhouse, that we had a good run."

"Don't make any rash decisions so soon after she's gone." Sissy picked up her cup of lukewarm coffee and finished it off.

"I hear cars coming," Gussie said. "We can't spoil this day with tears. That would make Blanche too angry to ever pop into our heads again. You go welcome the folks, Sissy."

Sissy hurried down the hallway, slung open the door, and stepped out on the porch. "Merry Christmas!"

"Merry Christmas to you." Becky waved. "What a lovely apron."

"Glad you like it. Gussie bought all four of us one," Sissy said.

"How sweet! Luke, darlin', you've got to get a picture of us four wearing them before we get them all messy," she told her son.

Luke, darlin'. Does that mean he is a big mama's boy?

Stop it, Aunt Bee scolded. *You already know him better than that. You're just trying to find a reason to break up with him so that he doesn't lose his job. Good God, girl. I taught you to fight for what you want and believe in, not roll over like a puppy that wants his belly scratched.*

Later that afternoon, Luke stood on the porch with Sissy and watched his folks' vehicle lead the parade of four cars leaving in the middle of the afternoon. He really liked the comfortable feeling surrounding him—his arm around Sissy's shoulders like they were a couple.

"A perfect Christmas day, even if it's two days early." He waved until all the cars were out of sight. "I'm going to help serve at the soup kitchen in Jasper the next couple of days. Want to go with me? We can always use an extra person."

"I've promised to have Christmas morning with Ina Mae and Gussie, but I could go tomorrow," Sissy answered. "You'll have to show me what to do. I've never done that before."

"Nothing to it. Just dip up food and then clean up the pots. I guarantee you'll have a wonderful feeling and a new appreciation for everything when the day is done," Luke said.

"Then I'm already looking forward to it," Sissy said. "Shall I wear my new apron?"

"Yes. That would dress up the whole place." He pulled her even closer to his side and kissed her on the forehead. "Did you feel that sizzle?"

"Of course I did," Sissy said. "It's like a dozen

Fourth of July sparklers are going off all around us every time we're together."

Seize the moment. That's what his mother had whispered when she had hugged him and said goodbye.

"Only a dozen?" He raised both dark eyebrows.

"Well, I didn't want to exaggerate," she teased.

"I guess we should save some of those sparklers for later." He spun her around and tipped her chin up for a real kiss—one that used up enough fireworks to fill a stand.

When the kiss ended, she took half a step back, and said, "I believe I need ice cream, or else a quick skinny-dip in the creek."

"Honey, we would make the water boil," Luke chuckled, "but I could go for some ice cream if there was peach cobbler underneath it." He opened the door into the house and stood to one side to let her enter first.

"Out! Out! Dammit, Ina Mae and Gussie!" Danny Boy screeched, and then started whistling "Turn Out the Lights."

Chester came limping from around the side of the house and flew up on the porch railing. He spread his wings, lifted his head, and crowed loudly. Not to be outdone, Danny Boy mimicked him.

"At least the children were good when we had guests," Luke said.

"They were probably afraid that they were

the targets when all that skeet shooting started," Sissy said. "I haven't seen Chester all day until right now, and Danny Boy hasn't made a peep."

"Smart kids," Luke said with a laugh.

Sissy went straight to the living room and opened Danny Boy's cage. He hopped out with his head held high like he was the ruler of a kingdom, sat on the table a few seconds, and flew over to a limb on the Christmas tree.

"Pretty boy?" Luke asked.

"Sweet Jesus!" the bird said.

Sissy covered a giggle with her hand. "Guess he's all mixed up with so many voices in and out today."

"Vodka!" He spread his wings and flew out to the kitchen.

"You've been a good boy all day," Sissy said as she followed him. "You deserve a drink even if it's not five o'clock yet."

Luke fell in behind her, and said, "Have I been good all day?"

"Oh, yes you have," she threw over her shoulder. "You want a bowl with a little vodka in it?"

"Never cared much for that, but I wouldn't turn down a glass of wine," Luke answered.

"White or red?" she asked.

"I like white best, especially with dessert," he answered.

Sissy thought of the T-shirts up in the closet that she still needed to wrap up for Christmas morning. "I love Jesus, but I drink a little," she muttered.

"What was that?" Luke asked.

Sissy explained about the shirts as she went on into the kitchen and poured Danny Boy's vodka first, then got down a bottle of zinfandel and two stemmed glasses.

"That sounds just like something Blanche would buy for Gussie and Ina Mae," Luke said. He raised an eyebrow at the glasses. "So, we're still in fancy mode?"

"Yes, we are. This is our Christmas Day, and it's not over yet. But to be honest, I usually drink it out of jelly glasses."

"Garden Club crystal." Luke smiled. "I've got about a dozen of those in my cabinet, and after a long day, sometimes, I wind down with a little wine."

She poured and then set the glasses on the table while Luke got both the pecan pie and peach cobbler from the refrigerator. "Cobbler with ice cream for me. What would you like?"

"Pecan pie with a scoop of ice cream," she answered as she brought pretty dessert bowls from the cabinet.

"Have I completely blown away your idea of what a preacher should be?" he asked as he carried everything to the table.

Sissy cut a slice of the pie and added a big scoop of ice cream to the top. "Yep, but I like it better than the image that I had from my grandfather. Does Jimmy have a little wine every now and then?"

"Yep, and he never turns down a glass of champagne on special days, like weddings or anniversaries," Luke told her.

Sissy handed him the ice cream scoop, and when he'd put two scoops on his cobbler, she put the carton back in the freezer. "I loved being here on holidays. Aunt Bee always made things so pretty for us."

"You were a little fancy last night at the program. You are a little common in your jeans today. Either one is beautiful." He smiled.

"Ina Mae and Gussie say I'm an old soul. I think you are a romantic soul," she said.

"I betcha if we looked up the two, we would learn that those two are the best match in the whole world." He dug into his cobbler and put a spoonful into his mouth. "Almost as delicious as your kisses."

Her green eyes twinkled. "Like I said, a romantic."

"I give it my best try." A wide grin made his blue eyes sparkle, too.

Chapter Nineteen

L uke thought he was dreaming when he heard Chester crowing and Danny Boy echoing it. In his half-asleep, half-awake state, he drew the pillow closer to his chest and tried to go back to sleep. Just a few more minutes, he thought, and then he would crawl out of the warm bed and get ready to go to the soup kitchen in Jasper. His neck knotted up and he reached up to adjust his pillow, only to realize that his head was resting on the arm of a sofa.

His eyes popped wide open to see a huge Christmas tree right there in front of him. He didn't have a tree in the parsonage, much less one in his bedroom. He started to remove his arm from the pillow, and then realized that it was a woman—not a pillow—that he was holding close to his chest.

"Oh, no!" he muttered.

Danny Boy must've heard him, because he began whistling "One Day at a Time," while the whole previous evening flashed before Luke's eyes in living Technicolor. He and Sissy had been watching a movie when she fell asleep with her head on his shoulder. He had leaned back on the sofa, and sometime in the night, he must have shifted positions and turned off the television, because now they were spooned together with her back to his chest.

"Rotten birds! Hush! It's not time to get up!" Sissy groaned.

Luke brushed her hair back and whispered, "Good mornin'. Are you going to make an honest man out of me?"

Her whole body jerked, and she jumped up off the sofa in a flash. "We didn't . . ." She looked down at her clothes. "What happened?" She scanned the room. "Are we alone?"

"We didn't." Luke sat up and covered a yawn with his hand. "We fell asleep and somehow stretched out together. And other than two birds, I think we're alone. Shall I make coffee? You want pancakes for breakfast or pie?"

"How can you talk about food when you probably are about to get fired for spending the night here with me?" Sissy began to pace the floor.

"We didn't do anything but sleep." Luke stood up and headed for the kitchen. "And if the church votes to fire me, then I figure it's God's will that I put in a soup kitchen here in Newton."

Sissy followed him out of the living room. "How can you be so . . ." She searched for the right word, but her mind was a muddle. "So . . . ," she stammered.

"So . . . at peace with whatever happens?" Luke set about making a pot of coffee. "I've decided

359

on pancakes. I'm a gourmet pancake maker. Dad says mine are even better than Mama's. If I'm ever running my own free kitchen for hungry folks, I'm going to make them every morning."

Sissy slumped down into one of the four chairs that sat around the table in the middle of Aunt Bee's—now her—big country kitchen. "Yes, on the pancakes, and yes, about that peace you mentioned."

Luke leaned his back against the cabinet. "I leave everything to God. That way I know it's not my decision but His."

The coffeepot made a dinging noise that let him know it was ready. He poured two cups, took them to the table, and handed one to her. They each took a sip at the same time, and then he bent and kissed her. "Been wanting to do that ever since we woke up, but morning breath can be a stinker, and I don't have a toothbrush here."

"There's extra ones in the bathroom upstairs." Sissy grinned. "I've never had coffee kisses first thing in the morning."

"We'll have to see to it that you have even more of those," Luke said. "But for now, I'm going to make pancakes. Do we have bacon or sausage in the house?"

"Both," Sissy said. "I'll cook the sausage while you make your Better Than Mama pancakes. On rainy days, Daddy made pandy cakes for me, when I was a little girl."

"Rainy days? And what are pandy cakes?" Luke went to the cabinets and began taking down the ingredients to make his pancakes.

"We cooked outside on the grills that campsites offered most of the time, but on rainy days, we had to make do with the tiny little kitchen in the RV. I couldn't talk plain at two years old, so *pandy cakes* was my phrase for pancakes. Roast beef was *roast beast,* and spaghetti was *busgetti,*" she explained as she brought out one of Aunt Bee's cast iron skillets. "Luke, you could go home now, before the sun comes up, and maybe no one would know that you spent the night here."

"I can't hide what I do from God," Luke said. "Are you ashamed to be dating a preacher?"

"Dammit! Out!" Danny Boy yelled.

"Absolutely not!" Sissy said.

"Are you talking to me or that bird?" Luke turned around, drew her close to his chest, and hugged her tightly.

"You," Sissy said.

"Then nothing else matters." Luke released her and went back to stirring up the batter. "But you might want to either feed those birds or let Danny Boy out to stretch his wings."

Sissy went to the utility room right off the kitchen and filled a scoop with chicken feed. She wished that she had as much faith as Luke did, and that she didn't worry about small-town politics. He could start a soup kitchen, and she didn't have a single doubt that he would be happy flipping pancakes and serving in that capacity. But if she moved to Newton and started a private practice, would the rumors ruin her business before she even got started?

She took care of Chester and then uncovered Danny Boy's cage and checked his food and water dishes. He didn't need anything, so she opened the door to his cage. As usual, he stepped out like a king, spread his wings, and cocked his head to one side.

"Pretty boy?" he said, and it came out more like a question than a statement.

"If you're talking about Luke, I agree wholeheartedly," Sissy whispered.

The bird took flight and she headed out of the living room right behind him. She made it to the kitchen just in time to see Danny Boy fly over and stick his crooked little beak into her coffee cup.

She stopped at the doorway and focused on Luke making pancakes and whistling. Was all this real, or had this past month been a figment of her imagination? Or had she been in a terrible car wreck? Maybe she was in a coma. Aunt Bee wasn't really gone, and she had not just spent the night with Luke. She stubbed her toe on the edge of a chair, and it hurt like hell.

Dreams don't produce that kind of pain, so this is real, she thought.

"Ouch!" she groaned.

Luke dropped the spoon into the batter and rushed to her side. "Are you okay? What happened?"

"I stubbed my toe." Sissy sat down in a chair and removed her sock. "Nothing serious. No blood. It just hurts."

Luke dropped to his knees beside her. "Can you wiggle it?"

She moved it around and said, "No broken bone. I'm fine, honest."

"Do you think we should go to the ER and get it x-rayed?" he asked.

"Nope," she said as she leaned forward and kissed him on the top of his head. "Thank you, Luke, for caring about me."

"You are important to me, and I don't want to see you hurting," Luke said.

"Dammit, Blanche. Need vodka," Danny Boy squawked as he took wing again and alighted on Sissy's shoulder. He bobbed his head as if he were keeping time with music and then hopped over to Luke's shoulder.

"Do you like pancakes?" Luke stood up very slowly so the bird wouldn't get spooked.

The bird crowed and then Chester echoed the sound out on the front porch.

"I guess that means I should make two extras."

Luke broke out into a laugh. "The children have spoken."

"Birds are not children," Sissy teased.

"They are in this house because that's what Blanche called them. She said she always thought she'd get a cat when she retired, but she wound up with two crazy birds instead, and they were as bad or worse than having kids in the house." Luke went back to his job and poured perfect little circles of batter on the hot griddle. "Sometimes we get what we need instead of what we thought we wanted. Speaking of that, I told the folks at the soup kitchen we'd be there at nine to help with preparations. Will that work for you?"

"Yep." Sissy browned the sausage patties and then drained them on a paper towel.

"Good! I can't wait to introduce you to all the folks over there." He flipped three pancakes out onto each of two plates.

She added a couple of sausage patties to each plate and carried them to the table. "Are those volunteers all affiliated with a church?"

"Oh, no! We've got a couple of bikers with tattoos and ponytails, a banker, a former Navy Seal, and some retired schoolteachers. The staff changes every year, but we appreciate whoever can come out and help." Luke refilled the coffee cups and followed her across the room. "I was the only preacher there last year, and I'm not sure that many of the folks even knew that. The important thing is not what we do or who we are at the soup kitchen. It's just that we've got two hands and are willing to help."

"Wouldn't it be nice if the whole world worked that way?" Sissy realized why Luke wanted to put in a kitchen of his own and help the needy right there in Newton. He had the money and a big unselfish heart to go with it.

"Amen, darlin'." He nodded in agreement.

Gussie was busy wrapping presents and wiping tears in between fights with the tape dispenser. This was the first Christmas without Blanche— the first holiday since Thanksgiving, when they were all together, the month before. So much had happened—both bad and good—that she felt like she'd been riding an emotional roller coaster for a whole month.

Ina Mae knocked once on the back door and then pushed her way into the kitchen. "I've got mine all done. What did you decide to do with Blanche's gift—" She stopped in her tracks and slapped a hand over her mouth. "I forgot to get something for Sissy. What is the matter with me? Thank God the gift shop is staying open until noon today."

"Take off your coat and stop fretting. I'll put both our names on my present." Gussie held up a picture album. "I got this for Blanche six months ago and put it aside. I thought that if Sissy makes up her mind to move over here, she could put pictures of all the folks she helps stay married, or maybe if our plan works, she can start a family album of her own."

"Why would you buy that for Blanche? She wasn't into scrapbooking, and all her family pictures are in shoeboxes according to the year. She did that after she inherited all that stuff from her mother. She said that she would never leave an unorganized mess for Sissy like what her mama left for her to deal with." Ina Mae set her wrapped present on the table.

"But she did by dying before she was supposed to," Gussie said with a long sigh. "She mentioned wanting to fix one with Sissy's pictures in it from the time she was a baby until the present day to give to her when and if she ever got married. Seems only right that we give it to Sissy. What did you get Blanche?"

"You know I never shop until the last minute," Ina Mae said. "Since I didn't have anything for her, I bought a fifth of Jack Daniel's at the liquor store when I was in Jasper last week. Sissy mentioned us taking a bottle out to the cemetery and pouring it on her grave after we open our presents on Christmas morning. One shot at a time. How much do I owe you for my half of the album?"

"Not one red cent. You took care of the whiskey," Gussie answered.

Her phone rang, and she dug it out of the bottom of her oversize black bag, which was still hanging on the back of a kitchen chair, where she had put it the night before when she had come home from the dinner at Sissy's place.

"It's Elvira," she groaned.

"Ignore it," Ina Mae said.

"If I do, she'll just keep calling until I answer the damn thing," Gussie swore as she touched the "Accept" icon on the screen. "Merry Christmas, Elvira."

Ina Mae pretended to stick her finger down her throat.

"Is Ina Mae over there with you?" Elvira asked. "I saw her truck go past my house a few minutes ago."

Gussie put the phone on speaker and laid it on the table. "Yes, she's right here. Are you all right?"

"No! I'm not all right," Elvira snapped. "I hate to say 'I told you so,' but I will in this case. Luke has gone to that gawd-awful soup kitchen, so I wouldn't have anyone to sit with me if I went to the hospital, but my heart hurts so bad that I might have a stroke, and it's all because of Sissy Ducaine."

"You should choose your words wisely from this moment on." Gussie's tone was ice cold.

"Hey, now"—Ina Mae sat down at the table— "why would Sissy be giving you a stroke? I thought you two had got to be good friends since she helped you with the decorations at the church."

"Don't play dumb with me, Augusta Sadler, or you, either, Ina Mae Garber. Sissy Ducaine tells y'all everything, so you know that Luke spent the night with her last night. It pained me to take this to the deacons this morning. I've already taken care of the problem because I didn't want y'all to try to talk me out of it by offering to let me join your club, either. So it's done." Her tone sounded downright smug.

"We wouldn't dream of bribing you." Ina Mae grimaced. "Where did you get your information about Sissy and Luke? Are you accusing them of doing something when you have no solid proof? If you are, you'll look pretty foolish and might even get kicked off the hiring committee."

"I saw it with my own eyes," Elvira said. "I was taking a little morning drive to watch the sun rise and drove past the parsonage. Luke's truck wasn't there, so I drove out to Blanche's place, and there it was before daybreak this morning. The house was dark, except for the lights on the Christmas tree in the living room window. Then the lights came on and I could see both of them through that same window. I was so upset that my heart started hurting, and I tried to call Luke, but he didn't answer."

"Good for him," Ina Mae mouthed.

"You were spying on them," Gussie said.

"Yes, I was," Elvira said, "and I'll do it again if I need to. Someone needs to take matters into their hands, and I'll be the one to do it. I rushed right home and called Jimmy first. He said that maybe Sissy had an emergency with one of those crazy birds or something. You'd expect him to take up for Luke since it's his nephew, but that's a lame excuse if I ever heard one."

Gussie laid her forehead on the table and groaned.

"Why are you telling us this?" Ina Mae asked. "Sissy and Luke are both grown adults."

"*You* brought Sissy here, so you tell her to go back to Louisiana. We've decided to give Luke one more chance, and if he doesn't stop seeing her, then we'll be looking for a new preacher. His contract is up on the last day of this year, so that will make it easy to do," Elvira said.

Gussie raised her head up. "If you want her or Luke to know that y'all are a bunch of petty-minded, old gossips, *you* tell them, and maybe the reason Luke didn't answer your call is because his phone was dead. Why don't you give them both the benefit of the doubt before you jump to conclusions?"

"How dare you talk to me like that! A preacher should see to it that his phone is never dead and always turned on in case someone like me needs him in an emergency. I've never been petty-minded, and I do not gossip. I've been a pillar of this community my whole adult life, and I sure didn't have a clubhouse where I could do God knows what. Oh, I do feel a heart attack coming on. I should call an ambulance. Goodbye!" Elvira ended the call.

"WWBD?" Ina Mae sighed.

"What does that mean?" Gussie asked. "I've heard of WWJD, but . . ."

"What would Blanche do?" Ina Mae said.

"Probably tell Elvira to go to hell," Gussie answered. "Are we going to say anything to Luke?"

"Yep," Ina Mae said. "I'm going to tell him exactly what's going on so he can be prepared."

Gussie gave the phone a dirty look. "Where are those brass knuckles and that bat when we need them?"

Chapter Twenty

Sissy helped carry three folding lawn chairs to the gravesite and set them up. Until then she hadn't realized that her aunt Bee's pink granite tombstone was located between Ina Mae's and Gussie's. It shouldn't have come as a surprise or a shock. They had done everything together their whole lives, so it was only natural that they would be buried side by side.

"Presents first." Gussie brought gifts from the back of her vehicle. "We made a clubhouse rule when we were little girls. Each of us could give the other two a Christmas gift, but they couldn't be expensive. When we were ten years old, we could spend no more than fifty cents on the present."

"There was a five-and-dime store in town back then, so we could buy trinkets for that amount. Now our limit is twenty dollars," Ina Mae explained.

Sissy jogged back to her car to get the shirts that she had wrapped that morning.

"You didn't have to do this," Gussie said.

"I only wrapped them. I found them in the closet where she must have put them. Aunt Bee told me about y'all exchanging gifts, so these are from both of us. Her, because she bought them.

Me, because I wrapped them, and wasn't sure if the three of us would be exchanging gifts since we hadn't talked about it," Sissy said as she sat down between them.

"All right then, before another Christmas, we will figure out how the three of us want to do things. You go first, Sissy." Gussie put a present in her lap. "This was bought for Blanche." She told the story of why she had bought it, and ended with, "You do what you want with it, but we thought if you decided to move to Newton, maybe you would use it to put a picture of the couples you help in it. That wouldn't go against confidentiality, would it?"

Sissy hugged the album to her chest. "What a beautiful idea. Y'all have your matchmaking album, and I'll have my therapy one. Now, you two open Blanche's presents."

The T-shirts brought about laughter from both of them that echoed through the cemetery and was so contagious that Sissy giggled so hard she snorted several times.

"Leave it to Blanche to put some humor in this day." Ina Mae wiped the tears from her eyes and handed Gussie a small gift.

"Oh, Ina Mae, I love it," Gussie said when she'd ripped the paper from a picture frame that held a photograph of the three little girls standing beside the door they had just painted. "Thank you so much. I had forgotten that Mama took a picture of us and had one printed for each of us. Now open my present to you."

Ina Mae opened it, and the laughter started all over again. Gussie had put a copy of the same picture in a gold gilt frame for Ina Mae. When the giggling stopped a second time, Gussie said, "I found mine and wanted to share it with you. Thought maybe in the moves you've made that you'd lost yours."

"All right, now let's get on with our party." Ina Mae reached out and laid her hand on the end of Blanche's tombstone that had just recently gotten the last date, the day of her death, engraved on it.

Sissy closed her eyes for a moment and visualized Aunt Bee right there with them. She was glad that her aunt hadn't wanted to be cremated and that they had a place to come remember her.

"Blanche, we've brought you a bottle of Jack Daniel's," Ina Mae said. "I thought about just sitting it up by the tombstone, but some lousy drunk would come by and steal it. Since you can't open it, we've decided to pour shots on your grave. Merry Christmas, my friend who is dearer to me than a sister could even be."

"Stop it, or you'll have us all crying," Gussie scolded. "Blanche would far rather hear us laughing like fools than weeping and moaning. Now, Ina Mae is the oldest." She pointed to the first tombstone to her left. "She was born on March twenty-fifth, on Easter Sunday that year, then Blanche was born on Mother's Day, and me, I came into this world on July Fourth. We were the holiday babies." She broke the seal on a full bottle of Jack Daniel's.

"Before we do this, and while we're here with Blanche, we've got something to tell you," Ina Mae said. "We called Luke and told him what was going on already. Has he told you?"

"No, I haven't talked to him since he left the house. I've got suspicions that I already know what it is," Sissy said. "Someone saw Luke going home really early from my house the past two mornings, didn't they?"

"Two mornings?" Gussie asked.

"The first night was an accident. We fell asleep watching a movie, and the birds woke us up before dawn. Luke made pancakes and we had breakfast and then we went to the soup kitchen. I loved helping out at the kitchen, by the way, and I can see why Luke has been talking about putting in one here in Newton, and not just for the holiday meals but every day. Last night, we just didn't want to say goodbye." Sissy stopped, took a long breath, and let it out slowly. "But I don't want him to get fired because of me, so like I told you earlier, I'm going home—"

"No!" Ina Mae raised her voice. "You can't let people walk on you, and we need you here."

"I'm not leaving forever," Sissy said. "Just for a few days to get things straightened out in my own mind. I feel like I'm too close and like Luke too much to think clearly while I'm here, so just a few days at home will be good. Then if I decide to move here permanently, I will get my apartment squared away."

"Blanche wouldn't run from a problem," Gussie said.

"Who says I'm running from it?" Sissy smiled. "I might be running right into the fire, but I'm packed and ready to go to Beau Bridge as soon as we finish up here."

"Have you told Luke?" Ina Mae asked.

"Not yet, but I will. Luke is waiting for me at the church. That's something I need to tell him face-to-face, not over the phone, and I didn't want to spoil the past two nights with him," Sissy answered. "But mere words can't begin to express how much your support through everything this whole month has meant and continues to mean to me. I couldn't have gotten through the funeral and everything that's happened since then without it."

"Right back at you, kiddo," Ina Mae said.

"Amen," Gussie added and then said, "And now for Blanche's present. We are each going to tell Blanche something with each shot we pour on her grave. Doesn't matter what it is. We'll just pretend she's sitting on top of that tombstone and that instead of pouring the whiskey on her grave we're handing it to her and she's downing it."

"I like that idea." Without even shutting her eyes, Sissy could envision Aunt Bee sitting cross-legged on the tombstone. She wore the bright-red dress that Ina Mae and Gussie had picked out for her burial, and not a single streak of gray roots shined in her freshly dyed red hair.

Gussie poured up a shot of whiskey and stood to her feet. "I'll go first. Elvira is a bitch. She's trying to ruin Luke's life and send him packing. We don't want him to leave." She poured the whiskey on the freshly mounded dirt, and then she handed the bottle and glass to Sissy.

"This is Aunt Bee's shot glass from the club-house, isn't it?" Sissy asked.

"Yep, special occasions call for the special glass," Ina Mae said.

Sissy's hands shook as she filled the tiny glass with whiskey.

Don't you waste a drop of good whiskey, and pour it out slowly. The vision of Aunt Bee on the tombstone faded, but a smile covered Sissy's face.

"I'm falling in love with Luke," she said and handed both bottle and glass to Ina Mae, who stood up and filled the glass a third time.

She held it up in a toast, and then began to let it dribble onto the grave. "Gussie and I beat the crap out of Walter. That's why he left Newton

376

and never came back. We told him the next time we *would* kill him and, like the sign on our clubhouse says, we'd feed him to the coyotes."

Gussie reached around Sissy and took the bottle and glass from Ina Mae. "She wasn't ever supposed to tell you that, but since you probably heard us telling Sissy, you already know it. We did it because your daddy wouldn't take up for you." She inhaled deeply as she poured her second shot on the grave. "Are you getting a buzz yet? These fumes are almost as intoxicating as drinking the whiskey."

Sissy poured her second shot onto the grave. "I want to live in Newton, but I need to be sure that it's not just a passing thing. If it's the direction I really want to go with my life, I'll need a place for my own practice."

Ina Mae took the bottle from Sissy. "We've tried to be nice to Elvira, but we're done with her. Gussie's right: she's a bitch, and she's out for blood where our Sissy and Luke are concerned." Her shot enlarged the wet circle on the grave.

"We can hardly bear to go into the clubhouse without you being there." Gussie sighed as she started the rounds all over again. "We need some direction about what to do."

"I'm glad that when I need you, you pop into my head and give me advice or scold me," Sissy said when Gussie passed the bottle to her.

Ina Mae held the bottle up when it was her turn.

"It's almost gone. I should have bought a bigger bottle, because we've got more to say. But if this is my last turn, then I just want you to pop into Sissy's head right now and tell her to not go to Beau Bridge. We're afraid she won't come back here to live, and we need her."

"We'll be here waiting for her, Blanche, when she makes up her mind. She's stubborn like you always were, but she's got a level head and she knows this is where her heart is." Gussie poured what would be her last shot into the glass.

"Merry Christmas, Aunt Bee." Sissy poured her shot on the grave and passed it over to Ina Mae. So much had been said and shared, and most of it had convinced Sissy that she did belong in Newton. Once she was there permanently, she would always have family close by to talk to, to drop in on for a cup of coffee anytime she wanted, or to bring a bottle of whiskey to Aunt Bee during the holidays. Now, it was just a matter of getting things squared away with her apartment and her job in Beau Bridge.

"I love my T-shirt." Ina Mae pulled her jacket back to reveal the writing: "I Love Jesus, but I Drink a Little." "If they tell Luke they aren't going to renew his contract, then we're going to wear them to church and sit on the front pew. And we'll talk Paul and Jimmy into sitting with us just to give Elvira some more juicy gossip." Her shot of Jack hit the ground.

"I'll end my last turn with what I said in the beginning: Elvira is a bitch," Gussie said and handed the bottle with the last few drops to Sissy.

"This is all of it, Aunt Bee. I just want to say that I've never met a man with a bigger heart or as sweet a nature as Luke," Sissy said as she poured the last of the whiskey onto the ground and set the bottle on the tombstone. Then she linked arms with the other two and they all three had a moment of silence.

"I think she enjoyed that present," Ina Mae whispered.

"I know she did. I can feel it down deep in my soul." Gussie nodded.

"Now what do we do with the bottle?" Sissy asked.

"We take it to the clubhouse and set it up on the cabinet as a memory of today," Gussie answered. "And one more thing, Blanche. We didn't let Jimmy and Paul into the clubhouse. We'd never do that, but we kinda have let them into our lives. We're still going on that Valentine's cruise, and we sort of asked them if they wanted to go with us—not in our beds, though!"

"God no!" Ina Mae gasped. "But as friends. It's kind of nice to have them around."

Gussie nudged Sissy with a hip. "Now what's this about falling in love with Luke?"

"Isn't that what y'all wanted when you started playing matchmaker?" Sissy teased.

"So, you figured it out, did you?" Gussie chuckled.

"How long did it take you?" Ina Mae asked.

"About a day," Sissy answered.

"Dammit, Gussie!" Ina Mae slapped the arm of her chair. "It really is time to stop this business. We've lost our touch."

Sissy hoped they thought she was smiling because she had caught on to their little plan, but the real reason was that she'd pulled the wool over their eyes with her own little matchmaking scheme.

"So you're going on the cruise after all?" Sissy asked.

"Do you think that would be a slap in the face to Blanche?" Ina Mae asked.

"Or that we shouldn't have asked Jimmy and Paul to go along with us?" Gussie asked before Sissy could answer.

"No, on both counts," Sissy answered. "Friends are wonderful, whether they're guys or women. As long as they don't build a clubhouse and write 'No Girls Allowed' on it. Now what's this about not keeping the Sunshine Club going?"

A slight breeze rattled the old scrub oak tree that had spread its limbs over the three tombstones. A few crispy leaves floated down to land on Blanche's grave.

"That's an omen that she understands," Ina Mae said. "We aren't making the decision about whether to abandon the Sunshine Club or not until after the new year, but right now every time we go into the clubhouse, we both start crying. As a therapist, what would you tell us, Sissy?"

"I would say not to make any important decisions until you are absolutely sure that's what you want to do," Sissy said. "When the time is right, you'll know what to do. My mama was a little bit superstitious, and she would say that you'd have a definite sign telling you what to do, and not to jump into anything until you do. Now, it's time for me to hug y'all and go see Luke."

"Would you call or text us when you get home, just so we know you are all right?" Gussie stood up and wrapped her arms around Sissy. "And don't worry about Chester and Danny Boy. We'll go out there a couple of times a day and take care of them."

"Of course I will, and thank you for taking care of the birds. I was going to ask you if you would do that for me." Sissy knew she had a family right here, but like she had just told them, this was not the time to make important decisions.

Luke had labored over his sermon for the next day, something he had never had to do. Always before, God had laid something on his heart that Luke felt was a message he should include in his Sunday sermon. But after what the deacons had said when they had met with him that morning, his mind was totally blank. He was still in a state of shock. For people, deacons at that, to jump to conclusions without even giving him the right to tell them what had happened just wasn't right— no matter what. His first thought when they gave him their ultimatum and didn't even let him explain was that he should hand in his resignation right then and there. But then he realized he would be doing something out of anger, and that wasn't right, either.

He removed his shoes, propped his feet up on his desk, and glanced at a picture of his parents and Uncle Jimmy taken on the day he preached his first sermon at this very church. He closed his eyes and tried to remember the excitement of that day, but all he could see was Sissy Ducaine—not the deacons, not Elvira, who had stepped up with her damning accusations—just Sissy. Was God sending him a sign?

He smiled at the vision in his head of Sissy sitting on the front row at the funeral parlor, waiting with Ina Mae and Gussie to say a few last words to her precious aunt Bee. The next picture that flashed through his mind was Sissy at the cemetery when she sent Gussie's hat flying, and the looks on their faces when Ina Mae caught it. His grin grew bigger at the memory of her and the two elderly ladies sitting on a pew the next morning in church. It was so evident that they all three had hangovers.

"Are you asleep?" Sissy asked.

He thought that it was all part of the memory and shook his head.

"Are you sure?"

He slowly opened his eyes and took his feet from the desk. "No, I was thinking about you."

"Oh, really?" She sat down in one of the wing-back chairs facing his desk. "I feel a little like Santa Claus in this chair."

"Well, it is Christmas," Luke said, "but why would that chair . . . oh"—he slapped his forehead—"because Uncle Jimmy sat in it when he was dressed up like Santa."

"You look sad," Sissy said.

"I am a little, but it will pass now that you're here," he said.

Sissy drew in a long breath, and he knew something wasn't right with her, either.

"Are you breaking up with me?" he asked.

"No, but I'm going home to Beau Bridge for a few days. I've got some thinking to do."

"Me too," Luke said.

"Want to talk about it?" Sissy asked.

He shook his head. "You will come back, won't you? I can't imagine spending New Year's Eve without you."

"We both need some time to analyze what has been happening, Luke. This has all been so fast and furious, and as a—"

He interrupted her when he pushed back his

chair, rounded the end of the desk, and scooped her up like a bride. She didn't fight against him but laid her head on his shoulder and put her arms around his neck. He sat down in the other chair and shifted her until she could be comfortable in his lap. They sat like that for several minutes in total and complete silence.

"As a therapist," he said, "your analytical mind is telling you this is all too fast, but my heart says that everything happens for a reason. We were brought together at this time in our lives so that we could meet each other and have this amazing relationship. You're right about us needing some time apart to sort things out, but that doesn't mean I'm going to change my mind about my feelings or that I'm not going to miss you every second of every day that you are gone."

"We can call, FaceTime, and text," she whispered.

"Yes, we will, and we'll tell each other how we are feeling, right? You won't hold back anything, will you?" he asked.

"Not one thing," she promised. "And now I'm going to kiss you, but it's not goodbye; it's a 'see you later' kiss. I hate goodbyes, and I never want to say that to you or hear it from you. Then I'm going to get up and walk out of here. I don't want you to go with me to my car, or call me for at least an hour, because this is the hardest thing, other than burying Aunt Bee, I've had to do in a very long time." She drew his face to hers for a long, passionate kiss.

Letting her walk out of his office sent half of his heart and soul with her that afternoon. If Sissy wasn't back in Newton by the end of the week, he planned to go bring her home—even if it meant begging on his knees.

In that moment, his sermon for the next day came to his mind. Clear as a bell. He picked up his yellow legal pad and his Bible and began to write a sermon about judging others.

Chapter Twenty-One

S issy could see dark clouds gathering in the southwest in her rearview mirror and hoped that they weren't an omen of bad things to come. Despite her master's degree in family and marriage counseling, she still retained just a little bit of her mother's superstition. Dark clouds meant there could be a storm coming in a person's life. Finding a penny faceup meant you would have good luck, but if the penny was facedown, then you were supposed to turn it over and leave it for the next person to have the good luck.

Her phone dinged, and she glanced down at the console, where she had laid it. She made a right turn into a lane leading up to a ranch house. The text was from Luke: I miss you already. Starting to rain. Be safe.

She sent back a message: Me too. No rain here.

Then she got back on the road, and even though that simple text made her want to turn around and go back to Newton, she kept driving. She turned on the radio and found her favorite country music station that played more of the older songs. She recognized the prelude of soft music of a single acoustic guitar starting "Love Will Build a Bridge," and the tears began to flow down her cheeks when she listened to the lyrics saying that their finest hour was when they stood together.

"Amen!" she said when the song ended.

She merged onto Interstate 10 at Lake Charles, and Garth Brooks began to sing "The River," one of Sissy's favorite songs. She kept time with her thumbs on the steering wheel and nodded with the lyrics that said there would be rough waters and mentioned the good Lord being her guide.

That's what Luke had been talking about that whole month, Sissy thought. Even if the waters weren't smooth and tough times changed the course of his life, he was going to be happy no matter which way the river ran.

"And now the last of our three in a row," the DJ said. "Here's an old one by Rascal Flatts. Give it up for 'Bless the Broken Road.'"

Like "'80's Ladies" was written for the Sunshine Club, this song had to have been written expressly for Sissy and Luke. Once again, she pulled over and picked up her phone. She found the song on YouTube and sent the link to Luke with a text: This is our song.

She listened to it three more times while she waited for a reply, and when it came, it was just a series of a dozen red hearts. Neither of them had actually said the three magic words—*I love you*—and she started to send back a text that said them, but her thumbs suddenly refused to move. Those words were special enough that they should be shared out loud and in person. She should be looking right into his blue eyes when she said them for the first time, not typing them into a text message.

She started the car and almost turned around and headed to Newton right then, but she had to be sure, had to know beyond a faint shadow of a doubt that this was the right thing for her. "Two days. I need just a couple of days to get everything in order, both mentally and physically, and then I'll go home to Newton and tell him."

Home.

As a child home had been whatever park her folks landed in between gigs; sometimes it was just a gravel parking lot next to a bar. As a college student, it had been her dorm room. For the past few years, it had been a one-bedroom apartment in Beau Bridge, Louisiana. Someone once said that home is where the heart is. If that was the truth, then her home had always been in Newton, Texas, because that's where her heart had always yearned to be.

"Why did it take me so long to realize this?" she asked herself as she drove past exits to small towns just off the interstate—Rayne, Duson, and Scott. She had clients from all those towns, but since she worked for a big practice, it wouldn't be difficult to shift them over to other therapists.

"Still, is it right for me to leave them?" she

asked herself. Some of them she had been seeing for months, a couple for years. "Are any of them as important as what is waiting for me in Newton?"

When she reached her apartment complex, she used her key card to open the front door and rolled her suitcase across the floor to the elevator. Bobby, the guy who manned the front desk on weekends, wasn't there. The desk sat empty and abandoned, but then it was Christmas Day. Even so, after she'd spent nearly a month in Newton, the place seemed barren anyway. She took the elevator to the second floor, rolled her suitcase out into the hallway, made a left turn, and felt like her shoes were filled with concrete as she made her way to number 213 and used her card again—this time to open her apartment door.

Nothing had changed except the ivy plant on the bookcase had died. She parked her suitcase and was about to call Luke and tell him she was home when her phone rang. She dug her phone out of her purse and checked the screen.

"I just walked in the door, Gussie," she said.

"You're on speaker with me and Ina Mae. We were getting a little worried."

"I stopped a couple of times." She sank down on her sofa. It didn't feel nearly as soft as the one at Aunt Bee's place.

"Was it hard to tell Luke that you were leaving?" Ina Mae asked.

"Yes, but I'm coming home—that would be Newton—as soon as I can," Sissy said. "I'm talking to my boss on Monday and hoping that she will count the last two weeks of my vacation time as my notice. I'll have some work to do, shifting my clients and taking care of my office, but it could be doable. It seemed like every song I heard on the radio was written to make me realize that Newton is where I belong. And this apartment seems so small and empty right now."

"Halle-damn-lujah!" Ina Mae shouted. "Hearing you say that this is home is the best Christmas present ever."

"Are you planning to start up a practice here?" Gussie asked. "God knows how bad we need someone like you here in Newton. We know that Blanche left everything to you, and you don't have to work another day in your life, but you are way too young and too smart to just quit what you are good at and take care of a couple of pesky birds."

"Got any ideas about where I might rent an office space?" Suddenly, Sissy felt like she could see a glowing light at the end of the tunnel. She belonged near her family and Luke, and she was going home—her mind was made up for good.

"Yep, we do!" She could hear the excitement in Ina Mae's voice.

"We want to give you our clubhouse for an office," Gussie said. "Ina Mae and I have talked about it and we even went back out to the cemetery to get Blanche's feelings on it this evening. We got our sign, like you were talking about, and we feel like this is what we want to do. We can remodel the old building however you want and have a sign put on the front door. We feel like Blanche would love that idea."

"Sunshine Family and Marriage Counseling," Sissy whispered, and then wondered if she'd even said it out loud.

"Great name, and that would be keeping a part of Blanche in it," Ina Mae agreed. "So, what do you say?"

"Yes, and thank you, but, Gussie, are you sure you want a business in your backyard?" Sissy's mind spun. Part of the furniture in her apartment could go in the new business. The clubhouse was a perfect size for an office. She had to stop and take a breath just to slow things down. "Have you decided on how much rent . . . ?"

"Chère, we will not talk about money," Gussie scolded. "I want you to come home where you belong. You'll inherit this place when I'm dead and gone anyway, so why not start now with the old summer kitchen? But I'm not planning on joining Blanche out there at the graveyard anytime soon, just so you know."

"Or me either," Ina Mae told her, "but you are also the sole beneficiary of my house and things when I go. However, I plan on being around long enough to spoil the grandchildren. Speaking of that, have you called Luke?"

"Not yet," Sissy said. "I just walked in the door when y'all called me."

"Well, hang up, for God's sake," Ina Mae said.

"Dammit, Ina Mae and Gussie!" Danny Boy said loudly in the background.

"Guess you know by that where we are, and, chère," Gussie said, "all three of us always hated goodbyes, so I'm just going to say *see you later,* and push the button to end this call."

Sissy laid her phone on the end table and took another look around the living room. Things could not possibly be working out any better—so when was the other shoe going to drop?

She made a quick trip through the bathroom, and then picked up her phone to call Luke, but it rang before she could even hit the button. When she saw that it was Annabelle, she panicked. What if something had happened to Holly? What if Annabelle needed her to come back to Newton right then?

"Hello," she answered.

"Sissy? Miz Ducaine? Martina?" Annabelle sounded as if she had been crying. "I'm not sure what to call you, but I had to tell you what happened today, and you said I could call anytime."

"Sissy is fine. Are you okay?" she asked.

"I'm fine. I'm better than fine. My grandmother

pulled through and got to go home today. Wes's parents came over to see the baby. His mama apologized and his father told Wes that they would not only take care of his education expenses, but they would also pay for mine," Annabelle said, "but Wes and I want to still come talk to you maybe every other week for a while."

"That would be wonderful," Sissy said, "and that's great news. I would love to work with y'all for as long as you think you need me."

"And, Sissy, if there's ever anything we can do for you, just tell us," Annabelle said. "I should go now. Holly needs feeding. Merry Christmas."

"Merry Christmas to you." Sissy ended that call and hit the speed dial button for Luke.

Luke had talked to Sissy for more than an hour after she got back to Beau Bridge. She had told him that she was coming home to Newton as soon as she could get things in order and that she already had a place for her practice. He loved the idea of keeping the name Sunshine in her new practice. If he ever put a soup kitchen in Newton, he just might follow her example and call it the Sunshine Kitchen.

He had a small glass of wine to celebrate after they ended the call. He had almost said "I love you" when she said that she would see him in a few days, but those words weren't something that a man said to a woman over the phone. They would have plenty of time for those kinds of declarations now that she was coming home.

"Maybe Valentine's Day," he said later that evening as he fell asleep.

He awoke on Sunday morning with a frown on his face and every bit as tired as when he had gone to sleep the night before. In his dreams, he had gone from one empty building to the next all around the square. He kept thinking that it was all crazy even as he was checking out the places because Gussie and Ina Mae had already given Sissy the clubhouse to turn into an office for her new private practice.

He sat up on the side of his bed and raked his fingers through his thick, dark hair. An old café located on the north side of the square had been the building he'd kept going back to in his dreams. He had argued with the Realtor that Sissy didn't need a big kitchen or a long buffet bar for a therapy practice, but the woman kept saying that this was the perfect place.

Luke finally smiled and nodded. "I hear you, God. I get the message loud and clear." He looked up the address of that particular piece of property, picked up his cell phone, and made a call to the Realtor who had it listed. Then he got ready to preach his last sermon at the Newton Community Church.

He felt totally at peace that morning when he took his place behind the lectern. God had visited men of old in dreams, and Luke was sure that his dream had led him to the right decision.

"Good morning, and I hope all of you had a wonderful Christmas yesterday," he began. "I celebrated the last two days in Jasper at the soup kitchen there, trying to give back to those less fortunate folks a little of the blessings that have been showered upon me, especially through this last month. I had a sermon written for this morning." He held up his Bible in one hand and his yellow notepad in the other. "I was going to preach about judging others, but when I awoke this morning, God had answered a prayer about a question I've been struggling with for quite some time. The question has been whether or not I should stay in Newton and continue preaching at this church."

He noticed that Gussie and Ina Mae were both nodding, and Elvira was shooting him another of her dirty looks.

"If I passed out a survey right now asking each of you to give your opinion on that, I feel like there would be those who wanted me gone, and others who would want me to stay. But really, it's not your yeses or noes that matter. It's totally up to God, and He has spoken to my heart. It has always been my nature to fight for what I believe is right and to stand up for myself, but if I did that in this situation, I would be fighting against God, because I truly feel like He has told me it's time to move on with my life. So, with that said, I'm resigning. My contract is up next Saturday anyway, so I'm just saving those of you who would vote to keep me the difficulty of trying to convince the ones who want me gone."

Several folks began to stare at the cell phones in their laps, and Luke could see their thumbs doing double time as they sent texts to whoever wasn't in church that morning.

"This is my last sermon, but I won't be leaving Newton. I plan to make my home here; however, I will be out of the parsonage by next Saturday. I have loved working with you folks, and I have made many good friends here. I like helping people, so I've got another project already in play. I'll see you all next Sunday, but I'll be sitting in the congregation, not here behind the lectern. As a very important lady in my life said just yesterday, I hate goodbyes, so I'll just say *see you later*. Now, Uncle Jimmy, would you please deliver the benediction to close the service, and would you also shake hands with the folks for me? I've got somewhere I need to be."

Chapter Twenty-Two

Sissy was busy packing her personal things into boxes when her phone rang on Sunday morning.

When she saw it was Luke, she answered on the second ring. "Shouldn't you be preaching right about now?"

"I did preach this morning, just not a very long sermon. I'm on my way to Beau Bridge to see you. I've got something to tell you that needs to be said in person, not on the phone, so could you do me a huge favor?" he asked.

"Anything," she agreed.

"Don't answer your phone unless it's me until I get there. I want to explain, not have you hear this from someone else," he said.

"All right," she said slowly.

"See you in a couple of hours, and thank you, Sissy," he said.

She sent a text to Gussie: Not answering my phone for a couple of hours. Luke is on the way over here to talk to me.

She closed her eyes for a moment and took a deep breath. The other shoe was about to drop—that much she knew. Aunt Bee had told her that hard work was the best way to pass the time, so

Sissy headed for the refrigerator. The leftovers she had stored a month ago were green with mold. There was no doubt that the milk had turned to clabber, and the lettuce was downright slimy. She would have to get the place completely cleaned out before she left anyway, so she might as well tackle this nasty job while she waited on Luke to tell her that they shouldn't see each other anymore.

What makes you think he's going to say that? This time it was Gussie's voice in her head.

"Because things have been going so well. As Aunt Bee has said before, everything can't be all rainbows and unicorn farts," Sissy said as she dumped a container of diced tomatoes down the garbage disposal and flipped the switch.

But you've endured enough storm clouds this month already. Her mother didn't pop into her head very often, so when she did, Sissy usually listened. *You lost your aunt Bee, which was hard enough, but then all these other things have been hard on your emotions, too. You are due for some good news, not bad.*

"Whatever it is, I'm still moving to Newton," Sissy declared.

Luke's call had come through at eleven forty-five, and that meant he would be in Beau Bridge sometime right after two o'clock. Sissy sent a text telling him her address.

Even though she kept busy and had cleaned the

refrigerator and the stove and had even packed what few things were in the pantry into an empty box, every minute that clicked off the clock seemed like an hour.

At one thirty, she stopped packing clothes, sat down on the side of her bed, and teared up when something dawned on her like a light bulb being switched on in her mind. Luke wasn't coming to see her because of something between the two of them. Theirs was as solid a relationship as any could be. He didn't want Elvira or anyone else to tell her that something had happened to either Gussie or Ina Mae. She had told him how hard it had been when she got the phone call about her aunt Bee, and he didn't want her to be alone when she got news like that again. Which of her friends had passed, she wondered, and the tears came even harder.

"Why didn't Gussie or Ina Mae reply to my text so I could be prepared?" She groaned.

Another funeral. Another grave beside Aunt Bee. And then the third member of the Sunshine Club would die of grief, for sure. In her profession, Sissy had already seen that happen too many times. A couple would be married for fifty or sixty years. One would pass away, and the other one wouldn't last six months. It was as if it took both their hearts to make one, and the one left behind didn't have the strength to go on. Aunt Bee, Ina Mae, and Gussie were as close as, maybe even closer than, a lot of married couples, so it was no wonder that when one of them died, the others couldn't survive.

She lay back and stared at the ceiling and then picked up her phone. She needed to know which one it was to prepare herself, but she couldn't make herself make the call. She was still in a state of numbness when the buzzer rang and jerked her back to reality. She jumped up from the bed, ran to the door, hit a button, and said, "Yes? Who's there?"

"It's me," Luke said. "Can you buzz me in and tell me your apartment number?"

She hit the "Enter" button and said, "Second floor. I'll meet you at the elevator."

She left her apartment door wide open and raced to the elevator, worried when she didn't hear the familiar creaking or see the light above the doors that would let her know when the doors were about to open. Then the stairwell door flew open, and there was Luke coming right at her.

Why was he smiling so big? How dare he look happy when either Gussie or Ina Mae was gone? Maybe they were just in the hospital, and everything was going to be all right. He covered the distance between them and took her in his arms.

"Which one?" she whispered.

"Which one what? Did someone call you after all?" he asked.

"Gussie or Ina Mae," she answered. "Which one is dead?"

"Oh, no!" He took half a step back and tipped up her chin. "I'm so sorry, darlin'. I should have said that everything was fine, but I wanted to be the one to explain things to you. I didn't want you to hear what happened this morning from someone else. Gussie and Ina Mae both had big smiles on their faces when I left the church. They are fine, and so is Elvira."

"Thank God, but I wasn't worried about Elvira. The devil and God will fight over who *has* to take that woman when the time comes, not who gets to have her." Sissy was so relieved that she was practically dizzy.

"Are we going to talk out here in the hallway, or can we go to your apartment?" he asked.

Sissy took him by the hand and led him the short distance from the elevator to her place. "Please excuse the mess. I'm packing to go home and start putting down roots. I've got some peanut butter and bread if you're hungry, and there's a couple of bottles of root beer that aren't outdated in the refrigerator."

"Later. Right now, I just want to look at you and hold you." He pulled her closer to him and kissed her with so much passion that she forgot all about the other-shoe business. The sizzle and sparks were still there, in double or triple fold.

When the kiss ended, she shoved a pile of

books off the sofa and motioned for him to sit beside her. "That kiss did not feel like an 'I'm breaking up with you' kiss."

Luke sat down beside her and took both her hands in his. "That was an 'I love you' kiss. I thought love at first sight was crazy, but I believe in it now, and it may be too soon to be saying the words, but I had to get them out of my heart today."

"I'm not sure if it was love at first sight for me"—she had to be honest—"but it was certainly lust and guilt all tied up into one package at first sight."

"Lust and guilt?" He grinned.

"Yep, lust because you are so damned sexy, and guilt because I thought I shouldn't feel that way about a preacher," she answered.

"I love you, Sissy Ducaine," he said.

"I love you, Luke Beauchamp," she said and meant the words with her whole heart. "Is that what you came all the way over here to tell me?"

"That's the most important part, but the rest of the story is this." He went on to tell her about his dream. "So I called the Realtor, and she said that she would meet me at the property before church this morning, which made me realize that I was right. The dream was God answering my prayers. I looked at the old building, and it needs some cosmetic help, but it's perfect for my new Sunshine Kitchen. I told the lady to take it off the market. I would buy it. Now, all I have to do is convince Gussie to let me rent one of her bedrooms since I have to be out of the parsonage by Saturday night."

"Oh, no, you will not!" Sissy said. "You can move in with me, and I love the name you've chosen for your soup kitchen."

"Just keeping the name in the family in honor of Blanche. And about moving in with you . . . I'm willing, but didn't you say that we shouldn't make rash decisions until a few months have passed after the loss of a family member or a good friend?" He tucked a strand of her hair behind her ear and brushed another sweet kiss across her lips.

"This is not a rash decision," she told him. "You don't have to worry about your job anymore. We've both got places to start our new journey in life, and we're two consenting adults." Down deep in her heart, she knew she was making the right decision when she stood up and tugged on his hand.

"Then the answer is yes, Sissy. I would love to move in with you, but . . ."

She led him down the short hallway to the bedroom and melted into his arms. "There are no *buts* or *maybes* in real love. No regrets. Just right now, and a wonderful future filled with endless love in front of us." She slipped his phone from his pocket and turned it off, then laid it on the dresser beside hers.

"Yes, ma'am. I like that idea of a future, but we don't have to rush into anything. I'm ready when you are, and you can take all the time you need," Luke said.

Sissy raised up on her tiptoes to kiss him. "We both know that time is something no one controls," she said as she closed the bedroom door with her bare foot.

Epilogue

Valentine's Day

A re we really doing this?" Sissy whispered outside the door of the small wedding chapel on the cruise ship. "I still can't believe we let Gussie and the rest of them talk us into going on this cruise with them, or that we're getting married on a senior citizens' cruise."

"I believe we are," Luke said, "and you got to admit, it's romantic."

"Everything is romantic between us." Sissy straightened the rosebud boutonniere on Luke's vest. "It's just that I never imagined getting married on a cruise ship or taking four elderly folks on a honeymoon with us."

"We met at a funeral, moved in together after only four weeks." Luke chuckled. "We're kind of like your folks. We do things our way, not the traditional way. Have I told you how beautiful you look today? I love the roses in your hair." He reached out to touch the circlet of white rosebuds that rested around one of her messy buns. "And this outfit is so you, from your hair to your toes."

Sissy smoothed the front of her white cotton eyelet sundress with a blue ribbon around its empire waistline. The dress barely skimmed her knees, and she was barefoot. "I didn't want the big white dress that would never be worn again, and, darlin', you are . . ." She searched for the right words.

"One sexy dude, right?" He winked at her.

"Took the words right out of my mouth," she told him. "There's the music and our cue to walk in together. I wish your folks could have been here."

"Mama gets seasick in a canoe. She would never make it for a week on a ship, but they're planning a big reception for us when we get home. I'm so glad the Sunshine Kitchen will be renovated by then so we can have it there." He opened the door to the small wedding chapel.

Like Luke said, they did things their way and walked down the short aisle together, her left arm in his and her right hand holding a bouquet of daisies.

Jimmy waited in front of an archway decorated with greenery. Bright sunrays filtered in from the porthole behind him, giving the whole area a surreal look. Paul stood to one side to serve as the best man. Gussie and Ina Mae, dressed in light-blue eyelet dresses with white sashes, waited on the other side.

Aunt Bee, this is for you, because you didn't get the wedding you wanted, Sissy thought as she handed her bouquet off to Gussie.

"Dearly beloved, we are gathered here today," Jimmy said to the empty chapel.

Sissy could visualize Aunt Bee sitting on the front row of white chairs with a big smile on her face as Jimmy went on with a shortened version of the traditional ceremony. They exchanged rings, and then he said, "I believe the two of you have written your own vows, so . . ."

Luke took both her hands in his and looked right into her eyes. "Sissy, I love you, and I tried to write vows, but there really aren't any words that are right for something as beautiful as what we have. I just want you to know that I love you today, tomorrow, and forever. I promise to honor and respect our love and relationship no matter what the universe hurls at us. We've got this, darlin'."

"Yes, we do, and I love you, too," Sissy said. "And I had trouble writing words on paper also. Like you once said to me, there are no *buts* in love, just *ands,* which means that we're adding to, not subtracting from, our relationship. I promise to honor *and* respect you, *and* to add lots of *ands* to us through the years." Sissy's heart was full and her soul at peace as she stood there with Luke.

"Well, then by the power vested in me by God and by the state of Texas, I pronounce you husband and wife," Jimmy said. "Luke, you may kiss your bride."

Luke bent her backward in a true Hollywood kiss. When it ended, Gussie handed back the bouquet, and Luke grabbed her free hand to lead her out of the chapel. Once outside and on the balcony overlooking the lido deck, where the pool was located, Sissy waited until the other four were down the stairs and waiting below them.

"Here it comes," she said as she turned around and tossed her bouquet over her shoulder.

The roses floated through the air and landed right in Paul's hands. He fumbled the bouquet like a football, and it flew right over to Jimmy, who almost dropped it. Ina Mae got a hold on it and was about to give it back to Jimmy when she stumbled, lost control of the thing, and it passed through Gussie's hands like a greased pig and fell down over the side rail of the deck and into the hands of a gray-haired lady.

"I caught the bouquet," she squealed, and held it high over her head. "I'm getting married next. Look, darlin', this means we're getting married."

The elderly gentleman with her dropped down on one knee and held out an engagement ring. "I guess there's no time like the present, then. Will you marry me, Joann?"

"Yes," she squealed again.

"Thank God for small favors," Gussie said, "but now you won't have it for the pictures."

"Who needs flowers?" Sissy said. "I've got a husband and a whole family to stand up together in the pictures."

Luke scooped Sissy up in his arms at the door of their cabin and carried her over the threshold into their balcony room. The sun was falling out there where the water met the sky, giving the whole room a golden glow.

"This is a modern-day version of riding off into the sunset, isn't it?" Sissy said.

"I planned it this way," Luke teased as he laid her on the bed.

"I wouldn't doubt it. I believe that you've got a hotline to"—she pointed out past the sliding glass doors—"and whatever you need is provided."

"Believing is the key." Luke stretched out beside her. "I believe I love you. I believe you love me. I believe we will be happy and that we'll get through whatever life throws at us together."

She rolled over on her side and planted a long kiss on his lips. "So, we're going to have some rough waters in the next fifty or sixty years?"

"Of course." He grinned as he tumbled her over onto her back. "We have to have the occasional argument so we can have awesome makeup sex."

"But not tonight," she whispered. "Tonight is our first time to make love as a married couple, and that is super special."

"I believe you are right, Mrs. Beauchamp." He

untied the blue ribbon from around her dress. "I'm so glad this isn't one of those dresses with nine million buttons that has to be undone."

"Me too, darlin'," Sissy said. "Me too."

Dear Reader,

My daughter, Ginny, was at a citywide yard sale a few months ago and found an old newspaper for less than a dollar. She brought it home to me because she was just sure that I could find some ideas for a book in those yellowed pages that were falling apart. Right there on the front page of the *Cheyenne State Ledger* from Cheyenne, Wyoming, in among the club and church events, was a tiny little paragraph about the next meeting of the Sunshine Society. I changed the name to the Sunshine Club and had the bare bones of the story in my head by the time Ginny left my house.

As I've said before, it takes a village to take a book from a bare-bones idea to the finished product you hold in your hands today. And I have many folks to thank who have helped me from start to finish on *The Sunshine Club*. My agent, Erin Niumata, and my agency, Folio Management, are amazing, and I can't thank them enough for continuing to be there for me. My editors, Alison Dasho and Krista Stroever—y'all are simply the best, and I love working with you both. All the folks on my Montlake team who proofread, copyedit, design my awesome covers, and do a fabulous job of promotion—I bow to

411

all your expertise. My husband, Mr. B, who is my biggest supporter, who doesn't mind having takeout so I can finish one more chapter—I love you, and here's to another fifty-five years together.

And to my readers! Y'all are the sweet icing on the cupcake. You are the folks who keep me in my writing chair for hours every day. I love your notes, your reviews, and your encouragement.

I'm one blessed author, and I appreciate everyone in my life who helps me be able to say that!

Until next time,
Carolyn Brown

About the Author

Carolyn Brown is a *New York Times*, *USA Today*, *Publishers Weekly*, *Washington Post*, and *Wall Street Journal* bestselling author and RITA finalist with more than one hundred published books. Her books include romantic women's fiction, historical, contemporary, and cowboys-and-country-music mass market paperbacks. She and her husband live in the small town of Davis, Oklahoma, where everyone knows everyone else, knows what they are doing and when, and reads the local newspaper on Wednesday to see who got caught. They have three grown children and enough grandchildren and great-grandchildren to keep them young. For more information visit www.carolynbrownbooks.com.

Center Point Large Print
600 Brooks Road / PO Box 1
Thorndike, ME 04986-0001 USA

(207) 568-3717

US & Canada:
1 800 929-9108
www.centerpointlargeprint.com